ABOVE HER, ONLY BLUE SKIES . . .

Some things were more valuable than money, and Jenny knew if she asked her parents for this loan, she'd end up paying them back with more than just money. Always before when she'd screwed up, flunked, or just plain failed, her parents had been there, bailing her out. And each time they rescued her, she could see the ever-sinking disappointment in their eyes. She was twenty-six years old. Too old to be running to her mom and daddy every time she got into trouble. It was time for her to stand on her own two feet. For no reason she could explain, a vision of Custer and his last stand flashed before her eyes. But that's what saving Blue Sky Air felt like to Jenny. Her last stand— the last chance she'd have to prove to her family that they were wrong about her. This time she wasn't only fighting for her self-respect, she was fighting for her and Steven's dream.

Jared Worth might have thought he had all the answers, but he was wrong. Jenny was in the driver's seat now, a place she intended to stay.

LAKE MAGIC

KIMBERLY FISK

BERKLEY SENSATION, NEW YORK

THE BERKLEY PUBLISHING GROUP
Published by the Penguin Group
Penguin Group (USA) Inc.
375 Hudson Street, New York, New York 10014, USA
Penguin Group (Canada), 90 Eglinton Avenue East, Suite 700, Toronto, Ontario M4P 2Y3, Canada
(a division of Pearson Penguin Canada Inc.)
Penguin Books Ltd., 80 Strand, London WC2R 0RL, England
Penguin Group Ireland, 25 St. Stephen's Green, Dublin 2, Ireland (a division of Penguin Books Ltd.)
Penguin Group (Australia), 250 Camberwell Road, Camberwell, Victoria 3124, Australia
(a division of Pearson Australia Group Pty. Ltd.)
Penguin Books India Pvt. Ltd., 11 Community Centre, Panchsheel Park, New Delhi—110 017, India
Penguin Group (NZ), 67 Apollo Drive, Rosedale, North Shore 0632, New Zealand
(a division of Pearson New Zealand Ltd.)
Penguin Books (South Africa) (Pty.) Ltd., 24 Sturdee Avenue, Rosebank, Johannesburg 2196,
South Africa

Penguin Books Ltd., Registered Offices: 80 Strand, London WC2R 0RL, England

This is a work of fiction. Names, characters, places, and incidents either are the product of the author's imagination or are used fictitiously, and any resemblance to actual persons, living or dead, business establishments, events, or locales is entirely coincidental. The publisher does not have any control over and does not assume any responsibility for author or third-party websites or their content.

LAKE MAGIC

A Berkley Sensation Book / published by arrangement with the author

PRINTING HISTORY
Berkley Sensation mass-market edition / January 2010

Copyright © 2010 by Kimberly Fisk.
Cover art by Julia Green.
Cover design by Rita Frangie.
Interior text design by Laura K. Corless.

ISBN: 978-0-425-23202-6

BERKLEY® SENSATION
Berkley Sensation Books are published by The Berkley Publishing Group,
a division of Penguin Group (USA) Inc.,
375 Hudson Street, New York, New York 10014.
BERKLEY® SENSATION and the "B" design are trademarks of Penguin Group (USA) Inc.

PRINTED IN THE UNITED STATES OF AMERICA

10 9 8 7 6 5 4 3 2 1

For Roger
Rachael, Brandon, and Colton
I love you all so very much

ACKNOWLEDGMENTS

Thank you to everyone at the Jane Rotrosen Agency, especially Christina Hogrebe and Andrea Cirillo for their guidance, support, and encouragement.

And to Kelly Harms for being there at the beginning.

To Wendy McCurdy for believing and giving me what every first-time author dreams of—a chance.

To Tracy Montoya and Pipper Watkins. Friends and critique partners extraordinaire.

And to Kristin Hannah. I will never be able to thank you enough.

ONE

❧

The drone of a single-engine plane drew Jenny Beckinsale's attention. Hurrying to the water's edge, she cupped her hands over her eyes and gazed upward. Bright sunshine had scrubbed the gray skies clean, and a sea of endless blue stretched before her. Her pulse quickened and her heart raced as her eyes searched the sky. Maybe . . . just maybe. . . . And then her mind remembered what her heart refused to forget: Steven was never coming home again.

She drew in a breath and let it out slowly. She was not going to fall apart. Not again.

Nearby, waves lapped against the weathered dock. Overhead, crows chattered noisily. And off in the distance, the hum of the plane continued on.

With renewed determination, she turned away from the shore, and her gaze fell on the home she'd inherited from her grandmother, then on the airplane hangar that had been built three years ago.

Sunlight glinted off the metal siding, making the green paint sparkle. A large sign, trimmed in gold, hung with prominence near the building's peak: Blue Sky Air. Underneath those black letters were smaller ones that read: Seaplane Charter Business.

A familiar sense of pride filled her. *We did it, Steven.*

"You done lollygagging?"

Zeke Phillips stood in the hangar's large opening wiping his hands on a rag. With his shoulder-length graying hair and stained mechanic's overalls, he looked like any other grease monkey, but Jenny knew that underneath his frumpy appearance was a sharp mind and a quick wit. And also one of the best seaplane pilots on the West Coast.

"You done fiddling with that engine?" she asked, sidestepping the concern in his voice, just like she'd been doing for the last nine months.

The left side of his mouth curved into a grin. "Just 'bout."

"Good. We have a charter at ten tomorrow."

"Since it's the *only* one on the books this week, don't reckon I'd forget it."

Jenny flinched and all but groaned at his emphasis of the word *only*. "Don't remind me."

"Don't s'pose I have to. But I think I should remind you that it's Wednesday." He glanced at his wristwatch. "I'd say you have about twenty minutes."

"Wednesday?" She started running toward the house. "You could have reminded me earlier."

"And miss the fun?"

Ignoring his laughter, she ran through the front door and up the stairs. The smell of the toast she'd burned at breakfast still hung in the air.

Her clothes were already half off by the time she reached her bedroom. Dropping her shirt onto the floor, she began to tug on the cuff of one pant leg as she hopped over to her bed. Clothes, books, and God only knew what else all but obscured the faded pink chenille comforter. Without bothering to push anything off to the side, she flopped down and finished wiggling out of her jeans. If she were late again this week, she'd never hear the end of it. She started to reach for a pair of capris, then stopped. She could still hear her mother's comment from last week: "Shorts, Jenny? Really. Couldn't you at least try?"

There was no use arguing with her mother that capris were not shorts. When Catherine Beckinsale made up her mind, that was it.

She grabbed one of only a handful of items hanging in the closet—a pink linen sheath with a designer label given to her as a birthday gift from her mother.

The dress seemed to mock her with its feminine perfection. Before she could change her mind and grab the pants on the floor, she slipped it on. It couldn't have fit better if it had been custom-made for her. She had to give her mother credit. Whatever Catherine did, she did to perfection. Whether it was raising her three children, running her own business, or picking out a gift for her youngest child.

Jenny glanced at her bedside clock.

Ten fifty.

Ten minutes until she was supposed to meet her mother.

Who ate lunch at eleven anyway?

Her mother, that's who. She scheduled their luncheons at that early hour so it wouldn't interfere with Catherine's schedule.

For the last nine months, Jenny had dreaded their Wednesday luncheons. But today—this Wednesday—was going to be different. Blue Sky Air had two charters scheduled, and somehow she was going to find a way to work that into the conversation. She knew it wasn't earth-shattering, but it was a start. And proof that her new advertising plan was working.

A quick search of her bedroom produced one sandal, and a few moments later, the second. She seemed to recall a delicate knit cardigan had been included with the dress, but she had no idea where it was. And there was no time to look. She also knew she didn't have time to find a pair of run-free nylons, so she slipped on her shoes and made it downstairs without a moment to spare.

She hopped into the Corvette—a luxury to her, but a

necessity to Steven. *If we're gonna land the big accounts, baby, we need to look like money. This car is just the ticket.* She smiled as she ignited the powerful engine.

"I'll be back in an hour," she called to Zeke as he came out of the hangar to wave good-bye. "But if something comes up, I'll have my cell phone."

Zeke chuckled again and rubbed a finger across his chin. "Never have needed to call you before, don't s'pose today'll be any different."

"Miracles happen."

As she hit Lakeshore Drive, she yanked hard on the gearshift and winced as the gears collided and ground. She wasn't sure what upset her more—knowing that Zeke's laughter was deserved or that in only a few minutes she'd have to endure yet another hour of *Oh, Jennifer, if only . . .* from her mother. A girl could only take so many *Oh, Jennifer*s, and at twenty-six, Jenny figured she'd received her lifetime quota.

Through the tall evergreens that hugged the shoreline, Jenny caught patches of glistening blue water and the jagged tops of the Olympic Mountains. Even in these last few days of May, snow frosted their sharp, uneven peaks. In less than five minutes, she was pulling off the road and onto the paved drive that led to her mother's restaurant— correction *bistro*—and art gallery. Sunlight filtered down through the massive firs and dappled the road as she wound her way down. Taking the final bend in the road, Hidden Lake came into view. As always, the sight of the lake made Jenny catch her breath. A lifetime of memories were in those waters.

She chose one of the angled parking spots on the far side of the building, not surprised to find several other cars already there. Even at this early hour, business was brisk.

Only her mother could open an art gallery and restaurant in a secluded bit of wilderness on the outskirts of Seattle and make it a resounding success. Catherine never failed at anything—except turning Jenny into the perfect daughter.

She glanced at her watch—11:09—then grabbed her purse and rummaged around in the bottom for an elastic band. With a couple of deft moves, she'd pulled her hair up into a messy bun. Not the best of looks, but the best she could do at the moment.

With a final grimace at her appearance, she twisted the mirror back into place and got out of the car.

Before Jenny reached the porch, the main door opened, and her mother stepped out. For just a moment, her mother's expression brightened as she caught sight of the dress Jenny was wearing. Then Catherine's sharp gray eyes narrowed in on Jenny's hastily done hair and bare legs, and the pursed expression Jenny knew only too well was back.

She should have just worn her capris.

"Jennifer, there you are. It was getting so late, I was beginning to worry."

As usual, her mother looked as if she'd just stepped out of the pages of a fashion magazine. Her auburn hair fell in a soft pageboy that framed her face and made her look younger than her fifty-seven years. A once-a-month trip into the city—that her mother believed was as sacred as church on Sunday—kept any traces of gray at bay. Her St. John knit pantsuit was as timeless and elegant as she was. Its soft plum color complemented her complexion. With the exception of her wide wedding band and tasteful gold hoops, she wore no other jewelry.

Even in the dress her mother had selected for her, Jenny felt dowdy.

After a quick hug, Catherine led them past the reception area and down the long hallway that served as an extension of the gallery. Art, ranging from modern to traditional to local pieces, was tastefully displayed along the corridor. The room's soaring ceilings, crisp white walls, and dark mahogany floors were the perfect backdrop for the unique and diverse collection. While most people remarked on the varied and exceptional works of art, for Jenny the special appeal of her mother's business would always be the smell. No matter what time of day she visited, there were always the most wonderful aromas drifting out from the restaurant's kitchen.

Their usual table along the far wall was waiting for them. As Jenny took her seat, she didn't bother to ask for a menu; she knew it wouldn't do any good.

As if reading her mind, her mother said, "André has outdone himself today. Salade Niçoise. The tuna is lovely."

Jenny gave the required: "It sounds perfect."

"André is a master in the kitchen. I don't know how the bistro would survive without him."

Jenny did. While it was true that the French chef her mother had charmed and wooed away from an exclusive restaurant in the heart of Seattle was a magician when it came to cuisine, Jenny knew that even if her mother lost André, her business would continue to flourish.

"Unfortunately, we'll have to hurry through lunch," her mother said. "A party of eight has reservations for noon. We would have had plenty of time if . . ."

If you'd been on time. The words were in the air as clear as if they'd been spoken.

"Well, no matter. You're here now." Her mother unfolded the pressed linen napkin and placed it on her lap. "Was there traffic?"

"The roads were fine." As they both knew.

Rush hour in Hidden Lake consisted of two cars going in opposite directions. It was just one of the many things Jenny loved about the small lakeside town. The only time there was ever a backup was when Mr. Wilson made his bimonthly run into town for staples: bread, milk, cheese, eggs, and a bottle of rum (for medicinal purposes, of course). And the only reason that caused a slight hiccup was because Mr. Wilson insisted on driving his tractor.

Thankfully, the waitress arrived with their lunch, stalling her mother from making any further comments on Jenny's tardiness. Jenny picked up her fork, but before she dug in, she paused in admiration. Not only did André's food taste out of this world, he managed to make a few bits of potato, a couple of olives, and some fresh fish look like art.

Spending an hour alone with her mother once a week might not be on Jenny's top one hundred list, but the food always softened the blow.

"How have you been?" Jenny asked in between bites.

"Frantic." Her mother said with a serene smile. "Business is up nineteen percent from this time last year, there's your father's birthday on Friday, our trip to Alaska, and the annual Seattle Art Museum charity ball is less than a month away." She laughed softly. "Remind me to say no next year when they ask me to chair again."

Jenny stabbed at a piece of hard-boiled egg. "You say that every year."

Her mother smiled again. "You're right, I do. But it's for charity, and as long as I organize my time accordingly, I'll be able to accomplish everything."

Criticism duly noted. Jenny pushed at a piece of seared tuna on her plate.

"I spoke with your brother this morning."

"How is Perfect Paul?"

"Jennifer, really."

"Sorry." But she wasn't. Living in the shadow of her "gifted brother" and "brilliant sister" had left her . . . faded. It was as if by the time the sun shone upon them, it lost all of its warmth when it finally reached her. She knew her parents loved her, but she often wondered how many nights they went to bed scratching their genius heads and wondering how they'd ever ended up with such a daughter.

"He's narrowed the candidates to two and believes he'll have made a decision by the end of the week," her mother said.

"How nice."

"His law practice is expanding so quickly, he can't keep up."

"Lucky for him." Jenny tried to sound sincere, but she could tell she'd failed when her mother arched one perfectly sculpted eyebrow in her direction.

"Really, Jennifer. You could at least try to show some interest."

Jenny stuffed a forkful of salad into her mouth to save herself from having to make any further comment. It wasn't that she didn't love her brother and sister; she did. It was just hard to keep up an enthusiastic front year after year when all their triumphs were put on display, and she had nothing to add to the ever-increasing collection.

"I told Paul I would help him with the welcome reception he's planning for the new attorney. André's already working on the menu."

Jenny took a large gulp of water.

"I heard from Anna on Sunday."

On to sibling number two: the brilliant obstetrician.

Perfect Paul. Amazing Anna.

And Jinxed Jenny.

"Anna was the head doctor on a delivery of quintuplets. Can you imagine? Your sister said it was the most rewarding experience of her career."

"What about Cody?" Jenny asked, referring to her nephew, Anna and Phillip's only child. "Is his hair still blue?"

"It's a rinse, dear. I've told you that before." Her mother took a small bite. "Anna believes it's only a matter of time before they promote her. Of course, with the promotion will come added responsibilities—"

"Are these new dishes, Mom? They're lovely."

"But your sister is more than up for the challenge."

"Was that a new statue I saw in the hallway?" She poked at a piece of fish with her fork, causing it to flake into small pieces.

"I suppose I should talk to André about a menu for Anna's promotion. I know nothing is official yet, but it's best to always be prepared."

"This is the best tuna I've ever had." Jenny scooped the fish bits into her mouth and made a great show of enjoying them. Actually, it *was* the best tuna she'd ever had. But considering that the only other kind she'd ever had came out of a can, that wasn't saying much. She was sure the great André didn't have the age-old debate of water versus oil-packed when he selected this fish.

"What do you think about a Polynesian theme?"

"For your rest—uh, bistro?"

"Don't be silly, dear. For Anna's promotion party. She's always loved the tropics."

"Maybe you should wait to see if she gets it."

"Don't be silly, dear," her mother said again. "Of course she'll be promoted. You know, the other day she sent your father and me several magazine articles that featured her . . ."

With a sigh, Jenny stared at the thin sliver of lemon floating on top of her water. Once her mother boarded the Paul and Anna train, there was no way to get her off. Not for the first time, Jenny reflected that lunch really should come with alcohol.

"And you, dear? How's your business doing?"

Jenny was about to give her standard, "Fine," when she remembered her earlier optimism. "We have a charter booked for tomorrow."

"Oh? A charter?"

The way her mother said it made it sound paltry.

"And we have another booked next week."

"That's wonderful, honey. Really." Her mother set her fork down alongside her plate. "But remember, my offer is always open. There is always a job waiting for you here."

Jenny was saved from answering by the ringing of a phone. Saved by the bell. Literally. She knew from past luncheons her mother would insist upon answering it. *Business first*, she'd say. But strangely, this time, her mother didn't move.

The phone rang again.

"Jennifer, dear. I believe that's your phone."

"My phone?" Her water glass clanked against her plate. She reached for her purse and nearly fell out of her chair in her haste. A muffled fourth ring spurred her on even more. Why were cell phones so darn small? Just as the phone rang for a fifth time, she located it and glanced at the number. Zeke. *Don't hang up. Please. Please. Don't hang up*.

"Zeke. Hello."

"Sorry to bother you at lunch—"

"No. No bother." She looked to her mother, did a poor job of covering the mouthpiece before saying, "It's Zeke, from work."

"Uh. Yeah. Well, some guy stopped by—"

"A customer?"

Her mother leaned in closer.

"He was rather persistent in seeing you, so I sent him on over to the restaurant," Zeke continued. "I hope that was okay."

"A client needed to speak to me right away and you sent him over here?" Jenny knew she was reiterating everything Zeke said, but she couldn't seem to stop herself. Finally her hard work was paying off, and it couldn't have happened at a better time. Now her mother could see Jenny as a businesswoman. She felt almost giddy.

"Should be there any moment. Like I said earlier, hope it was okay I sent him over."

"You did the right thing, Zeke. That's why I carry the cell phone." She knew she was laying it on extra thick, but she couldn't seem to stop herself. "And don't worry, I haven't forgotten our appointment this evening. Five o'clock, right?"

"Huh?"

"Oh, right. Five thirty."

"Have you gone daft, girl? What appointment? If you're talking about our weekly canasta game when my Mildred is at bingo—"

"The phone's ringing? Yes, of course you have to get it. All right then. I'll talk to you later." She hit the End button before Zeke could question her bizarre behavior any further. She knew she'd have some explaining to do when she got back, but just one look at her mother's surprised face was worth all the ribbing she'd get.

"Anything urgent?" her mother asked after a slight pause.

Jenny tried to tamp down her growing excitement but found it impossible to do. "There's an important client that needs to speak to me right away." It wasn't a lie. At this point, all of her clients were important. "I hope you don't mind, but he's on his way over here right now."

Her mother's expression turned to bafflement—as if she couldn't take in what was happening. "No. I don't mind at all."

Jenny knew she should make small talk with her mother, maybe even inquire further about her brother's search for a new lawyer or her sister's multiple birth delivery, but all she could concentrate on was the glorious call from Zeke. A customer. Needing to see her right away. Here. At her mother's restaurant. It was all just too wonderful. She'd known . . . she'd just known when she'd woken up this morning that her life was about to take a turn.

The wait seemed to take forever. And then, just when she didn't think she could take it any longer, a low growl vibrated through the restaurant.

Jenny, her mother, and several of the restaurant's patrons looked up to see what was causing the noise.

A huge, gleaming black motorcycle rounded the driveway's last bend and cruised into the parking lot. Sunlight glinted off the polished chrome.

The rumblings grew louder, rattled the windows. As the driver maneuvered the monstrous Harley around to the side of the building, Jenny lost sight of him. A few moments later, quiet descended.

Seconds crept by, and then there was the sound of the front door being opened . . . closed . . . boots thumping down the hallway. And then he filled her line of vision, and everything inside of her went still.

Oh my . . .

"Jenny?" her mother questioned, but Jenny couldn't respond. Something told her she'd just gotten her first glimpse of Blue Sky's newest client.

He strode into the restaurant as if he'd been there a thousand times before, pausing only when he reached where the hallway ended and the restaurant began. As he scanned the interior, Jenny couldn't help but take a thorough look at him.

He was tall—at least six two—and in his black leather jacket he looked like a walking ad for Bad Boy USA. His hair was as black as a starless night and short, almost as if he'd only recently begun to let it grow out. The short cut was probably the only thing that kept it from being a rumpled mess, since he'd been wearing a helmet. Then again, Jenny got the distinct impression he was one of those men who always looked good, whether they'd just gotten off of a motorcycle, out of the shower, or out of bed.

Bed . . .

The jolt hit her unexpectedly. It was the first time in over nine months her mind had gone down *that* path, and she felt a pinch of guilt. No, more like a good ol' slug.

He was one of those rare individuals who commanded attention whether they were in a boardroom or on a boardwalk. Or in a tiny bistro on the edge of a lake.

Her mother leaned close, whispered, "Sit up straight, Jennifer, and smooth your hair."

She barely heard what her mother was saying, because at that moment his gaze connected with hers. "Ms. Beckinsale," he said when he reached her table. His voice was deep and low.

"Y-yes." She cleared her throat. He was so close she could see the faint lines that fanned out from the corners of his eyes; something told her those creases hadn't been caused by laughter. More than likely, judging by his tan, they'd been caused by a life spent outdoors.

"Hello." He flashed her a killer grin, showing off his perfect white teeth. Spellbound, all she could do was stare. Dimly, she became aware of a movement to her left and belatedly remembered her mother. "This is my mother, Catherine Beckinsale."

He turned and gave her mother that same bone-melting smile. "Ma'am."

Jenny was surprised to see that her mother seemed rattled.

Catherine cleared her throat. "How do you do, Mr. . . . ?"

The visitor looked at Jenny when he responded. "Worth. Jared Worth."

He waited, as if his name would have some effect on her, but all she could think about were his eyes. They weren't brown, as she'd originally thought, but a deep, deep midnight blue framed by full, spiky lashes. And they seemed to reach inside to a part of her she'd kept buried for a long time.

There was a short pause, and then her mother filled in the silence. "Well, Mr. Worth, may I offer you something? A cappuccino? Espresso? Latte?"

He looked at her mother as if she were speaking Greek. "No." And then as an afterthought, tacked on, "Thank you."

Belatedly, Jenny's business manners kicked in. "Please, Mr. Worth. Won't you have a seat?" She motioned to one of the empty chairs at their table.

He continued to stand.

Seated, she tried not to feel at a disadvantage. Tried and failed. He was just too tall, too muscular, too good-looking. "I'm sorry I wasn't at the office when you arrived. I hope it wasn't too much of an inconvenience for you."

"No trouble at all."

"Were you able to find the restaurant all right?"

"Yes."

"Mr. Phillips mentioned that you needed to speak to me right away."

He glanced at her mother and then back to her. "I didn't realize you were busy. I can come back later."

She was never too busy for a client. "No, no. Now is just fine."

For a moment she forgot her discomfort as she imagined her company's bottom line floating away from the red zone and up toward the black. And her mother was here to witness it all.

He looked around the room. "Is there somewhere private we can talk?"

And have her mother miss this? No way.

"My mother is aware of my business dealings, Mr. Worth. Feel free to discuss whatever you need to in front of her."

"I think it would be best if we had our chat in private."

"Truly, Mr. Worth. There's no problem."

He let out a barely perceptible sigh, and it seemed to Jenny as if some of his bone-melting, megawatt-smiling, good-ol'-boy charm left him. "You're Jennifer Beckinsale, correct?"

"Yes. I believe we've already established that."

"The Jennifer Beckinsale who was engaged to Steven Harmon?"

Jenny wasn't sure if it was her or her mother who drew in the sharp, quick breath at the mention of Steven's name. It had been months since anyone had said his name out loud to her, and just the sound of it hurt. "Y-yes."

"The Jennifer Beckinsale who was partnered with Steven Harmon in a seaplane charter business known as Blue Sky Air?"

She tried to ignore the pain at hearing Steven's name again—tried to ignore her growing sense of unease—but she failed on both accounts. "I'm sorry, Mr. Worth, but I'm not sure what this has to do with anything. I thought you were here about a charter. About Blue Sky Air."

"I am."

"Oh." His answer should have brought a sense of relief. "Why don't you tell me your travel plans, and I'll have my associate, Mr. Phillips, get in touch with you. With summer just around the corner, I'm sure you can understand that our schedule is not as open as in the winter months." *Lies. Lies. Lies.* "But we will do everything we can to accommodate your travel needs. Blue Sky offers a wide range of travel options, from local trips in the Puget Sound area to frequent charters to the San Juans and British Columbia."

"I don't seem to be making myself clear. I'm not here to schedule a charter."

"You're not?"

"No. I'm here to discuss Blue Sky Air."

"You want to discuss my charter business?"

"No, Miss Beckinsale, I want to discuss *our* business."

"Excuse me?"

He let out another sigh; this one louder and more noticeable than the last. "I'm your partner."

She laughed, but somehow her laughter fell flat. "I don't have any partners. I am the sole owner of Blue Sky Air, and I don't think this little joke of yours is very funny. Now, if you're not here to book a charter, I think you should leave—"

"Christ." He rubbed his hand across his face, then zeroed in on her again. "You really don't have a clue what I am talking about."

"You have no clue what you're talking about, Mr. Worth. And it really is past time you were leaving." He was sick. Demented. He needed help. Any other day of the week she might have offered to drive him to a doctor's office . . . a hospital . . . a padded room with no door. But not today. Not with her mother sitting less than five feet away.

"I'm afraid it's you who doesn't have a clue," he said. "Look at the contract; you'll see that what I'm saying is the truth."

"I don't need to look at any contract. I am the sole owner of Blue Sky Air."

He muttered something under his breath, and Jenny had the sinking feeling she should be glad she hadn't been able to understand what he'd said. "You're exactly like Steven described."

"Excuse me?"

"Just like Steven said. All package, no product."

For a moment, she couldn't breathe.

He was lying. Steven would never have said anything like that about her. He'd loved her as much as she loved him. Anger jumped in front of her pain. "You need to leave. Now." She tried to keep her voice steady. Strong. But her emotions were too raw, and she felt the start of tears burn the back of her eyes.

She stood up, knocking her chair over in her haste. Without bothering to right the chair, she headed straight for the door; she couldn't get away from him fast enough.

But before she could reach it, he was right behind her.

"This isn't over." His voice was low and sent a shiver down her spine. "Instead of doing your nails tonight, read the contract. I'll be in touch tomorrow."

Without looking at him, she wrenched the door open and ran.

TWO

$\backsim$

Jenny stared at her brother across his large desk, feeling numb. "There has to be some mistake."

"I'm sorry, Jenny, but there isn't."

It was the same thing her brother had been saying ever since she'd burst into his law office unannounced, undone, and, undoubtedly unwanted (although he hadn't said as much). For all of Paul's faults, turning away a family member in need wasn't one of them. Of course, she was the only member of the family who was ever in need.

Within ten minutes of leaving her mother's restaurant, she'd known she had no choice but to go to Paul. Not if she wanted to get rid of Mr. Jared Worth.

Organization, especially filing, had never been one of her strengths. She knew trying to locate the original business documents—or any documents, for that matter—in her office would be an exercise in futility. But Paul would have them. Organization *was* one of his strengths. One of his *many* strengths. After Steven's death, and at Paul's unwavering insistence, she'd made copies of all her important financial documents, stuffed them into an old apple box, and given them to her brother for safekeeping.

"There has to be some mistake," she said again.

"Jennifer." The paternally patient tone of her brother's voice was beginning to wear on her. "There is no mistake. Jared Worth is your partner."

"But how?"

Seated behind his imposing mahogany desk, in a high-backed leather chair, Paul looked every inch the confident, successful lawyer in his handmade suit, blue silk shirt, and matching tie. The bookcases that flanked two of the walls and the tastefully framed diplomas only sealed the deal.

"Jennifer," he began in that same annoying tone once more, "have you heard anything I've said?"

"Yes." *No.* She'd pretty much tuned out after the first time he'd said *partner.*

"Did you, by any chance, read this contract before you signed it?"

"Of course I did." *Not.*

He sighed heavily. Sometimes it just didn't pay to consult an attorney who'd known you your whole life.

"Jennifer—"

"Please. No more *Jennifer*s."

"I blame myself for this."

That perked her up. It wasn't often her brother admitted any wrongdoing, and if he wanted to take the blame for this, she was only too happy to let him.

"I should have insisted on being the attorney to draft the documents."

"You did, but Steven wanted to use a friend from college."

"I should have been more insistent."

"His friend was an attorney."

"I am aware of that, Jennifer. At the very least, I should have been adamant on reviewing everything before you were allowed to sign."

She was just about ready to remind her brother that he had asked to see the documents before she signed them, but the moment he got to *allowed*, she clammed up. Her whole family thought she was a screwup. And quite honestly, she was tired of their assessment. She wasn't . . . not really . . . well, at least not always.

"Furthermore," Paul continued, "when I insisted on storing duplicates of your company's documents after Steven's death, I should have made sure to review them then."

Jenny wrapped her arms around her waist, wishing she would have spent those few extra minutes this morning searching for her sweater. She was bone-cold. She hugged herself tighter and tried to concentrate on something—anything—that could distance herself from what her brother was saying. From the moment she'd left her mother's, her emotions had propelled her forward, but hearing Steven's name spoken out loud so many times today was taking its toll. She wanted nothing better than to go back home, crawl into bed, and pull her comforter over her head. But that wouldn't stop tomorrow from arriving . . . or Mr. Jared Worth. No, she was going to have to figure this out today, heartache or no heartache.

"But I still don't understand how I could have a partner I've never heard of."

Paul leaned back in his chair, looking very much like their dad. Except her dad still smiled at her and teased her. Somewhere between Little League and law school, her brother had lost his sense of humor.

Several seconds ticked by before he said, "You're absolutely certain you don't recall ever hearing the name Jared Worth before?"

"No. . . ." But there was something slightly . . . familiar about his name. On further thought, she'd probably heard it on the news when they were discussing a recent escapee from the mental hospital.

Paul shifted forward, propped his elbows on the top his desk, and pressed the tips of his fingers together. His gold cuff links sparkled in his desk's high polish. "Let me try to explain this once more. Your initial start-up costs were provided by a loan."

"Yes." She wasn't that dense. "From the bank."

Instead of saying *Jennifer*, he just gave her the look. And that look was just as effective and just as annoying as hearing the word out loud.

"As I recall, you didn't obtain a bank loan until some ten months into the start of your business."

"It was a year," she said, certain of at least that one fact. She remembered it perfectly. Steven had come back from his meeting at the bank all smiles and laughter. He'd scooped her into his arms, twirled her about. *One year, babe. One year to the day we've been in business. And with this new loan, I've guaranteed us a sound start to the second.*

Her laughter had been as free and joyous as his. They'd celebrated by having dinner on the beach, and later, after the sun had disappeared and the only remnants of the fire they'd built had been a small pile of orange coals, they'd made love. It had been one of a hundred perfect nights she'd spent in his arms, and its memory was both unbearably painful and unthinkable to forget.

"All right, a year. So for the twelve months preceding, where did you think the capital was coming from to run Blue Sky?"

She hadn't thought. Steven always took care of the financial side of the business while Jenny concentrated on the bookings and office work. "I . . ."

Her brother pinched the bridge of his nose and let out another sigh.

She didn't know which were worse: the sighs or the *Jennifer*s.

"I don't know what else I can tell you, Jennifer."

The *Jennifer*s had it. By one.

He unsteepled his fingers and sorted through the small stack of papers on the edge of his desk. Locating the document he'd been looking for, he slid it across his desk toward her. "When Blue Sky Air was formed, you and Steven signed a loan agreement with one Jared Worth." He gestured to the document in front of her.

Could he stop saying that odious man's name?

"The loan was in the amount of one hundred thousand dollars."

"One hundred . . ." André's perfect salad didn't feel so perfect now. She felt sick.

"One hundred thousand dollars."

More than sick.

"The terms of the agreement were such that the entire balance was to be paid in full by the end of three years." Paul paused, glanced back down to the papers, flipping through several sheets. "You know, it's really rather remarkable."

"What is?" she asked, though she didn't really care.

"It's an interest-free loan. Very generous of him. I guess if there's anything positive to be gained from today, it's knowing that all you owe him is the original amount of—"

"Please, don't say it again." It was a mountain of a sum. Mount Everest to be exact.

How in the world was she ever going to get that kind of money? Even if the amount was in pesos, she'd have a hard time coming up with it.

"What if I . . ." She paused. "What if I can't pay him back?"

"Then he'll become your partner. Your equal partner." For several seconds, Paul looked at her. "Maybe your having a partner isn't such a bad idea."

"Are you crazy?"

His gaze was unwavering, and Jenny felt herself begin to squirm under his scrutiny.

"All I'm saying—"

"I know what you're saying. You think I can't run Blue Sky Air on my own. Well, I can. I am ." Blue Sky Air was all she had left of Steven. She wasn't going to let anyone take it away from her. It had been *their* dream. Hers and Steven's. "Mr. Worth will have nothing to do with my company."

"It was only a suggestion, Jelly Belly," her brother said in a soft voice. "I didn't mean to upset you."

The childhood nickname brought a fleeting smile and a

flood of memories. She'd long ago lost count of how many times her big brother had been there for her. "You didn't," she lied.

For a moment, Paul didn't say anything. "I've sunk a lot of capital into the construction of the new offices, but maybe I could—"

"No," she said, putting on a brave face. "But thanks. I mean that."

Too many times her family had bailed her out of one situation after another. She owed it to Steven—to herself— to find her own way out of this mess. Twenty-six years old. It was time to grow up.

She took a deep breath. "Is that everything?"

"Except for one detail."

She was almost afraid to ask. "Which is?"

"If you are unable to repay Mr. Worth in full by the date specified, as an equal partner, he could force a liquidation of assets to reclaim his investment."

"Liquidation of assets?" What was he saying? Liquidation of . . . Her gaze shot up, collided with his.

"Yes, Jenny, the plane." His eyes softened, his voice dropped a notch lower. "The property."

"No."

Foolishly, she'd thought this day couldn't get any worse. How wrong she'd been. She gripped her stomach tighter. "You mean I could lose Nana's property?"

At Paul's nod, she felt the start of tears. She blinked, trying to will them away. She turned from her brother and fought for composure. Through the window, Hidden Lake glistened in the unusually bright May sun. As she stared at the achingly familiar water, she felt her anguish grow. She could not lose her property. She *would not*. Nana had left it to her so she and Steven could start their business. But it was more than that. That house was a part of her. While her brother and sister had been busy with other pursuits, Jenny had spent time on the sandy beach with her grandmother. Building sand castles, wading in the lake's cool water. No matter how tough life got, she could always find solace on that little piece of land.

Hearing what her brother was saying was too much. She needed time. Time to think this through and more time in which to repay Mr. Worth.

But time was exactly what she didn't have. Because if what Jared Worth had said was true, he'd be back on her doorstep tomorrow.

* * *

Anna Adams stood in the middle of her master bedroom and listened to the din of the people below. She drew in a slow breath and fought to find her usual unruffled demeanor. But even as the voices changed, grew louder and slightly impatient, she knew they weren't the cause of this uncharacteristic apprehension. Her gaze strayed to the phone by the bed. She took a step toward it, only to stop short. What good would another call do?

A glance around the room assured her that everything was in its place. The intricately carved four-poster bed gleamed from a recent polish; faint traces of the lemony wax still hung in the air. Pressed Egyptian linens graced the bed. Silk curtains billowed around the windows. On the far wall an antique armoire housed a flat screen TV, and on the wall nearest the bedroom door hung the tapestry she and Phillip had purchased a little over thirteen years ago, during their honeymoon in France. A sharp pang of longing hit her, and she quickly looked away.

A knock sounded at the bedroom door.

"Yes?"

Marie, their longtime housekeeper and cook, entered. Spotting her employer by the bay window, she broke out into a huge grin. "They're ready."

"Thank you. I'll be right down."

"This is so exciting."

Anna tried to answer, but the words stuck in her throat. For over three months, she'd been looking forward to this day. She'd prepared for it, planned for it, shopped for it, but now that it was here, she wished she could sweep it away. Looking at Marie, she longed for some of that same excitement but knew it was as elusive as a peaceful night's sleep. All she could do was nod.

"It's too bad Dr. Adams couldn't be here."

Dr. Adams. To Marie, it didn't matter that both she and her husband were physicians. For her, Phillip would always be the only doctor in the house. "Y-yes."

"Your house. In a magazine." Marie clasped her hands together in front of her, her wide grin still in place. "I've told my whole family."

"I have, too." Anna felt a ghost of a smile hovering as she caught a tiny sliver of her housekeeper's enthusiasm. "And thank you again for all your hard work. The house looks beautiful."

Marie blushed. "It wasn't me. You have worked so hard." With that, she left, quietly closing the door behind her.

For several heartbeats, Anna stared at the closed door. She knew she should move, walk forward, walk out and greet the magazine crew, yet she lingered. Slowly, she made her way to the full-length mirror in her bedroom and gave her appearance one final check.

Her straight-legged black trousers and lace blouse with mandarin collar and ruffle trim was stylish without being stuffy. Instead of her usual French twist, she opted for a softer look, loosely gathering her dark blonde hair at the nape of her neck. A few strands floated free.

Like her house, she was picture-perfect. True, she wasn't a girl of twenty any longer, but at thirty-four, Anna prided herself on her appearance. A strict diet and even stricter exercise schedule kept her body toned and trimmed. Her skin was still as smooth and as soft as ever. But that perfection did not come without effort. Careful planning, excessive preparation, and dedicated endurance—that was her mantra. Anything could be accomplished if you worked hard enough and long enough.

Knowing she couldn't stall any longer, she left the bedroom and made her way down the hall, stopping at her son's door. She knocked once, waited a handful of seconds, then entered. Just as she suspected, he was sitting on his bed, earphones in, listening to his iPod. Even from across the room, she could hear the music. "Cody?"

He didn't answer.

Crossing the room, she gave his sneakered foot a gentle shake, fighting to keep the frown from her face. How many times had she asked him not to wear his shoes in the house? But she knew if she said something, they'd end up in an argument. And that was the last thing she wanted today. She couldn't stop the frown from forming when she once more caught sight of his blue hair. "Cody?" she said again, this time pulling out one of his earphones. The music blared louder.

He shot her a look. "What?"

"Please turn your music down."

He took forever to comply.

"The camera crew is here."

"So?"

"They're ready for us."

"So?" he said again.

She counted to ten. "It's time for us to head downstairs."

"No." He reached for the sketch pad next to him and flipped it open.

"Cody—"

"I told you, I'm not doing it."

"Come on, Cody. It'll be fun. It's not every day your house gets picked to be in a magazine." She heard the imploring note in her voice and stopped. She'd read enough parenting books to know that pleading would get her nowhere. She started again. "The camera crew would like our family in a few of the pictures—"

"Family. Right. Dad's not here."

"You know he can't be. We've been over this a dozen times. He's working."

"He's *gone*."

"I know it seems that way, honey, but Doctors Without Borders is an amazing organization, and your father—"

"Whatever," he mumbled before putting his earphones back in.

Anna stood there, staring down at her son. They'd had this same discussion more times than she could count, and each time, it ended the same way: with him shutting her out just as clearly as if he'd slammed a door in her face. Part of her wanted to force him out of that bed and make him come downstairs with her. But what good would that do? He would only continue to be sullen and angry, and wouldn't that just make for a lovely family—minus one dad—photo in a magazine read by millions? The best she could hope for was that when the camera crew made it to his room, he would be in a better mood.

"All right, Cody," she said, as if this had been her intention all along. "But be ready when the camera crew and I come up here in a little while."

She left without waiting for a response. Lately, she found that to be easier. She didn't know how many more *whatever*s and *fine*s she could take. She was halfway down the stairs when Marie met her. The housekeeper handed her the cordless phone.

"It's your mother. She says it's important."

"Thanks." Anna took the phone. At least she could share today's excitement with one of her family. "Hi, Mom."

"Anna, thank heavens. For a moment I thought you weren't home."

Not home. Right. Anna smiled into the phone. "You should see the new Aubusson rug I found for the living room. It'll look amazing in the photos—"

"It's Jenny."

"Jenny?" What did her younger sister have to do with today?

"Have you spoken to her?"

"No."

"We were having lunch and a . . . situation came up with her business."

Anna fought hard not to roll her eyes and harder still to keep from saying, *And what else is new?* If it wasn't one thing it was another with her younger sister.

After a small pause, her mother said, "I'm worried about her."

"You're always worried about her."

"Now, Anna, you know that's not true."

The noise from the magazine crew grew louder, and Marie reappeared at the bottom of the staircase. Anna motioned that she'd be right down. "I'm sorry, Mom, but I just don't have time for this right now."

Moments later, Anna clicked off the phone and made her way down the stairs. Alone.

THREE

Jared tore down the deserted road as if demons were on his heels. He laid hard on the throttle, pushed the bike to its limit. The weathered asphalt beneath him became a blur of faded gray, and the broken centerlines blended into one continuous yellow line. He blew past road signs and speed limits, gas stations and rest areas, giving them no more attention than he gave the landscape. Where he was headed—or not headed—didn't matter.

As the sun became a weaker glow of yellow and the wind picked up, a chill penetrated his jacket and stiffened his fingers, but still he didn't stop. No matter how hard he pushed, he wasn't able to outrun his thoughts.

What in the hell had Steven been thinking? How could a man go from being a top gun to flying sissy-assed seaplanes for tourists?

He didn't think, that's how. And Jared was certain if a drunk driver hadn't ended Steven's life, he would have been back in the cockpit of a fighter jet going at Mach speed by now.

A man's got to settle down at some point, Worth, Steven had often said.

Yeah, well, from everything Jared had seen, settling down and giving up were one and the same.

Ah, man, you don't understand. Jenny's different. She's—

Exactly like all the rest. Although Jared had to give her credit. He'd seen a lot of pampered princesses in his day, but Jenny had it down to an art. The flash of confusion, the soft puckering of her forehead, those pouty, full lips . . . all of it designed to make a man fall under her spell.

But it wouldn't work with him. He'd let himself fall for that kind of spell once. And it had been a disaster. He had never done anything as rash as Steven; he'd never gotten engaged. But for a few short months he'd let himself believe in the impossible. Believe he could be like the other guys. Believe he could be a part of something more.

What a crock of shit.

The rain turned hard, pummeled him. He flicked on his headlight then downshifted through a corner. It took him a moment before he realized where he was: right back where he started. He pulled onto the road's wide shoulder and shifted into neutral. The bike purred with a low growl as he took off his helmet and ran his hand through his hair.

From his spot on the low hill, he had a near perfect view of the town below. If you could even call Hidden Lake a town. Two short blocks of Victorian-inspired, lattice-dripping, rainbow-painted businesses that would have been appropriate in a child's theme park but looked only garish and out of place here. Businesses with names like John Dough's Pizza, the Best Little Hairhouse in Town, the Way We Wore, and a drive-through coffee stand called the Bean Counter.

He swore silently under his breath but knew it was his own fault he was stuck in this town. He'd blown it with Jenny; he saw that now. All he wanted was to collect his money and get out of town. He should have just told her that, but it seemed abrupt.

From everything Steven had said, Jared knew Jenny had no interest in the business. Opening and operating a seaplane charter had been solely Steven's idea. Jared was sure once Jenny knew he just wanted repayment, she'd be only too relieved.

But telling her that would have to wait until tomorrow. He'd tried going back to her house, but she was nowhere to be found.

From what he could tell, the only place to stay in town was a bed-and-breakfast. Minutes later, he pulled up in front of a big Victorian house.

Even in the waning light, the house all but glowed under its layers of paint. Purple—and all its various shades— overpowered the entire three stories. A large sign was pounded into the front yard: Murphy's Bed-and-Breakfast. Except someone had drawn an arrow before the word *breakfast* and inked in the word *occasional*. Murphy's Bed-and-*occasional*-Breakfast.

He knocked on the front door. A few moments later, a loud "Door's open," came from inside, and he walked in.

Inside, every square inch was crammed with something either gilded, cherubed, or just plain ugly, but he'd spent nights in places a hell of a lot worse than this.

"May I help you?"

Jared hadn't heard the woman approach. A rarity for him. She was short, barely five feet. Her head was a mass of tight white curls, and an apron was tied around her round waist. With her bright, cheerful expression and age somewhere in the old lady territory, she put him in mind of Mrs. Claus.

"Mrs. Murphy?" he asked, remembering the name from the sign out front.

"Call me Lovie, dear. Everybody does."

He shifted the duffel bag. "I'm here about a room."

She dusted her hands off on her apron and shot him a broad smile. "Well, you're in luck. I just had a cancellation, so Clark Gable's available."

"Excuse me?"

"Clark Gable." A dreamy, faraway look crossed over her wrinkled features. "Each room is named after one of my favorite movie stars." She sighed. "Let's see. There's Errol Flynn . . . Cary Grant . . . Rock Hudson . . . Gary Cooper, and of course Clark." Another sigh. "You'll be sleeping with him."

Not hardly. "You sure you don't have any Rita Hayworths? Marilyn Monroes?" he asked with a grin.

She gave a deep laugh, sending her ample girth bouncing. "Nope. Just my boys. Now, how many nights will you be needing the room?"

"Just one."

She nodded and motioned for him to follow. At the foot of the long, oak staircase, she paused and faced him. "I could let you have the room for two nights, but that's it."

He expected to be stampeded by all the guests at any moment. "Just tonight."

"If you're sure . . ."

He had to admire her persistence. It was probably the only thing that kept the purple mausoleum afloat. "I'm sure."

"If you change your mind, you just let me know." She grabbed ahold of the thick, carved banister and hoisted herself up the first step. "Come on then, and I'll show you to Mr. Gable."

There was something just plain wrong about that sentence.

The staircase was tall and narrow. Hiking his duffel higher on his shoulder, he followed her shuffling feet. Forcing his eyes away from downstairs, he glanced to the wall on his right and found himself face-to-face with dozens of pictures. If the sheer number wasn't weird enough, then what was in the frames—or not in them as the case may be—was enough to seriously creep a person out. Someone had systematically gone through and massacred them.

He felt Mrs. Claus's eyes on him. "Nice photos."

"My family," she said with a sad shake of her head. "Reprobates, every last one of 'em. I told 'em if they didn't straighten out, I was going to get rid of them. My brother Bob thought I was joking." She cackled and motioned to what had obviously once been a family photo of a man, his wife, and three children. But the man's head was now only a hacked-out memory, and all that remained of him was an arm wrapped around his wife's shoulder. "He was the first to go." She cackled again and pointed out several more frames. "Then came my brother Doug, my sister Martha, sister Delle . . ."

The wedding pictures were the worst. A bride. A groom. But never both in the same photo. Jared was sure he heard the theme music from *Psycho*.

He was seriously rethinking his whole Mrs. Claus comparison.

"That's why I can't rent you the room for more than two days. At the end of the week, I'll be heading out to the family reunion."

"But I thought—"

Lovie Murphy stopped dead in her tracks and turned to face him. "Just 'cuz I can't stand my family doesn't mean I'm gonna miss the reunion."

And didn't that just say it all?

She started back up the stairs. "Do you have family in the area?"

"No."

"Oh, they live out of state?"

"No." He didn't have family. Period. In the state or out.

"Just passin' through then?"

He was glad when they arrived at a bedroom and her questions stopped. She opened the door to his worst Victorian-inspired nightmare.

"Tea will be in an hour. I've made my signature sour cherry coffee cake."

"Thanks, but I'm not hungry."

She patted his arm. "That's okay, dear. Come down anyway. It'll give us a chance for a nice chat—"

"I think I'll just crash. It's been a long day." True, but he wasn't the least bit tired.

She patted his arm again. "Well, don't you worry. I'll make sure to save you a piece of my coffee cake. You haven't tasted anything until you've tasted Lovie's sour cherry. Now, go on there and crawl into bed. I've sprinkled the sheets with lavender so you'll sleep like a baby." With assurances that he had everything he needed and one final pat to his arm, Lovie made her way out of the room and closed the door.

He stared at the lace-canopied bed with its lavender-sprinkled sheets and made a distinct detour to the chair by the window. With a conscious effort, he kept his eyes averted from the dark sky. Once, that wide-open blue had been his haven, the only place he belonged. Now, every time he looked at it, all he saw was his failure.

Setting his duffel bag on the floor, he retrieved his cell phone and turned it on. A few moments later, surprised to find he had service, he punched in the long-distance number from memory.

"Fitzgerald Realty."

"Eric, please."

"Just a moment."

There was a slight pause. "Hello?"

"Eric? Jared Worth."

"I'm glad you called; you're a hard man to get ahold of."

"What's the news?"

"Good."

"Tell me."

"I just got off the phone with the interpreter, and I'm happy to report that everything is a go on my end. By this time next week, Mr. Worth, you'll be sitting on your own private beach in Mexico."

With a sigh, Jared leaned back and propped his foot on a flowered footstool. "Perfect."

"The only detail left is for you to wire my office the funds so I can complete the sale."

Jared stared out the window, noticing for the first time he had a decent view of the lake. "No problem. You should have them by the end of the week at the latest."

"Excellent. Excellent. It's a one-of-a-kind piece of property, Mr. Worth, exactly what you wanted—which was no easy feat to find. We were lucky. Your own isolated bit of Mexican paradise. It's so remote, no one could find you, even if they knew where to look."

The realtor chuckled, never realizing how close to the truth he was. It was exactly what Jared wanted. To disappear to a place where no one would bother him. "How quickly can we close the deal?"

"Once I've received your wire transfer . . . two days. Three at the most. Why don't you give me a call after you've wired the money? I'll have a more accurate time frame for you then."

"I'll do that. And thanks." Jared ended the call. A tension he didn't realize he'd been carrying left him. By tomorrow afternoon, after he collected his money, he'd be on his way to a place where the sun was warm, the tequila was cheap, and no one knew how badly he'd fucked up.

* * *

The next morning, Jared was out of the house before anyone else was up. He left his money on the hall table, which had been set up as a makeshift desk complete with pink envelopes that reeked of perfume. The envelopes smelled as bad as his sheets. If he'd been in a sleeping frame of mind, he might have cared.

Instead, he'd spent the night in the chair by the open window. The fresh air was welcome but not the noise. Even in a town this small, the daily grind of people going about their business was more than he cared to hear. He'd tried shutting the window, but that only amplified Mrs. Murphy and the other guests visiting on the floor below him.

Twenty plus years ago, when he'd been nothing more than a kid, he'd have gone downstairs, eaten cake and drunk tea, even though he couldn't stand the stuff, and tried to fit in. It had taken him too many years to learn something he should have known from the moment his mother left him:

he'd never fit. Not with his mother, not at the orphanage, and not with the foster families they'd tried to place him with.

School and studying came easily. He'd breezed through high school, graduated just after he'd turned sixteen. Right after that, he'd left. Left. Not run. Just stuffed his few things into a paper sack and walked out the front door. No one tried to stop him. For a few years, he'd bummed around, taking odd jobs, eating when he could, living on the streets. By one of his favorite haunts, he'd seen a weathered recruitment poster. We Want You! For over a year, he'd cursed at that picture, knowing it was a lie. Then, for no reason he could identify, he'd walked into the recruiting office on his eighteenth birthday and found out the poster had been telling the truth.

With nothing to distract him, he'd funneled all his energy into his career, and it had paid off big. In record time he'd become one of the navy's top fighter pilots with medals and ribbons and accolades that even the broadest of chests couldn't accommodate. But then he'd risked everything and lost it all.

With a swift curse, he kick-started his bike. He wasn't going to think about that. Instead, he turned his thoughts to last night's call with the realtor. He knew Mexico wasn't a permanent solution, but it was the best he had right now. He needed to get away, find a quiet place where he could think, and figure out what he was going to do next, now that the F-18s he loved were no longer an option.

Damp roads and a clear sky were the only remnants of last night's shower. A quick glance at his watch told him it wasn't even seven. He bypassed the local drive-through coffee stand and hit the road. He needed to kill some time before he headed over to Blue Sky Air.

A handful of miles down the road, he pulled into a service station combo mini-mart. After filling his tank, he grabbed a cup of coffee, paid, and then headed back outside. A weathered picnic table was chained to a telephone

booth. Bracing himself against the table's side, he took the
lid off his coffee and inhaled. Damn, but there was nothing like a good cup of joe in the morning.

He blew the steam away and took a drink as he watched
the traffic. Only a few cars drove past, and fewer still pulled
into the station.

The minutes inched by. Finishing his coffee, he looked at
his watch once more: 7:10. Perfect. He'd wasted enough
time.

A short while later, he pulled off the main road. The
rumble from his engine echoed off the still lake and filled
the quiet yard. He angled his bike into a parking spot next
to a shiny red Corvette. As he cut the engine, he eyed the
extravagant car, trying to remember where he'd seen it last.
And then he remembered: yesterday, at the restaurant. It
didn't take much of a deduction to figure the car belonged
to Jenny.

Taking off his helmet, he got off the bike and surveyed
the area. When he'd been here yesterday, he'd barely
looked around. Now he took a longer look. And what he
saw confirmed his suspicions: without Steven at the helm,
the place was all but dead.

Yesterday, the plane had been in the hangar off to his
left. Today, it was anchored at the end of the dock. He
eyed it with contempt. Once more he wondered how his
friend had gone from flying jets to flying charters.

The hangar, like the home and yard, had an air of recent neglect. Trim was missing around the windows, and
on the side there was a gaping hole, which Jared could
only assume was meant for a door.

The house was as quiet as the rest of the place and also
in need of attention. The cedar-shingle siding was weathered and grayed, the trim in desperate need of a fresh coat
of white paint, and the roof in dire need of attention. But
even with all that obvious maintenance needed, he had to
admit that the sprawling home had a decidedly comfortable look, as if whoever built it took their cue from the
surrounding landscape and strived to find harmony be-

tween the two. A large front porch wrapped around the bottom story of the house. On the far end, several rocking chairs were grouped together. A gentle breeze coming in from the lake tipped and rocked the chairs. Just past the lawn's tall grass and on the beach, Jared could make out a large fire pit, the rocks black from years of use. And then there were the flowers. Normally Jared didn't give a crap about flowers—much less notice them. But it was impossible to ignore these. While the house and hangar needed some work, the garden was perfection. Even this early in the morning, the air was heavy with their fragrance.

Once, a long time ago, when he was just a kid, he'd dreamed about living in a place just like this. What an optimistic fool he'd been.

"It's you."

Jared turned toward the sound of the voice. Jenny stood in the doorway, one shoulder propped against the open screen door. She looked different than she had yesterday, as if she'd just rolled out of bed. But even sleep-rumpled, she was just as gorgeous. He couldn't help but think she'd look completely at home frolicking around Hugh Hefner's mansion in a bunny suit. Her honey blonde hair fell past her shoulders in a mass of untamed curls. Instead of the pink dress and high heels, she wore shorts and a faded gray sweatshirt that said Go Huskies! in purple letters. Her feet were bare, with one foot resting on top of the other. The only thing that reminded him of the made-up girl he'd seen yesterday were her hot pink toenails and churlish expression.

"Expecting someone else?"

"Hoping."

"For?"

A springy lock of hair fell across her forehead, and she pushed it back. "That you were a nightmare. And like all horrible dreams, when morning came, you'd be gone."

He laughed. "Sweetheart, I've been told I'm the stuff of dreams, but those women begged me to stick around."

Her lips tightened into a scowl. "I'm not your sweetheart. And before I can deal with an ego that big, I need caffeine." Without another word, she disappeared back inside the house. The screen door banged shut behind her.

Jared crossed the yard. She wasn't going to get rid of him that easily.

He walked into the house and saw her moving down a long hallway. He followed and entered the large kitchen in time to see her bang a teakettle onto a burner then turn and rummage in one of the cupboards.

She stretched to reach something on the top shelf, and Jared couldn't help but notice her legs. For all her scatter-brained faults, Jenny Beckinsale had killer legs. Long and tanned and the kind that could wrap around a man and suck him in.

"Are you always this rude?" she asked, turning to face him with a mug in one hand a box of tea in the other. "Roaring into people's driveways at the crack of dawn?"

"Seven thirty is hardly the crack of dawn."

She grunted—*grunted*—and plopped a teabag into her cup. For several moments she seemed deep in thought until she finally held out her hand toward him. "I want to see your driver's license."

"Excuse me?" It wasn't often a person surprised him, but in less than three minutes, she'd managed to do it twice.

"You heard me. Your driver's license. It occurred to me after you left yesterday that you may not be who you say you are."

"Are you kidding?"

"Do I look like I'm kidding?"

Jared thought about arguing further, but what was the point? All he wanted was to get his money and get out of here. If her looking at his driver's license would speed the process along, so be it. He dug his wallet out of his Levi's back pocket and tossed it onto the nicked and scarred butcher-block countertop.

Before she picked it up, she gave him a glare, obviously pissed he hadn't handed the wallet directly to her. *Too bad, sweetheart.*

While she took her sweet time studying his license, he

looked around. He couldn't see down the hallway to what he'd passed on the way in, but the kitchen was large—one of those country kitchens he'd seen on magazine covers at the checkout stands. But he got the feeling this was the real deal—no remodel job here. Wide planked floors, yellow walls, blue cupboards softened and sanded by years of use, and a large antique stove. The same wood floors that were in the kitchen stretched into the adjoining family room. A river rock fireplace dominated the far wall, and a bank of windows showcased a backyard full of more flowers. While the furniture was a little flowery for his taste, he had to admit that the plush sofa looked damned comfortable. Even with the faded flowery print, he could imagine sinking in and propping his feet up on the worn wooden coffee table while enjoying a beer.

"You're in the military," she said, bringing his attention back around. She was staring at his military ID.

Was, but he didn't correct her.

"Is that how you knew Steven?"

He didn't miss the way her voice dipped and stumbled across Steven's name. "Same squadron."

Slowly, she returned his wallet. "So you're a fighter pilot." It was a statement not a question, but either way, he wasn't answering. "I should have known."

The teakettle whistled, cutting off their conversation. And frankly, he was glad. That was one road he didn't feel like heading down again.

She shut off the burner and poured the boiling water into her cup. After doctoring it with two spoonfuls of sugar, she gave it a quick stir and then took a careful sip. The moment she did, her eyes closed, her mouth parted, and a long, low sigh whispered from deep in her throat.

She stood like that for several moments. Eventually she took another sip, and the whole eye closing, lips parting, long sighing was repeated.

Jesus H. Christ. It was like watching porn. Good porn.

"Sorry," she said after awhile. "I'm not quite human until I've had caffeine."

"That isn't caffeine." His voice was sharper than he'd intended, but the whole wallet search and X-rated tea show had set him on edge.

"Yes it is," she said, taking another sip.

"Look, I didn't come here to discuss your drink preference."

"I'm sorry," she said in a rush, her tone a one eighty from when she'd demanded to see his wallet. "I didn't offer you anything to drink. Can I get you something?"

"If it's tea, no thanks."

Her smile looked forced. "I think I have a coffeepot around here somewhere. It won't take me but a second."

"Don't bother. I won't be sticking around that long."

The top half of her disappeared into a lower cupboard. "I know it's here somewhere." There was a loud clanking, as if she'd knocked over a stack of pots and pans. "You really should try tea. Not only does it taste good, but a lot of varieties are also good for you."

With a resigned sigh, he snagged the leg of one of the stools tucked under the kitchen peninsula with his boot and pulled it out. "I thought everyone from Seattle liked coffee." He took a seat.

"Not me." *Clank. Clatter.* "I think that was the problem with the coffee stand I used to own. Aha. Look what I found." She reemerged, coffeepot in tow.

"Used to own?"

There was a moment of silence. "Yeah. I closed it."

Something in her tone told him she wasn't telling the complete truth.

She set the coffeepot down on the counter. "Right after my vintage clothing store closed," she said before heading over to the sink for water. It took her a few more minutes to locate a filter and grounds (just how old were they?) but before long, the smell of freshly brewing coffee filled the kitchen.

How many businesses had she owned? He was about to ask when a picture on her refrigerator caught his attention. He looked closer and saw the big smile of a sandy-haired guy who looked like Mr. All-American.

Steven.

"I'm sorry, you know."

She looked up at him, surprise evident in her sky blue eyes.

He didn't wait for her to say anything, mad at himself for bringing it up in the first place but knowing there was no way he could leave without saying it. "I'm sorry I wasn't at Steven's funeral. I wanted to be there."

He'd been stuck overseas in a desert so hot it boiled your blood. It had been the only time in his military career he'd fought for leave, but they'd denied him. There had been a situation . . . a crisis . . . a *something* . . . and they hadn't wanted their best pilot gone.

"Oh." The coffeepot sputtered. Hissed. And he could see how she struggled to find a breath. For the first time he wondered what it would feel like to have someone miss him as much as she obviously missed Steven. "I'm sure he would have understood."

Yeah, he would have. Steven was that type of guy. "Look." Jared stood, suddenly wanting nothing more than to get out of there. "We got off on the wrong foot yesterday. I'm not here to become your partner."

She all but sighed with relief. "You're not?"

"No. I'm just here to collect on my loan."

The relief he saw on her face was short lived. "I don't have your money."

"No problem." He slid the chair back under the counter. "We'll stop by your bank before I head out of town."

"Y-you don't understand. I don't have it."

"I wasn't expecting you to have the cash lying around. You can write me a check, or we can go to the bank and have the money transferred into my account."

She shook her head and worried her lower lip. "I don't have it. Here or at the bank."

"Get it."

She looked at him like he was crazy. "How? By turning over rocks? Chasing down leprechauns? Playing the lottery?"

"I don't care how. Sell something. Sell the plane. Sell this house. Sell your fancy sports car." Her deep blush told him his suspicions had been correct. Miss Playmate of the Month drove around in a fifty thousand dollar automobile while her house and hangar were falling down around her. Unbelievable.

Her bottom lip stilled. "And how would I run the business if I sold this property? The plane?"

"What business? From the looks of things, there doesn't seem to be any business."

Her eyes flashed all shades of mad at him. "I am not selling. Ever."

"Fine. Then find another way."

"There is no way I can—"

"I'm not interested in your financial problems." He could feel the Mexican sand slipping through his grasp. "Go to a bank. Or go to your parents. Steven told me how rich they were. Frankly, I don't give a rip what you do. Just do it."

She moved toward him, braced the palms of her hands on the counter. "What are you, a Nike commercial?"

This was all a joke to her. "Find the money, or I will."

"What's that supposed to mean?"

"You might have an aversion to selling, but I don't." He turned and left the same way he came in. Come hell or high water, he was going to get his money. He'd finally found what he wanted, and no one was going to stop him. No one. Not even a honey-haired goddess with a centerfold's body and hot pink nails.

FOUR

The minute the bell rang, Cody was out the door. He heard his teacher calling his name, but he ignored her. He knew what she wanted—what she always wanted lately. To rag on him about something: a bad grade, a missing assignment, a test he needed to retake. But there was no way he was going to stop and listen to that today.

Hitting the main hall, he stuffed his book and papers into his backpack, not bothering to stop at his locker. All he could think about was getting home and getting ready for the game. He was almost to the front doors when he heard his best friend.

"Hey, Code Man! Wait up." Parker jogged up beside him, bumped him in the shoulder.

"Heya, Parker."

"Ready for the big game?"

"Yeah. You?"

"Like duh." Parker grinned.

They headed outside. A group of kids were piled around the front steps. Several called out to them as they hurried past. Cody and Parker tossed hi's back without stopping.

"I heard Coach is putting Brady on third base," Parker said as they made their way across the grass.

"Sweet. If he sticks Mason there again, we're screwed."

"No kidding." Parker spotted his mom parked out front. "Wanna ride?"

"Nah, not today."

"Okay, dude." Parker opened the car door and threw his backpack on the floor. His younger brother and sister were in the backseat arguing about something. Parker glanced back at Cody and rolled his eyes. "See ya at the game."

"Yeah, see ya."

"Hello, Cody," Parker's mom said, leaning across to peer out the passenger side.

"Hi, Mrs. Nelson."

"Do you need a ride to the game this afternoon?"

Cody hiked his backpack farther up onto his shoulder. He shook his head. "My mom's taking me."

Surprise flashed across Mrs. Nelson's face. "That's great. I'm glad she'll get to see at least one game this season."

He smiled. "Yeah, me, too."

"Aren't you pitching tonight?"

"Yep."

"Honestly, I don't know how your mother finds the time. I can barely take care of these three, let alone hold down a job. And just last week Parker's dad and I heard your mother's name on the news. Again." She shook her head. "The *news*." Now Mrs. N. was the one with the smile. "Something about the delivery of a set of quintuplets. Your mother has such an important job. And your father. I'm just amazed—"

"Come on, Ma," Parker interrupted, exchanging a look with Cody. Mrs. N. would go on *forever* if they let her. "We gotta go."

"Oh, all right." She turned in her seat, said something to Parker's brother and sister, which instantly shut them up. "If you change your mind about that ride, Cody, just give us a call. It's no problem."

"Thanks, but like I said, my mom is driving me."

After they drove away, Cody hurried to the crosswalk, only to be held up by the dorky lady with her dorky sign and even dorkier orange vest. She acted like they were still in kindergarten. Finally, she walked out into the street, held up the stop sign, and waved him and the other kids across. He took off at a sprint.

Even though his house was only seven blocks from the school, his mom had never let him walk home alone before this year. She kept saying he was too young. No matter how many times he told her he wasn't a baby, she just ignored him and made sure Parker's mom or one of his other friends' mom gave him a ride. But at the start of this school year, Dad said since he was in eighth grade, he was old enough to walk home by himself. Cody couldn't believe it when Mom finally said okay. But every day one of the moms still offered him a ride.

By the time he reached Fircrest, he was out of breath. He slowed to a walk. Maybe he should have stopped off at his locker, gotten rid of some of the junk in his backpack. But he hadn't wanted to waste the time. Using his arm, he pushed at his backpack. A stupid book kept jabbing into his back.

A fat raindrop hit his white sleeve. He looked up and saw dark clouds rolling across the sky. Scowling, he started to run again. A few minutes later, he turned onto his street. When he hit his driveway, he slowed and headed to the side door, digging his key out of his backpack's front pocket.

He couldn't help but roll his eyes, like he did every time he saw the keychain. It was so retarded. Retarded and huge. Like his mom thought if she didn't buy him the biggest one possible, he'd lose it. And if the ginormous plastic house wasn't bad enough, she'd written his name and phone number on the back. If he lost it and a burglar found it, they'd know exactly which house to break into. Cody rolled his eyes again. Sometimes his mom was so weird.

He kicked the door shut behind him and immediately pulled off his tie. Attending Saint Charles with their stupid uniforms and stupider rules could have been social suicide; the only thing that saved him was that his buddies also went there.

He dumped his backpack in the laundry room, went into the kitchen, and picked up the phone.

"Dr. Adams's office. How may I help you?"

"It's Cody."

"Hi, Cody," his mom's receptionist said just like she did every school day. "You made it home okay?"

Duh. "Yeah. Can you tell Mom I'm home?" He didn't even bother to ask to speak to her, knowing she'd be busy. She was always busy.

"I sure will."

"Thanks."

He headed for his room. The house was quiet, like it always was on Marie's afternoons off. In his bedroom he found his baseball uniform washed, folded, and waiting for him on the corner of his bed. On top of the uniform, Marie had left a note wishing him good luck at the game.

Knowing he only had a half hour until his mom got home, he quickly changed.

Back downstairs, he found another note on the kitchen table, this one telling him to have an apple and some cheese for snack. And a glass of milk.

Riiight. He left the note where it was (just in case his mom wondered what he'd had for a snack), and, instead, dug around in the pantry until he found the box of Pop Tarts buried in the back.

His stomach growled as he put two in the toaster. He hadn't eaten his lunch today. He knew his friends thought it was because of today's game. And yeah, that was part of it, but the real reason he was so psyched was because his mom was going to be there. Neither of his parents had been to a game all season. He knew his dad wouldn't make a game because he was off to some country Cody couldn't even find on a map. Doctors Without Borders. Cody wasn't exactly sure what that meant, but when he'd tried asking his dad and mom about it, they gave him some vague answer that probably only made sense to people with brains as big as theirs.

He glanced at the clock. Fifteen minutes till Mom got home. He was just about to go into the family room and play a video game when he changed his mind. Getting his backpack, he dug out his math book and got to work on homework. Mom would be shocked. He'd made his way halfway through tonight's problems when the phone rang.

"Adams residence."

"Hi, Cody, it's Mom."

"Are you on your way?"

There was a slight pause. "Look, Cody, I'm really sorry, but I'm going to be late."

"That's okay. We don't have to be there until four thirty."

"I'm sorry, honey, but—"

"You can still make it, Mom. You have plenty of time."

"I'm sorry, honey, but there's nothing I can do. Something came up at work—"

"It's always work."

"Cody . . ."

He squeezed his eyes shut. Hard. He wouldn't cry. He wouldn't. "You promised."

"This is important." She didn't say anything for a long time, like she was waiting for him to say something. But he was done talking. No one ever listened anyway.

"I've already called Parker's mom, and they're going to pick you up," his mom said after the silence had gone on forever. In the background, he could hear someone calling her name. "Honey, I've got to go."

She paused again. Then, finally, "Bye, Cody. I'll get home as soon as I can."

He hung up the phone. After a moment, he rushed over to the table, grabbed his homework, and ripped it into a million little pieces.

He caught his reflection in the large mirror on the wall. Fat tears rolled down his cheeks. He ground his fist into his eyes. He was such a baby. A big fat crybaby. Who cared if his mom came or not?

He looked into the mirror again, saw his blotchy, tear-streaked face and the bright white of his uniform. Turning, he ran up to his room as fast as he could and ripped his uniform off. Shrugging into a pair of jeans and a hooded sweatshirt, he went back down and slipped on his favorite pair of sneakers. His mom hated these sneakers. She kept telling Cody to throw them away because they were so old and torn. But Cody wouldn't get rid of them.

Without wasting another moment, he tore out the back door and grabbed his bike out of the garage. Who cared about a stupid old game? With tears streaming down his face, he pedaled as hard and as fast and as far as he could.

* * *

Jenny stared at herself in the full-length mirror and tried to recognize the woman she saw staring back. Her face was pale, her hair limp, her eyes dull and rimmed in red, and the black suit she swore she'd never wear again hung on her frame, testifying to all the weight she'd recently lost.

From the time she'd turned fifteen, she'd done the ten-pound battle, trying everything under the sun to shed it. Low carb. No carb. High fat. Low fat. All fruit. No fruit. But what little weight she managed to lose would always come right back, refusing to stay off. Until nine months ago when, on a warm August night, a drunk driver blew through a stop sign and took from her the only thing she'd ever truly wanted.

Those ten pounds she used to think so important fell off her. And then another ten. She knew she was bordering on too thin, but most days she could barely manage to choke down more than a bite or two. The only real meal she ate each week was the lunch with her mom, and she only finished that because it was easier than the verbal battle that would follow if she didn't.

How could everything have gone so wrong in such a short amount of time?

The panic and despair she'd been fighting to keep at bay since Jared had left demanded to be let loose.

She would never sell. Never. She would brave the lion's den—or the banker's office, as the case may be—to save her and Steven's dream.

The drive into Hidden Lake had never seemed to take so long . . . or go so fast. Before she had fully gathered her thoughts and courage, she was maneuvering into a parking spot right out front of the bank. Purse and file folder in hand, she entered the bank. She stopped a few feet inside, letting her eyes adjust. The two tellers—Sue and Monica—called out a greeting. Jenny waved to them and the only other customer in the bank, Mr. Denton, but her mind was elsewhere. She scanned the cool, quiet interior looking for—

"Jennifer. What a pleasant surprise."

Slowly, Jenny turned. "Hello, Mr. Howard."

John Howard, president of Hidden Lake's one and only bank, stood less than five feet from her. As usual, the short man was impeccably dressed—a navy blue suit with a crisp white shirt and gray tie. His full head of brown hair was expertly styled and his black leather shoes polished to a high sheen. Even though he was only a handful of years older than she was, Jenny always got a paternal vibe from him. Maybe it was because he spoke to her in that same kind but I-know-what's-best-for-you manner her father did. Or maybe it was because of the way he always gave her a pat and soft squeeze on her arm whenever they saw each other. As if reading her thoughts, he reached out and gave her upper arm a friendly squeeze.

"What brings you into the bank on this fine day?"

"Actually . . ." Jenny paused, swallowed. "Do you have a minute? I was hoping we could talk."

His expression seemed to brighten. "Certainly. Shall we go into my office?" He stretched his arm out, indicating the way. As if she didn't know. It seemed as if every other month she was making her way down the short hallway and into his office.

She gave him a smile. "Thanks."

A new picture of his recent halibut fishing trip was on his desk, but other than that, his office was unchanged.

The same serviceable oak desk, bookcase, and filing cabinet crowded the small interior. The only thing that kept the room from feeling claustrophobic was the large window that offered an unobstructed view of Hidden Lake. She shifted her weight in the chair and crossed her legs. She didn't want to be here, but what other choice did she have? This was her problem, and she needed to find the solution.

"What can I do for you today?" Mr. Howard said, lowering himself into the chair behind the desk. "Your loan payment isn't due for another three weeks, so I know you're not here to ask for an extension already."

His tone and smile were sincere, but Jenny still felt herself turning red. "No, I'm not here about an extension, but it is concerning my loan."

"Yes?"

Her stomach tightened; her palms began to sweat. She had the sudden, insane urge to laugh and jump up, say this was all a silly joke, and flee the room. But this was no joke. And running away wouldn't get her anywhere or anything except an unwanted partner. She tucked her purse next to her on the seat along with the folder she'd brought in. She squeezed her hands together and resisted the urge to dry her palms off on her skirt. *Oh, Steven, I need you. I can't do this alone.*

But she knew she had to. Steven wasn't here . . . wasn't coming back . . . and it was up to her to keep their dream alive. She just wished she'd planned a little better for this meeting. Gone over the books . . . looked at the contract she'd brought along . . . ferreted information from her brother about how she should approach the bank. But as usual, she hadn't done her homework. She'd jumped in headfirst without stopping to look or question or seek advice. This time it was her voice in her head—not her mother's or her brother's—that said, *Oh, Jennifer.*

"I wanted to talk to you about a loan."

John Howard was all patience. "Go on."

Jenny took a deep breath and plunged ahead. "Well . . .

Blue Sky Air is at a critical point in its expansion. The new advertising plan we've implemented is showing great promise. Early bookings for the summer season already show a positive growth. Plus, we are confident that the weekend getaway packages we've negotiated with hotels and B and Bs on the nearby islands are going to garner strong interest. Blue Sky should see a sharp increase in profits this year." She didn't know why she was using plural pronouns, but somehow it made everything sound so much . . . bigger. More official. There was no *we* any longer. Just *she*. The new ideas had been hers. Succeed or fail, it all rested on her. But the business was showing an increase. This time last year she only had one scheduled charter. As of today, she had two, and in her mind that was a fifty percent increase. Sharp indeed.

The bank manager sat back in his chair and studied her. As the seconds ticked by, she began to squirm, feeling like a bug under a microscope. "This need for an additional loan wouldn't by chance have anything to do with the appearance of Mr. Worth, would it?"

"How did you—"

"I ran into Lovie Murphy at the Chamber of Commerce meeting this morning, and you know how she likes to talk. Before Sally had finished reading the minutes from our last meeting, Lovie had told everyone everything she could about her latest customer. Including his name."

"I don't understand. How did you know about him? About Jared Worth?"

"I've known about him for some time."

She couldn't have been more surprised if it had started snowing right then. "You have?"

He nodded, and his face took on that distinctive paternal look once more. "Naturally. Before a loan approval is granted, the bank requires a full and complete understanding of the lendee's standings. This includes Blue Sky Air's loan with Mr. Worth."

"So then you understand why I'm here."

"I'm not certain I—"

"I need a loan to buy out Mr. Worth's interest. I will not have a partner. What I mean," she quickly added just so he didn't think she was being completely unreasonable, "is that like I was saying, Blue Sky is at a critical point of expansion, and Mr. Worth and I do not see eye to eye on how the business should be run." Putting it mildly. Their differences, in a nutshell, were that Jenny saw Blue Sky continuing just as it had, while that man saw it de-winged, dismantled, and dissected into saleable bits.

"I'm sorry, Jennifer, but I just don't think we're going to be able to help you."

"But—"

"You know I have great respect for what you're trying to do, but for the bank it all comes down to numbers. Profit. Losses." The last word was said in a soft, sympathetic tone.

Neither of them needed a calculator to determine what column her business fit in. When she looked up and into his kind eyes, she knew there was nothing she could say to change his mind. Bottom line was bottom line.

With as much grace and maturity as she could muster, Jenny stood and stretched out her arm. "Thank you for your time, Mr. Howard."

He took her hand and grasped it softly. "I'm sorry. I wish things could be different. Come back in six months. If business is picking up like you say it is, there's a strong chance we can work something out. In the meantime, maybe your parents—"

"Thank you again," she interrupted, cutting him off mid-sentence. While everything in her screamed to run and run fast, she forced herself to walk sedately out of his office, out the front door, out into the sun's bright light. It wasn't until she was inside her car that she let the full impact of the refusal hit her. She tossed her purse and file folder on the passenger seat where they promptly slid off and onto the floor, spilling their contents.

"Perfect. Just perfect," she mumbled as she took in the mess.

In pure frustration, she leaned her forehead against the hard curve of the steering wheel and waited for the rush of tears, certain they would fall. But, strangely, the tears didn't come. It was as if she'd used up all of her tears over the last nine months, and now she had nothing left.

Slowly, she lifted her head and stared out her windshield. Ahead of her lay the road that led out of town to the western shore of Hidden Lake.

Maybe your parents.

The bank president's words came back to her. For a moment she contemplated starting up the car, following that scenic road to her parents' home. She tried to picture the scene in her mind. Walking up alongside the manicured lawn, the impeccably tended flower beds, to the Colonial-style entrance with its wide, white trim. She knew if she pleaded her case long enough, her dad would loan her the money.

But at what cost?

She continued to stare at the road ahead.

At what cost? She couldn't shake that thought.

Some things were more valuable than money, and she knew if she asked her parents for this loan, she'd end up paying them back with more than just money. Always before when she'd screwed up, flunked, or just plain failed, her parents had been there, bailing her out. And each time they rescued her, she could see the ever-sinking disappointment in their eyes. She was twenty-six years old. Too old to be running to her mom and daddy every time she got into trouble. It was time for her to stand on her own two feet. For no reason she could explain, a vision of Custer and his last stand flashed before her eyes. But that's what saving Blue Sky Air felt like to Jenny. Her last stand— the last chance she'd have to prove to her family that they were wrong about her. This time she wasn't only fighting for her self-respect, she was fighting for her and Steven's dream.

A car drove past, shaking her loose from her thoughts. She reached down and began to pick up the spilled con-

tents of her purse when the file folder caught her attention. As she continued to stare at it, something her brother
said came back to her. Quickly, she grabbed for the contract and scanned through the lengthy document. There,
toward the bottom of the second page, she found what she
was looking for. With an ever-increasing smile, she put her
keys in the ignition and brought the Corvette to life.

Jared Worth might have thought he had all the answers,
but he was wrong. Jenny was in the driver's seat now, a
place she intended to stay.

* * *

A short while later, Jenny pulled onto a well-concealed
dirt road at the head of the lake. Sunshine glinted off the
car's candy apple red hood, causing her to squint. She slowed
the car to a crawl. Potholes punctuated the dirt. Overgrown
brush stretched out from both sides of the road. With infinite care, she crept forward, maneuvering as best she could
to avoid the worst of the ruts and brush.

Not once had that insufferable man mentioned she had
four months left to pay off his loan. The jerk had put the
fear of God into her, making her think she had to come up
with the money immediately.

Instead of doing your nails tonight, read the contract.

She'd read the contract all right! Maybe he should have
read it a little closer. She let out an unladylike snort, and
her foot slipped on the gas. The car jerked forward. Hitting
the brakes, she regained control and began the slow crawl
down the road once more. Who did he think he was? She
wasn't the one who needed to read the contract, he was.

The dirt road was long and curvy but finally the lane
opened up, spilling out into a small parking area. Ahead
of her was the lake. In the early afternoon sun, the water
glistened and sparkled, but it wasn't the beauty of the vi-
brant blue surface that drew her attention, it was the motorcycle parked off to the left.

For the first time in over a day, she smiled. Score one

for the home team, aka the local gossip mill. Her neighbors had yet to let her down.

After reading the contract, she'd had only one thought: locate Jared Worth. But finding him had proven more difficult than she'd thought. She'd driven around for a half hour, checking all the spots she thought he might be, until she'd remembered that if you wanted to find out something in Hidden Lake, you needed to head to the diner. She'd been there for less than ten minutes when Mr. Wilcox had come in telling anyone and everyone who'd listen about that there fancy mot-e-cycle out at the head of the lake.

God bless Mr. Wilcox and his daily fishing excursion. Feeling better than she had all day, she'd paid for her Coke and headed out.

Parking was usually tight, but since the motorcycle was the only other vehicle here, Jenny had plenty of room. Briefly she wondered how Jared had found this spot. It was a locals' hangout, a place the tourists never found. With the sun out in earnest now, she left her windows down and her suit jacket in the car. She probably should have gone back to the house and changed out of her black suit, but she'd been too impatient. Normally she wasn't the confrontational type, but right now she couldn't wait to see the expression on his face when she told him to leave.

The thought made her smile.

The lake was deserted. She glanced around, hoping to spot him. Except for the motorcycle, there was no sign of him. With a sigh of resignation, she made her way down the short path to the beach. Her black high heels sank into the sand, and she slipped them off. The ground was warm beneath her bare feet, and she dug her toes deep into the sand, luxuriating in the feel. She glanced right and then left. Empty beach greeted her in both directions. For a moment she contemplated which way to go. To the right the beach narrowed against a stand of tall evergreens that abutted the water, allowing only a narrow path along the lake. Few people traveled that way. To the left the sand stretched wide as it flared and then curved back against the shore. There weren't any trees barring that path, and the sand was less rocky. Without examining her reasoning too closely, Jenny headed to the right, certain it was the path he'd taken.

She tripped and stumbled over the rocks and logs, silently cursing him all the way. She hadn't gone more than fifty yards when she stopped short and drew in a quick breath.

He stood near the water's edge, one foot braced on a fallen tree. His gaze was focused out across the water, and he seemed lost in thought. He'd ditched the leather jacket she'd seen him wearing yesterday, and his white T-shirt stretched taut across an impossibly wide set of shoulders before tapering down into the waistband of his Levi's. He seemed relaxed, as if he didn't have a care in the world, but somehow she knew his posture was deceiving. He tossed a small rock in his hand. The picture was so perfect he looked like a model for an elite outdoorsman magazine.

On second thought, there was too much unleashed power in his stance, too much command to be a model—
Oh, for crying out loud!

"Mr. Worth," she said louder and sharper than she'd intended, angry with herself over those outrageous thoughts.

"Miss Beckinsale," he said without turning, and she got the distinct impression he'd known she'd been standing there, staring at him, all along, even though he'd never glanced her way.

"We need to talk." She strove for a steady tone and feared she'd failed miserably.

Slowly, he took his leg off the log and faced her. "Do you have my money?"

"No." She began to fidget under his sharp gaze. "Th-that's why I'm here. I read over the contract"—*as you obviously didn't*—"and the loan isn't due for four months." She waited, expecting . . . secretly hoping . . . to

see some flicker of emotion cross his face. Surprise—
disappointment—anger. But his closed features gave nothing away. "Did you hear me? I—"

"I heard you." He tossed the rock into the lake, not
bothering to see where it landed.

"I have four months."

"I'm aware of that."

"Then why—"

"Why what? Why not wait? You're a sinking ship, lady,
and I want to find dry land while I still have the chance."

She took a step toward him. "You have no idea what
you're talking about."

"I saw the business myself, remember?"

"You don't understand. Everything is going to be different this summer. I'm going to do what Steven and I set
out to do. I'm going to turn Blue Sky Air into the Pacific
Northwest's premiere seaplane service."

"You?" He laughed; it wasn't a nice sound. "Sweetheart, you couldn't turn that business around if you had
four years."

"I am not your sweetheart, and I don't need four years.
I have four months. Come back then . . . or don't. I don't
really care."

"You'd like that."

"Immensely," she said with one hundred percent honesty.

"I hate to rain on your parade, but I'm not that accom-
modating. If you want to keep plucking away at this futile
dream of yours, then by all means, have at it. But you're
not taking me down with you in the process. Buy me out."

"You know I can't do that right now."

"Then we'll do what I suggested yesterday. Sell."

"Over my dead body."

His gaze was hot enough to start a forest fire. "Don't
tempt me."

"Oh . . . you . . . you . . ." Where was the killer comeback when you needed one?

"Listen," his tone went all reasonable and placating,

and for some reason, that upset her even more. Probably because he was beginning to sound like her family. "We sell, and each of us gets what we want. You don't want to run a business. I know it was Steven's idea, not yours."

"Don't presume to know what I want."

He continued, ignoring her. "I get my money, and you'd end up with enough cash to keep you in high heels and those fancy wheels you drive."

He could go to— "I'm not selling."

"We'll see about that."

"Intimidation isn't going to work with me, Mr. Worth. I have four months in which to repay you. And even if— even *when* I have the money long before the due date, I have no intention of handing it over until I absolutely have to." Without saying another word, she turned and began to walk away. She could feel herself quaking and knew that if she didn't get out of there soon, she was doomed. She'd put on a brave front, but that's all it was: a front. Because even though she'd told him intimidation wouldn't work, it had been a lie. He did more than intimidate her; he unnerved her. And that scared her most of all.

* * *

Jared watched her stomp away. Was she for real? Did she really think she was going to get away with this? He'd seen the state of the business. If he walked away and came back in four months, there'd be nothing left. She might not give a damn that she was sinking her own financial future, but he sure as hell gave a damn about his. Thanks to the military, that money was all he had left, and there was no way he was going to let her flush his dream down the drain with hers.

I am going to turn Blue Sky Air into the Pacific Northwest's premiere seaplane service.

He almost laughed again then realized there was nothing to laugh about. She had as much business sense as a bird.

As he watched her continue to make her way down the

uneven shore, she stumbled, then immediately righted herself, but not before one of her shoes fell out of her hands and onto the sand. Leave it to her to come to the beach in high heels.

As she bent down to pick up her shoe, he couldn't help but admire how her skirt stretched across her butt. It wasn't hard to imagine a big fluffy white bunny tail on that tight little ass.

He'd seen a lot of gorgeous women in his time, but he had to give Jenny Beckinsale points for perfection. Cotton Tail might not have a head for business, but she sure as hell had a body for sin.

He had no doubt that most men fell at her feet, eager to grant her every wish—but not him. Maybe once, a long time ago. But he'd learned his lesson the hard way, and since then, he'd done his damnedest to avoid pitfalls like her: gorgeous women who made him forget his past and believe he was a guy who could fit, could be the type of steadfast man they wanted. There was only one thing that mattered to him right now, and it had Mexico written all over it.

Jenny was nearing the opening to the path. With each ass-swinging, sand-flying step she took, he could feel his money disappearing. He told himself to let her go. To let her walk away. Getting tangled up with her would be the worst thing he could do.

But what choice did he have?

"Son of a bitch."

He caught up with her before she'd taken another step. He blocked her path, forcing her to stop. Her eyes widened to the size of saucers. "Tomorrow, oh seven hundred. I'll see you at the office. And, Cotton Tail, make room for my desk."

FIVE

Night settled on Hidden Lake. In the darkness, Jenny sat on her front porch, staring out across the moonlit water. Most nights she found an inner peace sitting out here, a peace she couldn't find anywhere else. In the quiet darkness, the lake possessed a serenity that was lost in the bright light of day. But tonight, no matter how hard she tried, the tranquillity she craved was nowhere to be found.

The wind rustled through the trees, and she drew her legs up, wrapping the afghan her grandmother had made around her. The rocking chair swayed at her movement. She rested her chin on her bent knees, wondering not for the first time how her whole life could be turned upside down in one short day.

Tomorrow, oh seven hundred. I'll see you at the office. And, Cotton Tail, make room for my desk.

She looked down at her left hand, to the diamond ring she still wore. *Steven* . . . But instead of the memories that usually filled her when she thought of him, tonight, she was full of questions. Why hadn't he told her about that loan? But before she finished the thought, she knew the real question wasn't why hadn't he told her, it was why she hadn't asked. She had access to all the books, to the business records and documents. There had been nothing preventing her from gaining full knowledge of Blue Sky's financial obligations. So why hadn't she?

Because it had been easier to leave it all in Steven's hands, to let him make the tough decisions. She had been an equal partner on paper but not in truth. And that reality was a hard pill to swallow. But Steven had seemed to prefer it that way. And so had she. While he'd been building Blue Sky, she'd been building their life. She had ideas for the business, but there were more important things, like dreaming of soon. Soon they'd be married. *Soon* they'd start a family. But *soon* had turned out to be as far away as the moon and just as unattainable.

A car pulled off the main road and made its way down her driveway. Headlights arced across the yard, momentarily illuminating the still lake before the car parked and the lights were doused.

On any other night, Jenny would have been surprised by a late-night visitor. She knew that by avoiding her mother's calls ever since the scene in the restaurant, it was only a matter of time before someone from her family showed up. Her only question was which one of her family members it would be. Her bet was on Dad. The peacemaker.

But it wasn't her dad, Jenny noted a few moments later as her sister made her way up the stairs. The porch was dimly lit, but even in the faint light, Jenny could see that Anna was as impeccably dressed as always. Only her sister could work a fifteen-hour day at the hospital and still look like she'd just stepped out of the pages of a high fashion magazine. Only Anna and their mother.

Anna's high heels clicked against the wooden porch as she made her way toward Jenny.

"Hey," Jenny said, trying hard not to tense.

Just for a day, she wondered what it would be like to

be her sister, to be someone for whom everything came easily. Marriage. Career. Raising her son. All Anna had to do was want something, and it was hers.

Her sister sat down in the rocking chair nearest Jenny. With only a small table and a couple of feet separating them, it was easy to see the perpetual look of disapproval and disappointment on Anna's face. "Hello, Jenny."

"Are you hungry?" she asked quickly, before Anna could start firing questions at her. Jenny wanted to turn the conversation far away from the topic her sister had undoubtedly been sent here to discuss. "There's some leftover dinner on the stove."

"You cooked?" Her sister didn't bother to hide her surprise or her alarm.

"Soup. From a can."

"Thank God," Anna said with a solemnity that bordered on hysterical. "The last time I ate your cooking, I was sick for a week."

"It wasn't a week." Only a sister could say something like that and get away with it.

"You're right; it was four days."

Jenny couldn't help it, she laughed. It was well-known—and a well-trotted-out joke at each family gathering—that she was a bad cook. No, not bad, horrid. She'd never given cooking much thought until after she and Steven had gotten engaged. Wanting to be the best wife she could possibly be, she'd set out to learn. The third time the fire department had shown up at her house, she grudgingly accepted defeat. Or, almost. Every once in a while she mustered up the nerve to give it another try. And each time she was met with the same disastrous results. It was humiliating, but at least now she was humiliated in private.

"If you won't eat my cooking, how about a glass of wine? Even I can't screw that up."

Anna smiled. "Sounds great."

Jenny disappeared inside the house and was back outside a few moments later, wine bottle and glass in hand. She handed Anna the glass of chardonnay.

"Thanks," her sister said, watching as Jenny refilled her own near-empty glass, which was sitting on the small table between them.

"Rough day?" Anna asked when Jenny took her seat.

"You have to ask?"

"No." Anna took a sip of wine. "Mom's worried about you."

"She doesn't need to be."

"Grow up, Jenny. She worries about you so much she doesn't have time to think about anyone else."

The reproach in her sister's tone was nothing new, but it stung nonetheless. "That's not true."

"Yes, it is."

Jenny fell silent. No matter what she said, her sister would find fault. But this time she knew there was fault to be found. She had a partner—one she had known nothing about. Revealing that to anyone was humiliating; admitting it to her perfect sister was unthinkable.

But Jenny knew she wouldn't have to admit anything. No doubt her whole family knew the entire story by now, thanks to her mother and brother.

Jenny sipped her wine. She knew her sister was expecting a recap of all the events from the moment *Jared Worth* had walked into her mother's restaurant and announced he was her partner to five minutes before Anna showed up. But Jenny wasn't in the mood to rehash all the mortifying details. If her sister wanted to know something, she was going to have to ask.

An uneasy silence descended between them. In the near distance, shallow waves washed against the wooden pilings, an owl hooted, and the widening distance between two sisters who'd once been so close became all the more clear.

"Jenny, I only have a half an hour," her sister said finally, breaking the silence.

"So go."

"You know I can't do that."

She could, but she wouldn't. Jenny wrapped the afghan back around her, still hurting from her sister's earlier comment. When she spoke, she lashed out. "How is my nephew? Flunked out of any other classes lately?"

"He didn't flunk."

"I thought a B minus was as good as failing in your house."

"Refusing to live up to your potential is as good as failing. Cody understands this. Learning to work hard from an early age is the only way to achieve success. What do you think Phillip and I should do? Wait until he's fifteen? Twenty?" Anna's gaze turned hard and direct. "Twenty-five?"

"I'm twenty-six."

Her sister's look said it all.

Jenny should just shut up and drop the subject. What did she know about raising kids? But lately her nephew had turned into a little monster, a fact only she seemed to notice. The one time she'd tried saying something to her mother, Mom had gotten so upset that Jenny would even suggest such a thing, Jenny had quickly and permanently dropped the subject.

"I went to Cody's last baseball game," Jenny said. "Mom told me he was going to be the starting pitcher, but he wasn't there."

For a moment, Jenny thought her sister looked rattled, but when she continued in her same condescending tone, Jenny was sure she must have imagined it.

"Cody had a prior school commitment and had to miss the game. But discussing my son is not the reason I am here; you know that. This is about you, Jenny. And your business. Success is not something that just happens. You have to be willing to work hard."

"And you think I don't?"

"No," her sister said with a brutal honesty. "I don't."

She should have been prepared for her sister's answer. Should have, but wasn't.

"Mom's upset you haven't returned her calls."

Jenny took another drink of her wine seeking fortification, finding none. "I've been busy."

"So I've heard. Just who is this Jared Worth?"

"I'm sure Paul told all of you exactly who he is."

"Of course he did," Anna said without the slightest pause. Discussing Jenny's life was a favorite pastime with her family. "But I'd like to hear it from you."

"There's nothing to say."

"That's not what I heard."

Of course it wasn't.

"When you and Steven started the business, you took out a loan from him?"

Jenny eyed the front door, wondering if she could make her escape. But she knew even if she made it inside, her sister would just follow. Anna hadn't become one of the country's leading neonatal obstetricians by backing down. Giving into the inevitable, and hoping it meant her sister would leave all that much sooner, Jenny answered. "Yes."

"And a condition of this loan was that he was made a partner?"

"Silent partner," Jenny amended, feeling a small bit of satisfaction.

"It doesn't sound like he's silent any longer," her sister pointed out, and what tiny bit of triumph Jenny had felt instantly evaporated.

"So, Jennifer, what are you going to do?"

Jennifer. Like she was two years old. And when was that damn wine going to kick in? "Anna, I just learned about the loan. I think I'm allowed a day or two to mull things over."

Her sister sat all the way back in the rocker and crossed her legs. "That's always been your problem, Jenny. You think and dwell but never act. You can't go through life sitting in the bleachers."

"Blue Sky Air is not some sideline hobby."

"So then, you have the money to repay this loan."

They both knew she didn't. Anna, being Anna, was just making her point. "I will," Jenny said with as much conviction as she could summon.

"Jenny," her sister said softly, "your record on running

a *profitable* business is far from stellar. How many times have Mom and Dad had to bail—"

"Not this time," she interrupted, remembering her failed vintage clothing shop, the coffee stand that had gone bust almost before it got started, and the secretarial job she'd lost because she'd misfiled a petition and the delay it caused had been costly. "Blue Sky Air is different. Besides, I have four months until the loan is due. I spoke with Mr. Howard at the bank, and everything is arranged. In a few months, when I show him how profits are up, I'll be able to get a loan and repay Jared Worth." She prayed she sounded more confident than she felt.

"Jenny . . ." The look on her sister's face left little doubt as to what Anna thought of that statement.

"This time is different," she said emphatically. *She* was different. Or, at least on her way to being different. Stronger. More determined.

"How's the website coming?" Anna asked.

Jenny's rocking chair came to a sudden halt. How was it Anna knew exactly where Jenny was most vulnerable? She struggled to find her voice, wanted to remind her sister of the new advertising plan she'd launched and the weekend getaway packages she had put together. But emotion clogged her throat, made it impossible for her to speak. The website. Like so many aspects of Blue Sky, the thought of returning to a project she and Steven had started all but crippled her.

"Fine," Jenny lied, finally able to speak. Thankfully, Anna let the subject of the website drop.

"Paul said this partner of yours was in the same squadron as Steven."

In the space of a day, her family had said Steven's name more times than they had in the last nine months. After the accident, as if by some tacit agreement, her family, neighbors, and friends had avoided any mention of Steven whatsoever. It was as if they believed that by acting as if he never existed, somehow her pain would go away, and she would forget. But Jenny would never forget. Each time she climbed into his car, smelled his cologne, or remembered how his arms felt wrapped around her, her heart cracked a little bit more. That was something she had learned since losing Steven—a heart didn't break all at once. It happened over time, bit by painful bit, until it completely shattered, leaving nothing left. Jenny could only pray that hers would shatter soon, because the pain was becoming more than she could bear.

"And here I thought you were done with flyboys. Is he at all like Steven?"

Like Steven.

The question took Jenny aback. She swallowed hard, fought to breathe. "No," she said, her voice hollow and achy. "He's nothing like Steven."

For a moment the pain of losing him lifted, and she saw him in her mind. She saw his bright open smile, heard his laughter, felt the warmth of his breath as he whispered something into her ear. Whenever they went out, he was the life of the party, telling joke after joke in his loud, booming voice that captured everyone's attention. He was as all-American as they came: handsome with his sandy blond hair and green eyes and a personality so open everyone loved him. Her most of all.

"Jenny? What's this Jared like? Mother seemed quite impressed, and you know what it takes to impress her."

Jenny tried to cling to the vision of Steven, but it drifted away, and another man took his place. She tried to block the image, but the effort was as futile as ignoring the man.

Against her will, her sister's question kept coming back to her. *What's he like?*

Honestly, she couldn't think of a way to describe him. She knew if one of her girlfriends ever saw him, they'd sum him up in three words: raw sex appeal.

But Jenny needed only one: *unsettling.*

Everything about him unnerved her. He was tall, with hair as dark as the night sky. And his eyes . . . Eyes that blue should hold warmth, or at least a hint of softness. But there was nothing soft about Jared. There was a hard ruthlessness about him that hinted at a life she couldn't understand, nor did she want to. Beneath that leather jacket, he wore a confidence like most men wore custom-made suits. And when he spoke, iron determination fortified his words. It was almost as if he was from another era, from a time when warriors ruled the land, and their cunning and strength determined their survival. Jenny had little doubt that if Jared had lived back then, he would have been a force to be reckoned with.

Who was she kidding? He was one now.

A shiver of apprehension ran through her. Even though she'd only met with him twice, somehow she knew: he was a man accustomed to getting his own way. And right now, Jenny was a roadblock he was determined to move.

Tomorrow, Jennifer.

She shivered again. One way or another, she was going to have to do the impossible. She was going to have to find a way to deter Jared Worth from his path.

She looked once more to her sister and said the only thing she could. "No. He's nothing like Steven."

*   *   *

Jared was mad as hell.

Not upset. Or furious. Or even pissed off. He'd passed those markers around three this morning.

Yesterday when he'd given Jenny his ultimatum, he'd known it was his only option. The only way for him to see his investment repaid. But that didn't mean he had to be happy about it. Plus, he'd thought Miss January would cave. When she hadn't, she'd surprised the hell out of him. Something that didn't happen all that often, if ever. But if she thought he was going to lie down and accept her terms, she had another think coming. For over fifteen years he'd been intimidating men who outranked, outsized, and flat-out outnumbered him. And he'd always come out on top. If she thought she could bluff her way past him, she was in for one rude awakening.

The conversation he'd had last night with his realtor came back to him, and he all but growled in frustration.

I'll try to stall and buy you some time, but get the money to me as soon as you can.

That's not how it was supposed to go last night. Last night was supposed to be about wire transfers. Sealing the deal. Signing on the bottom line. And getting the hell out of this town. Instead, he spent another night in lavender hell cursing the bargain he'd been forced into making. The more he thought on it, the more pissed he got.

Partner. In a tourist-taxing, travel-at-the-speed-of-a-snail, stuck-in-Mayberry, seaplane charter business. *Christ.*

With more speed than necessary, Jared pulled into Blue Sky a few minutes before seven. The bike's engine rumbled in the quiet, echoed off the lake. The first thing he saw was that wannabe plane at the end of the dock. The second, the Corvette.

His dark mood went to ugly black in less than a second.

What a goddamn waste of money. *His* money.

He parked in the same spot he had yesterday. The place was as deserted as a minefield. It was obvious no one was up. No one was working. No wonder there was no money to repay him. How did she think a business could survive— let alone thrive—if the owner didn't get her delectable little ass out of bed before noon?

Disgusted with the whole situation, he made his way toward the hangar. Briefly he'd toyed with the idea of going to the house and pounding on the door until Sleeping Beauty answered, but he discarded the idea as quickly as it had come. For one reason, he doubted she'd wake up. And second, even he realized he was too pissed-off to face anyone.

From his visit yesterday, he knew the office was located in the far corner of the hangar. His footsteps rang out against the concrete floor as he made his way through the dark, cavernous space. The office was unlocked. Big surprise. Letting himself in, he turned on the lights and looked around.

He swore again. Whatever he'd been expecting, this was far worse.

Boxes, stacks of papers, magazines, and even clothing for Christ's sake littered the room. The amount of shit was unbelievable. The top of the desk was buried under a mountain of God only knew what. The place was a disaster.

He shook his head. How in the hell did anyone get any work done in this chaos?

They didn't. That's how.

Ignoring the mess, he tried to see the office as it could be if it wasn't one big garbage can. All in all, it wasn't a bad space: large and bright. An expensive looking L-shaped desk was positioned against the far corner. Above it were two good-sized windows that faced the lake. Even in the muted morning light, the lake was a glistening, tranquil blue.

On the far wall, a brown leather sofa and two chairs formed a seating area but, like the rest of the office, their horizontal surface was covered in crap.

Tripping over a pair of high heels—*high heels!*—and an empty box, he made his way to the filing cabinets on the far wall. It took him less than a minute to discover the cabinets were almost completely empty. He would have laughed if the situation weren't so depressing.

"Jesus, Steven. What were you thinking?" But Jared knew exactly what—*where*—his friend's thoughts had been. They'd been on a pair of sky blue eyes and long legs. On a body with enough curves and swerves to make a man not give a shit about whether the office got cleaned or the filing got done.

It was obvious Jenny had brought other talents to the partnership. Talents he'd had no trouble envisioning last night—when he hadn't been cursing her.

Remembering the thoughts he'd had last night, something told him he should just leave, walk away from his money and this wreck of a business. But he'd never been one to take the easy road, and he wasn't about to lose his money. Besides, leaving would make her only too happy. And making her happy was the last thing he planned on doing.

Just the opposite, in fact. Sometime during the night, Jared realized she probably didn't believe him. But if she thought he'd just leave, she'd seriously underestimated him. Bluffing wasn't in his vocabulary. He'd give it two days . . . three at the most, before she went running to her parents begging them for the money to pay him off.

With that thought, his mood lifted, and he got to work. Buried under a mountain of paperwork, he found a small table with a coffeemaker and can of coffee. After a quick rinse in the bathroom sink, the coffeepot was good to go, and not long after, the smell of freshly brewed coffee filled the room.

With the help of caffeine, he made the desk his top priority. He worked nonstop, sorting through stacks of paperwork and piles of miscellaneous items. A lot of the stuff was junk. Some of it needed to be filed. And some of it just plain did not belong in an office. As he went to file some paperwork, he opened the drawer with the pitiful few folders. Intrigued, he pulled them out. As he glanced through them, he realized he was looking at a market strategy proposal for the company. And if his guess was correct, they were done in a woman's handwriting. Jenny's, undoubtedly. He continued to rifle through the papers, surprised to find some solid ideas. *Well, well, well.* Cotton Tail might have more to her than what met the eyes.

He put the folders back, along with the other paperwork he'd gathered and organized, and shut the file cabinet drawer. From what he could tell, none of those proposed strategies had been implemented. He wondered why the hell not.

He'd been working for nearly three hours when he heard footsteps slapping against the hangar's concrete floor. Moments later, Jenny entered the office.

Jared looked up. God, but she looked good. Too damn good. And totally pissed.

"Just what do you think you're doing?" she demanded.

"Good morning to you, too."

"Believe me, there is nothing good about this morning." She'd pulled her hair up into a ponytail, and with her every movement, it snapped back and forth like a golden flag.

Her anger was palpable, and Jared found himself responding. He'd been wading around in the pissed-off pool by himself for far too long—he more than welcomed the company. "Working. I'm not surprised you don't recognize it."

Her eyes shot sparks. "Leave."

"Gladly. Just as soon as you hand over my money."

"You know I don't have it."

With deliberation, he leaned back in the chair and propped his feet up on the edge of the desk—the *cleared* desk. Crossing his ankles, he steepled his hands behind his head. "Then I guess I'm staying."

"Don't you need to get back to your squadron?"

"I have plenty of time for this." It was the god-awful truth. He had nowhere to go. Nowhere he had to be. His whole life had been taken away by a military inquest.

She eyed his proprietary pose, and he could tell she wanted to take him out. "I have a business to run. How do you expect me to get any work done with you in the way?"

"Believe me, no one gets any work done in this pit."

"My office—"

"Is as organized as a landfill." He dropped his feet to the ground. "Just what time does this *Titanic* of a business open?"

Her chin stubbornly shot up. "Our hours are flexible."

He choked back a laugh. "More like nonexistent. Where's the guy I ran into yesterday? The one working on the plane? Why isn't he here?"

"Zeke has the day off."

"Of course he does." His tone was heavy with sarcasm.

"How I run my business is not your concern."

"Somehow I don't think these"—he reached for the stack of magazines he'd found—"have anything to do with running a business. Riveting as the articles are. And by the way, thanks for highlighting them."

"Give me those."

She made a move to grab them, but he easily evaded her.

"I don't think many clients come here looking for the 'Top Five Hair Removal Secrets,'" he read from one of the magazines. "Or," he thumbed down the pile. "'Six weeks to a perfect body.'"

Her face flushed pink.

This time, when she grabbed for the magazines, he let her take them.

"Every office has magazines."

"Lady, this isn't an office. It's a dump." He leaned back in the chair, enjoying watching her squirm. In a small way, it made up for all the garbage he'd just spent the last couple hours wading through. "It worked, just in case you were wondering."

She clutched the magazines to her chest and eyed him warily. "What worked?"

"The six weeks." He raked his eyes over her body, making sure he paused in all the right places to fully admire and appreciate her God-blessed assets. "You are perfect, Cotton Tail. I'll give you that."

Her face burned a crimson red. "Don't call me that."

"And if you need help with the other thing, you just let me know. I'd consider it my civic duty to volunteer."

He could see she didn't want to ask, could tell how hard she struggled. But in the end, curiosity won out. "What *other* thing?"

Before she knew what he was doing, he pulled one of the magazines from her tight grasp. There, on the front page and in letters large enough to grab attention at the grocery checkout stands, was the headline: "Ten Positions Guaranteed to Drive Him Wild." "Believe me, sweetheart, it would be a night you'd never forget."

"You are insane."

He flashed her a smile that had opened more bedroom doors than he could remember.

"Insane," she repeated, crossing her arms under her chest. The action molded her long-sleeved shirt tight against her, pulling the V neckline down until the tops of her full breasts were exposed. As clothing went, there was nothing provocative about what she wore. But try telling that to his body.

Jesus, what in the hell was wrong with him? He'd been tossing out sexual innuendos for more years than he could remember, and a helluva lot more explicit ones. Until now, they'd never boomeranged back around to him. But there was something about her . . . something that pushed him off center and made him think about things that were better left alone.

"Before you leave—"

"Who said I was leaving?" she interrupted.

He cut off his smile. She was tough; he'd give her that. But not tough enough. "Before you leave, I have something for you."

"You have nothing I want."

He hid his grin and opened the bottom desk drawer. It was full of crap. Female crap. Makeup. Nail polish. A plastic bottle labeled Polish Remover that smelled like shit. And a whole lot of other unnecessary stuff. Sliding the drawer all the way out, he upended it into one of the empty boxes he'd found earlier. The tiny glass bottles clinked together.

Too late, she realized what he was doing. Trying to stop him, she grabbed the box, and glass bottles of nail polish fell onto the floor. "What are you doing? You have no right."

"Lady, until you come up with my money, I have every right. And from now on, no personal shit in the office. And one more thing." He ripped a piece of paper off the pad he'd been writing on. "Here's a list of supplies I'll need to get this place into shape, and when you bring me my lunch, I like white bread. None of that whole wheat shit."

"Go to hell." Without taking the box or the slip of paper, she left.

Jared watched her go, smiling. Like taking candy from a baby. By this time tomorrow, she'd be begging her parents for the money.

* * *

Jenny slammed her front door behind her and instantly wished she hadn't. She grabbed her head and groaned. Drinking that bottle of wine last night had been a mistake. Naively she'd thought it would help. Help her get Jared out of her mind, help her deal with her sister, help her sleep. But it hadn't done any of those things. She'd spent yet another sleepless night walking through the dark and painfully quiet house, trying to forget.

There had been a time right after Steven's death when she'd wanted to go to sleep and never wake up. While she didn't wish for exactly that anymore, she did crave the sweet oblivion of sleep at night. Most days, that was the only way she could make herself get up, by promising herself that at the end of the day, she would be able to go back to sleep and forget, even if only for a few hours.

But last night, Jared had robbed her of even that small comfort. Because of him she hadn't been able to fall asleep until well past dawn. No doubt that was the reason she hadn't heard him arrive. She wondered how long he'd been there without her knowledge. Judging from the drastic change to the office, it had been a couple of hours at least.

Releasing her hair from her ponytail, she massaged her aching scalp and went in search of Excedrin. Locating the bottle in the kitchen, she downed two. She leaned against the kitchen sink and closed her eyes. God, what a mess. What a complete and utter mess. And what a coward she had been to flee, but there was no way she could stay in that office one more second.

She tried to block out the image of Jared sitting at Steven's desk, in Steven's chair.

It wasn't fair. Everyone told her the pain would fade, that as time went on, she wouldn't feel it so deeply. But they were wrong. The pain didn't leave. As weeks and months passed in agonizing slowness, she soon realized a person just learned to do whatever they had to, to get through another day. And for Jenny, that meant avoiding the places and people who reminded her most sharply of Steven.

It hadn't taken her long to realize she couldn't work in his office. Everywhere she looked, she saw him. It had been easier to close it off, to fill the space with as much stuff as she could so she didn't have to see . . . didn't have to remember. She started running the business from the front room in her home and avoiding the office at all costs. But now all her hard fought for distance was being stripped away, leaving her raw and exposed.

Tears pressed against the backs of her eyes and made her head throb all that much harder. Damn him for making her hurt like this. But she knew the real issue wasn't the office, it was the man himself. Because no matter how much she tried to fool herself, she knew the truth: it wasn't *what* Jared had done that had left her shattered—it was how he had made her *feel.*

Heat spread through her body again as she remembered how his eyes had raked over her with a boldness that bordered on obscene.

Believe me, sweetheart, it would be a night you'd never forget.

She forgot to breathe as she remembered his words, the way his eyes had darkened with something almost like desire. But she had to be wrong, she realized with painful mortification. She'd never been able to arouse anything more than a lukewarm of wanting in any man—not even Steven.

That thought smacked of betrayal and brought with it a deep sense of shame. What she and Steven had—or didn't have—wasn't up for comparison. And how was it that in the space of less than a day, Jared Worth had made her feel and remember everything she'd fought to forget? That scared her more than anything.

Needing to do something—anything—she turned on the kitchen faucet, held her hand under the soft flow, and waited for the old pipes to produce hot water. After what seemed like an eternity, the cold water slowly warmed, and she washed the wineglasses from last night and the few other dishes in her sink. Finishing, she rinsed out the dishrag and began wiping down the already clean countertops. It wasn't until she reached the toaster sitting in the corner that she paused.

I like white bread. None of that whole wheat shit.

A reluctant grin tugged at the corners of her mouth. It would serve him right if she brought him a sandwich. With her track record, he'd get botulism. Even the cheerful thought of giving him an awful disease couldn't propel her into action. She had her limitations, and after their earlier confrontation, she knew she was in no shape to confront a poodle, let alone a panther.

Her phone rang, startling her. Putting down the rag, she glanced at the caller ID. She groaned. Great. What a perfect way to round out a perfectly awful morning. She eyed the bottle of Excedrin and wondered how many constituted an overdose. "Hello, Mother."

"Jennifer."

It was an art, really, how one word could hold so much recrimination.

"I was starting to worry I'd never get ahold of you."

Not up to another verbal battle, Jenny gave in with all the grace and humility she could muster. "I'm sorry, Mom. I should have called you earlier."

The apology went a long way to mollifying her mother. "It would have been nice, dear, but I understand you've been busy." There was a pause, as if her mother was waiting for Jenny to fill in the silence. But when Jenny didn't rise to the bait, her mom went on. "I was calling about tonight. You haven't forgotten, have you?"

Tonight . . . tonight. Jenny flipped through her recent

memories like a mental card catalog. She struggled to remember, was just about to admit defeat when, "Dad's birthday party. Of course I haven't forgotten."

"I thought we'd have dinner at seven. Nothing fancy. Your dad wants to try out his new grill."

"Seven. No problem. And, Mom, don't worry about the cake. I've decided to surprise Dad and bake him one from scratch."

There was a short, horrified pause, and even after everything that had happened this morning, Jenny had the urge to laugh. "Just kidding. I'll see you at seven."

"Perfect. Oh, and Jennifer?"

"Yes?"

"Make sure you invite your new partner."

SIX

It was after eleven when Jenny pulled into her driveway. She took the keys out of the ignition, started to open the car door, then paused. Closing her eyes, she leaned back against the Corvette's soft leather seat and let out a deep sigh. She was exhausted. Sleepless nights, battling with Jared, and then having to endure four hours of interrogation by her family had wrung her dry. The Spanish Inquisition had to have been a walk in the park compared to what she'd endured tonight.

She'd known there would be a high price to pay for ignoring her mother's request to invite Jared to her father's birthday celebration, but there had been no way she'd been about to spend one more moment in that man's company than was absolutely necessary. Tomorrow would come soon enough.

Briefly, she deluded herself that he wouldn't show. Tomorrow was Saturday. But deep down, she knew better. He'd be here. After their encounter earlier today, it was only too clear he enjoyed wreaking havoc on her already shaky world.

She let out another sigh. Thinking of him—of today—

was a subject she'd been dancing around all afternoon. Remembering how she'd run like a coward didn't sit well. She wasn't proud of her reaction to finding him in the office, and it was a reaction she didn't plan on repeating. Somehow, before tomorrow morning, she was going to have a plan on how to effectively deal with him. Thank goodness for insomnia. At least she'd have plenty of time to figure out what to do.

Jenny grabbed her purse and the leftovers her mom insisted she take home and got out of the car. As always, the first thing she looked to was the lake. At this late hour and with no bright moon high in the sky, the water was nothing more than a smooth black canvas that stretched as far as she could see. But just knowing it was there, waiting for her, was all she needed. In the quiet she could hear the water brushing against the pilings.

She was halfway to the front door when she knew something was wrong.

The porch lights.

They were on.

For anybody else, that's how it should be. But Jenny could never seem to remember to turn the outside lights on when she left, a fact Steven and her whole family had berated her for on more than one occasion.

Panic squeezed her. The last night she'd come home and the lights had been on, her parents had been waiting for her inside her house.

"We're so sorry—" her dad had begun, only to be stopped by her mother's heartbreaking sobs.

"What?" Jenny had demanded.

"There's been an accident."

"Not Paul. Or Anna, or—"

"It's Steven," her dad had said softly, reaching out to her.

Jenny had stared at her father's outstretched hands, shaking her head, refusing to hear what he was saying. She backed away from his embrace, blocked out his words . . . her mother's cries. She felt frozen as if she were in some horrible nightmare and couldn't wake up. Then the dam burst, and she'd turned, started to run back to her car. "We need to go. Tell me which hospital."

Her mom's sobs had grown louder.

Her dad reached out, stopped her. Gathered her in his strong embrace. "Honey, he didn't make it. Steven's gone."

She didn't remember much after that. She didn't remember collapsing or her dad carrying her to the couch or her parents trying to console her. Later, she'd been told all of those things. What little she did remember were words like "drunk driver" and "he didn't suffer." And she remembered the horrific truth she'd learned that night: there were degrees of grief. Some sorrows could be compartmentalized, tucked into a corner of your heart where, while they still made you ache and pray for the time Before, you could go on. You were still whole. But other griefs destroyed you. Left you a hollowed shell of your former self. Before that night, Jenny had had everything. On nights when the pain became more than she could bear, she told herself she'd been lucky; some people went a lifetime without knowing the kind of happiness she had had. And some nights she almost believed it.

It wasn't until days later that she found out why it had been her parents who had to deliver the devastating news. Steven's driver's license listed his parents' home address, not hers. The police had gone to their house to deliver the news. It had been Steven's parents who had called Jenny's mom and dad, not wanting her to be alone when she heard. While she and Steven had built a whole life together, they hadn't been married. She was only a fiancée, not a wife. He had been hers, but only to a point.

The memories were overwhelming, and she leaned against the side of her house, tried to stop herself from shaking. She should leave. Get back in her car and drive away. But drive where? There was no outrunning bad news. She'd learned that the hardest way possible.

Drawing in a deep breath, she straightened and went to her front door. Opening it, she listened. At first, she heard nothing, and then a low murmuring came from the back of the house. Her stomach knotted, and fear coiled through her. Not again. Please. Not again.

The voices grew louder as she neared the kitchen, and a soft flickering of silvery light came into view. She went weak with relief.

The TV.

She'd forgotten to turn it off when she left. And apparently remembered the porch lights for once. She walked into the family room.

Someone rose from the chair. Someone she didn't recognize.

Screaming, she threw everything she had in her hands at him before turning and running as fast as she could back down the hallway. All she wanted was to get out the front door.

She was almost there. A few more steps and—

A hand clamped onto her shoulder.

She screamed again and then her Oprah-ism kicked in. "I have a black belt in jujitsu."

Was it go for the eyes first or the instep? Damn, she couldn't remember.

"Right," a horribly familiar voice said. "And I know ballet."

Jenny turned, already knowing what she'd find. Six foot two of pure, undiluted sex appeal. A stranger would have been preferable. Her heart was beating as fast as a hummingbird's. "I'm calling the police. Breaking into a house is against the law."

Jared leaned against the wall and crossed his arms over his chest. His black T-shirt molded to hard, well-defined muscles. "I didn't break anything. Ever hear of locking doors?"

Her heart was still racing. She didn't want to examine too closely if it was because she was still scared or because she was standing so close to him. "No one on Hidden Lake locks their door."

"Of course they don't."

"If you dislike being here so much, leave."

"Gladly. Just as soon as you give me my—"

"If you say *money* one more time, I'll scream."

He grinned, a crooked smile that had probably conquered half of the female population. "You already have. Twice."

"You are not funny."

"Believe me, Cotton Tail, I'm not trying to be."

She thought about reminding him—again—to stop calling her that demeaning name but knew it wouldn't do any good. Besides, she was positive he said it just because he knew exactly how much it annoyed her. Instead, she marched back into the kitchen and picked up the phone.

He was right behind her. She hadn't even heard him following her.

"This is your last chance," she said." Leave now, and I won't call the police."

"What are you going to tell them? You're throwing out an invited guest?"

Was this 911-worthy, or should she use the sheriff's office number? "Invited? I hardly think so." She looked at him, waited. "Are you leaving?"

"No."

The threat of calling the police had no effect on him. He'd probably been in trouble with the law so many times one little B and E would be nothing more than an insignificant blip on his mile-long rap sheet.

On second thought, she'd call her brother. Tonight she'd had to listen to her family tell her how having a partner might be a good idea. Once they saw he was a criminal, they'd have to reconsider their pro-partner angle.

She punched in Paul's number. The line was busy.

Could just one thing go her way today? Just one?

"No luck?"

She wanted to wipe that knowing smirk off his too-good-looking-to-be-true face. "This is your final chance."

"Sweetheart, you could give me a hundred chances, and I still wouldn't budge."

"I hear our jail is quite comfortable."

He walked around her, and she caught the subtle whiff of cologne. Really nice cologne. And something more—something that hadn't come from a bottle. Like sun-warmed earth, and a gentle breeze off the water. How long had it been since she'd been this close to a man?

He headed into the living room, sat back down in the club chair, and picked up the remote. She noticed an open beer on the table next to him.

Unbelievable.

"Be honest." He took a drink from the longneck bottle. "You're speaking from firsthand experience."

"Excuse me?"

"The jail. How many times have you been locked up?"

He really was an ass. Nice-smelling or not. With his back to her, she tried her brother's number again. Still busy. She looked at the kitchen clock. It was nearly eleven thirty. Who could Paul be talking to?

All threats aside, she really didn't want to call the police. Or her brother. The sirens would wake her neighbors, Bill down at the *Hidden Lake Tribune* would pick up the story from his police scanner and plaster it all over the front page, or at least page two. He'd never liked her ever since she'd told her best friend Maddy he'd been two-timing her in the eleventh grade. And her family would only make her life all that more miserable. The porch light debate paled in comparison to the locking her doors argument. Contrary to what she'd told Jared, some people on Hidden Lake did lock their doors—her parents and brother, to name a few.

Jared flipped through the channels. All five of them. "Ever heard of cable?"

"If you like TV so much, you should have stayed at Lovie's Bed-and-Breakfast. I hear she has cable."

"Mrs. Murphy closed up shop and left for a family reunion today."

A fact her mother conveniently forgot to mention to-night when she'd told Jenny where Jared had been staying. Jenny hadn't even thought to question how her mother knew this. Nothing escaped her mom's notice. "Seattle and the surrounding area has hundreds of B and Bs. I'll get you a list. And another of hotels."

He stopped surfing and settled on a late-night news program. Jenny got the impression he wasn't too interested; the sound was muted. "I told you I'm not leaving. I was invited."

"For the second time, I didn't invite you."

"I never said you did." He pulled a duffel bag out from alongside the chair. The bag looked as old as he was. He reached in and withdrew something.

It looked like a letter, but Jenny didn't care. The bag was the final straw. She couldn't believe it—he'd all but moved in. Ignoring the letter or whatever it was in his hand, she stepped forward, grabbed his bag, and planned to throw it out the front door. Along with him. But she forgot it was unzipped. Clothing spilled out along with his motorcycle helmet, landing right on her foot.

With a muffled curse, she looked down, ready to throw it across the room. Then realized it wasn't a motorcycle helmet. She stared at the fighter pilot's helmet at her feet and felt herself hurled back in time.

She thought Jared might have said something, but she couldn't be sure. Tentatively, she reached down, picked up the helmet. The hard plastic was smooth and cool to her touch. She ran her hands over the rounded surface, her fingertips finding a few imperfections: a scratch here, a small indentation there as if it had been hit by something. Or something had hit it.

Steven.

How many pictures did she have of him either wearing his helmet or carrying it tucked under his arm? It had been as much a part of him as the gold wings they'd pinned to his chest on graduation day.

But like so many of his things, it had been packed away and sent to his parents' house. They'd needed those tangible memories of their son. Jenny had understood, of

course she had. But that still didn't stop her heart from
hurting when the boxes had been carried out.

She traced the call sign imprinted on the helmet's side.
But the nickname beneath her finger wasn't Steven's.

Blood pounded in her ears, and her breath caught in
her throat. The house was eerily quiet as she slowly looked
to the man in front of her. "You're the Ghost."

It wasn't a question, but he answered anyway. "Yes."

"Oh God." She stumbled back, sank down onto the
sofa. "Why didn't you tell me?" Her voice seemed to come
from far away.

"I didn't think it would matter. It's just a damn call
sign. Nothing more."

There was something in his voice Jenny couldn't
identify—a distance. Detachment. But she didn't dwell on
it. Too many other things were pressing in against her.

"Your name." Her mouth was dry. She swallowed, tried
again. "When you first introduced yourself at my mom's
restaurant, you asked if I recognized your name. I didn't.
But the Ghost . . ." She trailed off, lost in a hundred different memories, a thousand different conversations she
and Steven had had.

*Jesus, Jen-Jen. You should see the Ghost fly. In the air,
he's magic. There's no other way to describe it. No one
can catch him. Hell, they can't find him. I've never seen
anything like him. No one has, not even the CO.*

And then there were other conversations, ones that Jenny
didn't want to remember. Conversations where she'd learned
of Steven's and Jared's friendship. Only, Steven had never
referred to him as Jared. Always by Jared's call sign. She
remembered one call in particular. It had come late at
night. She and Steven had been talking for over an hour
when his voice had grown weary, threaded with an unfamiliar vulnerability. *If not for the Ghost, Jen, I'd never make
it. It's only because of him that I'm going to pass and become a fighter pilot.*

Why hadn't Steven just called Jared by his given name?

But Jenny knew. To them, their call signs were everything: their name . . . their identity . . . their life.

The helmet seemed to grow heavier in her lap, and she set it on the coffee table in front of her. Cool air swirled over her legs, marking its absence. "The Ghost, I know," she said softly, struggling to say the next sentence. "Steven thought you were some type of god in the sky."

"Don't believe everything you hear. I had a job to do, just like everyone else."

She knew he was holding back, not telling her the truth. The admiration and awe that had been in Steven's voice when he spoke of Jared had held a respect and reverence few men achieved. And Steven didn't give praise where praise wasn't due.

She got up and walked over to him, holding out her hand.

He gave her a puzzled look.

"The letter."

"Never mind. It doesn't matter."

Somehow she knew it did. Without waiting for him, she reached out and took the envelope. She was almost certain what she would find, but even knowing didn't prepare her for the stab of emotion that pierced her when she saw the handwriting.

For several long moments all she could do was stare. The envelope was wrinkled and stained, and the postmark had all but faded, but the bold, heavily slanted writing was unmistakable.

"A letter from Steven." She was going to lose it. Tears burned the back of her eyes, and she knew it was only a matter of moments before they blurred her vision. "Wh-what does this have to do with me?"

"Read it."

She thrust it back at him. Was he kidding? Upstairs in her bedroom safely tucked away in shoeboxes were dozens and dozens of letters and cards and notes she'd received from Steven over the years. She'd read them all so many times she knew them by heart. But a few months back, she'd made herself stop. The pain of those concrete reminders was too much. "No." Her voice wobbled.

He looked at her hard, and something changed in his expression. The chair creaked as he got up and took the letter back. She thought she detected a slight hesitation, but she had to be mistaken. If there was one thing Jared Worth was not, it was indecisive.

"'Jared,'" he began to read, and Jenny tried to block out the words, but couldn't. "'If you're ever in my neck of the woods, our door is always open. I mean it, man. Jen-Jen and I would love to have you.'"

Jen-Jen. Her vision blurred. "Steven invited you."

"Yes," Jared said in a low voice, refolding the letter and putting it back in his duffel bag.

It was as if all the air had left the room . . . left her lungs. "Why . . . Why now?" She swallowed hard, rushed through what she needed to say. "If you've had that letter all along, *why* did you stay at Mrs. Murphy's in the first place?"

His expression was unreadable as he stared at her. "I didn't think I'd be sticking around."

She felt a shiver go through her. The man was ruthless. Determined. He'd do anything to get his way. Even stay in a house where he clearly wasn't wanted.

Every part of her screamed to throw him out, and if she couldn't, then call the cops or her brother. Front page news and lecture be damned. But she knew she wouldn't.

How did you fight the wishes of the man you still loved?

"There's a spare room upstairs. Third door on the right. You can stay in there." And then she couldn't say anything more.

* * *

Jared heard her bedroom door close.

"Son of a bitch." He got out of the chair and began to pace. The room was spacious with its soaring ceilings and exposed wooden beams, but even so, he felt caged in, trapped. Everywhere he looked, there were reminders of the people who had either lived in this house or had been loved by them. Dozens of pictures vied for space on the thick wooden mantel. Older black-and-white pictures in tarnished silver frames intermingled with newer color snapshots. On the far wall there was everything from wedding photos to baby pictures to graduation portraits.

Jared stared at them, easily identifying Jenny. Even as a kid playing on the beach or climbing a tree or riding a bike, she had the same big smile and bright blue eyes. In several pictures she was with an older woman who Jared guessed to be her grandmother. He was struck by how happy Jenny looked. It was a side of her he hadn't seen.

He paused at her graduation photo. Even then she'd been a knockout.

Near her senior photo were two others in identical frames. From the resemblance, Jared could only assume they were her brother and sister. Lovie Murphy had made sure he knew as much as she did about the Beckinsale family.

Jared thought about his own graduation. There'd been no photos, no memories, no celebration, which had been just fine with him. School had been a means to an end, nothing more. He could have dropped out—most of the kids in the system had. No one gave a shit. Oh, they acted like they did, said all the right things, but in the end it boiled down to too many unwanted kids and too few social workers. Looking back, he often wondered why he hadn't just given up like so many of the others. But even back then, he'd wanted more. A different life. A *better* life. Where the only person you relied on was yourself, not some damn handout from the state.

With a curse, he turned away from the pictures.

Who was he kidding? He couldn't stay in this house. Once, when he'd been a kid, he would have done anything for a place like this. A family that had roots that went deep and held firm even through the tough times. But not now. Now, all he wanted was to get his money and get out.

Draining the last of his beer, he headed into the

kitchen, intent on throwing the bottle away when he saw Jenny's wallet on the floor, along with a plastic container full of food. He picked them both up, putting the food in the fridge. For no reason he could think of, he held on to the wallet.

In the military, he'd been called everything from brilliant to bastard. Brilliant because he'd outmaneuvered, outflown, and plain outperformed any other pilot. Bastard because he didn't give a damn about what other people thought of him—not even his COs. He stared at the wallet in his hands, remembering the look of sheer agony that had come over Jenny's face when he'd shown her the letter from Steven.

Jared cursed again. He shouldn't be here. He should be in the cockpit of an F-18 thousands of miles up in the sky; it was the only place he belonged. But a few months back he'd broken his cardinal rule to remain detached, and that error cost him everything. He'd believed in a just world, where the strong protected the weak. The bureaucrats in Washington had other ideas. And because of that, Jared had tendered his resignation. He refused to let some politician thousands of miles away decide who lived and who died.

He set the wallet on the counter and threw his beer bottle away. He told himself the only reason Jenny was still trying to keep the business going was out of some misguided loyalty to Steven. Jared knew Steven wouldn't want Jenny struggling to hold on to something that was impossible for her to grasp. Soon—very soon, if Jared's guess was correct (and it always was)—Jenny was going to fold up shop. It was obvious she'd just about reached her caving point. And when she did, Jared would be right here.

Grabbing his duffel bag, he turned and headed up the stairs, deliberately ignoring the pinch of conscience every time he remembered the look in her eyes.

SEVEN

⤳

During the last nine months, sleep had become as elusive as an unbroken heart. Most nights, Jenny lay awake in bed, trying to avoid memories that somehow were more vivid in the ebony darkness. When her memories became too painful, she escaped outside to her front porch. There, cocooned in one of her nana's quilts and curled up in a rocker, she let the sounds of Hidden Lake wash over her, soothing her. It had always been that way, she and this lake. They had a connection, one that defied explanation. No matter how hard life got or how bumpy the road ahead seemed, there was a peace to be found rocking gently in the dark night, listening to the sounds of the water.

Except for last night.

Last night, she'd felt like a prisoner in her own home—her own bedroom. With Jared prowling around in her house, she wasn't about to venture out of her room for fear of running into him. Once a night was enough.

Though she wasn't even sure if he was prowling. Even though she told herself to ignore him, pretend he wasn't downstairs, her effort proved futile. She found herself straining to hear his every movement. But no matter how hard she listened, silence was all she heard.

As the minutes ticked into an hour, then two, she found herself becoming even more angry. Damn him. Damn him for doing this to her. Damn him for barging in where he so clearly wasn't wanted. And damn her for not being able to ignore him.

Her muscles grew tense, worrying that at any moment she would hear him right outside her bedroom door. The waiting strained her, made her body ache and her head throb. As the hours passed, she found herself wishing for rain. Wishing for the noise it would bring and obliterate the harsh quiet that permeated the house and free her from her unwanted vigil. But the dark sky remained quiet.

Not hearing him was a worse kind of hell than hearing him.

Close to dawn, she dozed, only to wake with a start. She lay there, disoriented, trying to figure out what had jarred her out of a fitful sleep. She glanced at her bedside clock. Six oh three.

You've got to be kidding.

She heard the noise again. Creaking on the stairs.

Grabbing her robe, she hurried out of bed. She made it to the top of the stairs in time to see Jared's tall outline disappear out the door. He had left. She leaned against the railing, waited for the expected flood of relief, but it never came. Because she knew without a doubt he'd be back.

Where did he go?

More importantly, why did she care?

She turned away from the stairs and went back into her room. She shut her door, harder than she intended. Somehow she was going to get that man out of her mind and out of her house.

She looked longingly at her bed. Right now, she'd like nothing better than to crawl back in and burrow under her thick, warm covers. But even as she had the thought, she knew she wouldn't. Who knew how much time she had before Jared returned?

She started for the bathroom, only to walk past it to the room Jared was staying in. Curiosity had her opening the door, peering inside.

The room looked exactly as it always did. Not a thing was out of place. The bedside table held the old lamp and picture of her grandpa fishing, just as it always had. The top of the dresser was bare except for a few more photos and another lamp. But that was it. Not even so much as a book or a glass of water altered the space. Knowing she was being nosy but unable to stop herself, she peeked into the closet. Empty. Chest of drawers. Also empty. It was almost as if he hadn't spent the night. And then she saw the bed. There was no mistaking that military precision.

As she turned to leave, something in the corner caught her eye. She took a few steps closer and realized it was his duffel bag. His *packed* duffel bag.

She couldn't help but smile. If he wasn't unpacking, he wasn't planning on staying.

All but humming, she left his room and headed to the bathroom.

She was in and out of the shower in twenty minutes—a record for her. Back in her room, she dressed in her favorite old pair of jeans and a long-sleeved cotton top. As she made her way to the kitchen, she twisted her hair up and around and secured the thick bundle with a claw clip. Thank goodness she hadn't needed to take the extra time to wash her hair.

The house was chilly and dark; no surprise at this ungodly hour. She turned on the lights, cranked up the thermostat, and she put the teakettle on to boil. What was it with Jared and his obsession with the predawn hours? All right, predawn might be stretching it, but from her limited association with him, he seemed to be one of those obnoxiously early risers. She chalked up another fault on his ever-increasing list. Normally, she'd be generous and blame it on his military background, but she was feeling anything but generous this morning. Besides, it was Saturday. Even Steven had known how to relax on the weekend.

The teakettle whistled. A few moments later, with a cup of tea, she leaned against the kitchen counter and stared out the large window. Light, misty rain fell from a bleak sky. She stared at the dark clouds, taking comfort in the fact that the weather matched her mood.

She stood in her kitchen, drinking her tea and fighting down the feeling of trepidation that had plagued her ever since she'd come home last night and found Jared in her house. Knowing her unwanted guest (and she used that word in the loosest way possible) could come and go as he pleased was just plain unsettling.

He had to go. It was as simple as that. But knowing it and making it happen were two completely different things.

The old avocado green clock that had hung in her grandmother's kitchen for as long as Jenny could remember ticked away. She mentally groaned, thinking about the long day that stretched out before her.

Her stomach growled, reminding her she hadn't eaten much yesterday, even last night at her dad's birthday party. Somehow, the hundred and one questions her family had pelted her with had killed any appetite she might have had. All anyone had wanted to talk about was Jared. A conversation Jenny was so not having. After an hour or so, her family got the hint, but even though his name hadn't been brought up again, she couldn't keep thoughts of him out of her mind.

She opened the fridge and saw the Tupperware container her mom had sent home. She didn't remember putting it in the fridge, but then, she pretty much didn't remember anything about last night except finding Jared in her family room.

Ignoring the leftovers—eating them would remind her of an evening of interrogation she'd rather forget—she reached for the carton of eggs. She got out a skillet from one of the bottom cabinets and set it on the stove.

Her breakfast was just about finished when the front door opened.

Jared walked into the kitchen like he owned the place.

"Mornin'." He flashed her a grin that should be illegal in all fifty states.

She tried not to stare; honest to God she did. But ignoring Jared was like ignoring the Sistine Chapel. Except while he might be pure perfection on the outside, his rotten heart was another matter entirely.

Dark stubble shadowed his face, and raindrops glistened off his black hair. Rain molded his navy blue T-shirt to his chest like a second skin, revealing defined muscles and a hard, flat stomach. A pair of black shorts revealed long, toned, muscular legs. He smelled like a fresh rain shower, crisp morning air, and clean, hard-won sweat. She felt a pull in the pit of her stomach.

Damn him for waltzing into her kitchen half-dressed and making her remember sensations she'd buried long ago.

He snagged the clean kitchen towel off the counter, wiped his face, then ran the towel back and forth over his short hair.

"That's a kitchen towel," she snapped, trying hard to ignore him. And failing miserably.

The towel paused at the back of his head. "Do you mind?" He flashed her one of his boyishly charming grins that didn't fool her for one second.

Yes, her mind screamed. *I mind everything you do.* But arguing about a stupid towel was the least of her problems right now. She had bigger fish . . . bigger flyboys . . . to fry. "No, of course not." She tried to sound like she meant it.

And then it dawned on her just what he'd been doing up at this early hour. "You were running?" The way she said it was more of an accusation than a question.

"Only a quick jog. Didn't have time for my usual seven miles."

She choked. Seven miles? Chalk up another of his faults: compulsive exerciser. In her book, that ranked right up there with puppy haters and serial killers.

She was about to let him know how crazy she thought he was when the smell of something burning had her hurrying to the stove.

She grabbed the pan off the burner and popped the toast up. One of these days she was going to have to get a toaster that actually worked. She looked down at the food. Burned toast and overdone eggs. She placed the blame for this latest culinary disaster exactly where it belonged: on a wide, muscled chest and a wolfish grin that sent a tingle of awareness straight through her.

She pulled a plate out of the cupboard and tried to slide the eggs out of the pan and onto the plate. They weren't budging. It took several hard scrapes with the spatula to unstick them. Nonstick spray my foot.

She eyed the eggs suspiciously. She couldn't be sure, but it looked like there were still a few bits of eggshells mixed in. Darn it, she thought she'd picked them all out. Oh well, she'd just make sure to be extra careful when she ate.

Her toast was another matter. She thought about making a couple more pieces but then abandoned the idea. She'd learned a long time ago that enough butter could cover a multitude of cooking blunders.

With her breakfast in one hand, she turned and came face-to-face with Jared. Well, face-to-chest.

How did he always manage to sneak up on her?

Her heart stuttered then kicked into overdrive. He was close. *Too* close. It had been hard enough to ignore him when they'd been separated by the peninsula, but now that he was mere inches from her . . .

How long had it been since she'd stood this close to a man who wasn't her father or brother?

"Somethin' sure smells good."

Him. He smelled good. Like fresh raindrops, crisp morning air, and everything forbidden.

"Thanks," he said, reaching for the plate between them. "I'm starved."

Embarrassed at where her mind had been and embarrassed at her horrible cooking, she was about to tell him to get his own breakfast, when she remembered the burned toast and ruined eggs. At that moment, all of her grievances toward Jared piled up between them. He'd barged into her life, into her business, into her *house* without so much as an ounce of remorse. It was no secret what he thought of her or how she ran her business, while she couldn't seem to keep her eyes or thoughts off of him. It took less than five seconds for all of those thoughts to converge into a good old solid fury.

She looked down once more to the plate between them and had never been more proud of her cooking skills. One taste, and he'd be gagging and running for the phone book, desperately seeking a new bed-and-breakfast—one where he'd get the kind of melt-in-your-mouth home-cooked meals Mrs. Murphy was famous for.

With a smile as bright as a July sun, she relinquished her breakfast, even going so far as to get him a napkin and fork from the drawer.

"Thanks," he said again, pulling out a kitchen stool and sitting down. He'd forked up a bite of eggs, then paused. "Is that orange juice?"

She looked at the hand-squeezed juice she'd made from two of the puniest oranges ever. She'd been going to throw it out. All that work, and all she'd gotten was a couple of sips of juice, seeds, and globs of pulp. She slid the glass across the counter toward him. "Have at it," she said with another bright smile.

He took a bite.

She held her breath as gleeful anticipation ran through her. Briefly she wondered how he'd manage to choke the rubbery eggs down. Of course, on further thought, she didn't want him *dying* just gone. She thought back to when she'd learned the Heimlich maneuver and ran the process through her head. Yes, she could do it. She could save this miserable lout when he choked on eggs that he'd insisted on eating. She would save him (unfortunately), but then, with his gratitude overflowing, he would ask her what he could do to repay her. *Leave*, she'd say with a serene smile.

Lost in her fantasy, it took her a moment to realize he was talking.

"Great breakfast. Best eggs I've had in a long time."

"What?"

"Great scrambled eggs."

Was he for real? "They're fried."

He shot her a smile, one that had undoubtedly been charming women of all ages since he was two. He polished off the OJ. "Fresh-squeezed. My favorite."

She stared at his plate—his *empty* plate. Not a rubbery bit of egg left. Or a partially eaten piece of burned toast.

He set his glass down on the counter and wiped his hands off on his napkin. "You sure can cook. After that meal, I can't wait for lunch and dinner."

She couldn't cook. Everyone knew that. Even *she* admitted it most the time. And lunch and dinner? Just who did he think he was?

"Hope you've eaten." He wadded up his napkin and dropped it onto his plate.

"I'm not hungry."

"Breakfast is the most important meal of the day."

Who was he, her mother?

"Besides," he continued, "you'll need to keep your strength up. We have a busy day ahead of us."

"I don't know what your day consists of, but I already have my schedule, thank you very much."

He ignored her. "I've spoken to Zeke."

Zeke? How did he know how to get in touch with Zeke?

She hadn't realized she asked the question out loud until he answered it.

"I met him the first day I arrived. When you were at lunch."

The way he said *lunch* made her cringe. Like she was blowing off work for some frivolous girl thing. Believe you me, if she could get out of lunch with her mother, she would. "How?"

"How what?"

"How did you know how to get in touch with my pilot?"

"*Our* pilot's number is on the side of your fridge."

She shot her fridge and the large sunflower magnet that held the list of numbers a furious look. She even had her parents' and Paul's and Anna's. Though why, she couldn't say. It wasn't like she didn't know them by heart.

"Why did you need to contact *my* pilot?" There was no *ours*, now or ever.

"I've called a meeting." Jared looked at his watch. "He'll be here in thirty minutes. Don't be late."

"It's Saturday." Not that she had any intention of attending his so-called meeting, no matter what day of the week it was.

"So?"

"So Zeke has the day off."

"He's been more off than on since I got here."

"Zeke sets his own hours."

"Now, why doesn't that surprise me? Either of you ever heard of a work schedule?"

His superior attitude was really starting to piss her off. "You are not going to barge in here and start changing anything. Zeke and I have a system."

"Not an effective one."

"You are not the boss."

"No," he said with a barely there patience that reminded her of a harassed parent. "I'm your partner, and we're having a meeting in half an hour. Changes need to be made." He picked up the towel he'd used earlier and ran it back through his nearly dry hair, dismissing her as clearly as if he'd said the words.

"We don't need any changes."

He looped the towel around his neck, holding on to the ends. "Plan, brief, execute."

"Excuse me?"

"Plan." He said it with infinite slowness. "Brief." Another infuriating pause. "Execute." He gave her that look she was fast growing to hate. "First, I devise a plan how to turn this train wreck around. Second, I brief you on the plan. Third, I direct you on its execution."

"You are insane." It was fast becoming her favorite saying around him. She turned to leave. No way was she staying around and listening to any more of this, and no way was she walking out of here without letting him know exactly where his place was around here.

"I cooked," she told him. "You clean. Dish soap is under the sink."

"KP isn't my specialty."

"Don't worry. It doesn't take much skill. You should be able to handle it just fine." She thought she heard a chuckle, but when she whipped back around, his face was a blank slate.

"Don't you want to know what my specialty is?"

"Absolutely not."

"Debriefing." A wolfish grin appeared that did funny things to her insides. "I'm nothing if not thorough."

His comment left her frozen in her tracks, blushing clear down to her toes.

He began to walk out of the kitchen but paused when he reached her. "Oh eight hundred. Don't be late."

Moments later she heard him heading up the staircase. From the sounds of it, he was taking them two at a time.

Jenny looked at the messy kitchen and wondered what had just happened. She eyed his empty plate, wanting nothing better than to throw it at his gorgeous, arrogant head.

Plan. Brief. Execute.

When pigs fly.

She grabbed her purse, cell phone, and a jacket and was outside and in her car in moments. Before she had cleared the driveway, she was punching in Zeke's number.

Unfortunately, his wife answered and told Jenny that Zeke was already on his way over to her place. Jenny then called Zeke's cell, which went right to voice mail. No surprise. He'd told her at least a dozen times how he didn't like the darn thing. She left a message anyway, explaining that this meeting was not her idea, and Zeke was in no way obligated to be there. He could—and should—take the day off as planned.

Jared could plan, brief, and execute all he wanted, but she and Zeke were not going to be a part of it.

Debriefing. It's my specialty.

It wasn't until she was nearly to town that she realized she had nowhere to go and was no closer to getting rid of Jared.

* * *

Jared was on his way to the bathroom to take a shower when he heard the Corvette start up. Cotton Tail was on the run. Now why didn't that surprise him?

Running this business was at the bottom of her list of priorities; the evidence was all around him. Her office was a nightmare, her dedication a joke. She had no set business hours—no set anything, as far as he could see. And when he offered to help formulate a plan (not that he had any intention of carrying that out), she ran away.

If Jared thought for one minute that she was serious and wanted to run the business Steven had started, he might have felt differently. But her actions proved she was not only incapable but unwilling to do what was needed to make this place a success.

As he waited for the hot water to make its way through the antique pipes, he couldn't help but smile. Somehow he'd known that by insisting on staying here, he would drive her over the edge. Or, more accurately, over to the bank or to her parents.

Stepping under the hot water, Jared almost felt like singing. By the time his shower was over, the money would be as good as his.

Damn, he loved it when things worked out exactly as he planned.

* * *

Early Monday morning, Anna strode briskly through the halls of Seattle Trinity Hospital. She nodded and smiled at the nurses she passed and several of her colleagues.

One of her residents jogged up beside her. "Dr. Adams?"

"Yes?" Anna tried not to let her impatience show. On any other day, she would have been fine with the interruption. Making time for the residents was near the top of her list; the only thing ahead of them was her patients. But today was a different story. Still, she gave the resident her full attention.

"I was wondering if you had a moment to discuss the patient in two fourteen."

"Of course." Anna began to walk once more. "Mrs. Keller. Third trimester. Twins."

"Yes." The young man hustled to keep pace. "Baby A seems to be in distress."

"What is the heart rate?"

"One twenty and has been steady, but has been down to ninety."

"Has a nonstress test been done yet?"

The resident flipped open the chart, read for a few moments. "No."

"Do it. And page me the instant you have the results. We want to keep those babies in the womb as long as possible."

"Yes, Doctor."

Before she released the resident, Anna asked him several questions, assuring herself he had a full and complete understanding of the patient's condition and needs. Mrs. Keller was under Anna's care, and as such, Anna would allow nothing less than absolute competency when it came to her patients.

"My meeting shouldn't last any longer than half an hour," Anna said as the reached the elevator. She hit the up arrow. "I'll be back down to check on Mrs. Keller then."

The resident nodded and was about to leave when Anna said, "And, Doctor . . ." He stopped and faced her. "I don't want to see you out of uniform again."

Perplexed, he stared at her.

She pointed to his empty lapel. Rules were meant to be followed. "Your hospital ID badge. Find it."

"Yes, Dr. Adams." He couldn't hurry away fast enough.

Anna had no doubt that when she checked in on him later, his ID would be in place.

She took the elevator to the sixth floor. As she made her way down the carpeted corridor, she could see outside through the large windows that lined the hallway. It was a dull, drizzly May day. Typical for this time of year. Veteran Seattleites knew that while they might get a few nice days during the summer months, the early fall was when the true beauty of the Pacific Northwest was revealed. But even the dismal weather could not dampen her mood.

At the far end of the hallway, she reached her destination. The door was closed, but that was to be expected.

She drew in a deep breath and smoothed out the nonexistent wrinkles from her perfectly pressed white coat. She put her stethoscope into one of the large front pockets, then ran a hand along her upswept hair. Assured everything was in order, she gave two short taps on the glass portion of the door.

"Come in."

Anna opened the door and entered. Seated behind a large mahogany desk in the spacious office was Dr. Shephard, her mentor and chief of staff of Seattle Trinity. In the nearly ten years she'd known him, very little about Dr. Shephard had changed. A few more wrinkles creased his skin, his hair had gone completely white, but his eyes were still as sharp as ever.

"Anna." He rose and came around the side of the desk, taking her hand in his. "Thank you for coming on such short notice. I hope it wasn't too much of an inconvenience?'

"Not at all." She took the seat he indicated.

"Can I get you anything? Coffee?"

"No, thank you, I'm fine."

Dr. Shephard refilled his cup and then came around to the front of his desk. Moving a picture of his wife aside, he sat down on the edge. "I know how busy you are, so let's get right to it then." He paused. "I'm sure you know why I've asked to meet with you."

She tapped down her growing enthusiasm. "I'm not certain," she hedged.

Dr. Shephard's smile was knowing. "Dr. Bernard," he

said, referring to the head of the neonatal unit, "has requested an indefinite leave of absence."

Anna clasped her hands in her lap and willed them to stop trembling. "I had heard something to that effect."

Dr. Shephard gave a short nod. "His wife's cancer has returned, and he has decided to take time off to be with her."

"I was very sorry to hear about Gloria."

"We all are, but I'm sure you understand what his leaving means."

Of course she knew. The position as head of the neonatal unit was open. From the first day she'd entered medical school and known obstetrics was the field she'd wanted to specialize in, that had been the position she'd aimed for. And to achieve it, she'd worked longer and harder than anyone else.

"You have a true gift, Anna. One I've rarely seen."

"Thank you," she said, warmed by his praise.

He smiled, and in that smile she saw the years he had been beside her, teaching, mentoring, and then the later years when he stood across from her in the operating room as her equal. "I couldn't be more proud of you if you were my own daughter." He shook his head and gave a low chuckle. "Lord knows I've spent more time with you in this hospital than I have with my own children, my own grandchildren, or my wife."

It had been a while since Anna had heard Dr. Shephard refer to his wife. Then again, they didn't socialize like they used to. In the earlier years, they'd often find time for a quick cup of coffee and a chat. Even the occasional dinner out—her and Phillip, Dr. Shephard and his wife. But as her hours and workload increased, the time for socializing had dwindled, then all but faded. She knew he understood why she had had to stop accepting his invitations. A doctor's life was nothing if not demanding.

"It's yours, if you want it," Dr. Shephard said.

Want it? She'd never wanted anything more. "I won't

let you down," she said, her voice not betraying even a quiver of her excitement.

"Of that, I have no doubt." Dr. Shephard set down his coffee, a small frown darting across his brow. "But, Anna, before you accept—"

Hadn't she already?

"Why don't you take a day or two to think the offer over?"

"I—"

"We have a calling, Anna," he said, cutting in with a smile of understanding. "It's one of the most noble things a person can do: help another. But it doesn't come without costs. This new position will require even longer hours, working weekends. More stress, less time for your family. And with Phillip away . . ."

"Everything will work out perfectly." She stood, excitement making it impossible for her to stay seated for one moment longer. She couldn't wait to call Phillip tonight. He was going to be so proud of her. "Thank you, Dr. Shephard. For everything. I would not be the doctor I am today if it wasn't for you. I don't need any additional time. Not only do I want this position, but my family is behind me one hundred percent. You have nothing to worry about."

Dr. Shephard stood and clasped her hand in both of his. "Somehow I knew that would be your answer."

She smiled. "How?"

"Because it's the exact same thing I said almost thirty years ago."

For the first time since entering his office, she let her elation show. Her smile grew until it spread across her face. They were alike, she and Dr. Shephard. She'd always known it. Driven, smart, dedicated. Someday, down the road, after he'd retired, his title and this office were going to be hers. One day she would become the first female chief of staff at Seattle Trinity.

"I won't let the hospital down, Dr. Shephard. I promise."

He smiled, but it didn't quite reach his eyes. "I know you won't, Anna."

The rest of the day flew by in a blur. The hospital, always short-staffed, was even more so without Dr. Bernard. By the time Anna pulled into her driveway, it was after eight. Letting herself in the side door, she set her coat, purse, and briefcase on the hall bench and made her way into the kitchen. The minute she stepped into the large granite and stainless steel space, she caught a whiff of something wonderful. Something that reminded her of an exquisite Italian bistro. Her stomach growled; she hadn't eaten all day.

Her housekeeper was at the sink, finishing up the dishes. Marie turned as Anna entered. "So?"

Anna could not contain her smile. "Yes."

Marie broke out into a huge smile. "Congratulations. But I never had any doubts."

Anna smiled as she sank onto one of the chairs in the breakfast nook. God, it felt good to sit down. She'd been going nonstop all day. "What would I do without you?"

Marie dried her hands and went to the fridge. "You'd forget to celebrate your promotion with cake." She pulled out a two-tiered coconut-dusted sugar confection. "Every celebration needs cake." Her eyes twinkled, daring Anna to say anything. Most nights, Anna had a roasted chicken breast or grilled piece of fish with a small salad. But Marie was right. Tonight was different. They were celebrating.

Anna eyed the beautiful cake. "And what were you going to do with it if I didn't get the promotion?"

"Hide it."

Anna laughed. "Is that manicotti I smell?"

Marie nodded. "And not one word about the amount of cheese I used."

Anna laughed again. "Deal." Manicotti was Cody's favorite—a fact they both knew. As always, Marie's thoughtfulness was appreciated. Anna couldn't wait to have this special dinner with her son.

"Thank you," Anna said again. "Is Cody in the family room?"

Marie set the cake on the counter. "No. He went to bed a half hour ago."

So early? That wasn't like him. He usually fought his bedtime with as much tenacity as a grizzly bear. "Is he feeling all right?"

"He said he was just tired."

"Did he eat dinner?"

"No. He didn't want anything."

Anna's forehead creased in concern. "I'm going to head upstairs and check on him."

"Shall I heat your dinner?"

"No." Anna gave her a thankful smile. "I'll get it later. You go on home. I'm sorry I kept you so long."

"No problem. Are you sure you don't want me to fix you a plate? It'll only take a moment."

"I'm sure." Anna smiled at her again. "Now, go home. And tell your family hi."

After Marie left, Anna headed upstairs, still worried about Cody. The only time he ever went to bed this early was when he wasn't feeling well.

When she reached the top of the stairs, the sound of music grew louder. Light spilled out from under his door, and she couldn't help but feel relieved. He was still up. With a perfunctory knock, she entered. He was sitting up on his bed, his sketch pad in hand and the stereo blaring— as usual. Walking over to his desk, she turned off the music, ignoring the angry look he shot her. Lately, anger seemed to be the only emotion she could elicit from him. That, and indifference. No one could do indifference better than a thirteen-year-old boy.

"Hey," she said, taking a seat on the end of his bed. "How are you?"

"Fine."

"Marie said you went to bed early. Are you feeling okay?"

"I'm fine."

"Are you sure?" she asked, leaning forward to feel his forehead.

He shot her another ill-tempered look. "I'm not sick."

"Just tired?"

He went back to working on his drawing.

"Can I see your sketch?"

His pencil paused mid-stroke, but still he didn't look up. "Maybe when I'm done."

A pang of regret wrapped around her heart. Once, he hadn't been able to wait to show her his drawings. Before she'd even stepped through the door after work, Cody had been there, flipping through his sketch pad, pointing out everything he'd drawn that day. As always, his talent amazed her. This son of hers who could draw anything while the only thing she could draw was a bath. Now . . . now Anna couldn't remember the last time he'd met her at the door or asked her to look at anything. And before tonight, when was the last time she'd asked him? "Okay," she said quietly, rubbing his sock-covered foot. "How was school?"

His pencil scratched against the pad as he made quick, deft strokes. "Fine."

"Did you have a lot of homework?"

"No."

"Tomorrow's your spelling test. Do you need help—"

"I already studied."

Anna leaned back against the footboard, working hard not to rise to the bait. Talking with her son was like pulling teeth. Slow and painful. "Marie said you didn't eat."

"I'm not hungry."

"Not even for cake?" When it was clear he wasn't going to answer, she wiggled his foot, waited until he looked up. "I got the promotion."

Silence.

"Come downstairs with me. We'll have a celebration. Just the two of us."

"I said I'm not hungry."

She tried to hide her disappointment. "Maybe this weekend then, after I get off work. We'll go out to a special dinner. You can pick the restaurant."

For just a moment, his mask of indifference dropped away. "But . . ."

"What?" she prompted.

"Nothing," he mumbled, pulling his legs up, away from her touch. Her hand slipped away.

"There's something in that nothing." She waited for the reluctant grin that usually followed the familiar saying, but tonight there was no smile.

"What about my game this weekend?" he finally asked.

Her smile froze. Carefully, she said, "I thought you could stay with Grandma and Grandpa this weekend while I'm at work. I know they'd love to watch your game."

"Work?" he said, anger and disappointment clouding his eyes.

"I'm sorry, Cody, but with this new job, I'm going to be working more hours. Weekends."

"So you're not going."

"No," she said, feeling the weight of his disappointment. She wanted to explain how important this promotion was to her career but knew that anything she said tonight would fall on deaf ears. Hopefully, in a couple of days, when he wasn't so upset, she could explain it to him. "I'm sorry. But there will be other games, you'll see."

"Whatever," he said, propping his sketch pad higher on his bent legs until it all but hid his face.

"Cody—"

"It doesn't matter."

Yes, it did. But what choice did she have?

She sat there, wondering what she could say to make him understand. But the plain truth was, experience had taught her that nothing she said right now would make a difference. "I'm going to call Dad. Do you want to talk to him?"

"Why bother? He can never hear me."

Cody had a point. Why hadn't she been more proactive about insisting Phillip get a satellite phone?

Because until the day he'd boarded the plane, Anna had been convinced he wouldn't go.

"I know the phone service isn't the best, but maybe tonight—"

Cody tossed his sketch pad and pencil on the table beside his bed and grabbed his iPod. Shoving the tiny earphones in, he scooted down in his bed and punched his pillow until it was a white puff beneath his head. "I'm tired," he said, pulling up his comforter.

He was shutting her out. Again.

She let out a quiet sigh, not knowing how to break through this barrier he'd erected. She looked at him, wishing he would look back. When he continued to ignore her, she reached out, wanting to hold him like she'd done thousands of times before, back when he was still her little boy. But the moment she reached out, he stiffened and shifted as far away from her as he could.

Silently, she drew her arm back. "Good night, Cody," she said. "I'll tell Dad you said hi." At the door, she paused before turning off his light. "I love you."

She waited, hoping. But just like too many nights before, he didn't say "I love you" back.

In her bedroom, Anna turned on the bedside lamp and slipped off her heels. Sighing, she flexed her toes before curling up against the headboard. Stacking several pillows behind her, she reached for the phone. All day she'd been looking forward to this call. She had no idea what time it was in Sri Lanka but didn't bother to check. Phillip had told her his schedule was crazy and unpredictable, and they worked nearly nonstop. She punched in the long number, and while she waited for the connection, she tried to block out the stilted conversation she'd had with Cody. Why did it seem that every time they talked, she came away feeling like the bad guy?

Finally, a scratchy, unsteady ringing began on the other end. The phone rang several more times, and just when she started to worry he wouldn't pick up, she heard Phillip's voice. "Hello."

"Phillip?" Static filled the line. "Phillip, is that you?"

"H-h-hello . . . can't hear . . . bad . . ."

"It's Anna." Her voice grew louder. "Don't hang up. Please." The connection was horrible, but she knew it wouldn't be any better if she hung up and tried again.

"Ann . . . ?" The word was drawn out and barely audible, but she heard it all the same.

"Yes, it's me. I have the most amazing news." She waited, but when she heard nothing but static, she plunged on. "I've been appointed Dr. Bernard's replacement." She paused again, waited. "Did you hear me, Phillip? I am Dr. Bernard's replacement."

"I . . . sorry . . . didn't hear."

Anna drew in a deep breath. "Dr. Shephard appointed me as Dr. Bernard's replacement," she said again. "It's a temporary appointment," she all but shouted, willing her husband to hear. "But we both know that's only a formality." She closed her eyes, remembering again the moment in Dr. Shephard's office. "It's happened, Phillip. It's really happened."

The connection hummed with static. ". . . congr . . . talk another . . ." And then the line went dead.

For the longest time, she didn't move. Phillip's last words ran over and over in her mind. Had he heard her?

Yes, she silently told herself. He had. He'd told her congratulations, she was positive. Just like she was positive he would call her tomorrow when he had a better connection.

But he didn't call. Not the next day, or the day after that. Four nights later, when she got home from work and saw the still untouched coconut cake on the counter, she picked it up and tossed it in the garbage.

EIGHT

⟁

Something had gone wrong.

Jared stood on the beach, his boots sinking into the sand, as he watched Jenny. She was at the far end of the dock, near the plane. They had a charter today; a husband and wife on their way to Victoria, B.C., for a long weekend. From the moment the older couple had stepped out of their car, they'd been enchanted by Jenny. While they were completing paperwork and paying for their charter, she'd talked to them like they were old friends. And they'd responded. Opened up in a way Jared had never seen between strangers before. When Jenny learned they were going to visit their daughter and new grandbaby, she'd insisted on going out into her flower beds and putting together a huge bouquet. The couple had been moved by Jenny's generosity. And as Jared had continued to watch Jenny in action, he had to admit she not only had a way with flowers but also with people. By the time the older couple boarded the plane, they were giving Jenny hugs and promising her they'd be using Blue Sky a lot more in the future.

For all her faults, Jenny Beckinsale was customer service at its finest.

The plane sputtered to life, and Zeke began to pilot it to the middle of the lake. As Jenny waved good-bye, Jared shook his head. He still didn't understand why anyone would pay to be jostled around like monkeys in a tin can. Then again, it looked like most people agreed with him. This was only their second charter this week, and no more were scheduled for the weekend. How the seaplane stayed afloat (pun intended) was beyond him.

A breeze blew off the lake and molded Jenny's blouse to her. He couldn't keep his eyes off her. Even with the distance that separated them, her perfection was unmistakable. He'd been surprised when he'd first seen her this morning. Unlike the casual clothes she'd worn the last couple of days, today, with a charter scheduled, she'd dressed up. She wore a long, fitted blue skirt that hugged her just right and a white blouse that every time he looked at it reminded him of crisp sheets and hot nights. Her high heels matched her skirt and accentuated her legs. She was stunning. Professional yet provocative. But it didn't matter what she wore; he was fast learning that he found her irresistible.

As he shoved his hands in the pockets of his jacket, he thought about the engagement ring she still wore. It was the only reminder he needed to keep his eye on the prize. The right prize: Mexico.

He squinted into the weak sun and turned to watch Zeke navigate west and prepare for takeoff. The clunky plane bounced along the lake like a waterlogged buoy, going so slow it was a wonder it ever managed to get airborne. There was no power. No grace or stealth. No roar of the twin jet engines.

It wasn't an F-18.

Jared silently cursed. Dwelling on the past wouldn't solve his current problem.

The soft click of heels on the dock drew his attention. Jenny was making her way toward him, but instead of pausing, she breezed right past, ignoring him. Just like she'd been doing ever since he'd moved in.

One look, and it was clear to see how much his presence in her life—in her house—was pissing her off. The more upset she was with him, the quicker he'd get his money, he reasoned. But something had gone wrong with his plan.

The front door banged shut behind her.

For nearly a week, he'd been more patient than he'd ever been in his life. When she'd stormed out of the house after that disastrous breakfast, he'd been certain she was running to her parents or to the bank to get his money. But as Sunday turned into Monday, then Tuesday into Wednesday, doubts settled. He brushed them aside, reminded himself it took time to get funds together. But tomorrow it would be one week since he'd set things in motion. And in anyone's book, that was plenty of time.

Last night, he'd finally faced the truth: Jenny had no intention of getting him his money.

All week, he'd put up with her crap. From her godawful breakfasts to her hot temper and cold stares, he took it all in stride. If putting him through her idea of hell helped ease the pain of handing over the money, he was more than happy to oblige. Besides, if she thought bad food would get rid of him, she didn't know shit about the military. And her coffee. At first, he'd almost kissed her when the coffeepot had reappeared. Lack of caffeine in the morning turned him into a real bastard, and when he'd opened the front door after a particularly grueling run, he'd all but sighed in pleasure at the smell. Then he tasted it. If her breakfasts were bad, her coffee was downright shitty.

How could he have been so blind?

He cursed himself a thousand types of fool for not seeing it sooner. Jenny wasn't just trying to make his life miserable while she got his money—she was just trying to make his life miserable. Period. Money had nothing to do with it. Well, if she thought he was just going to disappear over a few bad meals, she was dead wrong. Cotton Tail had pissed off the wrong person.

He blamed himself. He'd been taken in by a set of kiss-me lips, sky blue eyes, and a body that made a man think about only one thing.

"Damn it," he cursed and itched his leg.

He woke up this morning, ready to try talking to her once more, when he noticed his arms and legs covered in small bumps. Small, itchy bumps. And the more he scratched, the more they itched. During breakfast, Jenny kept glancing his way which, in and of itself, was odd, since she'd done everything she could to avoid him this past week. But this morning, she'd hung around. He knew she was there for the charter, to assist the passengers and help Zeke with any last-minute preparations. But for a short while he'd also been lulled into the false euphoria that she was about to hand over his money.

He couldn't have been more wrong.

All during breakfast, he'd been scratching his arms and legs, wondering what the hell he'd gotten into.

Twice she asked him if he was all right. Twice he'd told her he was fine. By the third time, he wised up.

"I saw you out pulling underbrush yesterday," she'd said after he'd gone after a particular nasty bump, her voice full of earnest concern, her eyes wide with innocent distress. "I hope you didn't get into any stinging nettles. They can be miserable."

Earnest and innocent his ass. Behind those baby blues lurked all the compassion of MiG on his tail. It was right then he realized he'd seriously underestimated his adversary. A fact that didn't sit well with him.

The lousy food. The crappy coffee. The silent treatment. And now—hives.

This time, he hadn't given her the satisfaction of an answer. He went outside and looked through the weeds he'd cleared. Halfway through the pile, he saw them: stinging nettles. And she'd known just what he'd been getting into and hadn't said a word.

So she wanted to play dirty. Nothing could have pleased him more.

As if on cue, a black SUV turned into the driveway. As it neared, the sign on the driver's side door came into view: Hidden Lake Properties.

Jared scratched at his leg and smiled. While he'd been working on the property, it dawned on him they were sitting on a gold mine. Literally. This piece of waterfront had to be worth a fortune. Jenny might have an aversion to selling, but Jared sure as hell didn't.

As a short, balding man with a slight paunch got out of the SUV, Jared made his way across the beach. Reaching the SUV, he extended his hand. "Mr. Owen?"

"Brad, please," the man said, shaking Jared's hand. "And you must be Jared Worth."

"Thanks for coming on such short notice."

"Happy to do it." Brad gave a short laugh. "I have to admit, even if my schedule hadn't been open, I would have rearranged it."

"Oh?"

"Never thought I'd see this particular piece of property go up for sale."

Jared was sure the realtor wasn't the only one. He glanced to the house.

"Times change."

"That they do. That they do," the realtor said with a brief air of sadness. "Now," he said, grabbing a briefcase from his SUV, "I've brought along some paperwork I thought would help us determine a fair market value." He paused, looked around. "I assume Jennifer will want to be present for this discussion?"

You bet your sweet ass. "She's inside."

"Great."

As they neared the house, Jared saw the telltale movement of the curtains. This time, he didn't bother hiding his smile. *You can run, Cotton Tail, but you can't hide.*

"Mr. Owen." Jenny was on the porch waiting for them.

"Jennifer." The realtor greeted her with a warmth and

familiarity that momentarily threw Jared. Then again, this town was the size of a walnut; of course they'd know each other.

Jenny shot Jared a hard, questioning look, then turned back to Brad, her mood doing a one eighty. "How's Linda?"

"Still volunteering at the school, even though the twins graduated ten years ago."

"Is Bryce still in California?"

Brad gave a good-natured grimace. "We're holding out hope he'll come to his senses soon and return back home to God's country."

Jenny smiled. "And Byron? Is he—"

"Let's go inside," Jared interrupted. Old home week was getting old. He hadn't called the realtor so he and Jenny could take a stroll down catch-up lane.

She pursed her lips and, without saying a word, made it abundantly clear she thought he had the manners of a feral dog.

He scratched his arm. Too damn bad.

She opened the door to let them in, but as Jared went to walk past her, she drilled him with a what-in-the-world-is-going-on look. He ignored her and followed Brad inside. With obvious reluctance, and a good deal of trepidation, Jenny directed them to the front living room, which was used as a waiting area for Blue Sky's customers. The furnishings were more formal than the family room in the back of the house and in better condition. Not that that surprised Jared. From what he could tell of the business, the room probably got used only about once or twice a week at the most.

Two wing chairs in a soft green fabric flanked the fireplace. Jenny sat in one, Brad in the other, leaving the camelback couch vacant for Jared. Brad placed his briefcase on the round coffee table between them.

"Can I get you anything?" Jenny asked Brad, ignoring Jared. "Coffee?"

"Just say no," he told the realtor.

Jenny scowled at him.

Brad looked from Jared to Jenny, assuming they were joking. But no one was laughing.

"If you drink her coffee," Jared explained, "you'll need your stomach pumped."

Brad laughed. "Ah, yes, now I remember. Has Jennifer ever told you about the coffee stand she used to own?"

"I'm sure Jared isn't interested," she said quickly.

Yesterday, she couldn't have been more right, but today, he found himself more than interested. Warfare 101: learn as much as you could about your enemy. "A coffee stand?" he prodded the realtor.

Jenny hunched down in her chair and crossed her arms over her chest.

Brad coughed a few times, trying to cover his laughter. "Closed down in less than two weeks. Has to be a record for this area."

"A real success, was she?"

Another few coughs from the realtor. Another bad job of camouflaging his amusement.

"I'm sure Mr. Owen has better things to do than discuss my past employment." Jenny angled in her chair and faced the older man. "Actually, I am curious as to why you are here."

"You don't know?" Brad fidgeted, clearly uncomfortable. "I just assumed . . . I mean, well, didn't you ask Mr. Worth to call?"

"No," Jenny gave Jared another one of her Sunday school teacher stares. When would she learn he was immune?

"Oh my," the realtor said.

Jared leaned forward and braced his arms on his legs. "Jenny and I are partners."

"Yes . . . I did hear something to that effect."

"As such, I have an equal stake in this property. In order to come current with some outstanding debts, I believe it is in the best interest of everyone involved if we put the land up for sale."

Jenny shot to her feet so fast, the chair rocked on its wooden legs, startling the realtor. "Over my dead body!"

Jared stared at her.

"Mr. Owen." She took a couple of deep breaths. "I'm sorry you've been called out here on a fool's errand. I have no intention of selling this land."

"I must admit, I hadn't thought so." Brad got to his feet and picked up his briefcase. "But when I received the call, well, you just never know," he said, making his way to the front door. He couldn't seem to leave fast enough.

"How dare you?" Jenny hurled at Jared the moment the door closed.

"How dare I what?"

"Don't play games with me. You now what I'm talking about."

"Obviously you haven't been hearing me."

"My hearing is just fine. It's yours that's in question."

For a moment Jared was sidetracked by Jenny in full fury. Her blue eyes were as hard and cold as ice, her breathing fast and shallow. Her chest rose and fell in rapid succession. He found himself captivated, and then his leg started to itch once more, and he remembered exactly why he'd called the realtor. Underneath all those gorgeous curves beat a devious heart hell-bent on his destruction. "I want my money."

"I want you to leave."

"Then we're in agreement."

"Like hell we are."

"Either we sell this land, or you get the money from somewhere else."

For a short moment, some of her anger seemed to leave. "I tried."

"Tried what?"

"Getting a loan."

"And?"

Her eyes flashed, all her anger back. "They turned me down, all right?"

Jared tried not to let that piece of news affect him. "Then go to your parents. I'm sure they'd be only too happy to help you out."

"No," she said with such finality that Jared knew it would do no good to push her.

"Sell that damn car."

Tears welled in her eyes. "That car was Steven's."

Jared hadn't known. For the second time that morning, his eyes flashed to her left hand. Jenny would no sooner get rid of Steven's car than she'd take off his ring. At the thought, an unexpected flare of jealousy blindsided him.

Christ. Jealous of his dead friend. He really was a bastard.

"Then we're back to square one. Sell the plane. The land. I don't care, you pick."

Jenny stared at him for a long moment. "This property has been in my family for over a hundred years. My great-grandparents homesteaded this land. My grandfather expanded and remodeled the house. Put in the original dock. This land is as much a part of me as my heart. I will never"—she paused for emphasis—"never sell. I have four months in which to pay you back, and I plan on using every last bit of that time." She walked out of the living room and out of the house. The screen door banged shut behind her.

He started to follow her. This was ridiculous—*she* was being ridiculous. Running away solved nothing. But before he'd even gone half the distance, he stopped.

The ties he thought Jenny had here—the ones with Steven—were easily healed compared to her family's history on this land. He'd seen the pictures in the family room; he should have known. But somehow, the still images failed to capture the emotional connection he'd heard in her voice.

He looked out through the mesh on the screen door. Jenny was on her knees in front of one of the flower beds, a garden caddy full of hand tools by her side. All around her flowers bloomed in a riotous rainbow. While she might be the world's worst cook, she could work miracles with flowers.

He watched her turn over the fertile dirt, pulling out

weeds, snipping off dead blooms. No matter where he was on the property, he could always smell the flowers.

My great-grandparents homesteaded this land.

I will never sell.

For just a moment, Jared wondered what it would feel like to belong to a family with that kind of history. Permanence.

He rubbed his hand across his eyes and through his hair. Jenny would never sell this land; he could see that now. And a part of him couldn't blame her. Once, he, too, would have held on just as tightly. But now he knew the truth; it didn't matter how hard you held on. Some things . . . some*ones* . . . would never stay.

Jared pushed open the screen door and made his way across the lawn to the hangar. He didn't look at her . . . he couldn't. Understanding what this land meant to her changed things. It made what he had to do all that much harder. But he wasn't giving up. There was always a next step. Another way. He just had to figure out what it was.

*   *   *

Anna had been at her new job for less than a week, but she already knew that with her promotion had come an even crazier, more hectic whirlwind of a schedule. And she loved every minute. From the moment she'd arrived at the hospital at six thirty (a full hour earlier than she normally started) she'd been going nonstop. She'd thought the extra hour would give her a much-needed head start on everything she had to accomplish, but it was already three in the afternoon, and there were still a full five hours of work ahead of her.

She grabbed a cup of coffee and headed into her office, desperately needing a break, no matter how short a one. Shutting the door behind her, she drew in her first easy breath of the day. Through the closed door, she could still hear the supercharged energy of the hospital. She sat down at her desk and took a drink of her coffee. The hot caffeine went a long way toward perking her up.

All day she'd been trying to find a spare moment to call her mom. But somehow the hours had slipped away. Anna knew if she didn't make time now, the day would fly by, and by the time she got home, it would be too late to call. She reached for the phone.

"Hidden Lake Bistro and Art Gallery. How may I help you?"

"Mom?"

"Anna, honey. How wonderful to hear from you."

"How was your trip?"

"Quiet." Her mother said that as if it was a bad thing. Which, to her mom, it was. She liked to be active every minute of the day (much like Anna), while her dad, now that he was retired, was content to pretty much take it easy. "Why Joe and Deb ever moved to Alaska is beyond me," her mom said, referring to their longtime friends. "But it was wonderful to see them again. Your father caught enough fish to last two lifetimes." She laughed softly. "Be prepared for a fish fry when he comes home."

"Dad didn't come back with you?"

"No. He decided to stay for an extra week or so. He and Joe are having too much fun pretending to be wilderness men." Her mom laughed again. "And like your father said, if he can't have a flexible schedule when he's retired, what's the good of being retired?"

That sounded just like her father. "You didn't want to stay?"

"No time. I'm about to launch a new artist, and I have to make a decision this week on the caterer and band for the charity ball. Why is it I never remember how much time that event requires?"

"You say that every year."

"Jenny told me the same thing."

"It's true. So, tell me, how many pictures did Dad take?"

"Let's just say you should factor in a couple of extra hours on your next visit," her mother warned, a smile in her voice. "By the time I left, he had enough to fill at least three photo albums."

"I might not have time," Anna said. "I got the promotion, Mom."

"Oh, Anna. I'm so proud of you."

The pride she heard in her mother's voice went a long way toward making her lingering disappointment vanish.

"I bet Phillip was just as excited."

Anna didn't answer. She still hadn't heard from Phillip, but that wasn't news she wanted to share, even with her mother. As days piled one on top of the other, Anna had put aside her pride and picked up the phone. Twice she'd tried calling Phillip. Twice she hadn't been able to reach him. She felt a flare of anger. Why did it seem as if she was the only one trying in this relationship?

"When do you start?" her mom asked.

"I already have."

"That was quick."

Anna explained about Dr. Bernard's wife, concluding with, "Understandably, he's taken a lot of time off lately, and so we're behind and understaffed. I'm going to have to work most weekends. Actually, that's the main reason I called. I have to work this weekend, and I was hoping you could watch Cody."

"Oh, honey, I would love to except I'm going to be in Seattle. Meetings for the charity ball." Her mom paused. "But Cody could always come with me. I know it wouldn't be much fun for him, but I wouldn't mind."

But her son would. And he'd make his grandmother's life miserable in the process. Plus there was his baseball game. Anna didn't even want to think of the fit he'd throw if he had to miss it. "Thanks, Mom, but I don't want to put you out."

"I'd love to have him."

"It's okay, Mom. Really."

"I hate to leave you in a bind."

"I'll think of something." The hospital paging system

went off, and Anna heard her name being called. "Maybe Paul could watch Cody."

"Paul's working weekends, too, since he hasn't found a partner." Her mom paused, then said, "What about Jenny?"

Anna wouldn't trust her sister with a goldfish, let alone her son.

"I know what you're thinking," her mother said.

Anna seriously hoped not.

"Give her a call. She'd love to help you out."

The hospital paging system sounded again. "Mom, I don't mean to rush off, but I have to go."

"Call your sister."

"I'll think about it," Anna hedged, wondering if her mom could hear the lie in her voice.

NINE

~

The calls had started at seven.

Jenny had wondered how long her reprieve would last. She knew she had at least a week while her parents were on vacation. And without her mother around to keep everyone up to date, Paul and Anna wouldn't find out until her parents returned home. Naively Jenny had thought maybe she'd even have an extra day or two after they got back from Alaska. But mere hours after returning home, her mother had been on the phone.

The local gossip mill must have been working overtime to get the news to her so quickly.

"Is it true?" her mother had immediately asked.

Still groggy with sleep, Jenny scooched up in bed, pulling her pillow with her. Checking caller ID could have saved her a world of hurt. Then again, knowing her mother, Catherine would have just driven over if Jenny hadn't picked up the phone. "Hi, Mom. How was your trip?"

"Fine. Relaxing. Your father decided to stay an extra week for more fishing." Her mother said *fishing* like it was one of the seven mortal sins. She also sounded anything but relaxed. "But don't change the subject. Is it true?"

Twenty-six years had taught Jenny that stalling only made the situation worse. "It's true."

"Jennifer. He's *living* with you?"

"Sort of."

"Either he is or he isn't."

Jenny squeezed her eyes shut, knowing a headache was only minutes away. "Only temporarily."

There was a long pause, and Jenny braced herself. She'd been so sure a week would have been plenty of time to get rid of Jared. That he'd be long gone before her parents found out.

"Hmmm."

Hmmm? What the heck did *hmmm* mean?

"Maybe this isn't as bad as I first thought."

Jenny's eyes flew open, and she jackknifed to a sit. "Excuse me?"

"Well, I've never liked you living out there all by yourself. You know that. It's too isolated. I really wish you would move back here. This is your home. And it's only a ten-minute drive to your place. An easy enough commute to your business."

Jenny's headache came on full force. They'd had this same discussion a hundred different times, a hundred different ways, and it always ended the same way, with her mother still holding out hope that Jenny would "come to her senses" and move back home.

"You have nothing to worry about," Jenny said, bringing the conversation back around. "I have everything under control. He won't be here that long."

"That's not what your brother told me."

"You've talked to Paul?"

"Naturally. He was kind enough to fill me in on everything."

Jenny had no idea what "everything" meant, but she wasn't about to ask. Turns out, she didn't need to.

"After Paul explained exactly who Jared Worth is and

what his relationship had been to Steven, I'm feeling much better about the situation." There was a pause while her mother took a drink of her ritual one cup of coffee in the morning. "I think it will be a good thing for you to have someone living out on the lake with you."

Jenny fell back against her headboard. "You're kidding, right?"

"You know your father and I are always here if you need *anything*, but if you choose to go your own route on this, well, like I said, I feel better knowing you have some . . . protection."

Jenny let the protection comment slide—the crime rate in Hidden Lake was practically nonexistent—but they both knew what *anything* meant. All Jenny had to do was ask her parents for the money to repay Jared, and he'd be gone.

She couldn't kid herself; she was tempted. Like she had been several times before. But unlike before, she was determined to find her own way out of this.

Jenny assured her mother that she had everything handled and not to worry. After enduring a few minutes more of her mother's advice, the call ended.

The moment she hung up, the phone rang again almost immediately. This time she had the presence of mind to check the caller ID.

"Morning, Paul," Jenny said.

"Mother called."

"Surprise, surprise."

"Sarcasm doesn't suit you."

Jenny couldn't disagree more.

"We're just worried about you, Jelly Belly," her brother continued. "You have to know that."

The familiar nickname and the concern in her brother's voice was her undoing. Her throat clogged with a week's full of stress and strain. "Don't be. You know Steven couldn't even stand to live with me full-time." She tried to hide her hurt behind a teasing tone.

"That's not true."

Tears welled in her eyes, and she wiped them away.

"You're right. He only kept the apartment above his parents' garage to escape my family's early phone calls."

Paul's laughter was a little too loud and a little too forced, but Jenny loved him all the more for it. "Could you blame the guy?"

Jenny felt herself start to get back onto even ground. "Heck no." She drew in a breath, then confided to her brother, "Jared's the Ghost, Paul."

There was a pause while the impact of her words sank in. "You're sure?" Paul finally said.

"Yes."

"Wow." Paul paused. "The way Steven used to talk about that guy. Remember that time we were at Steven's parents' house and Steven couldn't stop talking about how amazing the Ghost flew and Steven's dad finally interrupted and said there was no way anyone could be that good. Steven was silent for the longest time, and then he said the Ghost was."

"Yeah, I remember." She also remembered how Steven's voice had taken on an almost reverent tone when he spoke of the Ghost . . . of Jared. Steven had all but worshipped at the tips of Jared's wings.

"Hey, have you . . ."

Paul didn't even have to finish his thought for Jenny to know what he was asking. "No. Steven's parents are still down in Arizona. Half-here, half-there, remember?" She hadn't seen them since the funeral. A part of her had been relieved that they'd left so soon after the funeral. Bumping in to them would be another painful reminder of everything she'd lost. Everything they'd all lost.

All of a sudden, Jenny couldn't stay in bed a moment longer. "Listen, Paul, I've got a full day. I really need to go."

It wasn't the complete truth, but she had to get off the phone and now. She didn't want to talk about Steven, about his living and not living here. Or his parents and how Jenny hadn't found the courage to face them since the funeral.

"I'm here for you, Jelly Belly. Just say the word, and Jared is gone."

"Sweet, but slightly overprotective. You can back off, Paul. I have it handled. Really," she said, not sure if she was trying to convince him or herself.

Now, an hour later, Jenny sat the edge of her yard and buried her feet into the sand. Tiny pebbles and rough grains filtered through her bare toes and over her feet. It wasn't even nine in the morning, but already the lake was alive with activity. A bright Saturday in May that promised unseasonable warm weather would do that.

Shielding her eyes from the sun, she could make out several of her neighbors from her spot on the shore. A handful of fishing boats speckled the large lake as they trolled near the shorelines, while a group of teenagers braved the cold water for a few hours of waterskiing. Their rock music and loud voices echoed across the water. Each time they sped past Mr. Wilcox, their wake tipped and rocked his shallow aluminum boat. Grabbing the boat's side with one hand, he raised the other, fist clenched, and shouted out an obscenity that was thankfully obscured by the music.

Bracing her hands behind her in the thick grass, she tilted her face upward, closing her eyes against the sharp rays. Warm sun beat down on her, and the heady fragrance of her grandmother's flowers surrounded her. Not for the first time did Jenny wonder what her grandmother would say about the mess she was in.

Spilled milk don't clean itself.

Her nana's voice came to her swift and clear. How many times had Jenny heard that old saying? But even Nana had to see that this mess wasn't so easily taken care of. For days she'd been trying to figure out a way to improve the business's bottom line. But no matter how hard she tried, she couldn't figure out a way. And then there was her other worry: one very large, very intimidating, heartbreakingly handsome worry working in the hangar behind her.

With a small shake of her head, she tried to concentrate

on anything other than Jared. She listened to the music
blaring from the kids' boat, she listened for Mr. Wilcox's
raised voice, she strained to hear the lawn mower coming
from next door, but none of it did any good. No matter how
hard she tried, she could not force him from her mind.

Everywhere she went, *he* was there, making her feel like
an intruder in her own house, in her own yard. In her own
business. Whenever she turned around, she saw him watching her . . . judging her. She wasn't sure what unsettled her
more: the watching or the judging. Her whole life she'd
been judged by her family and had been found lacking;
she should be used to it by now. But there was something
different in the way Jared looked at her. His gaze held an
intensity she'd never seen before. Like he could look deep
into her soul and see her every doubt, her every insecurity.
And her every mistake.

Then there were the other times when those looks had
nothing to do with uncovering her darkest failures and everything to do with uncovering her deepest secrets.

He crowded her mind, made her forget—and worse—
made her remember. And each time her body responded
to him, she felt so much guilt. As if Steven were alive and
she was cheating on him.

A part of her wanted to pack her bags and run away
like she had as a child. Except, back then, she'd always
escaped to the safety of Nana's house. But the reality was,
she still felt safe here. Even with Jared here. Maybe because he was here. And that was definitely not something
she wanted to examine too closely.

After Steven had died, all Jenny had wanted was to be
left alone. When her family kept showing up, trying to
comfort her, she had been quick to push them away. She
told them she was happy living by herself on the lake.
And she was. She *still was*. But as much as she hated to
admit it, sometime during this last week, she had started to
find solace knowing someone else was in the house. There
was a strength about Jared that she couldn't deny. He possessed an air about him she'd never sensed in another

man. Not even Steven. It was there in the way Jared walked, the way he spoke, and the quiet restlessness that seemed to keep him on alert at all times.

Her hands bunched in the grass as she fought against the wave of guilt that rolled over her. How could she be so disloyal? She fought for and found a mental picture of Steven. In her mind she saw his sandy blond hair, his smiling face. But then his hair changed color, turned an ebony black. And his green eyes became hard blue sapphires.

Water skiers roared past, startling her. Waves slapped angrily against the beach and splashed across the sand.

She sat up and looped her arms around her bent knees, trying to stop her trembling.

Steven her mind begged, looking for forgiveness.

A loud bang came from the hangar, but she didn't turn around. Jared was inside doing heaven only knew what. Over the last week, he'd laid claim to the space, and Jenny seemed to be the only one who had a problem with that. Zeke took it all in stride, acting as if he enjoyed having another guy around the place. Several times Jenny found herself working up her courage to confront him, to remind him that this was her business, and she was in charge. But whenever she was near him, he threw her off balance and made her forget what she wanted to say.

She picked up a rock and tossed it in the water. Maybe her family and friends were right. Maybe she did need to get out. For so many months, she'd gone out of her way to distance herself from friends and even her family to the extent they'd allow it. Being around people only reminded her of everything she had lost. Living had been replaced by mere existing. Living meant you laughed and you loved. Existing was just basic survival. You could be numb when you just existed. Numb was good. Numb kept her from feeling a pain so crippling it would destroy her.

She needed Jared to leave. And it wasn't just because of the business. There was more: an awareness of him that scared her like nothing else since Steven's death.

He could not stay here for the next four months. She wouldn't survive.

A tall shadow fell over her, blocking out the sun. She tensed, not needing to turn around to know who it was.

"We need to talk." His deep voice with a hint of roughness was becoming all too familiar. So was the perpetual look of irritation in his hard blue eyes. She didn't need to be facing him to know it would be there. His tone said it all.

"Ignoring me won't work."

She'd beg to differ.

"It's about your Beaver."

She whipped her head around so fast her neck twinged in protest. From her spot on the ground, her eyes leveled on the five-button fly of a pair of worn Levi's. Embarrassment tinged her cheeks pink, and that was before she forced her gaze up. She swallowed hard. He wasn't wearing a shirt. Taking up her whole line of vision was his bare chest and a set of broad shoulders, tanned by the sun and defined by muscles. A T-shirt dangled from the back pocket of his jeans. "My wh-what?"

"Beaver."

Pink turned to bright red. "I don't—"

"The *piston* Beaver."

She looked up at him. "The *plane*?"

"Of course the plane. What the hell did you think—" He broke off as a slow grin curved his lips. "You have one dirty little mind."

"I do not." That was the truth. Or it had been until a week ago.

He shifted his weight and crossed his arms across his chest.

His grin was worse than anything he could have said.

She felt like a fool, sitting on the ground at his feet. Standing, she kept her eyes off the fly of his Levi's and off his bare chest.

She ducked her head and took her time brushing off the seat of her white shorts. God, please let him blame her red face on the sun. Unable to face him, she stalled, searched for the flip-flops she'd kicked off when she'd first gotten to the beach. She found them in the sand, right next to where she'd been sitting. Picking them up, she brushed off her right foot and was just about to put her flip-flop on when she lost her balance and wobbled. Jared's hand instantly closed around her arm, steadying her. Heat that had nothing to do with the sun infused her.

Unnerved by his touch, she turned all thumbs. She fumbled as she tried to put on her shoe . . . tried not to think about how long it had been since she'd felt the strength of a man's hand on her.

With more force than necessary, she shoved the second flip-flop on. The hard plastic bit the soft skin between her toes.

The minute she had both shoes on, he let go of her arm. "Now, can we talk about the Beaver?"

She finally met his gaze. While her insides were tied up in knots and her arm still tingled from his touch, Jared seemed completely unaffected. She should have been relieved. "Can you stop calling it that?"

"What should I call it?"

"Anything but . . ." She couldn't, she wouldn't, say it.

"The Beaver?"

She glared at him. "You needed something?"

"The *plane* is due for an oil change, and during yesterday's flight, Zeke noticed the hydraulic flaps seemed a little slow to respond."

"I can't help you."

"Big surprise."

His comment pissed her off. He had no idea how she and Zeke divided the responsibilities. "Zeke handles the maintenance on the plane. He's the one you need to speak with."

"I would, but he's not here."

"He has the day off. Not everyone deems it necessary to work seven days a week."

"Five would be nice. Hell, at this point I'd settle for four."

She clenched her jaw. "We don't have any charters scheduled for today—"

"Big surprise," he said again.

"We don't have a charter, so there's no need for Zeke to come in."

"And we wouldn't want to be ready in case someone called out of the blue."

That had never happened before, but she wasn't about to tell him that. "Then I would call Zeke."

"Listen, sweetheart."

God, she really hated it when he called her that.

"There's a lot more to this business than just flying the plane. I don't give a damn what you and your handyman do when I'm gone, but while I'm here, you'll run a business like a business should be run. The plane will be maintained. And sunbathing"—the look he gave her made her feel like she was wearing the tiniest of bikinis instead of a pair of shorts and a tank top— "is not part of the job description."

She hadn't been sunbathing, and he knew it. And more importantly, the plane was impeccably maintained. Immediately following yesterday's flight, Zeke had consulted with her about the hydraulic flaps. They'd both agreed that tomorrow, during the regularly scheduled oil change, he would also inspect the flaps. "At least I keep my clothes on."

The moment she said the words, she wished them back.

He rocked back on his heels and rubbed a hand across his bare chest. "I've never had any complaints."

"Then I'd suggest a hearing test."

"What?"

"I said you need a hearing test."

"I'm sorry, what was that?"

He was playing her. The jerk. "No one around here wants your opinions. Believe me."

"You'd better start, or damn soon there won't be a business."

She turned and headed for the house. Why did she bother? Conversing with Jared was like the worst version of a "Who's on First" Abbott and Costello skit. All they did was talk in circles, but even so, he always seemed to come out ahead.

Just as she reached the front porch, a car pulled into the driveway. Shielding a hand over her eyes, she looked up the hill and saw a silver Volvo. Fan-freakin'-tastic. A run-in with her sister was the last thing she wanted.

Dropping her hand, she made her way to the parking area and waited for Anna. It took forever. Mr. Wilson on his tractor drove faster than her sister.

Finally, her sister angled into a parking spot and turned off the engine. Jenny smiled, trying to muster up some enthusiasm. She saw her nephew was in the backseat. She waved. He didn't wave back. Great, just what she needed. Another ornery male.

Several moments passed before her sister got out of the car; Cody stayed put.

Jenny tried not to feel underdressed. Even on a week-end morning, her sister managed to look like she'd just come from a Paris boutique. The pale lilac skirt and matching fitted jacket had exquisite, exclusive, and expensive stamped all over it. "This is a surprise."

"Good one, I hope."

"Always," Jenny said and wished it was true. At one time it had been.

Anna looked around the yard. "Grandmother's garden looks lovely. She always knew you'd be the best care-taker."

If her sister's compliment hadn't instantly put Jenny on guard, then the affectionate tone would have. As far as Jenny could remember, the last time Anna had said some-thing nice to Jenny was when they were kids and Jenny had roasted Anna's marshmallows during their cookouts on the beach. But then Anna had outgrown Barbies and grown boobs and decided everyone needed a life plan by the time they were thirteen. Her tolerance for her younger, less driven sister had all but evaporated.

"Thanks," Jenny said warily.

Her sister looked past her, toward the hangar. "Zeke sounds busy."

It wasn't Zeke, but there was no way Jenny was going to tell that to her sister. She was sick and tired of having every aspect of her life analyzed by her family. "So, what brings you all the way out here?"

"Well, I—" Anna broke off midsentence. "*That* is not Zeke."

Jenny turned and saw that Jared—still shirtless—had emerged from the hangar. He grabbed something, then headed back in.

"Is that who I think it is?" Anna asked, sounding like a breathless schoolgirl.

"It's no one you know."

"I think I can make an accurate guess."

Yes, Jenny thought. Unfortunately, her sister could.

"You sure know how to pick them," Anna continued. "I'll give you that."

"I didn't pick him."

Anna grinned at her. "I would have."

"Anna!"

"What?"

"You're married."

"Married, not buried."

Something in her sister's tone caught Jenny, and she found herself looking more closely at Anna. But as she searched her sister's features, Jenny knew she must have been mistaken. The tentativeness. The trace of uncertainty Jenny had thought she heard had been an illusion. Anna had never had an unsure moment in her life.

"Come on, this I have to see."

Her sister was halfway across the yard before Jenny could react.

Jenny hustled to catch up, knowing there was no way she could stop her sister. For a woman who drove a good ten miles under the speed limit, Anna was a surprisingly fast walker. "Don't you mean meet?" Jenny asked when she reached Anna.

Anna flashed her a huge smile, the kind that Jenny hadn't seen for years—if ever. "Yeah, right. Meet." She smiled again.

The hangar's large front doors were open, and sunlight flooded most of the vast interior. Toward the far end, Jared was working on one of the hydraulic flaps. The muscles on his chest and arms bunched and rippled as he worked underneath the plane's flap. Every time he reached forward, his Levi's slipped a little lower on his hips, exposing more of his rock-hard abs and the thin, dark line of hair that spiraled around his navel and disappeared into the waistband of his jeans.

Jenny felt a sudden rush of anger, and it had nothing to do with his working on her plane and everything to do with him standing half-naked in front of them making her remember the way the heat of his hand had felt against her skin as he'd held her, steadied her, while she put on her flip-flops.

Anna let out a long-drawn-out breath. "*That's* your partner?"

"Don't call him that."

"I never expected him to be so—"

"Arrogant? Obnoxious? Overbearing?"

Her sister tore her gaze away from Jared. "Gorgeous."

He was turning them all into besotted fools. "Let's go," Jenny said and started to turn away.

"Not on your life. I've been dying to meet your partner ever since Mom described him."

Her sister had never been infatuated with a guy. Ever. Not even with her husband. She and Phillip had had the perfect relationship. They'd met, fallen in love, and gotten married all in six months. The fact that Anna was now ogling the man wreaking havoc in Jenny's life was just plain wrong. "He's working."

"I can see that."

"We shouldn't interrupt him. We both know how much you hate to be interrupted at work. Jared's the same way." Okay, she'd made that up, but it was probably true.

"I don't think he'll mind. I'm sure he's anxious to meet your family." Anna's look was a clear reminder that Jenny could have avoided this if she had brought him to their father's party.

Jenny considered dragging her sister back to the house. The last thing she wanted was for Anna and Jared to meet. For Jared and any of her family to meet for that matter. Like the rest of them, he had no trouble trotting out all of her flaws. She could just imagine what a field day he and her family would have comparing notes on all of Jenny's short-comings.

But before Jenny could act, Anna called out, "Hello." Her voice carried loud and clear.

Jared paused and turned their way.

Anna waved, and Jenny rolled her eyes. Her normally reserved and studious sister was making a spectacle of her-self. And that was before she motioned for him to join them.

Jared set down the tool he'd been working with and made his way toward them, wiping his hands off on the seat of his jeans. His long legs ate up the distance.

Jenny glared at him as he drew near. Glared at him and then at the shirt he still hadn't put on.

He flashed her sister one of the bone-melting grins he reserved for women other than Jenny. "I don't think I've had the pleasure."

"Dr. Anna Adams. Jenny's sister."

Doctor. Of course her sister had to throw that in.

"Jared Worth. It's nice to meet you."

"I'm sorry we couldn't meet last Friday."

"Friday?" he questioned, his brow creasing.

"Yes. At our father's birthday party. Jenny said you had a previous commitment."

Jenny found herself the object of Jared's full attention. While that might be most girls' dreams, it wasn't hers.

She made sure to tell herself that twice.

"Yes," he answered Anna, still looking at Jenny. "Maybe next time."

"Will you be staying long?" Anna asked.

"No," Jenny said at the same time Jared replied, "Depends."

Anna looked from one to the other, then laughed softly. "Interesting." She held out her hand. "I wish I could stay longer and chat, but I've got to get going. It was nice meeting you."

He shook her hand. "Likewise."

Anna smiled one last time, then finally followed Jenny back to her car.

"You didn't have to do that," Jenny said the moment they were out of his earshot.

"Do what?"

"You know what. Introduce yourself."

"Why ever not? He's your partner."

"Stop calling him that. And he's not going to be around long enough for it to matter if he meets any of you. He's leaving. Soon." They reached the car. Her nephew was still in the backseat listening to his iPod and doing a good imitation of ignoring the world.

"Hmmm," was her sister's only reply.

Jenny let the subject drop, like she always did when she and her sister disagreed. "Before you arrived I was just about to head inside for a glass of lemonade. Would you and Cody care to join me?" She didn't really care if her teenage mutant nephew ever got out of the car, but excluding him would be rude. Besides, she'd only have to endure his company for a short while until they left.

"Mix or homemade?"

Lusting over the enemy and insulting her culinary skills. Perfect. "Homemade."

"No thanks," Anna said on a laugh. "But I do have a favor to ask."

"A favor?" Jenny was certain her surprise showed. She couldn't remember the last time her sister had asked her for anything.

"I got the promotion."

Of course she had. "Congratulations." Jenny tried to put some enthusiasm behind the compliment.

"The new job means a lot of overtime. More hours. Longer days. Weekends."

"Sounds tough."

"Nothing I can't handle."

It was true, and they both knew it.

"I'm actually heading in to work now," she added.

"On a Saturday?"

Her sister let out a sigh. "Do you listen to anything I say? I just explained how I'll have to work weekends."

"Right," Jenny said. Frankly, her sister's work schedule didn't interest her in the least. She had enough to deal with.

"That's why I'm here." Anna paused. "I need you to watch Cody."

"What?"

Anna crossed her arms. "Believe me, you were my last choice."

"Thanks a lot." Not that Jenny wanted to watch her nephew, but the insult hurt, nonetheless.

"I didn't mean it like that."

"Yes, you did."

"I'm sorry. It's just that we both know you're not the most organized individual."

"If I'm such a poor choice, why not take him to Mom's? She loves having Cody."

"I would, except she's buried under work."

"And I'm not?"

Anna took a slow, sweeping look around the property. "No."

Jenny felt like a dartboard her sister kept taking aim at. "What about Paul?" It seemed to her that if her brother had time for early morning calls to pester his baby sister, then he obviously had time to watch his nephew.

"He works nearly as many hours as I do. You know that. Come on, Jen, it would only be for the weekend. Cody's excited to come to the lake."

Jenny glanced into the back of Anna's car. Cody didn't look at all excited. Like mother, like son. Anna had never fallen in love with the lake like Jenny had. She'd never liked the water or fishing with Grandpa or gardening with Nana. To her, it had all been an interference, a waste of time for a girl who only wanted to set the medical world on fire.

And then the full impact of her sister's words hit her. "Weekend? As in today *and* tomorrow?"

"And possibly next weekend, too. Until I can make other arrangements for the summer. He has a baseball game late Sunday afternoon and a book report due on Monday. Please make sure he gets that done."

Jenny looked back at her nephew. He was turned sideways in the seat, facing as far away from them as possible and slouched so far down on the expensive beige leather seat all Jenny could see was the top of his spiky blue hair. But that still didn't hide the fact that he wore a big Back Off sign.

"This was a mistake," her sister said, uncrossing her arms. "I told Mom you couldn't handle it. Forget I stopped by. I'll figure something else out."

Her sister opened the car door, and Jenny waited for the sense of relief she was sure would come. She didn't need this. She didn't need her nephew hanging around giving her attitude. Her gaze strayed toward the hangar. She had enough to deal with at the moment.

I told Mom you couldn't handle it.

She could handle it; she just didn't want to.

Through the open car door, Cody shifted his position, and their eyes met. But this time, instead of seeing a brooding teenager, she saw something else, something more: a kid trying his hardest to act like he didn't care. But each time Anna talked about him staying for the weekend, Cody seemed to collapse into himself a little more. It was almost as if he expected to be rejected. Watching him, Jenny felt a pull on her heart. If anyone in this family knew about building barricades and pretending not to hurt, it was her.

"He can stay," Jenny heard herself say.

TEN

Before her sister's car even crested the driveway, Jenny knew she had made a mistake. Why hadn't she just said no?

Because she'd never been good at turning anyone down, particularly not family and most certainly not her sister. And especially when her sister was asking her for a favor. It had been such a novelty, Jenny had said yes before she'd fully thought it through.

Twenty-six years old and still trying to prove herself to her family. Pathetic.

Anna's Volvo turned left onto Lakeshore Drive. Soon the silver car disappeared around a long, sweeping bend, and the only evidence of her sister's visit was the low cloud of dirt hovering above the gravel drive, two brown grocery sacks at Jenny's feet, and the sullen teenager standing next to her.

Jenny faced her nephew and put on a brave face. Just because she knew it was a mistake that Cody was here, he didn't have to. Besides, it was only for the weekend. Two short little days. How bad could it be? "Why don't we head inside and—"

"Don't bother."

His tone took her aback. "Don't bother what?"

Cody snagged his backpack off the ground and slung it over his right shoulder. The stuffed gray and white nylon hung low on his back, the shoulder strap extended as far as it could go. "You can stop smiling." He glared at her. "I don't want to be here any more than you want me." Without saying another word, he sulked off toward the house.

Jenny watched him go, his backpack thumping against his butt with each step he took. "Great," she muttered under her breath, already feeling the weekend lengthen. As usual, she'd been wrong. Cody hadn't been worried about Jenny not letting him stay; he'd been worried she would. A weekend at his aunt's was obviously the last thing he wanted. With a shake of her head, she looked down into the grocery sacks Anna had left. There was enough food to last a week. Evidently, Jenny could watch her nephew; she just couldn't cook for him. Carrying the paper bags, she followed Cody into the house. When would she learn to stop being such a bleeding heart?

She found him in the family room, sprawled out on the couch. She paused, readjusted the grocery sacks. As she stared at her nephew, she felt a pang of remembrance. She knew what it was like to be the kid of two hardworking parents, though unlike Cody, Jenny's dad had always been home at night. And when her parents had been gone, she'd spent the majority of the time here at the lakefront house with her grandparents. Those times had been magical. Working with Nana in the garden or trolling for trout with her grandfather on the calm waters of Hidden Lake. It didn't matter how full the freezer was or how busy her grandfather was, he would always make time to take her out during the crisp early mornings.

Maybe that was what Cody needed: for Jenny to show him the magic of the lake. When he'd been younger, they had gotten along so well. But in the last few years—in the last year—their relationship had gone sideways. Now Jenny wondered why she'd been so quick to blame everything on Cody turning thirteen. As she continued to look at him, she realized she was just as much to blame, if not more so. Nine months ago, she'd lost more than Steven. In her grief, she'd found it easier to become detached from her family—from everything. Maybe this weekend was a chance for her to start to change some of that.

She took a step toward the kitchen to set the grocery sacks down, then changed her mind. Nothing like the present to start on her new path. Balancing the heavier of the sacks on her hip, she walked into the family room. "Cody?"

He didn't look her way.

She tried again. A little louder. "Cody?"

That was when she noticed his iPod and the thin white wires leading to his ears. Even from here she could hear the music coming from his earphones.

Knowing it was the only way to get his attention, she stepped into his line of vision and motioned as best as she could for him to take out his earphones.

With obvious reluctance, he pulled one of the miniature earphones out and glared at her.

"Hey," she said, with more enthusiasm than necessary. "I thought maybe you'd like to help me unload all these groceries your mom packed. Looks like she's planning on you staying for a week," she joked.

He didn't find her funny. "I'm sure she'd leave me if she could."

He tried to hide behind a sarcasm only a thirteen-year-old boy could master, but Jenny could hear the hurt. "I'm sure your mom would love to be with you. But it sounds like this new job—"

"Whatever."

Talking about Anna would obviously get them nowhere right now, so Jenny dropped it. "Hey, what about these groceries?"

He glared at her before picking up the remote and surfing through the channels. "You do it. I told Mom I didn't want 'em."

The bags were getting heavy, but Jenny was bound and determined to make a connection with her nephew. "How about after I put this stuff away, we do something fun? There's a whole cupboard full of board games from when your mom and uncle and I were kids."

"Bored. Yeah, right."

Something told Jenny he wasn't using board in the same sense she was. "There's Monopoly. Life. Scrabble. Or Clue. That used to be one of your mom's favorites."

"Get a clue."

Jenny bit back a grin. Her nephew was turning into a real stand-up comedian.

"Are you kidding me?" He kept flipping through the channels, then looked at her. "Five channels. What am I supposed to do all weekend?" He turned back to the TV.

"If you don't want to play a game, there's a whole shelf full of books upstairs."

Cody didn't bother answering. He cranked up his music and continued to push the remote, as if somehow more television stations would magically appear.

She stared at him a moment longer, at a loss for how to reach him. Still thinking, she headed into the kitchen.

She'd taken less than half a dozen steps when her flip-flop caught on something. She staggered, tried to regain her footing, tried to hold on to the grocery bags, and failed. Her feet flew out from under her. The bags flew out of her grasp as she flung out her arms, searched for something to grab on to. She only came up with air.

With a thud she hit the floor.

Dazed, she lay there, unable to move. It only took seconds for the back of her head to begin to throb. She blinked once . . . twice . . . tried to clear the pain away. But she could already feel the start of a killer headache. Her back began to sting, and her bottom felt like she'd just gotten a beating. She had. By a hardwood floor.

When the kitchen stopped spinning, she went to push herself up, only to have her hands slip out from under her.

She fell back, crying out as she smacked against the floor once more.

She seriously considered just giving up and lying there until someone found her. The thought of doing another kerplunk onto the hardwood wasn't all that appealing. Then she realized she'd either be found by her nephew—not so bad—or Jared—*very bad*.

Carefully—so carefully—she sat up and looked at her hands, wondering what had caused her second fall. A white gelatinous mess covered her palms. Wiping them off on her shorts as best she could, she used her forearms and pushed her hair off her face. Except for her aching head and throbbing tailbone, she was fine. The groceries, on the other hand, were a different story.

The milk had landed on its side, lid off. White froth gurgled across the floor. A carton of eggs had landed facedown. Broken yolks leaked out and mixed with the milk. So much for the mystery of the white goo on her hands. Fruit had toppled from a bag, and apples and oranges had scattered across the kitchen like balls on a pool table. The bananas hadn't gone far. A box of Cheerios lay half-in, half-out of the milk. Using her foot, she nudged the Cheerios, boxes of mac and cheese, and a few Tupperware containers out of harm's way.

Still disorientated, she looked around the kitchen. What had she tripped over?

And then she saw it: Cody's backpack, abandoned right in the middle of the pathway.

She stood and sucked in a breath as a sharp pain shot up her spine. Grabbing a kitchen towel from the counter, she wiped off her hands and looked to the family room. Cody was still on the couch, still glued to the TV. She eyed him suspiciously. He couldn't have picked a better spot to leave his backpack if he'd tried.

She opened her mouth, ready to give him what for—then stopped. What was wrong with her? Cody would no more try to trip her than she would try to trip him. She blamed her preposterous thoughts on the heat . . . her sister's unexpected visit . . . and on the man who'd moved into her house and into her thoughts.

With more force than necessary, she jerked the backpack off the floor (paid the price as a fresh surge of pain pounded behind her eyes and her lower back) and set it on one of the high-backed counter stools before making her way back in to the kitchen and the paper towel holder.

"Cooking?"

She nearly dropped the wad of paper towels in her hand.

Jared stood near the end of the counter, a lazy half smile tilting the corner of his mouth.

He's wearing his shirt was her first thought. Her second, "Stop sneaking up on me."

"Sorry," he said, but they both knew he was anything but. He eyed the mess of milk and eggs, then turned his gaze back on her. "Scrambled eggs?" His smile turned full-blown, and her heart slammed hard against her chest. "My favorite."

"Very funny," she snapped, unnerved by her unacceptable reaction to him. It was something that was happening with more and more frequency. Ignoring him—or at least pretending to—because quite honestly, she found that was the only way she could be around him and keep her sanity, she tenderly bent down and began mopping up the mess. "What do you want?"

He reached over her and picked up the jug of milk. "Why do you assume I want anything?"

Want. How long had it been since she'd thought about wanting. Needing? Merely existing had become enough. When she only had to worry about making it through the day, she was safe. Because thinking about more than that— wanting more than that—left her raw and exposed. "Forget it." She swirled her paper towels through the wet mess a little faster.

For several moments, he didn't move or say anything, and Jenny could feel his gaze on her. She didn't draw an easy breath until he set the half-empty milk carton on the counter. But instead of leaving, as she'd expected, he picked up the rest of the groceries. Setting them on the counter, he tore off a hunk of paper towels and crouched down next to her.

"I didn't hear you leave."

They were so close she could feel the heat from his sun-warmed skin, could count his thick, spiky lashes. "Leave?"

"To grocery shop."

His hand kept brushing against hers, almost as if on purpose. She told herself the fall had made her delusional, made her read into something that wasn't there. But that didn't stop the warmth from spreading across her hand, up her arm, down her spine, each time their skin touched. "Oh. That. I didn't. I mean, my sister brought them."

"Your sister brought you food?" He sounded surprised, as if the thought of a family member bringing food to another was a foreign concept.

"For my nephew." And that's when she realized Jared didn't know about Cody.

Glad for any excuse to put some distance between them, she stood. "Cody," she called out as she tossed the soggy paper towels in the garbage under the sink and rinsed her hands.

"Cody," she said again, louder, remembering his ear-phones.

He rolled off the couch with as much energy as a slug. "What?"

"There's someone I would like you to meet."

He shuffled into the kitchen. When he caught sight of Jared, his eyes widened, and for a brief moment his cloak of teenage disdain slipped away. Surprised curiosity took its place.

Jared looked just as startled. He stared at her nephew like he'd never seen a kid before.

Jenny made the introductions. "Jared, this is Cody. Cody, Jared."

Jared stuck out his hand. "Nice to meet you."

Cody stared at Jared's outstretched arm. "Uh . . . um. Yeah. Whatever." He put his small hand into Jared's much larger one, and his thin arm wobbled as Jared pumped.

"Cody is my sister Anna's son. Anna was recently promoted, and her hours at work have increased. With her husband out of town, she needed someone . . . me . . . to watch Cody. He might be back next weekend, too." She clamped her mouth shut. She was rambling, just like she did every time she got nervous. But that's what Jared did to her—made her nervous. And he made her remember.

"I didn't know you had a nephew."

"There's a lot about me you don't know." But looking at him, remembering the flash of uncertainty that had come into his eyes when he'd first seen her nephew, had her thinking the reverse. There was a lot about him that she didn't know.

Jared faced Cody. "Must be fun to stay with an aunt who lives on a lake."

"My mom doesn't like me to be near water unless there's a lifeguard."

"Maybe Jenny could talk to your mom, get her to change her mind."

Cody shoved his hands deep down into the front pockets of his baggy cargo shorts. "Mom never changes her mind." He hunched his shoulders. "Aunt Jenny doesn't even have cable."

"That sucks," Jared agreed.

Cody scuffed his sneakered toe against the wooden floor. "Totally. Who doesn't have cable?"

"Have either of you ever heard of a book? Or a game of cards?"

They ignored her.

"We have over two hundred channels at our house."

"Sports package?"

"Yep."

"You and your dad must have a lot of fun watching the games."

Cody's sneaker halted, and he gave Jared a sideways glance. "My dad's never around."

Jared was silent for several moments. "Tough break," was all he finally said.

"Cody's father is a surgeon," Jenny explained, filling the sudden silence. "For the next few months, he's volunteering in the Doctors Without Borders program. Where is he now, Cody? Sri Lanka?"

"Who cares."

The contemptuous comment hung in the air like a stale odor.

"And Aunt Jenny doesn't have a dog either."

Cody made the comment with such appalling disbelief, Jenny wasn't sure which ranked higher on the World's Worst Aunt List—the cable or the dog.

"My mom says we can't have a dog 'cuz we live in the city, and they poop. But Aunt Jenny doesn't live in the city."

"No," Jared agreed. "She doesn't."

Jenny shot him a *thanks a lot* look. His *you're welcome* was anything but.

Jared looked to all the groceries on the counter. "Your mom sure packed a lot of food."

Cody shrugged. "Mom said not to eat Aunt Jenny's cooking."

A deep bark of laughter erupted from Jared's chest. "She would know."

Jenny looked at Jared, momentarily stunned by his transformation. She knew she should make a comeback, tell him he was free to leave anytime, but she was struck speechless. True amusement had softened his features, replaced the everpresent hard, cynical edge. His eyes, usually so guarded, were as clear and blue as her lake on a hot summer day. She'd always found him attractive, but looking at him now, seeing him like this, Jenny found Jared nearly impossible to resist.

"Well, kid," Jared said. "I'll see you around."

Cody moved away from the counter. "You're staying here, too?"

"Just for a few days," Jared answered.

"Jared's my . . ." Jenny started to explain then stumbled to a halt. *Her what?* She wasn't about to say—

"Partner," he easily filled in. "I'm your aunt's partner."

"Oh," was all Cody said. And while Jenny might feel like kicking Jared, she felt like hugging Cody. Here at least was one family member who didn't drill her with a hundred and one questions.

With every word he spoke, Jared inched a little closer to the hallway. His movements were slow and measured, and if she hadn't been paying close enough attention, she would have missed them.

"If you can't go on the water, I saw a basketball hoop on the far side of the hangar. Probably a ball around here someplace."

Cody slumped against the counter. "I play baseball."

"What position?"

There it was again, that movement.

"Pitcher and third base."

"If you brought your glove and ball, maybe your aunt could throw you a few."

Cody gave him a look like he'd just escaped for an insane asylum. Jenny was beginning to warm to her nephew. "Have you seen her throw?"

Maybe warm was too strong a word.

"That bad?"

"Worse."

Jared laughed again. "I feel for you, kid."

Jenny didn't feel for either one of them. Nothing like having two males around to rake her over the coals. She faced Jared. "You never did say why you came in."

He'd made it all the way to the arch leading to the hallway. "Forget it. It's not important now." He glanced pointedly at Cody.

"Humor me." She didn't know why she pushed.

"I was just about to start changing the Beav—*plane's*"— he shot her another one of those smiles that turned her insides upside down—"oil. Thought you could lend an extra pair of hands if you had nothing better to do." His tone suggested she never had anything better to do. "But since your nephew's here, I'll manage on my own."

"I told you—"

"Zeke handles the plane. I got it. But he isn't here, is he?" His smile disappeared. "Look, it's not like I want to work on the damn plane, but I sure as shit don't want it to malfunction on my watch either."

She wanted to tell him to go to hell. Instead she told him, "Stop swearing in front of Cody. And you don't have a watch."

"As long as I'm here, I do."

She bristled. "We've never had any maintenance malfunctions. Blue Sky Air—"

"Has been damn lucky. From what I can tell, you've been flying on a wing and a prayer. Your maintenance records are a joke."

That was a lie. The maintenance records were in perfect order, but she bit the inside of her cheek to keep from screaming the truth. The last thing she wanted was to get into a yelling match in front of Cody. Somehow she just knew that bit of information would find its way to her sister . . . then her brother . . . then her mother, and so on. But as hard as she tried, everything seemed to come crashing down at once. This sham of a partnership. Her sister. Her fall. An unhappy nephew who she had no idea how to entertain. A man who was not only stirring her ire, but who was also stirring a hell of a lot more.

Before she could think it through, before she could change her mind, she heard herself say, "Cody can help you."

* * *

Jared went cold. "That's not a good idea."

"Sure it is." Jenny looped her arm around Cody's narrow shoulders, giving him a gentle squeeze. "He'd love to help," she said, putting on an overly bright smile. "Wouldn't you, Cody?"

The kid looked like he'd rather parade through his school cafeteria in his tighty whities. But Jared kept his mouth shut. Just like he should have earlier. Engaging in stupid chitchat with the boy had been just that—stupid. Jared didn't do kids. Period. Hell, he barely associated with adults. If there was one thing his less-than-stellar childhood had taught him, it was to keep his distance, to disassociate from everyone and everything. But remembering what he should do had become damn near impossible around Jenny. Just like it had been when he was with Steven. No, Jared corrected himself, not like Steven. When he was with Steven, he sure as hell hadn't been thinking about what he thought about every time he looked at Jenny.

Guilt nailed him. Again. Only a lowlife would lust after his best friend's girl.

More than lusted, Jared acknowledged. His thoughts pretty much landed on the down and dirty. It didn't matter that Steven was gone. Jenny was still his. It was there in her eyes, in the soft timbre of her voice every time she said his name—and even when she didn't. And it was there on the diamond ring she still wore. "Thanks," he said at the hallway, "but no thanks. I've got it handled."

"But you just said—"

"I know what I said."

Cody stopped trying to break free of his aunt's embrace. "Forget it, Aunt Jenny. He doesn't want me."

A long-buried memory blindsided Jared. Damn it, he'd forgotten the kid was standing there. He tried not to look at Cody, but Jared knew he didn't even have to look to know what he'd see. He'd heard it.

Doesn't want me.

Cody stood at the edge of the counter, his shoulders stiff and erect, his chin pushed out into the air, his eyes flat and expressionless. From all outward appearances, he looked like he couldn't give a rip about the discussion going on around him. But all that indifference was just a farce. No one knew that better than Jared. He'd perfected that exact pose by the time he was nine.

Shit.

"Hey, kid, why don't you run out to the fridge in the hangar and grab us a couple of root beers?"

Cody looked like he was going to refuse, then shuffled his feet and headed out.

The screen door had no sooner banged shut than Jenny turned on him. "Don't order him around."

He faced Jenny, and every dirty thought he'd had while they'd been slipping around on the floor pummeled him once more. He wanted to strip off her clothes, lay her out on the hardwood, and do every sinfully delicious thing to her that had been haunting his dreams. "When did sending a kid out to get pop constitute ordering him around?"

Her eyes narrowed, and her full lips thinned into a hard line. It was an expression he was fast becoming all too familiar with.

Good. Stay pissed. Maybe it would keep his thoughts where they belonged.

She crossed her arms under her chest, pushing her breasts higher, exposing a fair amount of cleavage.

No, his thoughts weren't going anywhere. Nowhere they should.

"It's not even ten. A little early for a can of pop, don't you think?"

He dragged his gaze off her chest. "Are you kidding me?"

She stared at him like he was an idiot. And frankly, he was beginning to think she was right. Especially when he was around her. "No one drinks pop at this time in the morning. Don't you remember anything your parents taught you?"

"Right. My parents."

She looked at him for several long moments, and slowly the angry expression eased from her face to be replaced by one of puzzled confusion. "I'm sorry. I didn't mean—"

"Listen," Jared cut in. He knew that look, that I'm-about-to-ask-you-all-kinds-of-questions look. Questions he had no intention of answering. Long ago, he'd learned how to bury his past. But somehow Jenny seemed to see past all the walls he'd fortified over the years.

He had to get out of here. Out of this kitchen, out of this town. "I'm sorry about the kid," he said, turning the conversation. "About offering him a soda. I just wanted him out of earshot."

"Why?"

Doesn't want me.

"Because no kid should have to listen to two people arguing about him."

Jenny opened her mouth, then closed it, clearly baffled. "We weren't arguing about Cody."

"Don't bullshit a bullshitter."

She narrowed her eyes again. "Do you always have to be so vulgar?"

He almost laughed. If she thought that was vulgar, it was a damn good thing she couldn't read his thoughts. "Can't help it. I'm a guy."

"Like I haven't noticed." The moment the words were out, she took a step back.

He knew he should let it go. Leave it alone. Leave *her* alone. But just like every other time he was around her, doing what he should never worked out. He closed the distance between them. Awareness widened her eyes. "And here I thought you hadn't noticed."

"I've noticed. But not like that. I mean . . . you're not . . . we're not . . ." She blew out a long breath and gave him an exasperated look. "You understand, right?"

He was playing with fire, but he couldn't make himself stop. "You better explain it to me."

She rubbed her palms on the front of her shorts. "You're making this harder than it needs to be."

If she only knew what was harder than it should be.

His gaze followed the up and down motion of her hands. She was nervous, and he knew he was the reason why. He should back off, back away from her. He'd been around a lot of beautiful women in his day, but Jenny was different.

Beautiful, definitely. But there was something else . . . something more. All the years Jared had been in the military, he'd never received a letter, a care package. But Steven had. Lots of them. And the vast majority had come from Jenny. When Steven realized Jared never received anything, Steven—being Steven—insisted on including Jared during mail day. Whatever treats he'd been sent (now Jared understood why they'd been store-bought) he'd shared; he'd also read parts of his letters out loud. Before then, Jared had been able to endure mail days. When you didn't expect anything, you were never let down. But through Jenny's letters, Jared had glimpsed a way of life he'd long ago given up on. Her letters had been filled with stories about life on Hidden Lake. Listening to the world she'd weaved, it had been almost impossible not to fall under her spell. With distance, he'd managed to resist. But now, being here, being in the world she had unknowingly woven around him years before, Jared felt that allure pull at him. Felt Jenny pull at him.

He tore his gaze off her legs and changed the conversation back to where it should never have strayed from. Being around Jenny was becoming dangerous. "All I'm saying is, I know what it feels like to be passed around like you aren't wanted. To have grown-ups talk about you like you weren't even there," he said with a candor that was unexpected, even to him.

"Cody's wanted," she said softly. "I just thought he'd have more fun with you. You were a kid once. A teenage boy."

"I was never a kid." His words were light, and his smile was bright. The combination had never failed to reroute a woman's thoughts to where he wanted them to go. But Jenny wasn't biting.

She searched his face. "What do you mean—?"

The screen door opened and banged shut.

Startled by the sound, her eyes widened and she moved away from him as if only just realizing how close they'd been standing to each other.

"Here," Cody said as he entered the kitchen. He handed Jared a root beer.

Jared took the can automatically, though what he really wanted was a straight shot. Maybe two. In less than a handful of minutes, he'd revealed more to Jenny than he'd ever told anyone else.

Before his aunt could tell him no, Cody snapped his can open, and a fizzy hiss filled the suddenly silent room. With his can of pop halfway to his mouth, Cody looked to each of them. "So, did you figure out who gets stuck with the booby prize?"

Jenny avoided Jared as she wrapped her arm around Cody's shoulders, gave the top of his head a playful tousle. "You are a prize, kiddo. Don't forget that," she said sincerely. "So here's the deal. I need to do some work in the office for a couple of hours, but then I'm all yours. You can either hang out in here with me or work on the plane with Jared. It's up to you."

* * *

Through the screen door Jenny watched Cody follow Jared across the yard. Jared walked like a man with a purpose, a man who knew exactly who he was and what he wanted. His long legs made the distance seem short, while Cody hustled to stay abreast. For every one step of Jared's, Cody took two. His small head was cocked to the side, turned toward Jared, and even from here, she could tell Cody was jabbering away. From the stiff set of Jared's shoulders, Jenny had a pretty good idea her nephew was nailing him with one question after another. She probably should feel bad for Jared. Probably, but she didn't.

She braced her arm near the door, squinting into the bright sun. Twice she'd headed out to call Cody back, and twice she'd stopped herself. He'd made it more than clear he wanted to spend the afternoon outside with Jared. But that didn't stop her from feeling guilty. Less than an hour ago, she'd vowed to be a better aunt, to find a way to bridge the gap between them. But then Jared had walked into her kitchen, and all of her good intentions had flown out the window.

She rested her head near her shoulder. He infuriated her . . . annoyed her . . . flustered her. But most of all, he scared her. Around him, she was finding it impossible to stay numb like she had for the past nine months. Each heated look he gave her seemed to thaw her heart a little more. When he'd first arrived, Jenny's only worry had been about Blue Sky. Now . . . now she had a far greater scare.

Jared reached the hangar first and disappeared into the long shadows. A few moments later, Cody followed.

Jenny dropped her arm and went into her office. She turned on the computer, and as she waited for it to boot up, her gaze slid to the desk's bottom drawer. Staring at it, her heart began to race and her palms sweat. She reached out, intending to open the drawer, only to draw back her hand. She sucked in a deep breath. Ever since Steven's death, she'd been avoiding this moment.

She lifted her gaze and stared out her window to the hangar. Even though she couldn't see Jared, she knew he was there. Where he would stay until she repaid him. And while she still had four months to come up with the money, she was beginning to realize there was no way she would survive that long. His loan and the letter from Steven might have brought him here, but it was up to Jenny to make him leave.

Steeling herself, she opened the desk drawer and withdrew her camera. The moment her hand closed around the cool metal, her heart kicked into overdrive. Her breathing became short and choppy, and she fought hard to drag slow, even breaths into her lungs.

She stared at the camera, marveled how something so light could feel so heavy. But then she knew. It wasn't the camera itself that weighed so much; it was the memories it held. She tried not to think about the last time she'd held the camera in her hands . . . the last time she'd snapped a picture. She tried . . . and failed.

She'd been outside, under a hot summer sky. Steven had been getting ready for a charter.

Snap some pics of me taking off, Jen-Jen. We'll need 'em for the website.

She'd clicked away, nearly filling the memory card, never realizing that would be the last time Steven would ever fly. A day later, he'd been gone.

As the pictures uploaded into the computer, tears pooled in her eyes. Each image cut deeper than the last, but she refused to look away. She drank them in. The first dozen or so were close-ups of Steven. Silly, candid shots of him smiling, goofing off. She soaked up each picture, finding it all but impossible to move on to the next. When a new photo loaded on to the screen, she laughed out loud. It was another shot of Steven, one of him just before he was about to board the plane. With his hand braced on the door, he'd turned around and stuck out his tongue at her. The camera had caught it all: the sunny day, his sandy blond hair that always needed to be trimmed, his bright green eyes, and that big-as-the-sky smile. She laughed again, even as fresh tears filled her eyes.

For months, she'd avoided looking at these pictures, not wanting to feel the pain of them. And while her heart still ached, there was also an unexpected joy. She was shocked to realize that looking at the still images of him didn't crush her like it once would have. Now, instead of remembering only the pain, she was also remembering all of the good times, too.

She wiped at the tears on her cheeks and finished saving the images. Then she picked up the phone.

"Barb," she said when the line was answered on the other end. "It's Jenny Beckinsale. I'm ready to finish the website."

* * *

"Son of a bitch," Jared swore as the wrench busted free and his knuckles scraped against a bolt.

"You shouldn't swear. My mom says so."

Jared picked the wrench off the hangar's cement floor and looked at the back of his hand. Welts were already beginning to form. A thin gash beaded with blood. He sucked at the wound. If he'd been paying attention to what he was doing and not to the kid, he wouldn't have made such a careless mistake. But Cody hadn't stopped yammering since they'd left the house almost an hour ago. "Yeah, well, your mom isn't here, is she?"

"She never is. Neither is my dad." Cody pushed off with his feet and sent the office chair careening across the open expanse of the hangar.

Jared braced himself for the inevitable crash. When he'd first brought the chair out for Cody to sit on, he'd never considered the wheels to be weapons of mass destruction. He was quickly rethinking his tactical error. "Sounds like they both have pretty important jobs."

"That's what everyone says."

Jared refitted the wrench on the bolt.

"What did your parents do?" Cody asked.

The wrench paused. "Nothing much." *Nothing at all.*

"I bet they didn't treat you like a baby. I'm thirteen. I don't need a babysitter." Again the chair went flying. "You're mom was probably cool."

"Yeah, cool." That was the last way Jared would describe Nancy.

"Your mom probably let you stay home all the time by yourself."

Jared nearly laughed. "Kid, my mom split when I was eight. I haven't seen her since."

The chair stopped. "Never?"

"Never."

"How come?"

Jared knew he should just shut up, but there was something about this kid, this place . . . *Jenny* . . . that was making him remember a past he fought hard to forget. "She didn't want to be a mom," he said with enough finality to end the conversation. Cody didn't take the hint.

"That sucks." Using the toe of his tennis shoe, Cody

spun the chair in a circle. "Do you want to see her?" he asked when the chair stopped.

"I saw a small rowboat behind the hangar," Jared said, sidetracking the conversation. "Why don't you ask your aunt if you can take it out?"

"I can't go on the water, remember?"

No, Jared didn't remember. The only thing he wanted to remember was a way to get the kid out of here.

Cody leaned down staring sideways at Jared. "Do *you* have a dog?"

"No."

"A cat?"

"No."

"Why not?"

"Because."

"Because why?"

Christ, did the kid ever shut up? Jared retightened the wrench on the bolt. He glared out the hangar's door, toward the house. He scowled against the bright sun, scowled at the woman who had put him in this position. Babysitting hadn't been part of the plan. And Jenny damn well knew it. But the minute Cody had said *booby prize*, Jared felt himself cave. And like a predator, she'd sensed his weakening and pounced. "Just because."

The chair rolled away and then came back to a stop near where Jared was working. From under the plane, he looked up at the kid. There was nothing about Cody that should stir up memories from Jared's past. Nothing at all. So why was it the more time he spent with the kid, the more old memories resurfaced?

"There are worse things than not having a dog and parents who work," Jared said.

"Yeah? Like what?"

Hadn't the kid been listening?

Like having a mom who screwed so many guys she didn't know who your dad was. Or who split one day while you were at school. It had taken Jared over a week to realize Nancy was never coming back. He'd held on to hope like some pathetic fool clinging to a waterlogged life ring. Not even when the small amount of food they'd had in the house had run out, or the power had been shut off, would Jared let himself believe his mom wasn't going to return.

His grip tightened on the wrench, and he put everything he had into it. His muscles bunched and bulged, and he was surprised the damn bolt didn't just snap off.

Cody kicked at the empty oil pan. "Mom's missed all three of my baseball games."

"Tough break," Jared said with a heavy dose of sarcasm.

The kid didn't notice.

At least his mom hadn't missed the last three decades of his life. Well, not quite three. Jared would give Nancy that. She'd waited until he was in second grade to split.

There was no stopping the memories now. As if in vivid Technicolor, they sputtered to life and began to play and replay over in his mind.

It was ironic, really, the day his mom chose to leave. She couldn't have planned it better if she'd tried. On the same day she hustled out of town, Jared had been called into the principal's office. Back then, he'd had nothing to fear from the principal. School had come easily to him. More than easy. He'd excelled in every subject. While his classmates were still working their way through elementary equations, Jared was breezing through work two to three grade levels above. And that was exactly what Mr. Larson had wanted to talk to him about on that fateful day.

You're gifted, son. Your test results have only proven what your teacher has seen all along. We're recommending you skip the third grade and possibly the fourth. We'll need your mother's permission, of course, but once she sees these scores, I know she'll be as proud and excited as the rest of us.

Proud and excited. Yeah, that's what Nancy would be.

Even at eight, Jared had had a hard time not laughing.

The last thing his mother had been was proud and excited over her son.

How many times had Jared been forced to listen to how she *coulda been something if only she hadn't gotten knocked up*. She'd been planning on going to cosmetology school; she was going to be *somebody*. Then *some bastard* had gotten her pregnant, and she had been forced to give up her dreams.

Some bastard. That was the only name Jared had for his father.

From what Jared could see, the only thing Nancy had been forced to give up was having to get off the couch. With Jared around, she had someone to wait on her hand and foot.

Still, even knowing what his mother was going to say, he hadn't been able to hold back his excitement when he got home from school. But by that time, Nancy was already gone. For two weeks, he'd been able to lie. To keep his mother's disappearance a secret. But in the end, it didn't do any good. He never knew how they found out, but one day Child Protective Services had shown up, and just like that, he was thrown into the system, along with hundreds of other kids whose parents hadn't wanted them.

Jared had always known the truth: Nancy had never cared about anything except her next drink, her next man. But knowing it didn't make it any easier for an eight-year-old to swallow. While most people might think he'd been given a raw deal—tossed like a Frisbee from one foster home to the next—Jared knew the truth. His mother's leaving had taught him the most valuable lesson of his life: the only person you could depend on or trust was yourself.

He'd learned quickly how to work the system. Another thing he could credit his mother for. From years of living with her, he knew how to put on a front. How to build a facade that to the outside world looked as if everything was okay. The state, the social workers, even the foster families he stayed with all bought it hook, line, and sinker. No matter how hard people probed or how far they

tried to dig, Jared never let them in. And in time, that facade became more than just a pretense. It became who he
was.

But somehow Jenny was able to see him clearer than
anyone else.

She'd found a way to get to a place inside of him that
no one else had. The more he was around her, the more he
was beginning to remember all those stupid fantasies he'd
had as a kid. Of how he'd wanted to find a home where he
could belong . . . where he could fit. Where there was someone waiting just for him, wondering about him. Wanting
to hear from him. He shook his head. By the time he was
on his sixth foster family, he should have learned. And he
had. Until his first year of flight school. He'd come home
one day and found the gal he'd been seeing had moved in.
He should have told Lisa to leave right then. To this day
he still wasn't sure why he hadn't. But, in the end, it didn't
matter. Three months later she'd stormed out, telling him
he was a coldhearted bastard who didn't know the first thing
about caring for anyone other than himself.

She'd been right. He did have a heart of stone; it was
the only way he knew how to survive.

But now Jenny was getting under his skin and into his
mind and dredging up all of those improbable ideas he'd
once had.

Jared eased off on the wrench. "There are worse things,
kid, than your parents missin' a few games. Trust me."

"Like you would know."

The bolt came free. Why didn't he just drop the subject? When it came to this kid, conversation was quick-
sand. "Yeah," Jared agreed. "You're right. I wouldn't."

"I bet your parents never missed any of your games."

Positioning the oil pan, Jared removed the plug. "Nope,"
he said with a hundred percent honesty. His mom hadn't,
because she couldn't drag herself off the couch long enough
to get him signed up, let alone take him to practices. And
by the time Jared was placed in the system, he'd lost what

little interest he'd had in organized sports. He wasn't about to buy into some social worker's bullshit about "getting involved" and "being connected."

Involved and connected didn't work for Jared. Except in the cockpit of an F-18.

"See?" Cody whined. "Parker's mom never misses a game. And his dad's there most of the time, too."

Jared glanced sideways. Was this kid for real? So his parents missed a few baseball games. So what? He was clothed, fed, and had plenty of expensive toys. Jared hadn't missed seeing the backpack full of them earlier. "Listen, kid—"

Cody kicked at the oil pan, and thick black liquid sloshed over the sides. "You're just like all the others."

Jared glanced at Cody's expensive shoes. "Shit." Oil pooled in the laces, ran over the expensive leather. "Shit," he said again.

Cody looked at his ruined shoes. "My mom won't care. She'll just buy me another pair."

Jared scooted out from under the plane. He pointed to the workbench. "Grab some rags. You're gonna help me clean up this mess."

Cody glared at him. "Get it yourself. I'm not your slave." He ran out of the hangar.

Jared watched him disappear and cursed himself for being ten kinds of fool. He should have stuck to his original plan and kept his mouth shut. No, he thought. His original plan had been to stay as far away as possible from the kid. And that's exactly what he should have done. Getting mixed up with Cody and his problems wasn't Jared's deal. Getting his money and getting the hell out of here was.

Still, he couldn't help but wonder if he should go and find the kid. Talk to him.

But about what?

He had nothing to offer.

Turning away from the hangar's exit, Jared got back to work. Without any distractions, he finished his work in no time. Halfway through updating the maintenance log, he heard the angry *slap-slap-slap* of flip-flops against the hangar's concrete floor.

"What did you do?" Jenny fired at his back.

He didn't bother to turn around. "I'll treat that as a rhetorical question."

Just what the hell did she use to make herself smell so damn good? Years back, he'd been stationed in Hawaii. That was what Jenny smelled like. Coconut oil, exotic flowers, and sun-heated skin.

"Cody hasn't said a word to me since he stormed back into the house."

"You can thank me later."

"I heard that."

Jared made the last entry in the maintenance log and turned around. And as always, he felt like he'd been punched in the gut. She didn't just smell good, she looked good. Better than good. For just a moment he let his fantasies run wild. He wondered what it would feel like to nuzzle the side of her neck . . . trail kisses up and down her throat . . . wrap his arms around her and pull her close while burying his face deep into her thick blonde hair. And those lips. Too many times he'd fantasized about what they would taste like, look like after he pushed his mouth against hers, smeared off her lip gloss until her lips were puffy and bruised because of him.

No wonder Steven had given up everything to be stuck in this godforsaken town. Why he'd quit flying jets and started puttering around in a damn seaplane. Jared realized most men would consider themselves the luckiest saps on the planet if they had the chance to throw everything away and spend the rest of their lives with a girl like Jenny. Bad cooking and all. But then those suckers still believed in happily-ever-afters.

"You were supposed to. The kid didn't shut up the whole time he was with me."

"He's sensitive—"

"He's spoiled rotten."

Jenny crossed her arms under her breast. Jared really wished she wouldn't keep doing that.

"He's going through a tough time."

"Tough shit."

Her foot began a staccato beat against the concrete. "You can make it up to him at dinner tonight."

"I wasn't the one who insisted he come out here. I'm no damn babysitter."

"He wanted to be with you."

"Right." Jared bent down and began to pick up the tools.

"I'm grilling hot dogs."

His hand stalled on the wrench, and he shot her a sardonic look.

She didn't even pretend to misunderstand. "Even I can't screw up hot dogs."

He placed the wrench in the toolbox. "Don't bet on it."

"You can apologize to Cody then."

When hell freezes over.

"I also thought we could watch a movie and play a game after dinner."

He'd rather chew glass. The whole domestic scene wasn't for him. Spending more time with the kid would be intolerable; spending additional time with Jenny, unbearable. As it was now, he couldn't keep his eyes off her mouth. His fingers all but burned with the need to run his hands through her hair, over her body. He wanted to forget she was still in love with Steven, forget that starting something up between them was a bad idea.

As he stared into her angry sky blue eyes, he knew she wasn't going to give up. If this last week had taught him anything, it was that she was tenacious. But that didn't mean he had to stick around.

"Fine."

Surprise briefly brightened her features before doubt set in. "Really?" Her voice was heavy with distrust.

"Sure," he said smoothly. "Give me a half hour to finish cleaning up, then I'll be in."

She hedged, staring long and hard into his face.

Nothing in his expression gave her anything to cling to. "Okay. See you then."

"See you then," he said as she made her way back to the house.

Less than ten minutes later, he was on his bike and roaring out of the driveway.

ELEVEN

It was well past ten when Anna pulled into her driveway. Streetlamps cast long shadows across the lawn and the mullioned windows that stretched across the front of her house. As she waited for the garage door to open, she knew she should be exhausted, but all she felt was exhilarated. Today had been hectic . . . crazy, and at times, completely overwhelming, but most of all, it had been wonderful. Finally, everything she had worked for was coming true.

When the garage door finished opening, she eased her Volvo in next to her husband's Mercedes. As she turned off the engine, she couldn't help but glance at Phillip's car.

Even in the dim light from the single overhead fixture, it was easy to make out the thin layer of dust covering his Mercedes. She frowned.

Why hadn't Phillip thought to cover his car before he left? Usually so meticulous, the oversight was uncharacteristic. To say he was particular about his vehicle was an understatement. *Obsessed* was a more accurate term. Whenever he'd had the chance, he'd been outside, washing and waxing and buffing that car until she'd tell him to stop before he rubbed the black paint clear off; she'd only been half joking. But now, his pride and joy sat in the garage, collecting dust.

Had he really been gone for three months?

When Phillip had told her he was considering accepting a position with Doctors Without Borders, Anna had at first felt a swell of pride. It was a noble sacrifice, what her husband wanted to do. All of their friends, family, and colleagues had said so. But as his excitement continued to grow, hers began to quietly dim.

We have so much, Anna, he'd said in his soft voice, the voice she'd fallen in love with, the voice that had calmed and soothed hundreds of terrified patients. *It's time we gave back.*

But it wasn't a *we* that was giving back, it was a *he*. He alone was going to be the one to leave, to travel to a place of such profound poverty it had made Anna's stomach clench in guilt. But her guilt had been two-pronged—a fact she'd barely been able to acknowledge. Guilt because she knew Phillip was right, they were blessed and it was right to give back. But guilt, too, because she didn't want her life to change. She and Phillip had worked hard for everything they had. And now he wanted to throw it all away. Or, if not discard it, then shelve it.

For how long?

The question haunted her.

She leaned her head back against the leather seat and closed her eyes, remembering their last night together. It had been late; Cody had fallen asleep long before. They'd been sitting in bed, Phillip reading, she watching Letterman. Or had it been Leno? As she'd pretended to watch TV, all she'd been able to think about that night was how much she didn't want her husband to leave. She'd wanted to tell him to stay, to stay with her and Cody. But she'd been unable to vocalize that need—afraid to hear what his choice would be. In the end, all she'd been able to say was, "Are you sure?"

"What if it was Cody, Anna?" he'd said, taking off his

glasses. "What if he needed help, and there were no doctors to save him? I *have to* go."

Hearing him, she'd felt selfish and small and had assured him he was right.

The next morning she'd driven him to the airport and hugged him good-bye. It wasn't until she was driving home that she realized how easily they'd both been able to abandon their embrace. She told herself it was because she knew he wouldn't be gone that long. She was embarrassed now to realize how smug she'd been, believing that her husband—a man who'd only known privilege and comfort—couldn't possibly survive the horrific conditions in a third world country. But as the days turned into weeks and then months, Anna had to face the truth: not only could he survive, but maybe this trip wasn't so much about giving back as it was about getting away.

Angry with her train of thought, she gathered her purse and briefcase and made her way to the house. The garage door rolled closed behind her with a familiar whine.

Why had she let her mind wander down that all-too-familiar path tonight of all nights? Today had been the highlight of her professional career, and she wasn't about to dampen her excitement with memories that only went around and around, never finding a beginning. Or, more importantly, never finding an end.

The house was dark and stuffy from being closed up all day. Making her way through the kitchen, she cracked open the window above the sink and turned on the lights. As she continued through the downstairs, she dropped her purse and briefcase on the table in the foyer and picked up the mail that had been dropped through the slot in the front door. After leafing through it, she tossed the small stack into the glass bowl on the hall table and tried not to feel a stab of disappointment. Again, no letter from Phillip. Then she saw the flashing light on her answering machine. Like a teenage girl, her heart thumped hard against her chest. She hit the Play button.

But it wasn't Phillip's voice that came through the tiny

speaker. "Hi, honey. It's Mom. Call when you get a chance. Love you."

The message clicked off, and for several long moments Anna stood there, staring at the machine.

A rush of emotions filled her: disappointment, sadness, guilt, anger. And she wasn't sure which one was justified, or if any were. She knew it wasn't easy for Phillip to have access to a phone. But a part of her couldn't help but wonder if he really wanted to call, wouldn't he be able to find a way?

The last handful of times they'd talked, she'd been the one to initiate the call. And they'd all been dismal failures. Bad connections. Bad timing. Bad everything.

As she looked at the phone, she tried to convince herself to pick it up, to try again. But even as the thought crossed her mind, she knew she wouldn't. She wanted him to be the one to make the next move. While she knew marriage wasn't about keeping score, she also knew it took more than one person to keep a boat afloat. And lately she felt like she was the only one trying.

She grabbed the cordless phone and headed back into the kitchen. More out of habit than hunger, she opened the Sub-Zero refrigerator. God bless Marie. The fridge was stocked with all of her favorites. Cool air washed over her as she stared at the food, trying to make a decision. In the end, even though she hadn't eaten all day, she closed the doors, and, instead, poured herself a tall glass of wine.

Hitting speed dial, she waited for her mom to pick up. On the fourth ring, the answering machine kicked in, and Anna left a quick message.

The house was so quiet—unnaturally so; the only noise was the fridge humming quietly in the background. When was the last time she'd been home alone? Usually the moment she walked through the door, a dozen things demanded her attention. But tonight, there was nothing but peace and quiet.

Taking her wine and the phone, she went into the family room, kicking off her pumps along the way. She groaned with pleasure as her stocking feet sank into the thick white carpet. As she sat down in one of the matching chairs, she heard the crinkle of paper beneath her.

She pulled it out. It was one of Cody's sketches. A drawing of a dog. For months he'd been barraging her and Phillip for a puppy. His hints had been none too subtle.

Just like all of the drawings he'd done lately, she hadn't seen this one. She marveled once more at his talent, a skill he most definitely had not gotten from her. His artistic ability had come directly from his father.

When she and Phillip had first started dating, he'd given her all kinds of notes with what he called scribbles. Now, she saw them for what they truly were: art. His talent had blown her away. No matter how many times she'd tell him he had a true gift, he'd brush her praises aside and say that if he could become a doctor and heal people, that would be a true gift.

As their relationship had grown, she'd found notes and drawings from him everywhere: tucked in her college text-books, hidden in the library where she'd worked to help pay her tuition, and then later, left on the pillow next to hers after a night of lovemaking.

She pushed all thoughts of Phillip aside and had her sister's number halfway dialed before she realized how late it was. Cody would be fast asleep by now. She set the phone on the small antique table next to her. She couldn't believe the whole day had passed without her talking to him. She'd tried calling during her one brief break but hadn't gotten an answer. Tomorrow, she promised herself, she'd get in touch with him first thing in the morning.

She took a drink of wine and wondered how her sister was dealing with the needs of her thirteen-year-old nephew. If she knew her sister—and she did—she knew the day hadn't gone smoothly. Jenny had never dealt with respon-sibility well. Or at all.

Even when she was little, Jenny had loved to fly high, never worrying about how far she'd eventually fall. And why should she? Always there had been someone to catch her. First their parents, then Steven. And now, just when it looked like she was about to crash, another savior had come to her rescue.

And what a rescuer he was. Anna considered herself a levelheaded person, but at her first glimpse of Jenny's new partner, she'd seriously gotten light-headed. Phillip was a distinguished-looking man. Steven, Mr. All-American. Jared. Jared was . . . gorgeous. There was no other word to describe him.

Leave it to her sister to land not only a partner but one who looked like a god.

Jenny had no idea what sacrifice and hard work meant. She'd never had to learn. And Anna was beginning to fear that Cody was falling into the same trap. He'd always been an outstanding student, but lately his schoolwork was barely passable, his attitude even worse. He didn't care about anything but drawing and baseball.

Anna looked down at his sketch once more. She knew she'd told Jenny she'd try to find someone else to watch Cody next weekend, but the more she thought about it, the more Anna realized that maybe what both Jenny and Cody needed was a sharp dose of reality. For Jenny to understand—even if only for a few days—what it meant to have to worry about someone other than herself. And for Cody to see what it was like to live in a house where disorder reigned. Maybe by spending a little time with his fly-by-the-seat-of-her-pants aunt, he'd come to appreciate his mother a little more.

For the first time since she'd gotten home, Anna smiled.

* * *

Where in the hell was the bar in this town?

Twice, Jared had cruised down Main Street looking for the local honky-tonk. Twice, he'd had to endure reading Hidden Lake's idiotic business names as he scanned the windows for a bright neon sign. But nowhere between John Dough's Pizza, the Best Little Hairhouse in Town, HosPETal, or a half-dozen other stupid-ass business names had he found the one thing he wanted.

God help him if the tavern was called Buds and Suds. He'd rather give up his left nut than toss back a couple of beers in a bar named Buds and Suds.

Then again, drinking at a Buds and Suds would be a helluva lot better than heading back to Jenny's and eating burned hot dogs and playing games. Not that the charred food bothered him; he'd been eating her cooking all week. But he wasn't about to go back to her house and act out some domestic scene she had concocted.

Family dinner. Play games. Talk to the kid.

Yeah, right.

He was a total fuckup where families were concerned.

We're sorry, Jared, but this isn't going to work. Don't worry, I'm sure your next foster family will be the one.

But the next one never was. He'd lost count of how many *we're sorrys* he'd heard during the eight years he'd been a ward of the state. It hadn't taken him long to see how life with a foster family would pan out. Soon, it became all too apparent that there was something missing in him. Something that came naturally to everyone else. Finally he wised up and stopped trying to fit.

Why did Jenny refuse to see what was so obvious to everyone else? That's why he'd left her house earlier today. Why he jumped on his bike and tore out of her driveway as if he was being chased by demons.

And maybe he was.

He'd made a mess of it with the kid, just like he knew he would. But somehow she thought if they all sat around, talked, everything would be okay. But Jared knew it wouldn't. It would just get worse. Like it had every other time he'd ever tried to get close to anyone.

So for hours he'd shot down unfamiliar roads, not caring where they led, only caring that they led away. He opened up the bike and let the speed and the wind drive out his frustrations. But no matter how far he went or how long he drove, he knew he wouldn't be able to do the one thing he wanted: leave. For good.

About an hour after he'd left her place, he'd called his realtor. The place in Mexico was still available. But for how long? With each day that passed, the possibility of losing that land grew stronger. Jared knew he shouldn't give a shit. He tried to reason with himself that if that land sold, they'd find something else. But he knew that wasn't completely true. It had taken months to find this isolated spot. If it sold, it would undoubtedly take them another handful of months. And Jared didn't have that kind of time. He wanted to get the hell away—far away. Where he could try to forget that he was no longer a fighter pilot. And where he could forget Jenny.

He pushed the thought away.

As much as he wanted to get the hell out of this town, out of Jenny's life, he knew that wasn't an option. He did a U-turn on the deserted stretch of road and headed back to Hidden Lake. The peaks of the Olympics were a violent orange and red as the sun set.

For the second time that night, he came to Hidden Lake's one and only intersection and tried to find a bar. Braking to a stop, he looked up and down Main, trying to figure out where to go from here. Decorative streetlamps cast yellow cones of light up and down the street. Though why the town wasted the electricity was beyond him. There wasn't a soul—or car—in sight.

As he sat at the deserted four-way stop, he looked to the left, then the right, then back to the left. But even as he did, he knew there was only one place he really wanted to see.

Slowly, he looked up. Overhead, an ebony canvas stretched out over him. Bright stars sparkled against the dark sky, and a sliver of a moon shimmered across the still lake. Staring at the sky, with a soft wind stirring through the tall trees, he felt his chest tighten. Once, he'd owned that sky. Now . . . now he was nothing.

Pulling his gaze down, he revved his engine and thought

about his options. To his right was the lake and Mrs. Murphy's B and B. The darkened windows and drawn shades told him she was still out of town. Straight ahead was Lakeshore Drive, the winding road that hugged the shore and was populated with homes. To his left was the main road that would take him back out of town. And behind him, the way back to Blue Sky Air.

Screw it.

If this town didn't have a bar, he'd find a place that did. He wasn't about to show back up at Jenny's house too early. He wanted to make damn sure she and the kid were fast asleep when he returned.

Gunning the bike, he turned left and roared out of town.

Less than half a mile out, a break in the trees caught his attention. Slowing, he turned off the main road and into a large gravel lot lit up by a handful of Mercury vapor lights. On three sides, tall evergreens surrounded a parking lot. A huge structure took up nearly three-quarters of the cleared space. The aged siding told him the building had been around for quite some time, but it had been well-kept.

There wasn't a neon light in sight or even a Buds and Suds. The only name he saw was a crude, white hand-painted sign that read: The Sawmill. On any other night, Jared would have turned around and left. But in this town, with the parking lot packed, the doors open, and twangy country music spilling out, Jared knew he had found Hidden Lake's one and only bar.

After angling into a parking spot, he pushed down the kickstand with his boot heel and swung his leg over the bike. Without the rumble of the v-twin engine, the music was even louder. He made his way up the wide wooden steps to the open door.

Only in Hidden Lake would a tavern be called the Sawmill. But then, the more Jared looked around, he got it. The Sawmill had obviously once been part of a working lumber mill.

The vast interior was constructed almost solely of wood. Huge clear-cut cedar beams stretched from one side to the other. Thick wide planks covered the floor. Under the bar's lights, they glowed with a soft sheen from years of use. In the center, an enormous U-shaped bar was in full swing, as were the pool tables off to the right and the dance floor to the left. As he stared at all the couples crowded on the floor, he couldn't help but wonder what it would feel like to dance with Jenny, to wrap his arms around her and pull her tightly to him, until all her soft curves were pressed against him. He wondered if it would be as good as he imagined and then knew it would be better. A hell of a lot better.

He jerked his gaze away.

Even with all the activity and noise, people began to note his arrival. Jared walked toward the crowded bar unfazed by the attention. With his military lifestyle, he was always the stranger rather than the regular. Finding an open spot at the bar, he waited.

It took only a moment for the bartender to make his way over. A white apron was tied around the large man's belly, and the overhead lights gleamed off his bald head. When he spoke, Jared couldn't help but think that his thick black mustache looked like a caterpillar. "What can I get ya?"

"Anything on tap."

"Bud?"

"Works for me."

The bartender disappeared and then was back with a large frosted glass foaming with beer. Jared dug out his wallet, but the bartender waved him off.

"Aren't you that new partner of Jenny's?"

Nothing like the small-town gossip mill. "Short sentence only."

The bartender barked out a laugh. "Then this one is on the house."

"Thanks."

The bartender moved on, and Jared made his way through the crowd. Toward the far end of the dance floor, he found an empty booth near a propped-open door. The fresh air felt good, and the open door helped diffuse the god-awful music. Why did every tavern—no matter what continent he was on—think country music was the only thing people wanted to hear?

Back in the far corner, the lights weren't quite as bright, and the high-backed booth afforded him some privacy. For the first time since leaving Jenny's, he began to relax.

He took a long drink and leaned back against the red vinyl. He tried to tune out the whiny song about somebody being done wrong or some such crap, but the more he ignored it, the more his own thoughts pushed through.

Or, more accurately, one thought.

This time there was no pushing it away.

Jenny.

Steven had been right; she was one tight little package. But Jared was quickly discovering there was more to Cotton Tail than met the eye. Gorgeous, hell yes. But stronger than he'd anticipated. He'd been sure that moving into her house would be enough to drive her to Mommy and Daddy to beg them for the money to pay him off. But she was standing her ground, proving him wrong. And her passion was as intoxicating as it was surprising. Instead of caving at the first spark of opposition, she seemed to grow more determined. She stood her ground, fought for what she loved. Her home . . . her business . . . her family. A grudging smile tugged at his lips as he remembered how she'd stormed to Cody's defense. Every kid should have family like that. And then there was the information Zeke was unknowingly feeding him, about the new business ideas she had created and was implementing.

Jared took another drink. But was it a passion and desire to keep the business going that propelled her forward, or was she still clinging to Steven's dream?

Steven had made it clear that the charter business had been his idea, his dream, and Jenny had just been along for the ride.

But was that the truth?

Yes, he told himself. The business had been Steven's

vision. Jared would be doing Jenny (and Steven) a favor by forcing her to see the truth now, before she lost everything.

"This seat taken?"

A tall man wearing a suit slid onto the bench seat across from him.

Great. Exactly what he didn't want: company. "Listen, mister, I—"

Before Jared could finish, a waitress sashayed over to their table. Her jeans were tight, her shirt was low, and her smile was almost as big as her hair. "Hiya," she said. Then, without taking her eyes off him, she said to the man seated across from him, "Hi, Paul."

"Hey, Tammy. How's your brother doing?"

"Good. Got a new job over in Redmond. Likes it real fine."

"That's good."

"Yeah."

With her eyes still glued on Jared, she leaned forward and made sure he had a clear view of her ample cleavage. "Thought you could use a refill 'bout now." She set a fresh beer down in front of him.

Jared wasn't even halfway through his first, but he gave the curvy brunette a smile and a thanks as he reached for his wallet.

"Forget it," she said, flipping her hair, batting her eyes, and motioning for him to put away his wallet. "We'll even up later." She flashed him another wide smile. "Bye." She turned and started to walk away, hips swaying to the music. She'd taken a half-dozen steps before she stopped and, as an afterthought, called over her shoulder, "See ya later, Paul."

The jukebox kicked over to another song.

"So, *Paul*," Jared said, sliding the full beer across the table, "something tells me you're not here for idle chitchat."

Paul tipped the beer in a silent acknowledgment, then took a drink. "It's Beckinsale," he said, wiping the foam off his upper lip. "Paul Beckinsale."

"As in Jenny's—"

"Brother."

So much for his small bit of peace and quiet.

"Ron told me you were here."

"Ron?"

"The bartender."

"Remind me to thank him later."

Paul almost smiled. Almost. But there was a tightness to him that Jared knew didn't bode well for their discussion ahead.

"You're the lawyer, right? Steven told me. So, what's on your mind?"

"Jenny."

Obviously. "Specifically?" Jared said with a bluntness that tended to shock most people. Paul didn't flinch at Jared's directness.

"I spoke with Jenny today."

Jared just waited.

"I don't like this current situation."

Jared ran his thumb through the condensation on the outside of his glass. "What situation would that be?"

Whatever civilities Paul had been trying to maintain vanished. He pushed his beer off to the side and tried to stare Jared down.

Jared had to give the lawyer credit. He looked to be in okay shape, but years of easy living had left him soft where it mattered the most. He was no match for Jared. Jared wasn't proud of some of the things he'd had to do in his life, but they'd kept him alive. And those fighting instincts, once honed, had never left.

"You know damn well what I'm talking about," Paul said through clenched teeth. "You. Living at her house."

"I'm only too happy to leave."

"Perfect," Paul said after a small hesitation. It was obvious that wasn't the answer he'd been expecting.

"I'm only too happy to leave," Jared repeated, then clarified, "once my loan is repaid."

"Jenny said something to the same effect. She also told me to back off."

"That was decent of her. Personally, I would have told you to fuck off."

Paul gave a reluctant smile. "If you weren't causing my sister such hell, I think I could almost like you, Worth. Steven had a lot of great things to say about you."

"Steven said great things about everyone. That's the type of guy he was."

"True. But there was something different in his voice when he spoke of you." Paul looked out toward the busy dance floor then back to Jared. "He really idolized you."

A sharp memory jabbed at Jared, reminded him of just how far he'd fallen. "Believe me, I'm nobody's idol."

"You don't have to convince me."

Another waitress approached their table, this time carrying a large plate of nachos. Once more, the waitress ignored Paul and focused her sole attention on Jared. "Thought you looked kinda hungry."

Jared had to give the owner credit; only knockouts waited the tables. But while the plate of crispy chips and oozing cheese looked appetizing, especially considering what he'd been eating during this past week, he was fast realizing that coming into the Sawmill hadn't been the escape he'd hoped for. Anonymity in a small town was unheard of. And that was before he factored in Jenny's brother. "Thanks, but—"

"No buts." She smiled and set the plate down on the table. "The Sawmill is famous for their nachos. It's almost a law you have to try them before you leave."

Jared knew he wouldn't eat them. As soon as he could, he was outta here. But still, he reached for his wallet a third time. And once more he was told to put it away.

"They're on the house. A welcome gift for Hidden Lake's newest resident."

Resident was a bit of a stretch. "I'm not planning on sticking around that long."

"Our loss." She crossed her hands in front of her stomach and cocked a hip out to the side. "Maybe after you and Paul get done talking, you'd like to dance."

They both knew the offer was for more than just a dance.

Jared had had more than his fair share of women in his day. It wasn't something he was extremely proud of, but, then again, it wasn't something he was ashamed of, either. The saying was true: a set of dress whites and gold wings could get you a bed anywhere. Anytime. And for years he'd taken what women had offered. And he liked to think he'd given back more than his fair share. But several years ago he'd realized he was never going to find what he was looking for between the sheets with a beautiful stranger.

Hell, he wasn't even sure he knew what he was looking for.

"That's a real nice offer," he said to the stunning redhead, "but I have to be heading back soon."

She tried for the pouty lip look. "Maybe next time."

He nodded. "Yeah. Maybe."

"That happen to you often?" Paul asked after the waitress had left.

"What?"

"Getting hit on every five minutes." Paul grabbed a chip loaded with cheese. He popped it in his mouth and then wiped his hands off on his napkin. "Hell if I know what women see in you, but stay away from my sister. She might have told me to back off, but I'm not going far."

"Is that a threat, Counselor?"

"Call it a warning."

"Jenny can hold her own."

"She's not one of your usual groupies, Worth. I remember other things Steven told me about you, too, so don't try to pull any of your stunts on her. She's not accustomed to a player like you."

"If you're trying to insult me, you'll have to do better than that."

Paul stood. "Just remember what I said."

Jared watched Paul walk away. Pain in the ass notwithstanding, he wondered if Jenny realized how lucky she was to have a brother who cared. For that matter, a family who cared.

She's not accustomed to a player like you.

All week Jenny had been doing everything in her power to avoid him. She stayed away from the hangar, cooked those horrid meals when he was out running or out working. And she'd disappear up into her bedroom long before bedtime just to avoid spending time with him at night. Oh, she'd asked him to join her for dinner tonight, but that was only because she had her nephew as a buffer.

Everything he'd tried up to this point had failed. He thought again of his call with the realtor. Jared needed to turn up the heat where Jenny was concerned, and Paul had unknowingly given him the answer.

She's not accustomed to a player like you.

Images flashed through Jared's mind. The day in the office, when he'd pulled out the magazines. She'd been pissed, but she'd also been flustered. Sexually flustered. Just like she had been today in the kitchen. With a new clarity, he saw how she shied away from him every time their bodies had touched.

Little Bunny Foo-Foo might act like she was immune to him, but her actions told him otherwise.

Moving in with her had been a good first step. Moving in *on* her would be even better. The closer he got to her, the farther she'd run. Right to Mom and Dad.

Jared grinned and drained the rest of his beer.

But even as his new plan went through his mind, he couldn't shake the image of a pair of sky blue eyes and a smile that made it hard to remember she was Steven's girl.

TWELVE

◡

Jenny heard the deep rumble of Jared's bike just after midnight. The monstrous engine growled as it came down the driveway, rattling the windows and, even more rattling Jenny. What had she been thinking, waiting up to confront him?

She'd been so angry when he roared off after promising to talk to Cody. Now, hours later, she realized how foolish she'd been. She was the bunny he kept calling her, and confronting him would be like taking on the Big Bad Wolf.

Even she would lay odds on the wolf.

The noise grew louder as the bike drew up alongside the house. Once, twice, the engine revved, and then silence fell.

She scrambled off the couch, tossing the afghan on the rounded arm of the sofa. She hurried through the family room, shutting off the TV before hustling into the kitchen, where she shoved the ice cream toppings away and all but threw the dirty bowls into the dishwasher.

At least that had been one thing she had done right tonight with her nephew. He'd enjoyed the ice cream. Then again, who didn't like Rocky Road?

After a quick glance around, assuring herself everything

that needed to be done was done, she flipped off the lights and hurried down the hallway. As she rounded the stair landing, she reflected that even if Jared had stuck around, there wasn't much he could have said or done to improve her nephew's mood. She should know; she'd tried just about everything and failed.

Archaic. That was the word Cody had hurled at her like a wrecking ball when she'd pulled out Monopoly; that and a few others she wondered if his mother knew about. She'd coaxed him into giving the game a try. Big mistake. She'd tried a different board game with the same result. When she got out the cards, he shot her a look that said *don't even*, so she'd put them away without even taking the deck out of the box.

After that, they'd been like two strangers in the same house. Cody had gone up to his room to sketch and listen to his iPod while Jenny had stayed downstairs watching TV. The only reason she knew what he was up to was because she'd made the mistake of checking on him. He'd made it more than clear that a thirteen-year-old didn't need to be checked on.

Halfway up the staircase, the teakettle began to whistle. *Crap.*

She ran back down the stairs and turned off the stove. She was halfway down the hall when the front door opened and six foot two inches of leather-wearing, bike-riding, bad-boy testosterone walked through.

She froze in her tracks. Maybe he wouldn't see her. Maybe he'd head straight up the stairs to his room. Maybe—

"Hello."

"H-hi."

"You're up late."

He smelled of warm night air, weathered leather, and a handful of temptation. "I wasn't. I mean, I was, but I forgot to do a few things so had to come back downstairs." She was rambling, wishing he'd move so she could get past. "I was just heading back to bed."

A wicked smile lit his eyes as he took in her appearance.

He ran his gaze slowly up from her bare feet, past her pink flannel pajama bottoms, to her white tank top, where he lingered. Under his intense scrutiny she felt like she was wearing nothing more than a see-through negligee.

"Don't let me stop you."

But he did. He was.

She chewed on her lower lip. Less than a few feet separated them. Hardly any distance at all. All she needed to do was take a few steps forward.

Bunny. Wolf. Bunny. Wolf.

The refrain grew louder in her head.

Squaring her shoulders, she told herself to knock it off. To grow up. She walked toward him.

He reached out and rested his hand on the stair rail in front of her, blocking her path.

She stumbled to a stop, her pulse going into overdrive. He was so close. Just one tiny step forward and they'd be touching.

"I ran into your brother tonight."

Slowly she lifted her gaze, up his muscular chest, past his strong jaw, until her eyes found his. His head was bent down, his full attention directed at her. A spark of something she didn't want to examine too closely heated his blue, blue eyes. "Paul?"

"Do you have more than one?"

Jared's face was so close she could feel his warm breath on her cheek. "Where did you see Paul?"

"The Sawmill. You coulda clued me in."

"On what?"

"The name. Had a helluva time finding the place."

"Something tells me you're the type of guy who could find a bar in a desert."

Jared grinned. "Is that so, sweetheart? And just what type of guy would that be?"

The type of guy that tied her up in knots and made her remember what it used to feel like to be held by a man. Caressed by a man. Wanted by a man. "I'm not your sweetheart."

"You sure 'bout that?" He put his other hand on the rail behind her. He pressed in closer, his arms on either side of her, boxing her in. The heat from his body penetrated her and the scent of him was even more intoxicating. She couldn't shake the feeling that there had been a fundamental shift in their relationship.

No, she had to be wrong. She leaned back until the hard edge of the stair dug into her back. "How many times have you used that line?"

"More times than I can count."

"And how many times has it worked?"

A wicked smile transformed his face into one of pure seduction. "More times than I can count."

"It's not going to work," she said with a bravado she was far from feeling.

"You sure about that?"

"Yes."

He was so close the opened edges of his leather jacket brushed against her chest, causing all kinds of warning bells to go off inside her head. But what she didn't know was if all that clanging was warning her that what was about to happen was something very, very bad or something very, very good.

She swallowed hard, ran her tongue over her dry, parched lips. "Intimidation by harassment."

He slanted his body, slid his hands down the post until they were even with her waist. "You need to be more specific. There are all kinds of harassment."

His wide chest covered her, but the weight of him was anything but unpleasant. She ran the tip of her tongue over her lips again and his gaze followed the movement. "Just so we're both clear here, what type are we talking about?" she said.

"I think you know."

Just when she knew she couldn't endure another moment of being this close to him, his hands dropped away from the railings, and he stepped back. Instantly she felt the loss of body heat.

Without his arms blocking her way, she had an open path to the stairs. Everything inside of her told her to run. But she forced herself to move at a normal pace. On the third step, she stopped and turned. "I meant what I said, Jared. It's not going to work."

"We'll see about that, Cotton Tail. We'll see."

She couldn't reach her bedroom fast enough.

Jared watched her go. It wasn't until he heard her door close that he leaned against the stairs and let out the breath he'd been holding. Christ. He ran his hand across his face, through the side of his hair. This was going to be a hell of a lot harder than he thought.

⁂

The minute she closed her door, Jenny grabbed a UW hoodie off her bed and slipped it over her head. She tugged at the sleeves until they were past her wrists, then pulled at the hem, making sure it covered as much of her as possible. She didn't care that it had been a hot day and continued to be a warm night. She didn't care that she was overheated. *We'll see about that, Cotton Tail. We'll see.*

Her heart thudded against her chest, and her breath came out in short little gasps. She felt like she was suffocating. Drowning in a pair of midnight blue eyes.

She went to her window and swung it all the way open. Like she'd done a thousand times before, she sat on the narrow ledge, one leg in, one out. Leaning back, she gulped in deep breaths of fresh lake air as she tried to control her erratic breathing. A week. That was all it was supposed to take. One week, and he should have been gone.

Once more she saw the way his eyes had taken in every inch of her. She wrapped her arms around herself, felt the bulky cotton sweatshirt beneath her hands. The extra layer of clothing should have made her feel safer.

She turned her face toward the dark lake, let the night air caress her skin, blow through her hair.

He wasn't budging. Not without his money. It was the same realization she'd come to earlier today in her office.

But somehow, in the shadowy darkness of her room, that reality became much clearer.

Her breasts began to tingle, almost as if he were still pressed against her. She hugged herself tighter, tried to force the sensation from her body.

The sound of the lake came to her. She closed her eyes, listened to the gentle lapping of the waves against the shore. Time became a blur. She grew numb from sitting on the hard wooden windowsill, but still she didn't move.

For as long as she could remember, it had just been her and Steven. The two of them against the world. They'd met before they could talk. Became playmates before they could walk. Their love had been gradual, building slow and steady over time. Like the fortification of a strong foundation that would never give way.

Promise me, she'd say to him each time before he left. *Promise me you'll come home.*

Baby, I'll be back. We'll have a lifetime together, you'll see.

And he'd been right, he had come home. But he'd also been wrong.

He'd quit flying jets. Quit flying too fast, too high, too dangerously. And foolishly, she'd thought that after he'd stopped, she could stop worrying.

They were supposed to grow old together. Have babies and raise them here on the shores of Hidden Lake. Now he was gone, and every dream she'd ever had was buried along with him. She knew their type of love didn't just disappear. That even though Steven wasn't still with her, her heart would always be with him. Or so she'd thought. But after tonight . . . after the way she'd felt held between Jared's arms . . .

Steven, tell me what to do?

But the only sound she heard was a night bird calling to its mate. This time, he wasn't going to be her soft place to fall. This time, there was only her. And her heart that wasn't as impenetrable as she'd thought.

THIRTEEN

Jenny woke to the smell of frying bacon.

She groaned. Not because of the tantalizing aroma wafting up from downstairs but because one look out her window told her she'd once again been woken up before the sun had even risen.

What was it with that man and his obsession with pre-dawn hours?

She fluffed her pillows, burrowed under her comforter, and closed her eyes, determined to go back to sleep. But after ten minutes, she wiggled to a sit. Blast him. She knew Jared did it on purpose, made plenty of noise to wake her up. Any other time, he prowled around the house as silent as a panther. She thought back to the first time he ate her cooking and how worried she'd been that he'd choke on her eggs. Then, she'd charitably promised herself she'd save him. Now, letting him choke to death seemed like a much better solution.

Yawning, she stretched, wincing at the sting in her back. The hours of sitting on the windowsill had exacted a toll, but not nearly as big a one as the worries that had plagued her all night. She hadn't been completely unaware of her reactions to Jared this past week. But up until last night, they'd been minor: a tiny flutter in her tummy, a little blip in her heartbeat. But last night, all that had changed. Her little blips and tiny flutters had gone to full-fledged longings.

It wasn't him, she tried to tell herself. She would have reacted the same way to anyone she'd let get close. But even as the thought went through her mind, she knew it was a lie.

She flung her covers aside, got out of bed, and peered down the hallway. With the coast clear, she hurried to Cody's bedroom. Last night hadn't exactly gone as planned. She definitely wasn't going to be up for an aunt of the year award. Reaching his bedroom, she quietly opened the door. Just because Jared was intent on jolting her out of bed so early didn't mean Cody shouldn't have the luxury of sleeping in.

The room was dark, but enough light filtered in from the hallway for Jenny to see his empty and unmade bed. Where was he? She rushed out of the room and was partway down the stairs when two distinct male voices could be heard from below. Pausing, she listened.

The voices were coming from the kitchen: one low and deep (Jared's) and the other one high-pitched with the occasional squeak (Cody's).

She let out a breath she hadn't realized she'd been holding. She knew she'd overreacted, but seeing his empty bed had brought her own childhood back. She couldn't remember how many times she'd fled to Nana's house after arguing with her parents. And while she and Cody hadn't actually argued, they sure hadn't gotten along, either. She stood at the railing for several more minutes, trying to make out what the two of them were saying. But while their voices were too muffled, she could tell that Cody was doing the vast majority of the talking. Again. She smiled.

Knowing her nephew was fine, she headed back upstairs to the bathroom. With Jared banging around in the kitchen doing heaven only knew what, and Cody keeping him company, Jenny planned on splurging on a long, hot shower.

The minute she opened the bathroom door, she knew something was wrong. At first glance, everything looked exactly as it should. Her favorite dark purple towels were still draped across the towel bar; her industrial-sized bottle of raspberry bubble bath still sat on the aged marble floor, right next to the claw-foot tub, along with the basket that held her loofah brush and coconut milk extract shampoo and conditioner. And then she saw the telltale items that proved someone else had put their mark on her space.

Alongside her elegant bottle of shampoo was a cheap ol' bottle of Suave. A plain white toothbrush next to her purple and green one, and a tube of Colgate by her minty fresh Crest. Spurred on by a growing sense of doom, she opened the mirrored cabinet above the sink. Someone had shoved all of her products (even her box of tampons) to the bottom two shelves, leaving the top shelf open. It didn't take a genius to figure out who had done it.

Everything was in precise order. Lined up like little traitorous soldiers on the white shelf. A can of shaving cream and a razor, a box of Band-Aids (the plain, boring ones; she liked the ones with pictures), a tube of Neosporin, Speed Stick, dental floss, and a small black comb.

All in all, it wasn't much. But it was the idea of him taking over even one more bit of space in her home. It was as if he was saying, "I'm here for as long as it takes."

Filled with righteous anger, Jenny scooped up all Jared's things and marched down to his room. His *temporary* room. His door was ajar. She gave it a little bump with her hip, and it swung wide.

She hadn't been in this room since the first morning after Jared had moved in. Like then, the room looked unused; the only difference—the same one as before—a bed made with military precision. Undoubtedly he was one of those neat freaks who had all of his clothes neatly folded and put away.

Her mother would be so proud.

Jenny dumped everything onto the tight-as-a-pin duvet. She was about to do an about-face and leave, when her curiosity got the better of her. After listening to make sure no one was coming up the stairs, she walked over to the dresser and opened the top drawer. Empty. The second drawer, empty. All the dresser drawers were empty, as well as the closet.

She stood in the middle of the room, stumped. He had no trouble putting his stuff in her bathroom, but he couldn't put away a single item of clothing?

Then she saw his duffel bag. Just like the first time she'd entered his room, it was propped up in the corner, still packed. She shook her head in total confusion. But then, everything about Jared rattled her.

As she took her shower, thoughts about last night kept coming back to her. She refused to think about the feelings he had stirred awake in her and, instead, focused on the more important topic at hand. The old pipes pinged as she squirted tropical passion body wash onto her loofah scrub brush. Even after a night of turning over all the different possibilities in her head, she kept coming back to the same one: she had to turn Blue Sky's profits around. The extra advertising and vacation packages she'd implemented before Jared arrived were good. As was updating the website, but she needed more.

She knew she didn't have much business experience when it came to Blue Sky. That had been all Steven. He'd handled most aspects of the business while Jenny had been only too happy to play a supporting role. The division of responsibilities had seemed to please Steven, and that had been all that mattered to her. Over the years, she'd had a few ideas but had never pursued them. What had been the point? Steven was the brains, the one with all the ideas. Hers had been too farfetched to even share.

The water began to turn cold, and she quickly finished. Wrapping her hair in a towel turban-style and slipping on her robe, she went back to her room and sat on the bed.

Plan. Brief. Execute.

Jared's infuriating words came back to her. She wanted to throw them back in his face, tell him he was wrong.

But as much as she hated to admit it, they held a truth. She did need a plan. And a way to carry it out. But like hell she'd brief him on anything she was going to do.

She looked out her window and saw the sun rising over the uneven peaks of the distant mountains. Today was going to be another glorious day. And not only because of the weather; Jenny was determined to figure out a new plan on how to get rid of Jared. Feeling almost transformed, she quickly dressed in white capris and a turquoise top. As she slipped on a pair of blue flip flops, she couldn't help but remember yesterday when Jared had helped her put on a different pair of flip-flops. Then her gaze lifted to the end of her bed where she'd tossed the hooded sweatshirt, and she was remembering more. Remembering last night. The two of them near the staircase.

Ever since Steven's death, Jenny had shut herself away. She'd stopped hanging out with her friends . . . going to all of her and Steven's familiar spots. It had been the only way she'd known how to protect herself from the pain. But the irony was, her seclusion hadn't worked. She learned that heartache found you no matter where you were. Just like memories. And she didn't want to outrun them anymore. Steven had been the love of her life. He would always have a special place in her heart. But maybe her mother was right. Maybe it was time for Jenny to reenter her old life.

She picked up the sweatshirt off her bed and folded it. As she put it away in her dresser, she told herself that the only reason she'd responded to Jared like she had was because he was the only person she'd let in. No, that wasn't right. She hadn't let him in—he'd forced his way into her life. But either way, it didn't matter. What did matter was protecting herself. She wasn't about to risk her heart on a man who kept his duffel bag packed and had one foot out the door.

She went to her bedside table and picked up the phone. "Maddy?" she said when her best friend answered. "What are you doing Monday night?"

Maddy laughed. "Monday margaritas?"

"Absolutely."

"Just tell me where and when."

"How about my place? We can build a fire on the beach."

"Sounds perfect. And, Jenny?"

"Yeah?"

"It's about time."

"Yeah," Jenny said again, knowing it was true.

Feeling better than she had all week, she headed downstairs.

The closer she got to the kitchen, the stronger the smell of bacon, freshly brewed coffee, and something else, something almost like baking bread, made her stomach growl.

As she rounded the end of the hallway, she stopped at the edge of the kitchen, not quite believing what she was seeing. Jared was at the stove, cooking. His back was toward her. Cody was seated on a stool at the peninsula, a plate full of food in front of him. Hearing her, he turned, his cheeks bulging like a squirrel with nuts.

"Hey, Aunt Jen," he said around a mouthful. A streak of blueberry syrup ran across his cheek while powdered sugar coated his lips and dusted his T-shirt like freshly fallen snow. "Ya gotta try these," he said, pointing to the waffles on his plate. "They're the best." He stuffed another forkful of blueberry waffles into his mouth and gave her a smile.

She didn't know what surprised her more: Jared cooking or Cody smiling.

"Good morning," Jared said, looking over his shoulder. "One or two?"

She sucked in a breath. No one had a right to look that good so early in the morning. He wore an untucked white collared shirt with the sleeves rolled up, a pair of worn Levi's, and several days' worth of stubble. "One or two what?" she asked, trying to keep her eyes off his backside.

"Waffles." Steam billowed up from the waffle maker as he opened it.

Forcing her gaze off him and onto what he was doing, she started to salivate as she eyed the food. Great. Her appetite had been nonexistent for nine months, and *now* it decided to return? "No thanks. I'm not hungry."

Ignoring her, he forked two of the fluffiest waffles she'd ever seen onto a plate, smothered them in butter, and topped them with blueberries. He even sprinkled powdered sugar on top. If that wasn't bad enough, he placed a couple of thick slices of bacon onto the plate before sliding it across the counter.

"Eat," he said in such a friendly tone she grew instantly suspicious. "Breakfast is the most important meal of the day."

She seemed to remember him saying something to that same effect his first morning here. But back then, his tone hadn't been friendly, and his smile hadn't been warm. Her stomach kicked over. "You've obviously been talking to my mother."

He smiled and poured himself a cup of coffee.

She took a seat, not because she was going to eat but because it put more distance between them. She tried not to breathe in, tried not to stare at the melting butter pooling in the little squares.

"They're *sooooo* good, Aunt Jenny." Cody looked at Jared like he was a culinary god.

"I'm glad you like them," she said to the little blue-haired Benedict Arnold. She knew her cooking sucked, but she'd thought she'd redeemed herself last night with the ice cream. Obviously it took more than pulling a cartoon out of the freezer to warm up her nephew.

She eyed the perfectly cooked waffles and crisp strips of bacon in front of her. "What are you up to?" she asked Jared, noticing that his fresh-squeezed orange juice didn't contain one seed or glob of pulp.

He took a drink of coffee. "Aren't you the suspicious one."

"Damn—darn right," she quickly corrected, remembering Cody. "And just when did you learn to cook?"

"Have you ever tried military rations?"

"No."

"Eat those for several years, and you'd do anything for a good meal. Even watch a few TV shows, read some cookbooks." He leaned his butt against the countertop. "That was the thing I'd always enjoyed most about leave."

"Food?" she asked, more surprised than she cared to admit.

"Good food," he agreed with a grin that had her stomach growling again, but not because of the waffles in front of her. "Great food."

"And you've been eating *my* cooking all week?"

When he laughed, a funny tingling sensation settled in the pit of her stomach. It was almost as if he'd let down his guard and, for a moment, let her in. *This* Jared was impossible to resist.

"I hate to tell ya," he said, a grin still crinkling the corners of his blue eyes, "but as far as cooking goes, you suck."

She couldn't help it; she grinned. She'd had the exact same thought not a minute ago.

"Yeah," Cody chimed in, still stuffing his face. "I thought my mom was kidding when she told me not to eat anything you cooked."

She bumped shoulders with her nephew. "Thanks a lot."

"Mom says it's best to be honest."

"Remind me to thank her when she picks you up tonight."

"Like I'm gonna tell her she was right about something."

Jenny eyed the plate of food in front of her once more before pushing it away. It was the principle of the thing, she told herself. Somehow, in her mind, eating Jared's cooking would be like agreeing to this farce of a partnership.

And she couldn't help being suspicious of . . . everything he'd done lately. Last night, finding his things in the bathroom, and now this. Him cooking.

"Hey, Code," she said, getting off the barstool. "Don't forget. We have a baseball game this afternoon. So after breakfast, you need to get on your homework."

He stopped chewing long enough to shoot her a look that took no words to decipher.

"I promised your mom you'd have it done before she picked you up tonight."

Without saying a word, he turned to Jared and did a whole *females* look thing, complete with the rolling of the eyes.

Jenny ignored the look. It wasn't her fault she had to be drill sergeant and make sure he got his homework done. And just when did the two of them become so chummy? She was about to let out her frustration, then stopped. Maybe she deserved his attitude. She still felt guilty for dumping him on Jared yesterday.

"I know this weekend hasn't been exactly what you wanted, but after you finish your work, and I finish mine, we'll do something fun. Promise."

Slowly, he pivoted on the stool. "For real?"

"For real," she said with a smile.

His grin was slow in coming, but when it did, Jenny felt her whole insides glow. "See you in a bit."

"Yeah," he said, still smiling. "See ya."

She didn't dare glance at Jared before she headed outside. *That smile. That laugh.* They captivated her and made her worry that even reconnecting with her friends would not be enough to keep her from falling under his spell. A breeze blew in off the lake, and she rubbed her arms against the chill. She should have grabbed a sweatshirt before heading out. But she hadn't wanted to take the time. She knew Jared would be busy in the kitchen with Cody for a little bit longer, and she wanted to be alone for what she had to do.

Her steps began to falter as she made her way across the hangar to the office Steven had used. Briefly she closed her eyes and drew in a fortifying breath.

As she reached out to open the office door, her hand wavered. Everything inside of her told her to turn around and run. Leave this place that held too many painful memories. But she knew she couldn't. Inside this office had to be the solution to her problem, the way to turn Blue Sky around and get rid of Jared. Steeling herself, she turned the knob and opened the door.

A rising sun hit the large windows and illuminated the space in a soft yellow glow. For a moment, Jenny felt disoriented. Like she was at the wrong place. This wasn't her and Steven's office any longer. Everything about it had Jared's stamp of precision and organization.

She made her way to the desk. Just like in the medicine cabinet, everything was in perfect order: the pencil sharpener, the stapler, the tape dispenser, and all the other usual gadgets an office needed. But there were other things on the desk, too. And seeing them brought back a dozen memories.

Tears blurred her eyes as she traced her finger over the small replica of the F-18 fighter jet she'd bought Steven. With a clarity time could never diminish, she remembered the look of pure joy on his face when he'd opened the gift. Next to the jet were two Star Wars action figures. She laughed softly. Steven had always been a total sci-fi geek. Moving away from the desk, she took in the rest of the office and couldn't believe what she saw. In a short time, Jared had managed to turn a storeroom of an office into a clean and orderly space.

Seeing all the changes, Jenny wasn't quite sure how they made her feel. For so long, she hadn't been able to come near this office. Or, if she did, it was only to fill it with more stuff. Anything to keep her from seeing it as it had been when Steven was alive. But Jared had changed all that.

She wanted to feel angry at what he had done, or, more

truthfully, she wanted to still be numb and not feel a thing. But seeing the office as it should be, as she should have kept it, made her feel ashamed. She owed it to Steven— and herself—to be stronger. With a renewed determination, she began to search the filing cabinets until she'd located the files she wanted. As she stared down at the manila folders in her hand, it seemed like a lifetime ago when she'd first sat down and tried to come up with marketing strategies to improve the business. She'd shown them to Steven, and he'd looked them over and said they'd figure out which ones were best. But then Steven had died, and the thought of going back through those notes without him was more than she could bear.

Before she closed the door behind her, she took one more look at the office. Before today, she would have thought it impossible for her to walk back into this space and not fall apart. But she had. She'd not only gone into the office, she'd also gone through the files she and Steven had set up. With a sense of strength she hadn't felt in a long time, she closed the door and headed back to her makeshift office in the house.

As she shut herself in the front office, she could still hear Jared and Cody. They were either still in the kitchen or had moved over to the family room. Either way, they were busy for the time being, and that left Jenny to work on her new plan.

She sat down at the small desk and turned on her computer. As it hummed to life, she opened the top file she'd gotten from the office. This file contained a list of all the businesses in the area that used Blue Sky's competition. Nothing had ever come of the list, though not for lack of trying on Steven's part or hers. What made her think she could succeed now was beyond her, but as she stared down at her calendar and saw how few bookings Blue Sky had, she knew she needed to do something. She started by picking up the phone.

Two hours later, she hung up for the last time. Burying her face in her hands, she could only be thankful no one else was around to witness her stupidity. Humiliation burned her cheeks, made her body shake. It was Sunday. No businesses were open. With her face still buried in her hands, she shook her head, unable to believe how foolish she'd been. Any other businessperson would have known not to try to call today.

Still filled with mortification, she put her file away and shut down her computer. Total and complete embarrassment had her wanting to hide out for the rest of the day. But knew she couldn't. That was what she had been doing for the last nine months, and look where it had gotten her. She was down, definitely, but not defeated. Tomorrow was another day. Besides, she had an appointment with her nephew.

Leaving the office, she found Cody sprawled out on the couch in the family room watching TV. "Hi," she said, doing a quick glance around, relieved not to see Jared.

Cody seemed startled. He swung his feet off the end of the sofa and sat up. "Hey."

"Sorry. Didn't mean to scare you."

"No. It's not that. It's . . . it's just that . . ."

She sat down on the edge of the coffee table. "It's just what?"

"Nothin'. Never mind." He looked a little sheepish.

"If you can't confide in your aunt, who can you confide in?"

"My best friend Parker."

"True. But then he doesn't have the goods on your mom like I do."

That got a smile from him. "Mom doesn't like me to have my shoes on the furniture."

"Yeah, well she always hated it when I borrowed her clothes. Especially her cashmere sweaters. Who knew they had to be dry-cleaned?"

"Aunt Jenny?"

"Yeah, Cody?"

"I have no idea what you're talking about."

Jenny laughed. "No. I guess you wouldn't. But what I'm

trying to say is, be comfortable when you're here. This house is meant to be lived in. So plop your shoes up on the couch anytime you feel like it. Okay?"

Cody looked puzzled. After a few moments, he said, "Okay."

As casually as she could, Jenny asked, "Where's Jared?"

"He said he had to go out for a bit."

Perfect. "Now about our date."

"I'm not allowed to date until I'm sixteen."

"Funny. Funny."

He just grinned.

"So, have you ever been fishing?"

"No." He drew the one word out, made the two letters sound more like ten.

"It'll be fun, you'll see. We'll take the rowboat out and—"

"I can't go on the water, remember?"

This time it was Jenny's turn to smile. "I've got the goods on your mom, *remember*? If she catches us, I'll just remind her of a few of the stunts she pulled as a kid."

"You gonna tell me any of them?"

Jenny gave the toe of Cody's shoe a playful kick and held out her hand. "Not today."

* * *

By the time Jenny had gotten the small rowboat from behind the hangar and to the shoreline, she was hot, grimy, and rethinking the whole fishing idea. And that was before she'd slipped in the wet sand. Her white capris weren't white any longer, and sweat had matted her hair to her scalp. Really a great look. Thank God no one besides Cody was around to see.

Using her forearm, she brushed a hunk of damp hair off her damp forehead and shot her nephew a look so full of reproach she was sure he'd finally get the hint and jump in to help.

Fat chance.

"How about a little help here?"

Halfheartedly he gave the small boat a shove with his foot.

Caught off guard by his effort to finally lend a hand (well, a foot, really), she wasn't prepared. The front of the boat lurched forward, banged into her legs, and sent her flying. She landed butt down in the cold, shallow water. "Ayyyy," she yelped and jumped up. Only her flip-flops were no match for the rocky bottom, and down she went again.

"Au-aunt Jen-Jenny." Cody started to laugh. "Th-that w-was s-s-so f-f-f-funny."

"Yeah, real funny." She flung wet sand and small pebbles off her hands before firmly planting her feet and grabbing hold of the boat to pull herself up. She couldn't help but think that twice now, she'd fallen flat on her ass when her nephew was near. She tried to brush the dirt from her pants but gave up. What was the point? She was wet, covered in lake goo, and a real comedian if Cody's laughter was any indication.

She glared at him. He didn't notice. He was too busy holding his sides and laughing. She slapped an orange life jacket around his neck.

That got his attention and finally shut him up.

"Aw, come on, Aunt Jenny." He looked at the big fat orange U as if it was a pink boa. "What if one of my friends sees me?"

"They'll thank me for keeping you safe."

"This is so *retarded*." Cody tugged at the neckline. His little chin jutted up, stuck there by the big fat orange vest.

"Better safe than sorry." She winced. Great, now she was starting to channel her mother.

Ignoring his continual complaints, she told him to hop in the boat. Once he was settled, she gave the rowboat one last shove and then did her best to jump in. Her "jump" turned out to be more of a scramble, grab, pull, pray, move. By the time she ended up in the boat, her stomach hurt from hurling herself over the hard aluminum side. Somehow she didn't remember fishing being this difficult when her grandfather had taken her out. "You want to help me row?"

Cody pulled out his iPod and plopped the two tiny speakers into his ears. "Yeah. Right."

She clenched her lips and kept her mouth shut. They were going to have fun, damn it, lousy start notwithstanding.

She grabbed the oars, centered herself on the middle bench, and forced herself to concentrate on all that was good. Sunlight glistened off the pristine blue water, a trio of ducks quacked and bobbed near the shoreline, one of them butt up. Off in the distance a Jet Ski zipped around the lake, shooting up a steady arc of water. And on the seat below her, her nephew sat listening to his music and doing his utmost to ignore her. Even through his earphones she could hear the music's steady hard rock beats. She drew in a breath, reminded herself that they were going to have fun, and then reached back in her memory for everything her grandfather had taught her about rowing.

Firm grip on the handles.

Nice smooth strokes.

Don't dig too deep.

Just like riding a bike. But a hundred feet out, she wasn't smiling any longer. Sun beat down on the top of her head, and her eyes ached from squinting. Her throat was parched, and her arms burned. Her back began to prickle, and she knew a sunburn was in the works. All in all, it was shaping up to be a winner of a day.

She looked at her nephew and realized she hadn't made him put on sunscreen. Crap. If he went home with his skin even the slightest flush of pink, Jenny was going to catch hell from her sister. But at least he was better prepared for their outing than she. He wore a baseball cap, the bill pulled as low as possible on his forehead she was certain so he wouldn't have to look at her. Sunglasses covered his eyes, and unlike her capris, his khaki shorts were dry as a pin. He wore a black T-shirt under the orange life jacket and the color combination made her think of Halloween.

She pushed the oars through the water, trying to ignore the throbbing in her arms. "Are you having fun?" She raised her voice to be heard over his music.

He looked up, but she couldn't read anything behind his dark glasses. He tugged at the orange vest again. "A real blast."

She faked a smile. "Good. I knew you'd like it."

He went back to ignoring her.

She looked around. Off to her left, there was a small inlet that her grandfather had always sworn was the best fishing hole in the whole lake. Jenny eyed the distance. It was at least twice as far as they'd already come. No freakin' way. She pulled the oars in and grabbed one of the fishing poles.

From beneath his bill, Cody looked up.

Jenny opened the ancient green tackle box and grabbed a pink bottle of bait. "Have you ever baited a hook?"

Trying to act cool and uninterested, he pulled out one of his earphones, and she repeated the question. "Remember? I've never fished."

"It's really easy." The jar was rusty, and it took her several tries until if finally twisted free. She found the end of the line, thankful a hook was still attached (a little rusty, but usable) and began to thread little pink eggs on.

"You mean we aren't gonna use worms?"

"No."

"Why not?"

"Because . . ." Because the thought of stringing those poor, live, squirming, slimy things onto a hook made her stomach crawl. "Because I've read that this bait is more effective."

Even through his sunglasses, she could see he wasn't buying it. They got their hooks baited, and Jenny tried to show Cody how to cast, though it had been so long since she'd gone fishing, she was as rusty as the bait bottle. Still, they managed to get the lines in the water with a satisfying kerplunk.

"Now what?" Cody asked.

"We wait."

"For how long?"

"For however long it takes the fish to bite."

If possible, his chin jutted even farther into the air. "Like that's gonna happen. A fish eatin' something that's pink."

"I would."

"Yeah, like what?"

Jenny thought for a moment. "Cotton candy."

Cody stuck his earphone back in. "Well, you're not a fish. They like worms."

Jenny tipped her face up toward the sun and kept an eye on their lines, watching for any telltale movement. As the minutes ticked by, she couldn't help but compare how what she was doing now was exactly the same thing she was doing with Jared. keeping one eye on him at all times. The Jet Ski zoomed by and rocked the boat. Her stomach plunged and lurched just like it had last night when he'd had her pinned up against the railing.

I'm not your sweetheart.

You sure 'bout that?

Yes, she was sure, but she couldn't help wonder what it would be like to be his just for one night. One night where she'd feel his arms around her, his mouth on her, his weight between her thighs. Guilt collided with desire and twisted her stomach into a knot. She didn't want to remember what it felt like to lie naked next to a man, to feel the hard length of him pressed against her. Especially not a man like Jared. A flyboy who had no roots, only wings.

"Aunt Jenny, I'm hungry."

Heat crept up her neck and over her cheeks. She knew she was beet red and could only hope Cody blamed her inflamed skin on the sun and not on her licentious thoughts. She was hungry, too, but not in the same way. "I . . . um . . . I didn't pack anything to eat."

"Anything to drink?"

"No," she said, knowing she was the world's worst aunt. She'd forgotten sunscreen, food, and drinks, and she'd been having illicit thoughts about Jared while her nephew sat less than two feet away. "Do you want to head back in? It doesn't look like the fish are biting." Not that she'd know. She'd stopped looking at the poles around the time she'd started thinking about Jared on top of her, inside of her. "We can always come back out next weekend and try again."

"Whatever."

She took that to mean yes. She reached for her fishing pole, and then everything happened at once. Cody stood up and grabbed for his pole at the same time that the Jet Ski roared past again. This time it was so close, the little boat nearly tipped over from the wake. Without thinking, Jenny jumped up and grabbed a handful of vest and held on to Cody for dear life. His pole went over the side, and even as Jenny was yelling at him to forget it, to let it go, he was bending over, trying to reach it. Both their weight went to the left side, and water sloshed over the side. Panicked, she pulled Cody back and forced him to sit. By the time it was all over, they were both panting hard, and the fishing pole was sinking away. And an oar was floating off.

Jenny groaned. This. Could. Not. Be. Happening. Was it possible for this day to get any worse?

And then she heard laughter coming from the shore. She closed her eyes and groaned again. She didn't need to look to see who it was; she'd recognize that deep baritone anywhere. Maybe if she sat here long enough, the sun would just burn her up and end her misery.

"Jared!" Cody hollered, waving madly, starting to stand up again.

Jenny felt the boat rock, and her eyes shot open just in time to pull Cody straight back down. "Don't you dare," she said as she snuck a peek toward the shoreline. Jared stood there with his feet planted a shoulder's width apart. No wonder she hadn't heard him leave. He was dressed in running shorts, a T-shirt, and tennis shoes. Remembering her earlier thoughts, she blushed all over again.

"We need his help."

"No, we don't."

Cody pointed to the oar that kept floating farther and farther away. He crossed his arms across his puffy orange chest and let out a loud *"Huh."*

Jenny looked around. She didn't need to be saved, no matter what Cody or her family thought. She could manage on her own. She picked up the one oar she had left and stretched out as far as she could, hoping she'd be able to nab the other oar. But no matter how far she stretched, the oar stayed out of reach.

"Need any help?" The deep timbre of his voice easily carried across the water to them. And so did his amused arrogance.

"No," she hollered back, shooting Cody a *keep quiet* look. Using the one oar, she began to paddle, but no matter how many times she kept switching the oar from side to side, she ended up going in more of a circle than a straight line.

"You sure you don't need help?"

She gritted her teeth and dug in, determined to reach that damn oar if it killed her. "Positive."

But no matter how hard she rowed, she didn't make any forward progress. Finally, she gave up and dragged the heavy wooden oar back into the boat.

"How much longer are we going to be out here, Aunt Jenny?"

As long as it takes. "Don't worry. I've got everything under control. We'll be back on shore in no time."

"Good. 'Cuz I really need to get back."

A terrible suspicion stole over her. "Uh, you don't have to use the bathroom do you?"

"No. I'm thirsty. And I gotta finish my homework before we leave for my game."

"You're not done with your homework?"

"No."

She didn't want to ask the next question, afraid of the answer. "Have you started?"

"No."

"Cody . . ."

He didn't say a word.

"Cody Adams, I'm—" But she was fresh out of threats and fresh out of ideas on how to retrieve the oar. She had the sudden urge to throw her nephew over the side and tell him to swim out and get it, then she wondered just how old that life vest was and would it even still float?

"Looks like we won't be stuck out here much longer."

She looked in the direction he was pointing.

Jared was shrugging off his shirt and pushing off his running shoes and heading for the water.

"No way." A girl could stand only so much humiliation in one day.

Without pausing to fully think it through, she dove over the side. Icy cold water sucked the air straight out of her lungs, and she surfaced, gasping for breath.

"Aunt Jenny!"

"I-I-I'm f-f-f-fine." Goose bumps ran up and down her body, and she couldn't stop shaking. She bobbed in the water for a moment, trying to catch her breath and sight of the oar. Just when she spotted it, she heard the long, even strokes of Jared swimming toward her. She spared a glance his way and gasped—not from cold—but from surprise. The man swam like a fish.

Determination fueled her on. Her breaststroke was awkward and choppy, and she refused to put her face in the freezing water. Slowly she gained on the oar. But Jared was right behind her. She thrashed her arms faster and sucked in air, along with some lake water. Five more strokes, and she'd have it.

Jared reached the oar moments before she did. Panting, she drew up alongside, unable to believe he'd beat her. Her head start had been huge. So much for girl power.

He turned the oar around, until the fat end was facing her. She grabbed it like a lifeboat, not caring that it did little to hold her up. Her breathing was fast and uneven, his slow and rhythmic, like he'd just walked across the yard. And while her teeth chattered away, he wasn't acting the least bit cold.

In one stroke he was by her side, an arm around her waist. Water swirled around him as his leg brushed against hers. The corners of his mouth slid upward in a slow, sexy grin, drawing her attention to his mouth and then down to his broad shoulders. "And here I didn't think bunnies liked to get wet."

FOURTEEN

In a blaze of orange and pink, the sun set behind the ragged tops of the Olympic Mountains. Long shadows stretched across the lake. Frogs sang. And a blazing fire shot sparks into the dark night.

Jenny looked around the fire pit. Instead of just having Maddy over for Monday margaritas, Jenny had decided to include a few more friends. If she was going to jump back into her old life, she was going to do it with both feet. Yesterday, after she'd returned from Cody's baseball game, she'd called Maddy again and asked her to bring her husband, Don. Then Jenny had called Sharron and Rob and also invited them. The four of them had arrived a couple of hours earlier, and with the fire crackling on the beach and a canopy of stars above them, it felt just like old times. Or almost. Jenny glanced at the empty seat on her left. Out of habit she'd brought six chairs down to the beach instead of only the five they'd need.

She knew tonight would be difficult, a minefield of emotions. It was the first time she was getting together with friends since Steven's death. As she'd poured margaritas for the girls and handed beers to the guys, she couldn't help but feel a little guilty, like she was doing something wrong. But then she'd glance over at the extra chair, and a sense of peace would come over her. Almost as if Steven were there, telling her, *Yes, you're doing the right thing. It's time to move on.* But she didn't think he meant moving on with Jared.

Not for the first time did her mind stray to him. And each time she thought about him, she grew warm. She'd worried about how she was going to handle tonight, with Jared and her friends here. But, thankfully, Jared had unknowingly taken the matter into his own hands. Earlier, he'd left on his motorcycle, and she hadn't seen him since.

And here I didn't think bunnies liked to get wet.

Warm grew to hot as she remembered what he'd said to her in the lake yesterday. Remembered how his hands had slipped beneath her soaked tank top and found bare skin. How his hands had wrapped around her waist and held her close as they'd both paddled to stay afloat. Limbs had intertwined as cool water washed over heated skin. Something had shifted in the way Jared was treating her, and she wasn't sure she liked it. On second thought, she was worried she liked it too much.

The voices of her friends floated around her. Don and Rob were deep into a friendly argument over which they found more challenging—sturgeon fishing or halibut—while Maddy and Sharron chatted about all things baby. Jenny had forgotten that, how since both of her friends had had children a couple of years ago, kids were the main topic of choice. When they'd started talking, Jenny had braced herself. Not long ago, she'd been certain she and Steven would be planning for a family about now. But the sharp sense of loss she'd expected never materialized. Instead, in its place, only a tender memory of what could have been resided.

"I couldn't believe it either," Sharron was saying. "My back was turned for less than a second, and before I knew what was happening, Amber had gotten into the Vaseline and smeared it all through her hair."

"That must have been miserable to get out," Jenny said, drawing her legs up and wrapping her arms around her denim-clad knees. She braced the soles of her tennis shoes on the chair's seat.

Sharron took a drink of her margarita. "Tell me about it. Washing an eighteen-month-old's hair once is bad enough. Having to do it three times in one day—a nightmare."

They laughed, and Jenny once more felt a sense of peace. *This* was right. She was doing the right thing.

"What about Taylor?" she asked Maddy.

"A terror on two legs," Maddy said with a smile full of love. "That boy of mine is never still. What I wouldn't give for energy like that."

"Hear, hear," Sharron said. "I—"

Whatever she'd been about to say was cut off by the deep, throaty rumble of a motorcycle coming down the driveway. And with that sound, Jenny's sense of peace flew right up into the starry sky.

Conversation ceased as four pairs of curious eyes looked at her. Maddy was the first to speak. "Who do we have here?"

Jenny couldn't answer. Her gaze followed her friends' to the lone figure on the bike. Her heart seemed to catch, stutter, then kick into overdrive as she watched Jared park alongside the Corvette. She knew there was the chance he'd return while her friends were still here; she should have insisted they meet up somewhere else. Tonight held enough challenges without having to deal with Jared and the tangled mess of emotions that always plagued her whenever he was near. But she'd desperately wanted to be on familiar ground for this first reunion.

Slowly, she unfolded her legs and sat up. "No one important," was all she could say.

The engine fell silent, and the bike's single headlight doused. Once more the fire was the only light. But even in the darkness, Jared's tall form was unmistakable as he swung his leg over the bike and removed his helmet.

"That doesn't look like 'no one' to me," Maddy said,

eyeing Jenny. "This wouldn't happen to be your infamous partner? The one the whole town is buzzing about? I wondered if he'd make an appearance tonight. Don," she said to her husband, "go over and make sure he joins us."

Jenny felt her insides drop. "I don't think that's a good idea."

Maddy gave her a twinkling smile. "After everything I've heard about him? I do."

"So do I," Sharron said, walking over to the nearby picnic table and refilling her margarita.

Don and Jared made their way toward them. Jared wore a pair of faded Levi's, a dark shirt, and his black leather jacket. His boots sank into the sand with each step. It was practically the same outfit she'd seen him in all week. There was absolutely nothing about it that should trip her heart and cause her breathing to come a little quicker. Nothing at all.

Jenny was saved from having to make introductions as Don took over. When Rob and Jared were introduced, Rob stood and shook Jared's hand. "Nice to meet you."

"Likewise." Jared withdrew his arm and shoved his hand halfway down the front pocket of his Levi's. "I didn't know you had friends over," he said, looking to Jenny. Firelight softened his features, and she felt the weight of his deep blue stare all the way to her marrow. "I'll leave you all to it. It was nice to meet everyone."

She should have felt relieved. He was leaving just like she wanted. But as their gazes stayed connected, something passed between them. That look tugged at her and had her saying, "Why don't you join us?"

Jared looked as surprised as she felt.

"Yes, stay," Maddy chimed in. "We're harmless."

"I wouldn't say that," Sharron joked. "But no one will bring out a guitar and force you to sing 'Kumbaya' or 'Michael, Row the Boat Ashore.' You have my word."

"There goes my fun for the evening," Rob joked.

Jared hesitated. It was so brief, Jenny was sure no one else caught it. Then he stepped around her and took the only vacant seat, the one next to her.

Don grabbed a beer out of the cooler and handed it to Jared.

"Thanks," Jared said, reaching across Jenny to grab the bottle. His arm was so close that if she leaned forward just a fraction, his sleeve would brush against her.

"What do you think of Hidden Lake?" Maddy asked.

Jared popped the top off his beer. "Small."

Sharron nodded her head. "Give me a big city any day."

"Are you from around here?" Maddy asked.

"No."

"Where did you grow up?"

He took a drink. "No one place in particular."

Maddy shifted in her seat. "How long do you plan on staying?"

Jared's deep blue gaze sought and found Jenny's. "Depends."

There was a world of meaning in that single glance, and Jenny wasn't the only one who noticed. Out of the corner of her eye, she caught Maddy and Sharron exchange a knowing look.

Don laughed and wrapped his arm around Maddy's shoulders, pulling her close. He gave her a kiss on her forehead. "You'll have to excuse my wife. Before she decided to stay home with our son, she was a newspaper reporter. Always looking for a story."

Maddy gave him a playful jab in the ribs.

"I ran into Paul last week," Don said to no one in particular. Then he turned to Jared. "He told me you and Steven were in the same squadron. The Fighting Eagles, right?"

"Falcons," Jared said, raising his beer and taking a long drink. "Fighting Falcons."

"Steven always was a sucker for speed," Maddy said, smiling gently at Jenny.

Jenny returned her smile, feeling only a small tug on her heart. "Yes, he was."

"Remember that old Thunderbird his parents bought him our sophomore year?" Don said. "A rusted-out hunk of shit if there ever was one. But he loved that car."

Yes, he had. So had Jenny. She'd lost her virginity in the backseat.

"Isn't that the car you two took drag racing?" Maddy asked her husband.

Don laughed. "We caught a bucket load of shit when we got home that night."

Maddy shoved her hands into the pockets of her fleece coat. "If Taylor ever pulled a stunt like that, disappeared for hours without a clue to where he was, I don't know what I'd do."

"I do," Don said. "You'd send me out to find him."

Maddy nodded. "Sad, but true."

Everyone chuckled.

From there the conversation took a turn down memory lane. Don trotted out one crazy story after the other about the stunts he and Steven had pulled all through school while Rob added a few stories from more recent years. Never ones to stay quiet, Maddy and Sharron jumped in, adding their versions to the mix. Soon, everyone was laughing and talking and telling one silly childhood story after another. Everyone except Jared.

Jenny glanced his way. In the warm glow of the fire-light, she searched his profile, but his expression gave nothing away. He listened to the stories, smiled, and laughed in all the right places. But he never added a story of his own. Not a single childhood memory about summer camp or how his parents had grounded him for staying out too late. No mention of siblings or pets or a torturous family road trip. Not once during the whole evening did Jenny get a single glimpse into Jared Worth's life. She couldn't help but sense he was keeping a part of himself separate. Distant.

She glanced around their small group, certain someone else would have also picked up on it, but no one had.

She couldn't shake the feeling that Jared's childhood had been anything but normal.

A log fell in the fire and sent a shower of sparks upward.

Rob pushed up his sleeve and glanced at his watch. "I

hate to be the party pooper, but we'd better get going. We only have the sitter until nine thirty."

"Is it that late already?" Don stood and held out his hand to Maddy.

She took his hand. "When did nine get to be late?" she said jokingly as she stood up.

Don shrugged into his flannel shirt. "The minute we became parents."

Sharron laughed in agreement.

When Maddy and Sharron tried to clean up, Jenny shooed them away. "My party, my mess." They argued, but she was adamant.

Before Maddy climbed into the passenger side of their truck, she gave Jenny a hug. "Tonight was good."

Jenny returned the hug. "Very good."

Maddy stared at her a moment longer. "Don't be a stranger."

"I won't."

"And, Jenny?"

"Yeah?"

Maddy motioned to Jared. "Go for it. I would."

Maddy was still laughing when Don climbed into the truck and drove off. Sharron and Rob's car was right behind them.

Jenny watched until their taillights had disappeared. Turning, she made her way back to the beach, telling herself it was because she needed to clean up. But the moment she saw Jared's solitary figure down near the lake, she knew that wasn't what had brought her back.

Slowly, she made her way toward him.

He looked so alone, standing at the water's edge, staring out across the flat, dark surface of the lake. Jenny didn't know what it was—the soft night air, the starry sky, the glow of the campfire in the near distance—but something made her want to reach out to Jared. To walk up to him, put her arms around him, and hold him tight. Assure him he wasn't alone in this world.

The idea was so preposterous, she stumbled in the sand.

In an instant, Jared was there, reaching out, holding on to her arm and steadying her. Under his hand, heat infused her skin.

"I like your friends," he said as the breeze blew through his hair.

She wondered if he could feel how erratic her pulse had grown. "They liked you."

Even in the darkness, she could see him shrug, as if he didn't believe her words.

He let go of her arm. Instantly, she missed his touch. He reached down and picked up a rock from the beach, tossing it a couple of times in his hand before throwing it into the lake. In the still night they heard the soft kerplunk as the rock hit the water.

Jared stared out at the dark lake for several moments before shoving his fingers down into the pocket of his Levi's and slowly turning to her. "May I ask you a question?"

"Turnabout is fair play."

He laughed softly then looked back out across the lake, not saying anything for the longest time. "What the hell is 'Kumbaya'?"

She started to laugh, then stopped, realizing he was serious. "You don't know?"

He kicked at a fallen log near his boot. "No."

Looking at him now reminded her of an earlier thought she'd had tonight. When she'd wondered at just what kind of childhood he'd had. "Weren't you in Scouts?"

He shot her a puzzled look.

"Cub Scouts. Boy Scouts."

He laughed, but the sound held no mirth. "No."

What type of childhood had he had? The question kept circling back around to her. "'Kumbaya' is a folk song sung at just about every Scout campout there is. Don't ask me why."

He nodded, and once more she was struck with the desire to reach out and touch him. Hold him. Instead, she found herself confiding, "My nana always told me this lake was magical. That this water could heal almost anything."

He tucked a strand of hair behind her ear. "Has it healed you, Jenny?"

He said her name like it was a caress. "Yes," she answered. Then, "Almost." She searched the shadowy planes of his face. "What about you, Jared? What do you need healed?"

"Nothing."

"I think you're lying."

His dark face gave nothing away. "Believe what you want."

"I don't know anything about you."

"There's nothing worth telling."

She knew he was wrong.

Shallow waves rolled up the beach then washed back out.

"Tell me about your childhood."

She waited, and when the silence became too much, she said, "Please."

"Leave it alone," he said in a low, toneless voice.

Boldly, she placed her hand on his chest. Soft cotton covered a wall of hard muscles. "I can't."

He reached up, as if to pull her hand away. But, instead, his hand closed around hers. The warmth of him seeped through her shirt and onto her skin right above her heart. The weight of his hand kept hers there for several moments before he pulled hers away.

"Cody told me you haven't seen your mother since you were eight. Is that true?"

He cursed softly. "Believe me, you don't want to hear about my childhood."

"Yes," she said quietly, "I do."

Silence stretched out between them.

"Is it true?" she asked again when he didn't answer.

He looked at her. Even in the semidarkness, the intensity of his blue gaze shot straight through her.

"One question, remember," she said.

"You already asked your question."

She shook her head.

"About if I was in Scouts."

"That didn't count."

He reached out and cupped her cheek in the palm of his hand. "Why not?"

The feel of his hand on her stole her breath. "One real question. Please."

He rubbed his thumb underneath her jaw. "One real question."

Are you going to break my heart? But she feared she already knew the answer. "When was the last time you saw your mother?"

He let out a ragged breath and took his hand away, averting his gaze to the lake. "When I was eight."

"But how? Why?"

He shoved his hand back into his pockets. "What do you want to hear? That one day my mother left and never came back? Threw me out like an old pair of shoes?"

"Jared . . ." She couldn't imagine the type of childhood he was describing. "Where did you live?"

"Drop it, Jenny."

But she couldn't. "Where?"

He angled his head and looked at her. "Has anyone ever told you that you are stubborn?"

"I prefer tenacious."

A reluctant grin tugged at his lips.

"Where?" she asked for the third time.

"I grew up a ward of the state."

"What about your father?"

"What about him? Nancy never knew which one of the many guys she'd been sleeping with knocked her up."

"What about foster homes?"

"Didn't work."

Even though his tone was expressionless, his words tore at her. She felt the sting of tears. *No father. No mother. No home.* No child should have to endure anything so painful. "I'm so sorry."

"Don't be. It was a long time ago. It doesn't matter."

"Yes, it does."

"Don't," he said again, his voice low and harsh.

"Don't what?"

He tipped her chin up. Wiped away her tears with the pad of his thumb. "Pity me."

She searched his dark eyes. "I'm not." It was the truth. "I was just thinking how amazing you are. To have endured so much and instead of letting it crush you, you excelled."

"Jenny," he said her name like a prayer. "What am I going to do with you?" He didn't wait for an answer; instead, he pulled her against him and slowly lowered his mouth to her. The touch of his lips on hers stole her breath. She didn't think; she reacted. She wrapped her arms around the back of his neck and sank into him. She tilted her head back and opened her mouth. He growled low in the back of his throat and deepened the kiss. Spirals of hot desire started low in her stomach and spread outward until her whole body was on fire. She stretched up on her toes to fit herself more firmly against his warm, hard body. His hands wrapped around her and lifted her tightly against him. He buried his face in the side of her neck, whispered her name over and over, before reclaiming her mouth in a kiss that seared her all the way to her soul.

In the end, it was Jared who pulled back. "Go," he said, "before I do something we'll both regret."

* * *

As Jared watched Jenny run to the house, he wondered where in the hell he'd found the strength to pull away from her. Raw desire ate at his gut. She intoxicated him, filled him with a wanting that all but overpowered him. Holding her, he'd almost been able to delude himself that the type of future he used to dream about was still a possibility.

I was just thinking how amazing you are. To have endured so much and instead of letting it crush you, you excelled.

The cool night air washed over him, tried to cool his overheated body. If she only knew the truth. He hadn't excelled; he'd fucked up. Again. It was the same thing that happened every time he let his emotions get involved.

He looked up at the inky dark sky. If he'd only stayed detached, he'd still be up there and not down on the ground kissing Jenny with a fervor he prayed would drive everyone else from her mind—would drive Steven from her mind. But how was a man supposed to stay detached when innocent people were being slaughtered? How was he supposed to buy into a set of rules that were based solely on politics rather than what was just?

He walked back to the fire, doused it. As he watched the wood hiss and steam, he lost the battle to forget about his past . . . forget about the day he lost everything.

There had been nothing unusual about that day. He'd been flying a regular mission, just about ready to head back to the carrier, when his radar had picked up something. He was on fumes, but that hadn't stopped him from investigating further. What he found made his stomach turn. Refugees were being slaughtered by the hundreds as they fled from attack. It was an all-out massacre. Witnessing what was happening, Jared didn't think about anything but saving innocent lives. Not his CO's command nor the rules of engagement. He'd done what he thought was right; he provided air support until the refugees found safety. But by doing so, it had cost him his career. His life.

The front door slammed shut. He dropped his gaze from the sky and looked out across the dark yard to Jenny's house. He would not make the same mistake again. *Stay detached.* It was the only way he knew how to survive. But as he continued to stare at her house, something told him that this time was going to be a hell of a lot tougher than anything he'd faced before.

FIFTEEN

As the following week unfolded, the weather took a turn. Heavy, dark clouds rolled in and hung low in the sky. The sun turned weak and the air cold. The rain came slowly at first, a splattering of droplets here, a heavier mist there, almost as if Mother Nature couldn't make up her mind. Even though the calendar read June, no one was surprised by the weather. Those few bright, sun-filled days at the end of May had been an unexpected gift, something every Seattleite had known and not taken for granted. Summer clothes might have been brought out and worn, but no one had packed away their jeans and sweaters. As Jenny stared out the front window, she couldn't help but think how the weather perfectly mirrored her mood.

She ran a finger lightly across her lips, remembering how it had felt to be held by Jared, kissed by him. Within his arms, she'd come alive. Gone were the doubts that had always plagued her before. Instead, with Jared, she'd become a woman she didn't recognize. Someone confident, bold. Someone who knew they were exciting a man as much as he was exciting her. The evidence had been in Jared's every fractured breath, in the way he'd said her name over and over again, like he couldn't quite believe it was her he held in his arms, her he kissed. But then he'd ended their embrace and pushed her away.

Go, before I do something we'll both regret.

And she had. She'd run away, scared and burning with raw humiliation. She tried not to think about what would have happened if he hadn't stopped their kiss. But she knew. She would have given herself to him wholly and completely and not thought about the consequences until much, much later.

And she would have regretted it. She, better than anyone, knew there was no future with a flyboy with itchy feet. Steven had loved her wholeheartedly, and still he hadn't been able to commit to her fully. They'd been engaged but each time Jenny had pressed for a wedding date, he'd put her off. She wasn't about to make that same mistake. She wasn't going to give her heart to someone who didn't want the same thing she did. She and Jared were business partners, nothing more. The sooner she paid him off, the sooner she could get on with her life.

The front door opened, and she heard the stomping and wiping of shoes on the front mat before the heavy *clomp clomp* of footsteps came down the hallway. She tensed, fearing it was Jared, then relaxed when Zeke came into view.

Poking his head into the office, he braced one hand on the doorjamb. "We're ready to take off."

"Tell the Johnsons to have a good visit with their nephew. And be careful up there."

"Aren't I always?" The creases in his weathered face deepened into a grin. "Besides, it's only a quick trip to the San Juans. I'll be back 'fore ya know it."

"Still, be safe."

He went to push off from the doorframe, then paused, his smile going slack. "You okay?"

She tucked her hair behind her ear and fought for a true smile. "Never better. Just a little tired."

Her false bravado didn't seem to convince him.

"I'm fine," she reassured him. "Now scat. We don't want to keep paying customers waiting."

Concern still softened his eyes, but he let the subject drop. Several minutes later, she heard the seaplane start.

Alone, she let the facade fall away. She massaged her forehead and tried to stave off the feeling of doom as she stared at the calendar on her desk. She tried to ignore all the open spots in the schedule but found it impossible. True, with summer nearing, there were a few more charters on the books but not nearly enough. All week she'd worked on ideas to bring in business, to improve Blue Sky's bottom line. She'd lost count of the number of calls she'd made . . . the number of people she'd talked to. Each business she'd reached, the conversation had ended the same way: thanks, but no thanks. No matter how hard she tried, nothing she did made a difference.

Panic unfurled. Now, she silently acknowledged, the stakes were even higher. Yes, she was still determined to prove to her family that she was capable of running a successful business, but now there was so much more at risk.

What do you want to hear? That one day my mother left and never came back?

That night, when she'd stood next to Jared by the edge of the lake, something vital inside of her had changed. Jared wasn't a man who opened up often—if at all. Yet he'd opened up to her. Told her things she knew, just knew, he'd never revealed to anyone else. That meant something. That meant a lot of somethings.

She picked up a pencil then made the necessary notes in her ledger regarding the day's charter. She closed the book and rubbed her temples, knowing that her headache had nothing to do with Blue Sky and everything to do with Jared. No matter where she was or what she was doing, he was there. It was as if he had decided to put out an all-strike attack on her senses. And he was winning the battle. She tried to avoid him, but he made that impossible. Twice, he'd caught her in the hall after a shower. She'd thought she was alone, that she was safe to dash the short distance from the bathroom to her room. But the minute she'd opened up the door, covered only in a towel, he was standing directly in front of her. His gaze devoured her like she was a candy store of pure sin, and he wanted to taste every last piece.

And it didn't end there. Whenever they were together, his body had a habit of accidentally touching hers. Though something told her those were no accidents. His arm would brush against her side as he reached for his coffee. Every so often, he'd show up in her office and lean across her shoulder to see what she was working on. His warm breath fanned across the back of her neck, his chest pressing against her back.

In the evenings, he'd insist on joining her on the couch. As they talked about the business, his shoulder would rub against hers, and the hard length of his thigh would press against her thigh. Each touch was a shockwave that went straight through her. When she finally escaped him and reached the safety of her room, she realized they'd talked very little about the business and more about her. Without her even realizing it, he had a way of steering the conversation until she ended up confiding things to him she hadn't told anyone else. Not even Steven. She rubbed her hand across her forehead again and closed her eyes. She couldn't explain it or even understand it. How had he made her open up and let him in that far to her soul?

Except for the night on the beach when she'd held nothing back, Jenny had thought she'd done a good job of hiding her reactions to him. But last night had changed all that. She'd been sitting on the couch when Jared had walked into the room. Earlier, he'd built a fire in the large river rock fireplace. The fire snapped and popped, and rain pattered against the windows. The warm glow from the fire and the single lamp near the couch had been the only light in the room. She'd started to get up, to head to her bedroom, because being near him was her own personal kind of sensual hell. But as she stood, he took hold of her wrist. Gently, he turned her hand over and lightly ran his fingertip across her palm, caressing a scratch she'd gotten earlier that day.

"What happened here?" he'd asked, the firelight softening his strong jaw and warming his blue eyes.

Her heart had beat a little faster, and she'd gotten light-headed as his fingertip traced the outline of the cut. "Nothing," she said, feeling a pull in the pit of her stomach. She wasn't about to admit to him that the knife she'd been using to cut her sandwich had slipped when she'd heard his voice. That's all it had taken, just the sound of his voice for her to lose all concentration.

"Looks like it needs a Band-Aid." And then he'd raised her palm to his mouth and lightly kissed the small sore. The feel of his lips against her skin had nearly sent her over the edge once more. A tingle had started in her palm, then spread up her arms, across her breast, until it pooled deep in her belly. The moment she'd recognized the feeling for what it was—pure, undiluted desire—she'd snatched her hand away.

For so many years, her dreams had been filled with a sandy-haired man with an open smile and twinkling green eyes. But lately, as she twisted and turned in bed at night, Steven's image was replaced by another's: a man with hair as dark as the ebony sky, a mouth too sensual to resist, and deep, deep blue eyes that spoke of on open wanting but also hid a world of secrets.

"Jenny? We're here."

The sound of her sister's voice startled her back to the present. Jumping up, she went out to the hallway. There, Anna and Cody waited for her. It was Saturday, and that meant another weekend with her nephew.

"I didn't hear you pull in."

"We've been hanging outside for a few minutes. Cody wanted to watch the plane take off."

Jenny smiled at her nephew. "Hi, Cody."

"Hey, Aunt Jenny." He looked only marginally happier to be here this weekend.

Anna set his small carry-on–size suitcase on the floor.

"When I talked to Mom this week, she said you were so preoccupied at lunch on Wednesday, you hardly said a word."

"Seems like the two of you would have something better to talk about than me."

"*You're* all Mom ever wants to talk about."

"We both know that is so not true," Jenny replied curtly.

"I didn't mean to start an argument." Anna let out the barest of sighs. "Cody has a another game this Sunday. Can you take him."

It wasn't a question. Once again, her sister just assumed that Blue Sky was a recreational pastime. Jenny wanted to refuse, to tell her sister she needed to start understanding that Jenny's job was just as important as hers.

"Big surprise," Cody said with more disdain than Jenny thought possible in a thirteen-year-old. "Another game you're gonna miss."

"Cody—" her sister started.

"Forget it," he snapped and stomped off to the family room.

Anna smoothed her perfectly done hair and gave Jenny a smile. "Don't worry. He's just going through a stage. The game is at two. Will you be able to take him?"

Jenny looked down the hallway to where her nephew had disappeared. She couldn't shake the feeling that under all that malcontent was an aching little boy. "Yes, I'll take him."

"You're a lifesaver. The game is on Whitman Field this week." Anna dug in her designer purse and pulled out a slip of paper. "Here's the address. And, Jenny?"

"Yes?"

"Please make sure he completes his homework this weekend. He was up until ten last Sunday."

Not waiting for a response, Anna breezed past her and headed toward the family room. Jenny followed but at a slower pace. Her sister was nothing if not consistent.

"Bye, Cody. I'll see you Sunday night."

He didn't answer, and when Anna leaned down to give

him a parting kiss to the top of his head, Jenny saw how he tipped away to avoid the contact.

Anna straightened, smiled one last time at Jenny, then was out the door. Several long moments passed before Cody spoke.

"Thanks for taking me to the game, Aunt Jenny."

All of a sudden, he seemed so young and forlorn, she wanted to get up and hug him. But she knew he wanted that as much as he'd wanted to wear the orange life jacket. How many times had he told her he wasn't a baby and didn't want to be treated like one? Still, she found it hard to stay seated. "I'm looking forward to it." She searched for something else to say. Something that would help ease that look of hurt in his eyes. "You packed light this time."

"Huh?"

She motioned to the backpack next to him on the couch. "Only a backpack and a small suitcase. Where are all the bags of groceries? Or does your mom trust my cooking now since you came home alive last week?"

A tiny crack of a smile appeared and brought out his right dimple. "No. I told her you weren't doing the cooking, Jared was."

"And she trusts him, without even trying what he's made?"

"Yeah."

"Sisterly love."

Cody giggled, and his smile made her feel like she'd accomplished something worthwhile for the first time this week.

"Oh. Aunt Jen?"

"Yeah?"

"It's my turn to bring snacks to the game for the team." *Thanks, Sis.* "This doesn't involve cooking, does it?"

Cody laughed harder. "Naw. Just some pop and candy."

Jenny highly doubted that, but she'd figure it out tomorrow. And the more she thought about Cody's game, the more excited she actually got. For a few hours at least,

she'd be away from Jared and all the emotions he kept
stirring awake inside of her.

*   *   *

Sunday morning, Cody woke to the sound of the plane
starting. Jumping out of bed, he shucked off his pj's and
pulled on his jeans, T-shirt, and the Mariners hooded sweatshirt he'd worn yesterday. He hurried down the stairs, trying to be as quiet as he could. Aunt Jenny's door was still
closed. Cody sure didn't want to be the one to wake her.
He'd never seen anyone so grumpy in the morning.

The minute he stepped out onto the porch, he sighed in
relief. The rain had stopped. His game wouldn't be canceled. But when he looked to the end of the dock where the
plane was anchored, he frowned. The cockpit was empty,
and the plane was silent, but he still heard the whirring
noise. Looking around, he finally spotted Jared at the far
end of the hangar using a Weed Eater.

For a moment his chest hurt like it had when Troy
Reed had accidentally nailed him with a fastball. Before
Dad had left, he'd mowed their lawn and trimmed around
the backyard fence. His mom kept telling Dad he didn't
have to do that; they could hire someone. But Dad had
said he liked being outside after a long week of being
stuck indoors. Now, ever since Dad had left, a guy in a red
truck came once a week and took care of their lawn.

Cody still didn't get why his dad went away. There
were plenty of sick kids here that needed his help. No
matter how many times his parents explained it to him, it
still didn't make sense. He sat down on the top stair and
picked at a piece of chipped wood.

It wasn't fair. His mom worked all the time, and his
dad was gone. They tried talking on the phone, but there
was this funny echo and a lot of static that made it hard
for either of them to hear. His dad sent letters, and Cody
wrote back, but it wasn't the same. It wasn't anywhere near
the same.

The small sliver of wood tore free, and he began to dig at another one. As much as he hated how his mom wouldn't let him stay home by himself, at least Aunt Jenny spent time with him. Even if it was doing the dorkiest stuff. Like last night. Right after dinner, she brought out another one of those board games. Cody smiled, remembering how Jared had winked at him and said they should be spelled b-o-r-e-d instead of b-o-a-r-d. Jenny had told Jared to go clean up his mess in the kitchen and put away the chili that nearly killed them because it had been too spicy. Cody had thought it tasted good, but he kept quiet. In a weird way, he liked hearing them argue. Well, not arguing. No one got mad or yelled or anything like that. They just talked. Like his mom and dad used to. Now, his house was always so quiet.

After dinner, Aunt Jenny had dragged out Monopoly and insisted they all play. Even though the game was so stupid, and he'd never tell Parker or any of his friends what his aunt forced him to do, he kinda had fun. And even Jared had joined in their game last night. He said he'd never played Monopoly before, but Cody didn't believe him. He'd kicked their butts.

"Hey. You're up early."

Jared was at the bottom of the stairs, the Weed Eater in his hand. Cody hadn't even heard it shut off.

"Aunt Jenny and I have to go to the store and get snacks." He wasn't about to admit he'd run outside, hoping to see the plane take off. It sounded lame, even to him.

"That's right. Your game is today. You must be excited."

"Sorta." Cody dropped his gaze. "I didn't get to practice pitching this week." And he didn't want to suck. Not today. Not when there was going to be someone in the stands cheering just for him. "Do you wanna . . ." He dropped his gaze and stubbed the toe of his sneaker against a nail sticking up on the stair. "You wouldn't want to come to my game, would you?"

Jared was silent for so long, Cody didn't dare look up.

Of course Jared didn't want to go. "Never mind. It was a stupid idea."

"I want to finish the yard work today."

"It's okay, I understand."

"If I had an extra pair of hands, it would go a lot faster."

Cody's gaze shot up. "You mean you'll come?"

"You any good with a lawn mower?"

His dad had always told him he was too young to use theirs, but Cody had watched him use it a hundred times. It looked super simple. Besides, he was older now. "Yep."

"All right then, sport. Have you had breakfast?"

"Yep," Cody said again, fibbing for the second time. But he didn't want Jared to send him back inside.

"Let's get crackin'."

Cody jumped down all three stairs at once. "If we finish early, do you think . . . do you think maybe I could pitch some balls to you? You know, to warm up for today?"

"You sure you don't want to ask your aunt?"

"She throws like a girl, remember."

"She is a girl."

"Exactly."

Jared laughed. "Yeah, I think we'll have time to toss a few."

Cody felt the hard squeeze in his chest begin to lessen. "Sweet."

* * *

Jared had barely gotten Cody started on mowing the lawn when Jenny came barreling out the front door. The door smacked shut as she stormed across the yard, her pink robe flapping open in a V from her belted waist down.

She took his breath away. He'd never fully understood that phrase until he'd met Jenny. Oh, he'd seen a lot of gorgeous women in his day and slept with more than his fair share. But never had anyone gotten under his skin the way she had. He was a fuck 'em and forget 'em type of guy.

And he made damn sure the women he slept with knew that right up front. He didn't do relationships; hell, he barely ever spent the night. Not that he'd ever heard any complaints. He made sure everyone he left was as satisfied as a well-petted cat. Maybe that was his problem. It had been a while since he'd gotten laid. Maybe if he went back to the Sawmill and found a willing partner, he'd be able to get Jenny out of his mind. But he didn't want just any woman; he wanted Jenny. It didn't matter if she was yelling at him or ignoring him; he wanted her.

And that kiss. All week he'd tried to forget it, tried to erase it from his mind. But he knew he'd never be able to.

As she drew near, the morning breeze brought the scent of her to him. Her hair drifted toward him, and if he wasn't already as hard as a rock, the smell of her would have shot him from soft to stiff in five seconds flat.

"Have you ever heard of sleeping in?"

Jared set the Weed Eater on the ground and braced his right arm on the handle. God, she was magnificent when she was angry. "Nine isn't sleeping in. That's comatose."

Her hair was a mass of long, wild curls, and her blue eyes blazed. "Only in your mixed-up world."

"You've obviously forgotten the conversation we had about work hours."

She planted her hands on her waist, drawing his eyes to her hips. "And you've forgotten that it's Sunday. *Sunday.* Even God rested on the seventh day."

"God doesn't pay the bills."

"And neither does mowing the lawn."

She had him there. But working himself to the point of exhaustion helped with all his pent-up sexual frustration.

Her brow wrinkled as she stared at the Weed Eater. "If you're not—" Then she saw Cody. "You're making *my nephew* mow the lawn?"

"I'm not making anyone do anything."

"He's thirteen."

"Exactly."

"Thirteen," she said again, a little bit louder. No, a lot

louder. "Plus, he's wearing tennis shoes. And where are his eye protectors and earplugs?"

"It's a lawn mower not a machine gun." By the time Jared was thirteen, he'd been doing a heck of a lot more than just mowing lawns. If memory served him correctly, one foster family had him splitting wood with an axe before he was ten.

"He could get hurt."

He was about to tell her he could just as easily get hurt crossing the street or riding his bike, but then he thought better of it. He was definitely no expert on the subject of kids. Hadn't he made a mess of things with Cody the first time they'd met?

"Fine. I'll tell him to stop."

Just then the lawn mower shut off, and Cody yelled out to her. "Hey, Aunt Jen." His smile was as big as the lake out in front of them. "Guess what?"

She smiled back at him. "What?"

"Jared let me mow the lawn." His enthusiasm was hard to miss. "And guess what else?"

"What?"

"He's gonna come to my game."

Her gaze snapped back around, and her smile thinned. "Don't even think about it," she hissed under her breath, making sure Cody couldn't hear.

SIXTEEN

"Aunt Jenny," Cody yelled through the front door. "We gotta leave *now*."

"Hold your horses. I'm coming." Grabbing the two bags of snacks off the kitchen counter, Jenny made her way outside. She started toward the Corvette only to stop short when she saw Cody climbing into the passenger side of Zeke's pickup. "Wait," she yelled, but he didn't hear her. The door slammed shut. She headed for the truck, ready to tell him to hop out, he was in the wrong car, only to draw up short.

The driver's door opened, and Jared stepped out. He wore a pair of soft, faded Levi's, a V-necked cotton shirt with the sleeves pushed halfway up his forearms, and a pair of Aviator sunglasses. His hair was still wet from the shower he'd taken after mowing the lawn.

No way.

She reached the side of the truck in record time. "I thought we agreed you weren't coming."

He rested his arm on the bottom of the door's open window. "I never agreed to anything. You just assumed."

"The answer is no."

He dropped his arm from the door and stepped toward her. She backed up, then realized what she was doing and stopped. He wasn't going to intimidate her. Or, at least, he wasn't going to see how much he unnerved her.

"Then you tell your nephew. For some reason, the kid wants me there."

Jenny paused, weighing the truth of his statement. All week he'd been doing everything he could to get under her skin; she was certain this was just another one of his antics. Avoiding Jared, she peeked her head into the cab of the truck. Cody was grinning from ear to ear.

"When I told Zeke we couldn't all fit in your car or on Jared's motorcycle, he said we could use his truck. Cool, huh?"

"*You* asked Zeke?" Her stomach sank.

"We needed a way for all three of us to get to the game. Jared said he'd help me warm up. And Zeke said he didn't mind."

Jenny drew in a breath. She knew when she was licked. Turning, she faced Jared again.

He stood closer than before. She tried to back away from him but ran into the hard side of the truck. "You win. But you'd better be on your best behavior."

He leaned forward, took the grocery sacks from her and placed them in the front of the pickup's bed. "I'm always at my best, Cotton Tail."

"Stop calling me that."

He grinned but didn't say anything, only motioned for her to get in. As she climbed into the old truck, it dawned on her she would be sitting on the middle of the bench seat, right next to Jared.

The next twenty minutes were pure torture. Each time Jared shifted, his hand bumped against her, touching her thigh.

"Behave," she hissed under her breath, shooting him glares from beneath her lashes.

"What?" His innocent tone didn't fool her for a second.

By the time they pulled into the Whitman ball fields, it was 2:05. Five minutes late. She hustled Cody out and grabbed the snacks while Jared got Cody's baseball bag. They rushed to Field A, only to find it empty.

Jenny looked around. "Don't tell me we're at the wrong place."

"No, this is it," Cody said as he took his bag from Jared and set it on the ground.

"But it's after two. Where is everyone?"

Crouching, Cody unzipped his bag. "The game doesn't start till three."

"Three? But your mom said two."

"Coach likes us here a half hour early."

But they weren't a half hour early. They were an hour early. Jenny gritted her teeth. It was just like her sister to give her an earlier time to make sure Jenny wasn't late. And it was just like her sister to think nothing of using up more of Jenny's day. She readjusted the sacks in her arms. "So," she said to Cody, masking her annoyance. "Looks like we have a half hour to kill."

Cody paused and shot Jared a hesitant glance. "You still want to catch some pitches? I mean, if you don't want to, it's okay."

Jenny looked at Jared, afraid he would refuse.

"Sure, kid."

Cody pulled two gloves and a baseball from his bag. "Here." He handed Jared the larger of the gloves. "This one is my dad's, but you can use it if you want."

Jared took the glove and turned it over several times in his hands. "Thanks." His voice was low as he stared at the glove. "I'll make sure to take good care of it."

Cody grinned, and the two of them headed out to the field. Jared's long, confident strides had Cody doing a half jog, half run to keep up.

Setting the snacks next to her, Jenny took a seat in the bleachers. She tried to keep her eyes off of Jared and on Cody but found it nearly impossible to do.

"Why don't we just toss a few easy ones first, to get you warmed up?"

"Yeah," Cody agreed, jogging a distance away from Jared. "That's what Coach always says."

Worn Levi's hugged Jared's long legs, and muscles flexed beneath his shirt as he tossed pitches back and forth with Cody on the green field. Cody laughed as Jared threw a miss and as her nephew ran to get the ball, she thought about their trip to the grocery store earlier today. He'd still thought they should go with pure junk food. She thought bottled water and a piece of fruit. They'd settled on Gatorade and chocolate chip granola bars.

"Looking good," Jared said. "How do you feel?"

"Great," Cody answered.

"Ready to take it up a notch?"

"Yeah."

Jared positioned himself behind home plate and smacked the inside of his glove with his bare hand. "Okay. Let's see what you got."

Cody jogged out to the pitcher's mound. He dug into the dirt, making a grove for his foot, and then with a windup move that reminded Jenny of a major league player, he nailed one right across the plate and directly into Jared's glove. It landed with a satisfying thump.

"Nice one," Jared said, standing and tossing the ball back.

Cody threw about a dozen more pitches that sailed straight down the middle. Several times after a pitch, Jared would shake his gloved hand.

"Whew. That's some heat."

"You wanna see my curve ball?" Cody hollered to Jared.

"Bring it on."

Lifting his right leg high in the air, Cody brought his arm back and let the ball fly for all it was worth. It sailed a good six feet above Jared's head.

Cody's shoulders slumped, and he kicked at the mound

of dirt. "Sorry," he said as Jared retrieved the ball. "Guess I don't have a curve ball."

"Don't give up, kid. You'll get it."

"You think so?" Cody asked.

"I know so." With an easy toss, the ball sailed back into Cody's mitt.

As Jenny watched Jared with Cody, something warm and unexpected nestled next to her heart.

Soon, Cody's team and their opponents started showing up. People began to fill the seats around Jenny. She smiled and said hi, even though she didn't know anyone. And just like when she'd had Maddy and the rest of the gang over, it felt good to be with a group of people.

As Jared jogged off the field, Jenny couldn't help but notice how several of the women eyed him. A stab of jealousy took her by surprise. What did she have to be jealous about? He wasn't hers. And she didn't want him to be. Right?

Oblivious to the stares he was receiving, Jared climbed the bleachers two at a time and joined her. He smelled like the fresh outdoors and everything she knew she shouldn't want. "That was really nice of you," she said after a slight pause, trying to even her breathing.

He used the sleeve of his T-shirt to wipe his forehead. He shrugged off her words. "It was nothing. I promised him earlier I'd help him warm up."

It wasn't nothing. It was a major something that wrapped around her bruised soul and settled right next to her heart. She swallowed and looked away, only to come eye to eye with a gorgeous brunette staring hard at Jared. Jenny found a different spot to focus on, regained her equilibrium, then looked back to the emerald green field. "Sounded like you knew what you were talking about out there. You must have played baseball."

"No."

Cody's team ran out onto the field. Nine kids in blue and white uniforms fanned out across the field as they took their various positions. Cody settled in on the pitcher's mound.

"Football?"

Even though she was still looking straight ahead, she could feel his gaze on her.

"No," he said again.

"What sports did you play?"

"None."

She turned and looked at him, while her mind remembered every painful detail he'd told her about his childhood. She knew he didn't want her pity—but would he accept her comfort? She wished she was brave enough to find out. Instead, she tried to joke her way past the emotions eating her up inside. "And here I thought all little boys couldn't wait to get their hands on a ball."

"Some of us preferred to get our hands on more important things." His gaze went directly to her cleavage.

"Behave," she reminded him under her breath while her heart did somersaults. "That was the deal, remember?"

"Your deal." His grin was as wicked as it was inviting.

She quickly steered the conversation in a different direction. "I want to apologize."

"For?"

"Getting so upset when I saw Cody helping you this morning. It's just that he seems too young to do that kind of stuff. But then I saw how happy he was helping you. Besides, I should have realized you'd make sure he was safe."

Jared pulled at the leather strings on the baseball glove he'd been using. "No, you're right. He is too young."

"Did you do that kind of stuff when you were his age?"

"Yeah."

"Like?"

He twirled the glove in his hand. "Like a hell of a lot harder things than mowing a damn lawn." He motioned to the field, ending the discussion. "They're done with warm-up. I'm gonna go grab a Coke before the game starts. What would you like?"

She wanted to ask him more, but one look at the hard set to his jaw, and she knew he wouldn't answer. "A Diet Coke would be great."

Even behind his dark glasses, she could feel the heat of his gaze. "Diet is the last thing you need. You're getting a regular one."

She watched his broad shoulders disappear into the throng of people standing in front of the concession stand. From all outward appearances, Jared appeared to have everything. But more and more, Jenny kept glimpsing a different side of him. A boy who grew up without a home. A teenager who did jobs more suited for an adult than a kid. A man alone who seemed to isolate himself from almost everyone and everything. Even as she tried to stop it, her heart reached out to him. He was making her life a living hell, but it didn't seem to matter. No matter how hard she tried, she couldn't stop herself from wanting to fill the emptiness she glimpsed in him.

Jared returned with their drinks, and for the next two hours Jenny forgot her worries as she watched the kids play their hearts out. Cody pitched through five innings and reached base safely three out of his four trips up to bat. In the end, his team won by a score of eleven to three.

"Great game," she said as they made their way back to the truck after handing out snacks. Jenny didn't hear a complaint from the parents about her food choice, so she took that to be a good sign. "You looked like a real pro out there."

"Thanks," Cody said, quickly turning to Jared. "Didja see that double play Parker made in the second inning?"

"Just like a major leaguer."

"Yeah." Cody twisted off the top of his Gatorade and took a long swallow. "We creamed 'em." He took another drink. "Thanks for the warm-up. It really helped."

"Glad I could do it. Thanks for inviting me. I had a fun time." There was nothing but truth in Jared's voice.

When they reached the truck, Cody put his bag in the bed of the truck and hopped in the passenger side, leaving Jenny stuck in the middle again.

Seeing her hesitation, Jared just grinned.

"Behave," she warned him for the third time, unable to

forget the look of joy on Cody's face when he talked to Jared.

"Always."

"Never." She climbed in. Jared slid in next to her and started up the truck. "How about we celebrate with some pizza?" she said.

"As long as you aren't cooking," they said in unison.

She bit back a smile. "And here I was even going to suggest we go out for ice cream, too." Then she laughed, because she knew they'd end up having both.

It was nearly dark by the time they arrived back home. As they pulled into the driveway, Jenny saw her mom emerge from her beige Mercedes.

"It's Grandma," Cody said.

"Yes, it is," Jenny said, trying to keep the worry out of her voice. She wondered what had brought her mom over so late.

"Hi, Mom," she said as they piled out of the truck. "Is everything okay?"

"Fine. Except I've been trying to reach you for over an hour."

"Sorry. I left the house without my cell. You're sure everything is fine?"

"Yes, sweetheart. I'm just here to pick up Cody. Anna has to work later than planned, and she'd like me to take Cody home so he can get to bed at a decent time for school tomorrow."

"Oh." Jenny let out a relieved breath. Ever since losing Steven, she tended to assume the worst. Whether it was a middle-of-the-night call, the sound of a siren, or someone—even her mother—showing up at odd hours. "I'm sorry we're home later than expected. We went out for pizza and ice cream to celebrate Cody's big win."

Catherine walked over and gave Cody a hug. "Congratulations. I'm sorry I couldn't be there."

"That's okay, Grandma. Mom told me you're working on some party."

Jenny's mom smiled. "That's right. But the *party* is

almost here, and then I won't be so busy. You and I will have to plan some fun stuff for the summer. But it's getting late, and we really should get on the road."

Cody nodded and turned to Jared. "Thanks again for all your help."

Jared tugged on the bill of Cody's cap. "Anytime, slugger.

"Just give us a sec," Jenny said, steering Cody to the house. "We'll have his things rounded up in no time."

Jared knew Jenny's second could be anywhere from ten minutes to an hour. Right now all he wanted was a beer and to be alone. But he could tell Jenny's mother had something on her mind. He leaned his back against the front fender and braced his boot on the inner rim of the tire.

"You went to Cody's game?" she asked.

"He invited me." Jared knew he shouldn't have gone. But hearing so much raw desperation in Cody's voice brought back too many childhood memories. There had been no way he could say no.

The porch light came on, but the single sixty-watt bulb didn't extend to the driveway. Even so, in the waning evening light he could see the resemblance between mother and daughter. During their first meeting in the restaurant, Jared had barely given Jenny's mom a second glance. As he waited for her to tell him what was on her mind, he noted she was still a striking woman for her age. But where Jenny was soft and too bighearted for her own good, her mother seemed tougher and less forgiving.

"May I be direct?"

"By all means." He shifted his weight, planted his other boot on the tire.

"Something tells me I can ask, but you may not answer."

Jared remained silent.

Catherine let out a sigh. "Jenny means the world to us, Mr. Worth. Or should I say Commander Worth. Paul told us you are a pilot in the military."

He wasn't a commander anymore. "Jared, please."

"Jared." Catherine gave a slight nod of her head. "We don't want to see Jenny hurt. She's suffered enough already."

"I have no intention of causing your daughter any harm, Mrs. Beckinsale. Jenny and I have a business relationship. That's all." That kiss sure as hell hadn't been about business.

"I guess I'll have to take your word on that."

"You have it."

Catherine Beckinsale's face seemed to relax ever so slightly. "Thank you," she said before opening the driver's side door of her car and reaching inside. She handed an envelope to Jared. "As Jenny's business partner, please accept this invitation to come to the museum's charity event. It's formal—black tie— so I'll understand if—"

"Will Jenny be there?"

"Yes." Catherine paused. "Her father and I plan to pick her up."

Jared pushed away from the truck. "Don't bother. I'll bring her."

Catherine would have said more, but just then Cody and Jenny came out of the house carrying his backpack and small suitcase.

"All ready," Cody said. "Bye, Aunt Jen. Bye, Jared."

"Bye, kiddo," Jared said. "Don't forget this." He grabbed the baseball bag out of the back of the pickup, waited for Catherine to pop her trunk, then placed the bag, backpack, and suitcase inside.

Cody opened the passenger door, then looked at Jared over the hood of the car. "Maybe . . . if you're not busy, you'd like to come to my game Thursday."

"I'll do my best," he hedged.

"Sweet." Cody slid into the car and shut the door.

Catherine gave Jenny a hug then turned and stared at Jared for several moments. He easily read the warning in her gaze.

"I'm bushed," Jenny said as her mom drove off. "Good night." She didn't wait for a response before hurrying into the house.

Jared watched her leave. He wanted to follow her inside. And not for the same reason he'd been staying close to her all week. This wasn't about the business or about getting his money back. There was only one reason he wanted to follow her: to be near her, to see her smile, to hear her laugh.

More lights went on inside the house. A warm glow spilled outward from the mullioned windows. Upstairs, the light in Jenny's bedroom came on.

Keep your eye on the prize, he reminded himself, thinking of Mexico.

But what if he was after the wrong thing?

Swearing, he turned and went into the hangar. Thoughts like that could get him into a hell of a lot of trouble. He grabbed a beer from the fridge and a heavy flannel coat off the workbench. As he left the hangar, he made his way to the beach. He dragged one of the camp chairs over to the cold fire pit. Slouching in the seat, he propped his boots on the charred rocks surrounding the pit, crossed his feet at the ankles, and twisted the cap off the Bud.

Stars packed the inky sky, and an owl hooted behind him. As he took a long drink, he listened to the waves sloshing against the dock and the rustling of critters in the underbrush. On the far side of the lake, house lights flickered through the trees. He kept his gaze straight ahead, refusing to look at the house behind him. The house that glowed like a damn Christmas card, making him feel welcome when he knew he was not.

My nana always told me this lake was magical. This water could heal almost anything.

Has it healed you?

Almost.

He might want Jenny with a passion that burned through him, but he knew he wasn't what she wanted. Today as he'd tossed the ball back and forth with Cody and sat in the stands with Jenny, he let himself fall into a fantasy. One where he was more than just a stranger passing through. Where he was a part of something, part of a family. A part of Jenny's life. He let himself wonder what it would be like to have her waiting for him when he came down from the sky. But he wouldn't be coming down from the sky. Ever again. Jenny and his days as a top gun were as out of reach as the stars overhead.

He took another drink. Silhouetted in the moonlight, the seaplane rocked gently at the end of the dock. He waited to feel the same disgust he did every time he looked at the bulky, cumbersome plane, but tonight, looking at the plane bobbing in the water, he couldn't make himself forget what it had meant to fly. He tried to push the memories away but found it impossible. With the wide-open sky overhead, he could almost hear the roar of the jet engines, smell the jet fuel. There had been a time when he'd been up in that endless sky going eight hundred miles an hour. He'd thought he could walk away, find a bit of peace on an isolated stretch of beach in Mexico. Now he wasn't sure.

In one gulp, he drained almost half his beer and pulled the invitation out of the front pocket of his jacket. The heavy card stock was intricately engraved. He glanced at the date. Two weeks from today the event would take place. His thumb rubbed over the embossed words, and he wondered what had prompted him to say he would go. But he knew. Just like he knew that he needed to get out of here, as far away from Jenny as possible, and from everything that reminded him of what he could never have.

I have no intention of causing your daughter any harm, Mrs. Beckinsale. Jenny and I have a business relationship. That's all.

He'd meant what he'd said. Hurting Jenny was the last thing he intended. If he could just walk away, he would. But if he left, he'd leave with nothing, and, more importantly, Jenny and this damn business she was trying so hard to keep afloat would still go under. He'd heard the calls she'd been making all week. He also knew nothing would ever come of them. Twice now, he'd seen how much her family worried about her. It was obvious they would do anything for her—even bail her out. Just like Steven had said.

Jared looked at the invitation again. Maybe this event was just the ticket. Maybe, with her family's help, she would finally accept the truth: there was no way she could save this business. The sooner she accepted that, the better off they'd both be. Then he could leave, get out of her life, and get her out of his mind.

He pulled out his cell phone and dialed a number he thought he'd never call again.

"Hello?" The voice was raspy from sleep.

"Hart? Wake up."

He could hear a female voice in the background: "Sugar, come back over here. I've got something special I want to give you."

"Worth, is that you?" Kenny Hart asked, apparently ignoring his female companion. "Christ, man. I've been trying to reach you for weeks. Hang on."

There was a rustling noise like Kenny had gotten out of bed and was pulling on some clothes. The woman whined some more as Kenny let her know she was free to leave.

Jared could only imagine the woman's frustration. Lieutenant Commander Kenny Hart was a top-notch pilot and certified ladies' man. For as long as Jared had known him, women had lapped up his good looks and open smile.

"Okay, Ghost. Talk."

"Hope I didn't take you away from someone important."

"They're all important," Hart said with a chuckle.

"Does she have a name?"

"Same as all the others. Baby. Only with you gone, I get the pick of the litter." Kenny paused. "Listen, Worth. I've been trying to get ahold of you for weeks. Hell, the whole squadron has. The CO's been looking for you. He wants to see you ASAP."

"I've got nothing left to say. The CO saw my ass for the last time when I resigned my commission. Now drop it," Jared said with a finality that left no room for further comment. "That's not why I called. I need a favor."

There was a long pause. "Shit, man. I've never heard you ask for anything. Name it, and it's yours."

SEVENTEEN

⌬

It was only Wednesday, and already Anna felt as if she'd put in an eighty-hour week.

"Dr. Adams," a resident called out to her, "you're needed immediately in the ER. Probable head injury. Mom is at twenty-seven weeks and unresponsive. Fetus may be in distress."

"Tell them to get an electronic fetal monitor on her stat. I'm heading down right now."

She rushed to the elevator and hit the down button. As she waited impatiently, her beeper went off. She glanced at the number. *Cody's school.*

In the ER, she took the chart from the triage nurse and studied it. "Get me an update on her vitals and the readout from the fetal monitor."

"Right away, Dr. Adams."

Anna picked up the phone and dialed Cody's school. Worry spread through her. His school had never found it necessary to beep her before.

The secretary put her through to the principal.

While she was on hold, Anna turned, the phone held to

her ear as the attending trauma physician handed her the updated information she'd requested.

"Thank you." She scanned the readout. "Keep monitoring the mother, and I'll be there momentarily."

The principal came on the phone. "Hello, Dr. Adams. This is Mr. Strickner. I'm calling regarding Cody."

A flutter of panic hit her. "Is he okay? Did he get hurt?"

"He's fine. Physically. I'm sorry to have to call you at work, but we've been trying to reach you at home, and our messages and notes have gone unanswered."

"I wasn't aware you were trying to get in touch with me."

"I thought that might be the case."

A door slammed down the hall, and the hushed sound of crying could be heard. Anna's shoulders stiffened. There could be only one reason she hadn't received the calls or letters. Cody had been hiding them from her. Her panic turned to anger.

"I've been approached by several of Cody's teachers," the principal continued. "They are concerned. There's been a distinct change in Cody's performance and attitude over the last few months. I was hoping you could shed some light on the situation." The principal paused, then continued. "Is there anything at home we should be aware of?"

A nurse rushed by Anna as the paging system went off. She looked down at the chart in her hand and felt her agitation grow. "No. Everything is fine."

"As you know, the school year is almost over. At this point, Cody is missing nearly half of his assignments in three classes. I've spoken with his teachers, and we are all in agreement that if he can complete the list of missing schoolwork that was sent home with him today, he will get credit and pass those classes. If not . . ." The principal let his voice trail off.

"Rest assured, Cody will have the assignments completed and turned in well before the end of the school year." Anna saw the ER resident hurrying toward her. "Thank you for the call. I'll make sure to take care of this."

She hung up the phone and rushed to ER Room Number Five.

Six hours later, Anna arrived home feeling every bit as frustrated and angry as she had earlier. "Cody," she called out the minute she entered the house.

Marie wiped her hands on her apron. "He's in his room."

"Thank you, Marie. I'm sorry it's so late."

"It's no problem." Marie untied her apron, folded it, and placed it in a kitchen drawer. "Your dinner is in the oven," she said. "Cody hasn't eaten. He said he wasn't hungry." Her face creased with concern.

"Thank you," Anna said again. "I'm sure he was just waiting until I got home." She wondered if Marie saw through the lie.

After Marie left, Anna made her way up the stairs. She didn't bother knocking on Cody's door. As usual, he was lying on his bed, tennis shoes and all, a sketch book in his hands and a bad attitude in his expression.

She came directly to the point. "I received a call from your principal today."

"Prickner."

"What did you say?"

"Mr. Strickner."

"This isn't a joking matter, Cody. You are on the verge of failing several of your classes." Anna didn't sugarcoat the seriousness of the situation, but Cody continued to look unconcerned. "Get me the list of missing assignments. I know you were sent home with it." When he didn't move, the irritation she'd felt since receiving the call boiled over. "*Now.* And consider yourself on restriction until this is resolved. No iPod. No TV. And no baseball."

That got his attention. "You are so unfair."

"I heard everything I needed to." She held out her hand for his iPod. She waited until he finally withdrew it from his pocket and tossed it on the end of the bed.

"You don't even want to hear my side of the story."

"Believe me, I heard your side. Actions speak louder than

words." She picked up the iPod. "Also, you'll be staying home this weekend. While I was supposed to be doing my job, I was on the phone hiring you a tutor. Ms. Thorton will be here each afternoon after school and on the weekends until all of your assignments are in."

She opened the door and stood with her hand on the knob. "Also, I know about the phone messages you erased and the notes from your teachers you never gave me."

"Yeah? So what? You're not home long enough to call anyone. Not even Dad."

"Cody."

"Forget it."

"Come downstairs and let's have dinner. We can talk—"

"I'm not hungry."

Anna stared at her son, at a loss as to what to do. "Fine," she said quietly. "Suit yourself." She shut the door and went downstairs to eat another meal alone. As she picked at the shrimp pasta Marie had made, she once more felt a stab of resentment toward her husband. How could Phillip have left her to deal with all of this?

* * *

Cody waited until his mom went downstairs, then he sneaked into her room. Carefully picking up the phone, he made sure she wasn't on the downstairs line. As quietly as he could, he dialed his aunt's number. Jared answered on the third ring.

"Hi, Cody. I'll get your aunt."

"N-no. I called to talk to you."

"Me?"

"Yeah." Cody sat down on the edge of his mom's bed. He could hear the TV in the background. "Don't bother coming to my game tomorrow."

"Canceled?"

Cody kicked at the leg of his mom's nightstand. "No. I can't play 'cuz Mom is a hard-ass, and school sucks."

"That bad?"

Cody squeezed his eyes shut and tried not to cry like a big baby. At least Jared didn't tell him not to say *ass*. "Yeah. Just because of some stupid assignments."

"Sorry, kid."

"Hey, Jared?"

"Yeah?"

"Have you ever screwed up so badly everyone was mad at you?"

"Too many times to count."

Cody stared at the silver-framed picture of his mom and dad on their wedding day. "I wish my dad was here."

"I wish he was there, too."

"If my dad was here," Cody started, feeling a lump form in his throat, "I wonder what he'd say . . ."

Jared didn't say anything for a moment. "I wish I knew."

"Did your dad ever leave you?"

"Your dad hasn't left you, Cody."

A tear ran down Cody's cheek. "That's what my mom says, but he's been gone a long time. Maybe he's not coming back." Cody wiped his face. "Tell Aunt Jenny for me, okay?" The tears were coming harder, and he had to get off the phone. "And tell her I won't be there this weekend either. I'm stuck here with a tutor."

"Hang in there, slugger."

Cody could only nod.

* * *

Jared hung up the phone. He flexed his hand, not realizing how hard he'd been gripping the receiver.

If he'd known the reason for Cody's call, he would have ignored Jenny's call from upstairs for him to pick up and let the answering machine get it.

If my dad was here, I wonder what he'd say.

Jared leaned back in the chair. God damn it. Why did the kid have to call him? Couldn't he see that Jared wasn't qualified to give advice, especially to a thirteen-year-old boy who needed his father?

"Was that Anna?" Jenny said, coming into the family

room. Lately, she'd taken to bundling herself from head to toe in her pink robe with only the bottom cuffs of her pj's peeking out from the hem. Wet hair hung down her back and over her shoulders. A few strands were beginning to dry and curl around her face. It didn't matter what she wore. Just being around her was enough to drive him crazy.

"No. It was Cody."

"Cody? What did he want?"

Jared forced himself to stop trying to find her breasts buried under the thick robe. "To tell us he can't play in his game tomorrow, and he won't be able to come this weekend." The telephone call should have made him feel relieved. The kid would be out of his hair.

Jenny walked into the kitchen and put the teakettle on. "How come?"

Jared wanted to blow off her question, tell her he didn't want to be dragged into her family drama. "Because he's missing some schoolwork, so your sister has him on lockdown."

"I doubt it's as bad as that."

Jared ran a hand through his hair. "Not according to Cody."

"He's been a bit of a handful lately. I'm sure Anna is doing the right thing."

Jared stood and walked to the fireplace. He picked up the poker and jabbed at the cold ashes. "It's only a couple of assignments. Cody seems like a good kid."

"Don't you think I know that?"

Jared turned from the fireplace and faced her. He knew it was none of his business, and he should keep quiet, but he couldn't. "It sounds like your sister is making a mountain out of a molehill."

"Believe me, Anna has never taken a wrong step in her life, especially where Cody is concerned. I'm sure she's doing the right thing. Besides, neither of us is a parent. What do we know?"

Jared stabbed once more at the half-burned log. "You're right." She smelled like fresh powder and tropical flowers.

He grew hard and felt his gut tightening. He wanted to lay her out on the couch and strip off that damn robe and lick her from the bottom of her feet all the way up to that soft spot on the side of her neck, making sure to pause in all the right places. She was driving him insane, and she didn't even know it. It was supposed to be the other way around. He was supposed to be making her burn up and melt inside. "You're right," he said again. "I don't know a damn thing about being a parent. But I know something about businesses. And all those calls you're making are a waste of time. Tell me, have you ever got past a secretary?"

The teakettle whistled, but she didn't make a move to turn off the burner. Instead, she stared at him through baby blues, wide with confused anger. "Why are you turning mean?"

She didn't know what mean was. He'd been waiting around for what seemed like forever for her to cave and go running to Mom and Dad. But she hadn't. She wasn't. Instead, she was working her ass off to save this business. If he'd been anyone else, he'd be damned impressed. But the more time he was around her, the less he thought about Mexico.

Anger at her—anger at himself—turned his tone icy cold. "Business is about the bottom line. Period. I've been through the office. I saw the files you worked up. If you're the businesswoman you say you are, you'll figure it out."

EIGHTEEN

⌇

Two days before the charity event, Jared stood outside the house and looked around. Ever since Cody's call, he'd done nothing but keep busy. He'd hung the new door at the side entrance of the hangar and trimmed it out; he'd power-washed the roof and cedar shake siding, repainted all the white trim, cleaned and restained the porch, fixed the leaky faucet in the kitchen, and about a dozen other projects. He'd organized and reorganized the inside of the hangar so many times it looked like a damn showroom. But no matter how many chores he gave himself, he couldn't keep his mind occupied and off of the hurt he'd seen in Jenny's eyes.

If you're the businesswoman you say you are, you'll figure it out.

After jerking on a pair of leather gloves, he hefted three brand-new two by six boards from the stack on the far side of the hangar, propped them on his shoulder, and made his way to the dock. The smell of freshly milled lumber filled the air as he balanced the boards with his right hand. Reaching the dock, he set the boards on the sandy ground. After power-washing the dock yesterday, he'd noticed a few boards that needed to be replaced. When he'd asked Zeke to borrow his truck for a run to the lumberyard, the old man had smiled and shook his head even as he'd handed over the keys.

"Son, those boards are just fine."

Maybe they were. But Jared needed a project, and this was as good as any. He'd not only bought the wood and screws but two five-gallon drums of water-resistant, environmentally safe stain. Resealing would be his next project.

The rain had finally stopped, and the sun was out. His T-shirt hung from his back pocket, and a tool belt rode low on his Levi's. He grabbed a pry bar and got to work.

Earlier, he'd dragged the radio out of the hangar, found a classic rock station, and cranked the volume as high as it would go. As AC/DC sang about the "Highway to Hell," sun beat down on his back, and his biceps bulged as he worked the boards loose. With all the work he'd been doing outside, his tan had deepened to a rich golden brown.

The first couple of boards popped off easily, but the others proved to be a bitch. Banging on the end of the pry bar with a hammer, he forced the bar under a board and strained until he heard it squeak free from the timber supports.

"This is a step up. From top gun to no fun."

Jared paused, the pry bar in his hand. "You never could follow directions worth shit."

Kenny Hart stood at the end of the dock, looking like he'd just stepped off the beaches of Malibu. Not for the first time did Jared wonder what the hell women saw in him. He was a pain-in-the-ass pretty boy who'd been crowding Jared's wings ever since he'd joined the squadron two years ago. Hart looked like he was modeling for a damn magazine in designer jeans, a foil-print T-shirt, and some high-tech shoes Jared would rather go barefoot than wear.

Jared looked around Hart to the parking lot. A glossy black Porsche glistened under the sun. "Your girlfriend lend you her car?" It was a sissy-ass car, and they both knew it.

"All the rental place had. Jealous?"

"Yeah. That's it."

Kenny turned the volume down on the radio. Jared considered it sacrilegious to mess with the Boss, especially when he was belting out "Born to Run," but obviously Kenny had no such compunction.

"What the hell are you doing here?"

"Would you believe I grew up around here?"

"No."

Kenny just shrugged, and Jared got the feeling Malibu Ken hadn't been lying.

"I came to offer my services."

Jared braced a foot against the dock and pulled back on the bar. "Services for what?" He grunted as the board began to work free.

"Best man, of course. I figure there was only one reason you'd need a tux. And I am the better man."

The board came loose. Jared crouched back, setting the pry bar down. He reached for his T-shirt and wiped the sweat off his forehead. "The day you outfly me, Hart, will be the day I'm six feet under."

"I am outflying you. You bailed, remember?"

"Shut the fuck up and hand me that board."

Kenny glanced at the stack of new wood. "Sorry. Might get a splinter, and then how would I stop the proud papa from holding a shotgun to your head during the ceremony?"

Jared shoved the shirt back in his right rear pocket. "There's no wedding."

Kenny took off his Oakley sunglasses. "Then why the need for a tux?"

"Who are you? The goddamn *National Enquirer*?"

"They'd probably pay me a pretty penny for the scoop on why the navy's top gun walked away at the height of his career."

Jared walked down the dock and straight past Hart. He

didn't stop until he was in the hangar and in front of the fridge. He opened it and pulled out a cold one. He twisted off the cap, took a drink, and shut the door with his foot.

Kenny didn't wait for an offer. He opened the fridge and grabbed his own bottle. "So, what do you think? Do I have a story for them or what?"

"Go to hell."

"Seems like you're already there." Hart twisted his own lid off and took a drink.

"Thought sissies like you needed a glass."

"No. But I'll take an answer."

Jared leaned his butt against the workbench. He was spoiling for a fight, and Hart wasn't biting. Seeing Kenny standing in front of him was like seeing everything he'd lost paraded before him. "You know the answer."

"You were given a raw deal, I'll give you that—"

"Raw deal? It was political, and I was left out to dry."

Kenny shoved a hand in his back pocket. "The CO's been busting balls to make this right. Talk to him."

"I said everything I needed to during the inquiry."

"Why didn't you let the squadron argue on your behalf? Every one of us wanted to be there."

"I fight my own battles."

"Maybe it's time you stopped being such a damn one-man show and remember that you're part of a team."

Jared laughed. "I hear Dear Abby is looking for an assistant. You'd be perfect."

"Looks like you need the job more than me. I'm still flying."

Jared pushed away from the bench and stood tall. "Give me the damn tux, and get the hell out of here."

"On one condition. You talk to the CO."

Jared didn't bother answering. He walked to the Porsche and opened the door. He scanned the interior, and when he didn't see what he was looking for, he popped the trunk. Ignoring the suitcase, he grabbed the garment bag and slammed the trunk shut. "Thanks. Now leave."

Kenny leaned against the side of the sports car. "Whose place is this, anyway?"

"None of your damn business."

"Humor me."

Jared glared at him. "No one you know." Steven had left the squadron before Hart had joined.

A grin spread across Kenny's face as he looked past Jared's shoulder. "I think I'm about to find out."

Jared turned and saw Jenny coming down the porch steps. He let out a low curse. Dressed in a white skirt and a pink T-shirt, she walked toward them like a queen. Her head was high, her shoulders back, and her hot pink toenails flashed in the sun as her flip-flops made a smacking noise against the bottom of her feet. Jared had seen a lot of women wear a hell of a lot less, but that didn't stop him from wanting to throw a blanket over Jenny and cover her from head to toe. Where was that damn robe of hers when he needed it?

Then he looked to Kenny, and Jared saw exactly where his gaze had gone. Jared saw red, and instead of wanting to cover Jenny, he wanted to punch Kenny square in the face.

Completely ignoring Jared, she smiled brightly at Kenny. "Hello."

"Hell*ooo*, gorgeous."

She laughed, and the sound tore at Jared's gut. Since the night of Cody's call she hadn't said one word to him. Not one. She'd even stopped yelling. It was better this way, he kept telling himself. Easier. When he left, she would feel only relief. But that didn't stop him from wanting her to smile at him just one more time. Once more, so the image of her hurt-filled eyes would leave him.

"I'm Jenny. Jenny Beckinsale." She held out her hand, and Kenny took hold like it was a life ring and he was a sinking man.

"Kenny Hart."

"Are you here for a charter? I don't have you on the

schedule." Her smile lit up the day, and she used her free hand to tuck her unbound hair behind her ears.

"A charter?"

The bastard still hadn't let go of her hand.

Jared shot him a look that Hart ignored. Jared took a step forward, and Kenny finally got the message. He dropped her hand.

She motioned to the plane at the end of the dock.

Kenny shot his gaze to Jared. "You have freakin' got to be kidding me."

"I take it that means no." Jenny's voice floated over to Jared like a soft breeze. He didn't care that she was talking to pretty boy. Hearing her voice was enough.

"Let's not be too hasty." Kenny put his arm around her shoulder. "Just exactly what are you chartering?"

She laughed again.

"Back off, Hart." Jared's voice was low and dead serious.

"I don't think so."

"Back off or get it torn off."

Surprise flickered briefly through Kenny's gaze before he dropped his arm from around Jenny. "I don't believe it."

"Don't believe what?" Jenny asked.

Kenny stared at Jared for a long time, then a slow, knowing smile curved his mouth. "Nothing, honey. I'll explain it another time."

Jared moved between them. "There won't be a next time."

Kenny gave Jenny a conspiratorial wink. "He's in a foul mood."

"Does he have any other?"

Kenny tipped his head back and let out a loud laugh. "Honey, you and I are going to get along just fine."

Twice that bastard had called her honey. Jared waited for her to give Hart what for, for her to tell him to stop calling her that, but his Jenny just smiled up at pretty boy and flipped her hair. *Flipped her hair.*

"I was just about to have some iced tea," she said to

Kenny in a voice so sweet Jared wondered where that had come from. She'd never spoken that way to him. "Would you care to join me?"

Kenny shoved his half-empty beer at Jared. "I'd like nothing better."

* * *

For over two hours they sat on the front porch, drinking tea and talking and laughing like long-lost friends. Jared tried to concentrate on what he was doing. But the third time the pry bar slipped out of his grip and he smacked his fingers into the board below, he gave up.

He glared at Kenny. What did that son of a bitch think he was up to? Iced tea, my ass. Hart was a hard-core party animal if there ever was one. And if he didn't stop smiling at Jenny like he wanted to take her straight up to her room and do every dirty thing Jared had fantasized doing to her, he was going to make good on his silent threat and punch the bastard right between the eyes.

Jared flexed his hand, warming to the thought.

He moved closer to the porch on the pretext of staking up some of her flowers. He didn't give a crap if the flowers fell over, but at least he was close enough to hear what they were saying. Or so he thought. While their laughter was loud, their voices were hushed. All he heard was bits and pieces of their conversation.

". . . tux . . ."

". . . Tomorrow night . . ."

"   you don't say . . ."

You don't say what?

Jared was being driven insane. And each time he looked at them cozied up on the porch, seated in rockers, he couldn't help but think how perfect they looked together. He clenched his teeth so hard, the back of his jaw felt like it was going to snap in two. And that was before Kenny shot him a big, Cheshire cat grin.

He really was going to have to punch the bastard.

Finally, Kenny rose and prepared to leave. But not before he engulfed Jenny in a hug that lasted way too long and had his hands riding on the top of her tight derrière.

The stake in Jared's hand snapped in two.

Jenny told Kenny good-bye then headed back inside the house.

Jared stopped Hart at his car. "Keep your hands off her."

"Possessive, aren't we?"

Yes. No. "She's not one of your bimbos, Hart. I meant what I said. Come near her again, and I'll lay you out flat."

"That's going to be hard to do."

"All it will take is one punch."

Kenny laughed. "Don't flatter yourself."

"Try me."

"As much as I'd like to, I'd hate to mess up my hands before tomorrow night."

Jared felt his scalp tighten. "You're not going." He knew Hart was referring to the charity ball.

"Sorry, Worth. Can't disappoint the lady."

"Stay away from her."

"She's already promised me a dance."

Jared's hand clenched into a fist. He knew his reaction was unreasonable, but knowing it didn't change how he felt.

Kenny grinned as he opened the car door. "If I didn't know better, I'd think you had turned into a one-woman guy."

NINETEEN

Jenny spent all of the next afternoon preparing for the fund-raiser. She showered, washed her hair, shaved her legs, and spent an exorbitant amount of time on her makeup and even longer on her hair. She lost count of the number of hairstyles she tried. Finally, she settled on a simple upswept style even her mother would approve of. The one thing she didn't have to worry about was her dress. As always, her mother had come through.

White and strapless, the designer evening gown clung to her every curve. The sweetheart neckline enhanced her cleavage, so much so that as Jenny stared at herself in the full-length mirror, she had a moment of trepidation. And that was before she saw how much the long, single slit in the back revealed. The shoes her mother chose were also perfection: white, with a touch of sparkle.

There was no denying the fact that she was nervous. Last year, she had attended the event on Steven's arm. This year, she was alone. Or almost alone.

She could hear Jared now, in the bathroom, getting ready. When her mother had told Jenny she'd invited him, Jenny had silently fumed. Of course her mother would invite him. Why not? She didn't know the havoc he was wreaking on Jenny's life, because Jenny had never told her. As far as her mother was concerned, Jared was a business partner, and that was it.

Jenny only wished that were true. Even as angry as he made her, she still found herself drawn to him more than she cared to admit.

Later, as she made her way down the stairs and with her mind still on Jared, she nearly missed the last two steps and would have fallen if Jared hadn't reached out and grabbed her. His arms encircled her waist, and she felt the heat from his palms seep through her, warming her in places that had long grown cold.

"Sorry." It was the first word she'd spoken to him in over a week. "It's just—" It's just that the sight of him in a tuxedo sucked all the air from her lungs and made her forget about something as insignificant as walking down the stairs. Jared in Levi's and a T-shirt was dangerous; Jared in a tux was deadly.

"Just what?"

She backed out of his arms, and he seemed reluctant to drop his hands from her waist. "I didn't see you."

He smiled like he knew she was lying. Then he took a small step back and ran his gaze from her upswept hair down to her high-heeled shoes. Slowly. As if he had all the time in the world. His gaze paused on her cleavage, and desire flared in his dark blue eyes. "I see you," he said simply.

"My parents will be here soon to pick me up. I think I'll wait out on the porch." Anywhere but right next to him, where the air all but sizzled between them.

"Your parents aren't coming. I told them I'd drive you."

Panic hit her. Being in the same room with him was one thing. Being in the same car, another. She couldn't stop herself from remembering their ride in Zeke's pickup. "I think we should take separate vehicles."

"Not a chance."

She made a sweeping gesture down the length of her dress. "Forget it. I'm not riding on your bike."

"I'm not expecting you to."

"Then I don't see—"

"Truce."

His voice was soft and low, and when she tipped her head up and looked in his eyes, it was like drowning in the bluest of waters. Or flying high in the bluest of skies. "What?"

"A truce. Just for tonight, if that's all you want."

"Why?"

"Because I know tonight means a lot to your family, and I don't want our . . . differences to ruin that for you. For any of you."

She dropped her gaze until it landed on the black studs on his white shirt. In that instant she realized she wanted it, too. Desperately. A night where they weren't at odds. She was nervous enough about her first big outing in almost a year. Raising her gaze back up to his, she smiled. "I'd like that very much."

He closed the distance between them, wrapped his arms around her waist, then slipped them up her side until they were cupping the bottom of her breasts. Before she could utter a sound, he pulled her up onto her toes and next to his chest, then his mouth came down on hers. Not soft or slow, but hard and hot. The kiss was as brief as it was intense, and if Jared hadn't been holding her, Jenny was sure she would have collapsed in a white puddle right there at the bottom of his feet.

"A kiss to seal the deal."

She fought to regain her breath. "I thought you sealed a deal with a handshake."

"Not us, Cotton Tail."

Her legs still wobbly, they walked out to the Corvette. Jenny was surprised when Jared didn't head straight to the driver's door. "No, please." She handed him the keys. "You drive." She lifted her dress and showed off her stilettos. "Have you ever tried driving in these?"

"Lots of times."

This Jared she didn't know. The Jared who charmed and smiled and kissed her like she was the only thing in this whole world he wanted.

As they drove through Hidden Lake, Jenny pointed out landmarks. The really important ones, she jokingly told Jared. Like where she'd taken her first ballet lesson and driver's ed class. Her favorite pizza place and the tiny movie theater that only ran vintage films. She knew she was rambling to fill the silence, to cover her awkwardness. But the weird thing was, the more she talked, the less awkward she felt. And Jared was the reason why. Instead of just nodding and pretending to listen to her silly stories, he was completely absorbed in everything she had to say. It was as if he wanted to know every single detail about her. And he didn't just listen. He asked all kinds of questions. About everything. His curiosity about her was endless.

"Okay," Jenny said with a soft laugh as they neared Seattle. "Now it's my turn."

He glanced over at her, his face illuminated by the dashboard lights. "My life has been dull compared to yours."

She laughed again. "I don't believe that for a minute."

With a little prodding, he told her about all the places he'd traveled and the things he'd seen. She was mesmerized by him, captivated by his voice and the stories he wove around her.

They talked about nothing and everything, and when the Space Needle came into view, Jenny felt a stab of disappointment. Instead of attending the fund-raiser, she wanted to stay right where she was, continuing to talk to Jared.

Parking was crowded, but Jared found a spot close by. As they got out of the car, a slight breeze blew the bottom of his jacket open, and she caught herself staring at him. In the weeks he'd been here, his hair had grown, and she found herself wanting to reach out and run her hands through the back of his head, where it brushed against his collar.

Jared had her through the doors and into the thick of the party before she realized it. Waiters, dressed in black pants and formal white jackets, moved effortlessly through the crowd, balancing silver trays on their hands. Jared snagged two glasses of champagne and handed one to her. He clinked his glass against hers. "To a perfect night."

She smiled and took a sip, knowing that even if the evening ended right now it had already been perfect.

On a dais at the far end of the museum, a dozen or so members of the Seattle Symphony provided the music for the night. Even in this large a room and with this many people, she could still hear the beautiful strains of their music.

"Jenny." Wearing a sapphire gown that perfectly matched her teardrop earrings, her mother was ravishing. She gave Jenny a hug and a kiss on her cheek. "You look lovely," she said before turning to Jared. "I'm so glad you could make it. Now come, mingle."

She steered them toward the crowd. For over an hour, Jenny met new friends and reacquainted herself with old ones. As they talked, she found herself relaxing and re-connecting. Jared was the perfect companion. Once, when she was talking with some very old and very dear friends, he'd tried to move away, to give them some privacy. She'd caught his hand, and when he looked at her, all she said was, "Stay. Please." And he did. She couldn't explain it. All she knew was that she found a strength in his near-ness, a comfort from his arm when it settled gently around her waist. She'd been so worried about tonight; worried about coming face-to-face with people she'd pushed away after Steven's death. But now she saw how wrong she'd been.

"Jenny." She turned at the sound of her brother's voice.

"My, don't you look dapper." It was the same thing she said each time she saw him in a tux. And each time, he smiled and crushed her in a bear hug.

"And you clean up pretty well yourself, Jelly Belly."

He gave her a peck on the cheek. "Worth." Paul stuck out his hand, and the two men shook. "Enjoying the party?"

Jared's gaze went right to Jenny and stayed there. "Immensely."

An awkward silence fell as the two men sized each other up. Trying to smooth over the moment, Jenny hastily asked, "Have you seen Anna?"

Reluctantly, Paul returned his attention to her. "I don't think she's arrived yet. How about a dance, little sister?"

"Only if you promise not to step on my feet."

He laughed as he took her arm and tried to guide her onto the dance floor, but Jared's arm was still around her waist. Jenny was caught between the two men. She looked from one to the other, confused. Then, with a sigh only she could hear, Jared's arm dropped away. Paul lifted the champagne flute out of her hand (the champagne flute Jared had made sure was never empty) and shoved it at Jared.

"You were rude," Jenny said to her brother as they danced.

"I'm beginning to not like that man."

"Oh, really? I didn't know you liked him at all."

"I'm not sure I did."

"Play nice," she half-jokingly admonished. "No big brother Neanderthalness. I'm here to have a good time tonight, and nothing is going to ruin my fun."

That drew a reluctant smile from Paul.

When that song ended, a son of a family friend asked her for the next dance. As he whirled her around, she learned that he'd gotten divorced, had a son, and wanted to know if she was interested in going out sometime.

So caught off guard by being asked out on a date, she missed a step and stumbled. "Let me think about it. Okay, Ryan?"

"Sure."

From then on she had a blur of partners. Her feet were beginning to hurt from being stepped on, and her head was feeling a little fuzzy from all the champagne. When the next song ended, she felt herself being swept out onto the floor with a flourish. Looking up, she smiled. "Kenny. I didn't think you were going to make it."

"And miss my dance with the belle of the ball?"

She laughed. "Hardly that."

He stared at her, his voice turning serious. "You really don't get it."

"Get what?"

"Jesus, he's a lucky man."

Confusion furrowed her brow. But before Jenny could say anything, a deep voice sounded from behind her. "Hart." Her heart leapt at the sound of the achingly familiar voice.

Kenny twirled her around until they faced Jared.

"I'm cutting in."

"Later," Kenny said.

"Now." Jared didn't wait for a reply but scooped Jenny into his strong arms.

"Hello," she said, slightly giddy from champagne. "I was wondering where you were."

"Watching."

"Who?"

"You."

Her whole body flushed at the look of raw desire in his gaze. "You should have been dancing."

His stare was direct and held a wealth of meaning and a promise that made her shiver, but not from cold. "There's only one partner I wanted."

"And who would that be?" she asked, knowing it wasn't only the champagne that was causing her to be so bold.

He pulled her close, pressed their bodies together, until she could feel every hard inch of him. "I think you know."

She did. They'd been dancing around this attraction for weeks. She wanted him. And now she knew without a doubt that he wanted her. She was done denying it.

Stretching up on her tiptoes, she wound her hands around his neck and brushed her fingers through the back of his hair like her hands had ached to do outside. Unlike her other partners, Jared danced with a slow, languid confidence. "Thank you."

He leaned down until his warm breath brushed across her. Even in a tux he smelled of the outdoors, of fresh air and sunshine and aged whiskey. "For what?"

For everything. For that kiss I can't forget. "For fixing the kitchen faucet."

He smiled. "How do you know it was me? Maybe Cody fixed it."

It was her turn to laugh. "Somehow I don't think so."

"And here I thought you thought he was a great assistant."

She blushed, remembering how she'd sent her nephew out to work with Jared in the hangar. "I plead the Fifth."

His voice lowered a fraction. "I can think of a lot better things to plead for."

Her heart slammed against her chest and heat spread through her, pooling low in the pit of her stomach. "Name one."

He pulled back until there was just enough room for a shaft of light to fit between them. "Come out onto the deck with me, and I'll show you."

She didn't resist as he led them through the crowd and onto the patio. Soft light spilled out from the double set of open French doors. In the warm night, the air was heady with the fragrance of the flowers that overflowed from the huge containers bordering the patio's perimeter.

Jared didn't say a word as he pulled her into a corner. His large body blocked her from anyone's view as he leaned into her. She met him halfway, pressed herself against him. His hand caressed the side of her face, his callused thumb rubbing her cheek. His hand slipped lower, down her neck, across her shoulder, until both his hands were on her bare back, the heat from his touch burning her, fueling her desire. He crushed her against him. Instead of the fiery hot kiss of before, he lowered his head slowly, trailed kisses along her forehead, down the side of her face until finally, *finally*, settling on her mouth. She gripped his strong shoulders, not knowing if it was for support or to make sure he didn't pull away. A hot ache started deep in her belly and spread outward. There were so many reasons why she shouldn't do this, but right now none of them mattered. He wove his hands through the back of her hair, and she felt the warmth of his fingers against her scalp. He worked the pins free, and her hair fell around her shoulders in a thick collection of disorganized curls. He ran his hands through the tangled mass and sighed with pleasure as if he'd been waiting forever to do just that.

"Jenny."

"Don't stop," she pleaded with a voice she didn't recognize, one husky from want and need. She didn't want him to end this like he had that night on the beach.

"As if I could." His mouth was warm and demanding, soft yet firm. She pushed her hands under his coat and over his shoulders, feeling the hard strength of him. He grabbed her waist and lifted her up on her toes. His tongue explored the inside of her mouth, driving her crazy with a carnal desire she'd never known. Her breasts began to ache with need and want and desire, and as if reading her mind, he reached behind her, cupped her butt in the palms of his hands, and pulled her even closer until she was crushed against his chest. Pinpricks of sensation tingled outward and hardened her nipples. One hand held her back while his other roamed over her bottom, down her leg, until he found the slit in the back of her dress. Reaching through, he pulled her left leg around his hip and anchored it there.

"God, I've been wanting to do that all damn night. Tell me. Tell me you want it, too."

She looked up at him through eyes half-closed with desire. A small slash of light illuminated his strong profile, and she ran her hand over his cheek. "I do."

"Do what?"

"Want this. Want you."

"God, Jenny." Her name was as much a curse as a caress. He slid his hand farther inside her dress, skimmed the underside of her thigh, before slipping his hand under her panties.

She sucked in a breath, and his hand stilled. She pulled

against his shoulders and kissed him with every bit of desire she'd been holding back, telling him without words how much she wanted him. His fingers fanned over her heated skin, and right then he made her forget everything but him. She forgot about the music, the ballroom full of people. His hand continued to deepen its caress. Her body went hot and wet all at once. As his fingers skimmed over her swollen flesh, she stiffened.

Oh God.

She pulled back, dropped her leg from around his thigh. Dampness pooled between her legs, and she felt a stab of shame and fear.

Without saying a word, she ran. She paused at the French doors, but she knew she couldn't go back into the party. Her lips felt swollen and puffy, and her hair was one long, disheveled mess. She rushed past the doors, past the light, and toward her car. But halfway through the parking garage, she realized Jared had the keys. She stopped, not knowing what to do. Tears stung her eyes, and right then she wanted nothing more than to curl up into a ball and cry.

"Jenny?" Her sister's voice startled her. "Oh my God. What's wrong?"

"Nothing." Tears made her vision blurry, but even through her watery eyes she could see Anna had just parked her car. Her keys were still in her hand. "Your keys. Please. I need to go home."

"Jenny." Her sister's voice was full of concern. "Tell me what's wrong."

"I can't. Please just give me your keys."

"I'll drive you."

"No!" She nearly shouted the word. "Please."

Anna stretched out her hand but didn't let go of the keys. "I wish you would tell me—"

Heavy footsteps thudded behind them, and they both turned at the same time. It was Jared.

Grabbing the keys from Anna's hand, Jenny jumped in her sister's Volvo and roared out of the garage.

All the way home she tried to keep the guilt at bay. She knew Steven was gone, but she couldn't shake the feeling she was somehow cheating on him. And then there was something else, something she'd never admit to anyone. Steven had been her only lover, and she knew she'd always been a bit of a disappointment in bed. He was generous and kind and giving, and Jenny had loved him with her whole heart, but she'd never been able to just let herself go like she knew he wanted her to. But tonight, in a crowded museum, where anyone could see, she had become a woman she didn't know in Jared's arms.

TWENTY

Not long after Jenny arrived home, she heard the Corvette pull in her driveway. A few minutes later, Jared knocked on her bedroom door, but she refused to answer. He called to her several times, and when she continued to remain silent, he tried the handle, but it was locked. She knew she was being a coward. She knew she should open her door and talk to him, try to explain. And she would. But not tonight. Even now her body still hummed and burned for him. She closed her eyes and let her tears fall onto her pillow. Guilt still tore at her, but so did another thought. For six years she had been engaged to Steven. Six years she'd waited for him to find roots.

Flyboys fly. How often had he told her that? She would have waited a lifetime for him to settle down, and when he told her he was getting out of the military and wanted to start the business in Hidden Lake, she knew all her dreams had been about to come true. Now she was falling for another flyboy. But unlike Steven, this one would never have roots. The evidence was right before her—in the duffel bag he never unpacked. She was on the verge of falling in love with Jared, and she couldn't let that happen. He'd break her heart, and this time she knew she'd never get it back together.

Jenny wasn't surprised when the phone rang first thing the next morning. She was even less surprised that it was her mother.

"Jenny, Anna told us what happened last night."

Jenny didn't say a word. Anna didn't know what happened, but seeing Jenny in such a state, she'd probably guessed.

"Honey, do you want to talk about it?"

"No."

Her mother sighed. "Your father and I talked this morning, and we want to give you the money to buy out your partner."

For one dizzying moment, Jenny considered accepting their offer. Even though it was the last thing she wanted to do, she knew she had to get Jared out of her life and quickly. For so long she'd been trying to make a success of Blue Sky on her own, but now she didn't know if her heart was strong enough to survive him.

"Think about it, honey," her mom said when Jenny continued to remain silent. "We're here to help whenever you need us."

"Thanks, Mom."

Not long after, she heard Jared head out for his morning run. While he was gone, she took a shower. As she dressed, she thought about her parents' offer. It would be so easy, just like it had been every other time she'd let them bail her out. She knew her family was waiting—*expecting*—for her to once again fail. But this time, she wasn't going to. Blue Sky had become more than just a tie to Steven. It had also become a huge part of her. She'd never worked so hard for anything in her life.

Tell me, have you ever got past a secretary?

I saw the files you worked up.

If you're the businesswoman you say you are, you'll figure it out.

Jared's words came back to her. She hated to admit it, but he'd been right. All those calls she'd made had gone nowhere. She was just a voice on the phone. Why should anyone take her or her business seriously?

Pulling off the jeans and sweater she'd just put on, she got out her one and only business suit. As she put it on, she noticed that it didn't hang on her like it had a few weeks ago. She didn't know why, but this pleased her. Somehow, the gaining of a few pounds made her feel as if she was getting back to her old self. To brighten the black outfit, she put a pink shell underneath then hurried down to her office. There, she found the files and spreadsheets she had been working on. She placed them in Steven's old briefcase, then started for the door, only to realize she needed to make one important call before leaving.

Picking up the phone, she dialed her parents' number. When her mom answered, Jenny said, "Thank you so much for the offer, Mom, but no thanks. I know what I need to do. And please tell Dad thanks, too." She hung up filled with a new determination.

But twenty minutes later as she pulled into the underground parking garage, she wasn't feeling nearly as confident. Her stomach ached, and perspiration dampened her underarms. The large glass and steel building that housed North American Timber, LLC, was imposing to say the least. Scanning the directory, she found the name she was looking for. She took the elevator to the twenty-fifth floor.

After much persuasion and nearly an hour wait, she was escorted in to see the president and CEO, Mr. Kragen. She was tired of trying to get in through the bottom end. This time, straight to the top. She was so nervous she barely took in her surroundings except to note the large desk and bank of floor-to-ceiling windows.

"I have only ten minutes, Ms. Beckinsale." Mr. Kragen said after his secretary had led Jenny into his office. "Please don't waste my time."

Sweat trickled down her back, and what little courage

she had all but deserted her. She wanted nothing more than to get up and run, but the thought of another failure kept her firmly in place. "I would like to discuss your air travel needs."

"We already have a service."

"Yes," Jenny began, taking one of the seats in front of him. "But I believe Blue Sky Air could serve your needs more efficiently."

The older man leaned back in his chair and crossed his arms over the front of his opened suit jacket. "And how is that?"

"I am aware that you and several of your executives commute to British Columbia three times a week."

"Correct."

"Unlike the current charter you are using, Blue Sky has a more scenic route. We circle over Snoqualmie Falls and go up the Cascades."

Mr. Kragen unlocked his hands and sat forward. "If we wanted scenic, Ms. Beckinsale, we'd go on a vacation."

Jenny felt herself floundering. She could feel his growing impatience and knew he was moments away from asking her to leave. Once more, failure seemed imminent. Then she saw Jared's face and heard his words.

You're a businesswoman, figure it out.

This time, his tone wasn't biting but encouraging. As if he was challenging her to stretch her wings and find her way. "You're exactly right, Mr. Kragen. I jumped the gun by starting to explain a few of our vacation packages. Our company would like to offer one to you free of charge so you can experience all Blue Sky Air has to offer. But first, let me tell you how we can be of benefit to your business."

"Go on."

Those two little words gave her more courage than she thought possible. "As we are both aware, the current charter business you use is in the heart of downtown Seattle."

"A fact we find very convenient."

Her confidence took a little nosedive. "Convenient, yes.

Except during weekdays and rush hour traffic. Exactly the same time you are commuting. And as we both know, the congestion on I-5 causes major delays. I'm sure you have experienced them."

"More often than I like."

She shifted her weight in the chair. "That is the reason I believe Blue Sky would be a more convenient choice for your company, as we are located off of I-90. You would be traveling opposite of congestion. Also, if my research is correct, and I believe it is, two of your corporate officers live closer to Blue Sky Air than the current company you are using."

Mr. Kragen braced his elbows on the desk. "You have done your homework, Ms. Beckinsale. I'm impressed. But while you have made some valid points, we have had a long and successful relationship with Emerald City Charters. We will be continuing to use their services."

The familiar heavy weight of failure pressed down on her. Mr. Kragen scooted his chair back, and she knew it would only be mere moments before he dismissed her. *Business is about the bottom line. Period.* "Wait." Her voice seemed loud in the room. "Please."

"Ms. Beckinsale—"

She didn't stop. "With the current rise in fuel costs, I am also aware that Emerald City Charters is charging your company a fuel surcharge. Our company has no such surcharge in effect. Additionally, to prove to you our heartfelt belief that Blue Sky Air is the only charter company that can fully and most conveniently meet your needs, we are prepared to offer you a twenty percent discount for three months. If, after that time, you feel your needs are not being met, we would expect you to return to Emerald City Charters." She smiled. "But I do not foresee that happening."

Thirty minutes later, with a signed contract in her hand, Jenny walked out of North American Timber. It wasn't until she got into her car that she let out a loud yell. She couldn't believe it. *She* had landed the biggest account

Blue Sky had ever dreamed of having. Three guaranteed charters a week to Canada.

Getting her cell phone out, she punched in the first number that came to her.

On the second ring, Jared answered.

* * *

When Jenny pulled into her driveway that evening, the glow of a campfire down on the beach immediately caught her attention. Her foot came off the gas, and the vehicle slowed to a crawl. There was only one person who would have a fire on her beach at this time of night. The same person who had held her in his arms last night and had caused her to burn with a need so hot and sharp her stomach clenched into a tight knot every time she thought about it. Which she'd tried not to do all day. And it had worked . . . some of the time . . . hardly any of the time. Silhouetted in the darkness and backlit by the fire, she saw Jared's achingly familiar profile.

Her breath came out all at once in a whoosh. Sooner or later, she knew she would have to face him. Last night she'd fled like some sixteen-year-old virgin who'd been felt up for the first time. She owed him an explanation. She only hoped she'd be able to give him one that didn't reveal too much.

Gravel crunched under her tires as she eased the vehicle into her normal parking spot and set the emergency brake. She gathered her purse and briefcase, then opened the door and slid down the seat.

Jared stood a few feet away from her.

She drew in a breath, and her heart bumped against the inside of her chest. The hangar's outdoor lights were on, and he looked so good she held on to the door handle for support. Gone was the tuxedo and, instead, he was back in Levi's, a soft cotton shirt, and his leather jacket stretched wide across his shoulders. "Hi."

"Hi." He closed the small distance between them. "Here, let me take that." He reached out and took the briefcase from her hand. His fingers brushed across her skin, and all her hard work to forget the memory of their kiss vanished in that one touch. "You're home late."

"I . . . I got stuck in town."

He was so close she had to look up to see him.

"Collecting cars?" He gestured behind her to the used black SUV she'd driven home.

She smiled at him tentatively, grateful for his patience. She knew he wanted answers, and yet he was thinking of her first, letting her find her way. "No. It's Blue Sky's newest *and only* vehicle. I traded in the Corvette." Just saying the words made her ache but not as badly as she had imagined. It had been time to let go of the Corvette. It was time to let go of a lot of things from her past.

"You've had a busy day."

"There's a lot I would like to tell you." She glanced at the fire, then back at Jared. "Give me a second to change and then meet you at the fire?"

"Sounds good."

She hurried into the house and up to her room. Quickly, she changed out of her suit and pulled on a white T-shirt, a soft pink zip-up hooded sweatshirt that said BUM across the front, and a pair of matching sweatpants. She slipped her feet into white Nikes.

Then she went back outside. The bright hangar lights were off. It was then that she realized Jared had left them on for her, to make sure she didn't stumble through the dark when she got home. She felt something warm squeeze her heart. It had been a long time since someone had done something so simple but thoughtful for her.

A full moon, stars, and crackling fire provided the only light she needed. As she walked through the sand, she found the hushed darkness inviting. "Thank you," she said as she eased down into the chair next to him. There were three other chairs around the fire pit, but she didn't take the easy way out and sit across from him. She owed him that much at least for her behavior last night.

"For what?"

"For leaving the lights on." *And for being so patient with me.* The fire crackled and popped, and the yellow and orange glow danced across his face, highlighting his dark hair and drawing her gaze to his eyes.

"Thank you for the call."

"I'm sorry I sounded so giddy. I just couldn't believe I landed the account. And when I grabbed for my cell, I punched in the first number that came to my mind." She looked across at him, and this time, she wished the night wasn't so dark and the light so dim, because she wanted to be able to read his expression.

"I was your first call?"

"Yes."

He stared at the logs on the fire. "I'm flattered. More than flattered." His voice was deep with a husky sincerity she hadn't heard before. He turned and smiled at her. "I've never been anyone's first before."

She laughed softly. "I doubt that. But if it's true, I've had enough for the both of us."

"Care to tell me one?"

She swallowed hard. There were a hundred firsts in her life she could tell him about, but she chose the only one that mattered at this moment. "Last night was the first time I let a guy get to third base and then panicked and ran away."

"Technically, I only got to second base."

"Are you sure?"

He turned and faced her. "Yeah, pretty damn."

She remembered his mouth on her, the heat of his hands as he slipped his fingers under her panties. She was pretty positive that was third base, but she wasn't about to argue. "Still a first."

Jared stood and stirred the logs on the fire. Fresh flames jumped and licked the sky. "Not quite the reaction I was expecting."

"Not the one I expected either."

He poked at the burning logs once more before sitting back down next to her. "Care to tell me what went wrong?"

A small breeze blew the smoke toward the left of her, away from them. She looked up into the ebony darkness and star-filled sky but then realized that those things made her think even more of Jared. Desire twisted her up inside, and she fought to find a truth. Or at least a partial one. She could never reveal the full reason she'd behaved the way she had last night. "I didn't mean to lead you on, if that's what you are thinking."

"Frankly, I haven't known what the hell to think."

"I . . ." She turned in the chair, and the metal bar bit into the backs of her legs. "Steven hasn't even been gone a year. I guess I'm not ready for anything beyond a working relationship. I hope—"

"You don't have to say any more."

"But—"

"I mean it, Jenny." He looked at her and braced his elbows on his knees. "I get it."

A silence fell between them. The fire crackled and popped. The waves rolled in against the shore. And for some reason she couldn't explain, Jared's abruptness bothered her more than she cared to admit. "What do you think of the Suburban?" she asked, struggling to find safe ground.

"A better business choice than the Corvette. But it must have been difficult to let go of something that had belonged to Steven."

"Very," was all she could say. Trading in the car had been nearly impossible. But as hard as it had been, it had been the right choice. A sound business decision, just like Jared had said, and one she should have made months ago. "Here." She dug in the pocket of her sweatshirt and pulled out the spare set of keys she'd tucked in there before leaving the house. "So you don't have to keep borrowing Zeke's truck for all those trips to the lumberyard."

He palmed the keys, seeming to weigh them in his hand. "You knew about that?"

"How could I not?" She made a sweeping gesture around the place. "I've never properly thanked you for all the work you've done here. The place hasn't looked so good since . . ." She laughed. "Well since I don't know when." She crossed her ankles. "You want to hear the best part?"

He tucked the keys in the front pocket of his Levi's. "Definitely."

"With the amount I owed on the Corvette and the price of the Suburban, it was a straight trade. No car payment. God, that feels good."

"As good as the account you landed?"

"Hell no." She laughed again, and so did he.

"Do you want to tell me about it?"

"You mean you're not sick of hearing about it? After I practically screamed the details in your ear?"

Jared made a joke of putting his finger in his ear and vibrating it back and forth, like he'd gone partially deaf. "The details were a little fuzzy. But the high pitched screams came through loud and clear."

"Sorry."

"I'm not. Now tell me."

And she did. She told him everything. About how nervous she was, how long she had to wait, and about how she almost blew it. "You're a huge part of the reason for today's success," she said after a slight pause. "I kept thinking about things you've said to me. How it's all about the bottom line and to think like a businessperson."

"This success is yours, not mine. You should be incredibly proud of yourself."

"Thank you." But even as she said it, she knew. He *was* a part of this success. A vital part. For years, Steven had been her soft place to fall, but what she hadn't seen until now was that sometimes all that softness made you so content, you didn't feel the need to get up. She wasn't blaming Steven. Not at all. He was everything she'd wanted him to be, but Jared was . . . different. He was strong and solid, and she had no doubt he would catch her, but he'd also prop her right back up on her feet and force her to walk alongside him. "Do you want to hear what I have planned for tomorrow?"

"Absolutely."

"A meeting with International Trust and Loan. Besides several other places in the world, they have banking headquarters based in Seattle and Canada."

"Planning to steal all the competitor's clients?"

"Absolutely," she said, repeating him.

He smiled and threaded his fingers across his stomach. "Good for you."

She fidgeted in her seat and looked back up into the inky dark sky. "Can I ask you a question?"

"Anything."

She wanted to ask him if he had thought about last night as much as she had. But instead, she said, "Any advice for my meeting tomorrow?"

He grew still. "You want my opinion?"

"Yes."

He seemed genuinely flattered by her request. "During negotiations, first offer the no fuel surcharge. If they don't bite, then start with a ten percent discount and negotiate from there."

"So, in other words, don't jump out of the gate at twenty percent?"

"Not if you can help it."

She nodded, knowing he was right. She shoved her hands into the front pockets of her jacket. "If International Trust and Loan comes on board, too, I know my bank will give me the loan to repay you. You'll be able to get back to your squadron in no time." No matter how hard she braced herself, the words still cut.

He hesitated. "I'm no longer in the military. I resigned my commission."

Her gaze swiveled to his as shock hit her. "When?"

"Before I got here."

She tried to take it all in. "You're no longer a fighter pilot."

"No."

"Why?" *And why did you wait until now to tell me?*

He kicked at a burning log. "Because everything comes to an end."

It was a cop-out answer, and they both knew it. But she didn't ask him any more questions. She couldn't. Only one thought kept whirling through her mind: he was done with flying jets. What did that mean for her? For them?

Did it mean nothing, or did it mean everything?

When Jared steered the conversation back around to the business, Jenny let him. There was so much she wanted to say, to ask him, but she knew tonight wasn't the night. Her emotions were a tangled mess, and she needed time to sort through them. Tomorrow would be soon enough.

As they sat by the campfire talking, she not only lost track of time, but she lost herself in a discussion about the business. Jared was a master at drawing out her ideas. He listened to everything she had to say with the same attentiveness and intensity he had last night. And just like last night, she found it intoxicating. Their discussion turned lively, a mutual sharing of ideas and thoughts. He complimented her on the redesigned website. He suggested they update the website to reflect North American Timber's scheduled charters. He went on to explain that since Blue Sky would only be flying two or three executives up at one time, and the plane had room for more passengers, they'd be able to increase their profits without expending additional capital. She wanted to highlight several vacation packages; he thought one would be good. They settled on two to start with: one in British Columbia and one in the San Juans. She also thought they should offer weekend and holiday scenic tours, especially during the whale migration. He agreed. She became immersed in listening to him, and if the look in his eyes was any indication, he was just as absorbed by her thoughts.

Back and forth their discussion went, until Jenny could barely keep her eyes open. Exhausted, she headed to her room, certain she'd fall asleep almost instantly. But one thought kept going through her mind.

I'm no longer in the military. I resigned my commission.

She stared down at the diamond ring she still wore. Moonlight glinted off the round cut diamond. For over six years, she'd worn this ring, pledged her whole life to one man. But Steven was gone, and nothing she could ever do would bring him back. Tears blurred her vision as she twisted the ring around her finger.

I'm no longer in the military. I resigned my commission.

Slowly, she removed the ring and placed it in her jewelry box.

* * *

Jared stared at the fire that was nothing more than a pile of coals. Deep admiration filled him. Against the odds Jenny had found her first big success. And from their discussion, he knew it was only the beginning. He was pretty damn positive she'd land tomorrow's account, too. And every one she went after. Not only did she have strong marketing plans and solid strategies for enticing customers away from Blue Sky's competition but she also had something more. She had a gift when it came to dealing with people. A genuineness that made people want to do business with her. And that couldn't be taught or found or learned. With the new accounts and the innovative ideas they'd discussed and would implement, she soon would be able to repay him. And wasn't that exactly what he wanted? But he couldn't help but wonder what it would be like to stay her partner.

She had called him first. That revelation still left him stunned. Not her parents or her brother or her sister. She'd call *him*. He tried to push it out of his mind, to tell himself not to read too much into it. He also tried to tamp down the memory of last night. But no matter how many times or how hard he tried, he could still feel the texture of her silky hair as it ran through his fingers, the taste of her on his mouth, her soft skin under his hand, and the hot wetness that had told him she'd wanted him just as much as he'd wanted her.

Steven hasn't even been gone a year. I guess I'm not ready for anything beyond a working relationship.

He stood and doused the fire.

Steven.

In one fell swoop, his pipe dream died just like the fire below him. While he might have fanciful visions of sticking around, he knew it could never work. Jenny wanted a forever type of man, someone who could put down roots, become a part of a family. A father. Someone like Steven, who not only had wings but who also had roots. He'd seen the look of hope that had flashed in her eyes when he'd told her he was out of the military. He knew she was thinking that maybe he'd be that guy—the kind that stuck. She couldn't be more wrong. The longest Jared had ever stayed in one place could be measured in weeks, not years. Yeah, the military had had him stationed all over the world, but he'd been anything but stationary.

While he might burn and ache for her, a business partnership was where it should begin and end. He remembered the plan he'd come up with in the bar and all but laughed. Kissing Jenny had nothing to do with a plan and everything to do with him not being able to keep his hands off her. He wanted her. *All* of her. Not just in his bed but in his life. But he knew the cold truth: every relationship he'd ever tried had ended in disaster. And he was beginning to care too damn much about her to screw up her life any more than he already had. But knowing all of that couldn't erase the taste or feel of her from his mind. Or the thought of her upstairs in a bed big enough for two.

TWENTY-ONE

◌

A few weeks after the charity ball, Anna found herself heading back to her sister's house. Her parents had returned her car to her two days after Jenny had run off with it. Anna had been grateful. Even though she'd told her sister not to worry about getting the car back to her, driving Phillip's car had proven too difficult. In so many ways. Since the car had sat for months, Anna had to call a mechanic to get it started. Then someone had to clean it from the inside out. Looking at the once-pristine vehicle, she couldn't help drawing a comparison between that damn car and her marriage. The car wasn't the only thing in their household that needed revitalization.

She glanced at Cody in the rearview mirror. As usual, he was doing his best to ignore her. She'd tried to convince him to sit up front with her, but he'd refused. Like he had been refusing every effort she made to reach out to him. Thankfully, school was out, and he'd managed to get all of his missing assignments turned in. Even though he'd only ended up missing two of his baseball games while he worked with the tutor, he still hadn't forgiven her.

When they pulled into Jenny's driveway, Anna nearly stomped on the brakes, sure she was at the wrong place. Four cars were in the parking lot, and a group of people were boarding the plane. But the obvious business activity wasn't the only difference. The place looked amazing. Beautiful. The yard was in pristine condition, the cedar shingles on the house had been cleaned and were once again a soft dove gray. Fresh white paint coated the window trim and the porch railing, and the garden was in glorious full bloom.

She'd barely gotten the car parked before Cody jumped out. He headed straight for Jenny, who was exiting the hangar, a stack of folders in her hand. Always beautiful, her sister still looked gorgeous but . . . different. She wore a flowered print skirt, white lace top, and pink flip-flops. Her blonde hair was piled at the back of her head in a mass of riotous curls. But as she bent down and hugged Cody, Anna realized there was something more to her sister today than her breathtakingly good looks. There was an air of self-confidence about her that Anna had never seen.

Slowly, Anna got out of the car and grabbed Cody's things.

"Hi, Anna." Jenny sounded genuinely happy to see her. "So, I guess we're stuck with the rug rat for a couple of days."

"Hey," Cody said, trying to sound offended, but his smile ruined the effect.

Jenny gave him a playful bump on the shoulder. "Just kidding, kiddo."

"I hope you don't mind. It's just that—"

"I know," Jenny said with a smile. "You have to work. I understand."

The plane started up, and they turned to watch as the pontoons parted the water and the plane taxied out toward the middle of the lake. Sunshine glistened off the water like Christmas tinsel. A few puffy, snow white clouds dotted the blue sky.

"Looks like you had a full plane today," Anna said over the noise.

"Almost. One empty seat."

"Only one?"

"Yeah." Jenny's smile was big and bright. "It's really wonderful, Anna. I know I should have called, but I've been swamped. In a very, very good way." She laughed. "Blue Sky has recently landed several new accounts, and I'm getting new bookings almost daily for the vacation packages I put together. Most of the information is on the website, but there are a few details I still need to iron out."

"Website? Accounts? Vacation packages?"

Jenny laughed again. "I know. A bit overwhelming."

Cody turned his eyes away from the plane. "Hey, Aunt Jenny. Guess what?"

"What?"

"My team made the playoffs. Can you come?"

"I wouldn't miss it for the world."

Anna stared at her sister. She hadn't asked a single question. Not when, where, or what time. Without hesitation, she'd agreed, and Anna knew Jenny meant it. She would be there, no matter what.

"Cool. Grandma and Grandpa said they'd be there, too. What about Jared? Will he come?"

A shadow crossed over her sister. It was there and then gone so quickly that Anna wondered if she'd imagined it.

"You'll have to ask him. But it's going to be a tight fit in the stands with your mom, me, Grandma, and—"

"Mom can't make it. She's gonna be at work. Just like Dad."

Jenny put her arm around Cody and gave him a hug. Cody leaned into her embrace, and Anna couldn't help but feel a pinch of jealousy. "You know your mom and dad would be there if they could."

Cody shrugged. "Whatever."

Jenny looked up from Cody and gave her sister a supporting look. "Jared's in the hangar. Why don't you go ask him about the game?"

After Cody left, Anna turned to her sister. "Thank you." Two little words, but for Anna, they were hard to say.

"For what?"

"For not making me out to be the bad guy."

"No one thinks you're the bad guy, Anna."

Anna set Cody's suitcase on the ground and shielded a hand across her eyes as she stared at the hangar. "My son does. He thinks my job is more important than he is."

"He's thirteen. Of course he does."

"I'm really proud of you, Jenny. You went after what you wanted and got it."

"So did you." Jenny stared at her sister for several moments. "I owe you an apology. I never realized what it took for a woman to not only survive but thrive in this world. It's all I can do lately to keep up with the new business demands. And I don't have a husband and a son. How you manage everything is beyond me."

I don't. I'm not.

Jenny wrapped her arms around her sister. For too long, Anna's arms remained still. How long had it been since they had given each other a hug? Anna couldn't remember the last time. As she slowly returned the embrace, she wondered what it would feel like to actually accept the support her sister offered. But she didn't know how. For too long, she'd relied solely on herself, not even reaching out to her husband.

* * *

In an uncharacteristic burst of hot, golden sunshine, the Fourth of July arrived. While Jenny assisted the group of tourists who were headed out for a scenic tour around the San Juans, Jared helped Zeke ready the plane. Jared smiled, remembering how worried Jenny had been about Zeke having to work on the holiday. When she'd confided her concerns to Zeke, he'd only laughed and told her he couldn't think of a better way to spend the day. Then he pointed to the brand-new Dodge Ram pickup his new raise and bonus had bought.

With the plane in the air, Jenny went into full dictator mode. She kept the commands flying until the Suburban all but overflowed with everything she insisted needed to be taken to her parents' annual party. When Jared had first been told about the family gathering, he'd tried to get out of it. Family affairs made him uncomfortable to say the least. But Jenny had dug her heels in and insisted that he accompany her. Why she wanted him there was beyond him. Ever since that night by the fire, their relationship had been exactly as she'd wanted: strictly business. But every day he felt the undercurrents of his growing desire. From the moment he'd met her, he'd been knocked on his ass by her beauty. Now he was being flattened by her tenacity and intelligence. Daily, Blue Sky was becoming a more profitable entity. Almost nightly, they discussed new ideas to bring to the table. Those nights were killing Jared. As he sat across from her at the table or next to her on the couch, it was all he could do to keep his eyes off her left hand. Her bare left hand. And when he wasn't thinking about the engagement ring she no longer wore and what the hell that could mean, all he could think about was stripping her naked, carrying her upstairs, and using every sexual skill he possessed to drive her beyond thinking. Beyond remembering that the only thing she wanted from him was a business relationship.

The drive to Jenny's parents' house took hardly any time at all. Cars packed the driveway and overflowed onto the narrow road, but a spot near the garage had been reserved for Jenny. The house was an impressive brick rambler that sat on the west side of Hidden Lake. As they walked around to the backyard with their arms full of food, lawn chairs, and fireworks, he was astounded to see how many people were at the party. An emerald green lawn stretched at least three hundred feet along the high-banked waterfront. Red and white checked plastic tablecloths covered the picnic tables spread out in clusters around the lawn. A game of croquet was in full swing as was a game of badminton. Paul lifted his racket and waved at them, missing a birdie. Jenny smiled and waved back. With his hands full, Jared nodded a greeting. Laughter mixed with the sound of music coming from the built-in speakers on the open back patio. Jared grimaced. Country, of course.

"What?" Jenny said, noticing his expression.

"Nothing," he said, trying his damnedest to keep his gaze off her cleavage. The minute he saw her walking out of the house in a pair of Daisy Duke shorts and a bikini top, he knew he was doomed before the party had even started.

"Here," she pointed. "Let's put the chairs by this table."

Behind a large barbeque, Jenny's dad was busy flipping burgers and rotating hot dogs. There were also clams steaming next to the barbeque. "Hey, Daddy," Jenny called out. "That sure smells good."

"Jelly Belly," her dad said, engulfing her in a bear hug. He wore an apron that said World's Greatest Cook.

Jenny pointed to her dad's apron. "He taught me everything I know."

Jared laughed as he shook her dad's hand.

"How about a beer?" he said, opening the cooler next to him.

"Thanks." Jared took the cold beer.

Her dad grabbed a couple of red plastic plates. "Now let me dish you up some food. How about a hamburger or hot dog? Or some clams?"

"I'm not hungry," said Jenny. She turned to Jared. "Do you want anything?"

You. "No, thanks. Not yet."

"If you see your mother, tell her I need more melted butter for the clams."

"Aunt Jenny! Jared!" Cody ran up to them, a hot dog in his hand.

"Hey, sport," Jared said.

Jenny hugged her nephew and rubbed the top of his head. "Hi to you, too. Your mom here?"

"She's coming later. After work. Are those fireworks?" he asked, eyeing the big bag Jared held.

"Yep."

"Cool."

"How about showing me where to put these until we need them tonight and then helping me grab a cooler and the other bag of fireworks out of the Suburban?"

Cody's eyes widened. "Another bag. *Sweet.*"

They left Jenny trying to find her mom and walked back to the car. Cody chattered nonstop about his upcoming playoff game and working on his curve ball. "You gonna play in the game later today?"

"What game?"

Cody rolled his eyes like Jared should know. "The baseball game we have every year."

"Here?"

"No duh."

Jared grinned at the smart-aleck answer. "I didn't bring a glove."

"I have my dad's you can use. Remember?"

Jared knew he should say no. The more time he spent with Cody, the harder it was becoming for Jared to stay detached. But instead of doing the smart thing, he said, "Guess I'm all set."

After they brought the cooler and fireworks to the backyard, Cody spied a group of kids his age and took off, calling over his shoulder, "Don't forget about the game later."

Jared stood at the edge of the lawn and took a drink of his beer. He watched Jenny dart in and out of the house and around the yard, doing dozens of tasks. Setting out food, greeting newcomers, making sure they had something to eat and drink. When a little girl smacked her foot with a croquet mallet, Jenny was there to soothe away her tears. Not once did he see her take a break.

When Jenny's mom called to her husband that she needed him in the house, Jared walked over to the grill. "Need me to take over?" he said to John.

"That would be great, thanks." Jenny's dad handed him the spatula and motioned to the tongs hanging off the side of the grill. "How about the apron?"

Jared laughed. "You better keep it." It wasn't long before Jenny joined him. As he cooked, she handed out red plastic plates loaded with thick hamburgers, plump hot dogs, steamed clams and corn on the cob.

"Hey, you're starting to cook like me," Jenny said, pointing to a charred hot dog.

He looked down, surprised he hadn't burned everything. She was the only thing he could concentrate on. "It's for you. I know how you like them."

She punched his arm. "Don't be a butt."

He wasn't being a butt; he was watching one. Hers to be precise. Instead of keeping his eye on the grill, he'd been keeping his eyes on Jenny's tight ass. He should have kept the apron to hide his reaction. Her mom called, and she was off again, running. While he was helping at the barbeque, Jared found himself visiting with people as they came to dish up. Surprisingly, even surrounded by so many people, he started to relax.

As the shadows began to lengthen across the lawn, the badminton net came down and the wire croquet hoops were pulled. Tables were pushed back as the undersized baseball diamond was formed. Jared was surprised to see Cody's mom arrive just before the start of the game.

Cody caught sight of her and ran over. They were too far away, and the music and voices from the guests were too loud to hear what was being said, but Jared could see Cody pointing to the baseball field, and then he held out a glove to his mom.

As Anna shook her head no, Jared's temper began to rise. Cody dropped the glove at his mom's feet and then walked away like an abandoned puppy.

Jared looked around. No one else seemed to notice the exchange. He knew it was none of his business, and he should just stay out of it, remember his philosophy to stay detached, but one look at Cody's heartbroken face, and Jared knew what he *should* do wasn't what he *had* to do.

He strode over to Anna.

"You don't get it," he said before she could say a word. "I know you have a job, but you also have a son. Stop buying him all those damn expensive gifts and do the one thing he really wants." Jared picked up the baseball glove and held it in front of her. "Get your ass in the game."

Jared turned and walked away, ignoring Anna's shocked expression.

* * *

As always, the game was a blast and a blowout. Cody and all the kids (especially since he'd recruited several of his teammates) slaughtered the adults. The little pyros were celebrating winning the bet. They were setting off fireworks as fast as they could light them on the platform Jenny's father had built years ago that hung out over the bank. Most of the parents were right there alongside their kids.

With the fireworks lighting up the sky, Jenny escaped into the kitchen. The empty house was pure peace after the hectic day. Plus, she needed time to think.

I'm no longer in the military. I resigned my commission.

She'd refused to let herself read too much into Jared's revelation. Instead, she'd thrown herself into her work. She'd funneled every bit of her energy into Blue Sky. She worked harder and longer than she ever had so that at night, when she crawled into bed, exhaustion would take over. But today, being here with Jared, watching him playing ball, play with Cody, mingle with their friends and neighbors, she couldn't ignore what he had said any longer. And she also couldn't ignore the fact that Jared hadn't said anything about leaving in quite some time. Did that mean he wanted to stay?

Just as she finished whipping up a blender full of margaritas, Anna walked into the kitchen.

"You're brave," Jenny said, glad for the distraction. Her thoughts were leading her down a road better left unexplored. "Leaving Cody alone out there with all those fireworks."

"Jared's with him."

Jenny tried not to react at hearing Jared's name. "Men

and explosives." She shook her head and handed Anna a salt-rimmed glass. "You look like you could use this."

"Thanks." Anna took the margarita like it was the Holy Grail. "I so need this."

"Yeah. Saw that slide into home. That has to be good for at least a double shot."

"Minimum."

Jenny laughed, poured herself a drink, and sat down next to her sister at the table.

They were on their third margarita when Anna said, "I saw you standing by the open kitchen window. You heard what Jared said?"

Jenny licked some salt off her lips. "Yeah. I did."

Anna grabbed the bottle of tequila and poured some straight into her margarita. "He's right, you know. I haven't been in the game of late. And I'm not just talking about today."

Jenny looked at her sister, not knowing quite what to say. She'd seen the hurt on Cody's face but hadn't stepped in. Anna had always seemed so in control, never taking a wrong step. But now, Jenny was seeing her sister in a new light. Anna struggled just like everyone else. "You're a great mom with a lot on your plate. It's impossible to be everywhere at once. Especially when you're in the role of both mom and dad."

Anna swirled the slushy liquid in her glass. "Remember when I dropped Cody off last time, and you said you wondered how I managed everything? Well, I don't. I haven't been. My job became too important." She let out a sigh and drained her glass. "I haven't been there for my son, and I'm pretty sure the reason Phillip left is because I pushed him away."

"Have you called him?" Jenny asked softly.

"Yes. No." Anna stared at her empty glass. "We've talked. But not about this. Not about anything important."

"Maybe it's time you did."

"What if . . ."

"What if what?" Jenny prodded.

Anna looked at Jenny, and for the first time she saw real fear in her sister's eyes. "What if he doesn't want me?"

Jenny's heart went out to her sister. "Of course he wants you. Phillip fell in love with you, proposed, and had a wedding all in less than six months." Jenny couldn't help thinking how her engagement had dragged on for six years.

Anna got up and poured herself another margarita. "You should have just gotten knocked up like I did. Then you, too, would have had to have a hasty marriage."

Stunned, Jenny could only stare at her sister. Finally, she said. "Call him. Promise me."

Anna looked out the kitchen to where the fireworks were going off. "I will," she said quietly. "And I'm going to make Cody's playoff game, no matter the consequences at work." She turned back to Jenny. "Now you have to make me a promise. Don't let Jared go. It's as plain to see as that hideous tattoo on Aunt Margaret's boob that you love him."

Jenny was beginning to fear her sister was right.

TWENTY-TWO

Long after Anna, Cody, and the vast majority of the guests had left, Jenny wandered down to the beach. She hadn't seen Jared, but then she hadn't looked too hard for him either. Her mind kept tumbling back to her sister's words. *You love him.* She'd wanted to tell Anna she had been wrong, Jenny hadn't been foolish enough to fall in love with another flyboy, another man who would always want wings more than he would want her. But the denial had died on her tongue. And instead of leaving a bitter taste as she feared, all she could remember was how sweet he'd tasted when she'd kissed him and had run her open mouth along the outside of his neck.

And he wasn't a flyboy. Not any longer.

"Hey, Cotton Tail." So lost in her thoughts, she hadn't heard him.

He sat down beside her in the sand and handed her a plate of food. "You haven't eaten all day."

It was true; she hadn't. She wasn't surprised he'd noticed. All day she'd felt his gaze on her, following her. Seeking her out.

She stared at the plate of food and realized there was only one thing she was hungry for. But did she dare?

"You're not eating."

She set the plate off to the side. She could either grab at this chance for happiness or live like she had been, safely cocooned away. Right then she realized she didn't want to live that way anymore. "This isn't what I'm hungry for. I want . . ."

Jared tipped her chin toward him. The warmth of his fingers reached all the way to her heart. "What?"

One word. One word, and there was no going back. "You. I want you."

"Jenny." His voice was husky with desire. He ran his thumb along her jaw then cupped the back of her neck.

He pulled her clear off the sand as his mouth came down on hers. His kiss was like the fireworks, hot and brilliant, and it made her want to *ahhh* in wonderment. Somehow she ended up on his lap. Lust and longing coiled low in her stomach, and she returned his kiss with a fervor she hadn't known she possessed. She wanted to touch him everywhere, run her hands across his shoulders, down his hard chest, and over his hard erection pressing into her leg. She tugged at the front of his T-shirt and pulled it loose from his jeans. Running her hands underneath, she felt hard muscles and hot man. But she wanted more. She reached around his waist, grabbed a handful of soft cotton, and tugged. His shirt came free, and she broke away from their kiss. "Off," she said with a foreign boldness.

With a low growl, he pulled her to her feet. Still holding on to her hand, he pulled her with him. She had to run to keep up. Then they were inside the Suburban and skidding out her parents' driveway.

Only the weak glow from the dash lights illuminated Jared's profile. Seat belt be damned, she half sat/half straddled the console between them and ran her hand along his rough jaw. She brushed her hand across his lips and felt him kiss her palm. He grabbed her around her waist moments before they took a sharp turn. Gravel spewed underneath the car as they skidded to a stop.

"You're going to get a ticket," she said, sliding even farther into his lap.

"Ask me if I give a damn." He wrenched his door open, and that's when she realized they were already back at her place. It felt as if the drive had taken mere seconds.

The steering wheel rubbed against her side, and he lifted her out of the SUV. He slammed the door shut with the bottom of his boot. Still carrying her, he headed for the house. His usual long, smooth strides were missing, and Jenny grabbed on around his neck to keep herself steady. "I can walk."

He leaned down and gave her a kiss as he continued to walk. Their noses bumped. "And take the chance of you getting away? Not on your life." And he meant it. He kept her in his arms as he unlocked the door. He took the stairs two at a time, and she had a moment of trepidation as they neared her bedroom door. Where? His room or hers? Her first flutter of panic started then settled to a little tingle when he headed straight for his room. His door was slightly ajar, and he used his shoulder to open it and then bumped it closed. He laid her on the bed as if she were made of porcelain.

"God. You don't know how many times I've envisioned you here, in my bed."

Her stomach clenched at his words, and her breathing grew short and choppy. He knelt down beside her, cupped her cheeks in the palms of his hands, and drew her up until his hot, insisting mouth found hers. She arched into him, wanting more, wanting it all. This time when she went to slip his T-shirt over his head, he didn't stop her. Speechless, she stared at him. He was perfect. Beautiful. And then she did exactly what she'd wanted to earlier. She ran her hands across his rounded shoulders, down his chest. He was hard and muscular and warm to her touch.

"Turnabout is fair play." Before she knew it, Jared had

her bikini top untied. He tossed it onto the floor. His blue eyes were all but liquid with desire as he took his time looking at her, like he'd been waiting for this moment forever, and now that it was here, he was going to savor every last drop. With the tip of his index finger, he drew a straight line from the hollow of her throat to her belly button. Her stomach contracted at the intimate caress, and all she could think was, *More*. Retracing his path, he dragged his finger back up and circled the outer fullness of her breast. She sucked in a breath of air, or she thought she did, but then she wasn't sure, because she felt like all the oxygen had suddenly left the room. His warm palm settled on top of her breast, and she gasped. Desire turned her nipples hard and heated her blood until she thought she was going to burst into flames.

She couldn't wait any longer. Her hands went to the top button of his Levi's, and she struggled to work them free. In one deft move, he popped them open. His hard erection jutted out against his white briefs, and she ran a hand down the soft cotton and hard shaft. He groaned, and that groan made her more brazen than she'd ever been. She sat up and pushed him back. She tugged at his jeans, but their position made it all but impossible. She rocked up onto her knees, and he followed suit. Kneeling on the bed, she pressed her breasts against his chest and skimmed her hands down along the hard planes of his back, the indentation of his spine, and under his briefs. She tugged and pulled again, then tipped her head up to look into his eyes. Raw, undiluted desire darkened their blue depths, while a smile played around the corners of his mouth. "Help," was all she had to say, and he slipped out of his pants.

He came back on the bed, completely naked and fully aroused. He knelt next to her again, and as he kissed her mouth, the side of her neck, the little hollow indentation at the base of her throat, he unsnapped her shorts but before he took them off, he slipped his hand into her panties and across the warm, slick skin between her thighs. At his touch, she came undone. She arched into him and held on

for dear life. Wave after wave of sensation rolled through
her, buckled her knees.

His hand stilled. "Jenny?"

Embarrassment flooded her. Just one touch. That's all
it had taken.

His hand was still. Wetness dampened her underwear,
seeped into the seam of her shorts. She knew he could feel
it. She buried her head in the crook of his shoulder. He
must think—

"Jenny."

She looked up at him feeling completely gauche and
self-conscious.

"It's only the first of many tonight, Cotton Tail." And
then with one kiss, he took all her fears away. He slid her
shorts and underwear off, and soon she was naked beneath him. The weight of him felt so right on top of her.
He reached to the nightstand, slipped a condom on, and
then fitted himself between her thighs. He slid into her in
one long, languid motion. She arched to meet him, found
his rhythm, and matched it. As he slid in and out of her,
pleasuring her in every way possible, he kissed her forehead, her eyelids, her nose, before settling his open mouth
against hers in a kiss so full and deep, she knew she was
about to lose it again. He quickened the pace, driving
against her until they both climaxed. Jenny could have
sworn she saw fireworks go off.

*   *   *

Jenny came awake slowly as if from a dream. She lay in
the bed, wondering what had woken her, then became aware
of the man beside her.

His breathing was slow and even. She knew he was asleep
without even looking at him. Carefully, she eased away
and got out of bed. She looked around for her clothes. She
saw her bikini top but couldn't find her shorts or underwear. She thought about going to her room and putting on
her nightgown, but then she saw Jared's T-shirt and slipped
it on. The soft cotton fell to mid-thigh and engulfed her in

his scent. She breathed in, and the memories of what she'd shared with him came flooding back.

She walked over to the window. A crescent moon hung high in the dark sky. Jenny leaned forward and rested her overheated cheek against the cool glass. Her breathing didn't betray her inner turmoil. But her heart was another matter entirely.

She blew against the window until a small circle formed. In the haze she drew a heart with her fingertip and then the initial J +. Her hand paused. Always before it had been J + S, but now she left it blank.

She closed her eyes and let the rush of memories fill her. She waited for the flood of guilt, of regret, but none of those emotions came. Instead, her body ached in a way that was as foreign as it was familiar. Even now, with the distance between them, she could still feel Jared's hands, his mouth, his body claiming her. Longing pooled in the pit of her stomach, spiraled down, and left her with a need that defied description.

Even with her eyes closed, she knew he was standing behind her.

Slowly, she opened her eyes, and their gazes met in the window's reflection. His warm breath cascaded over her hair, down the back of her neck. Goose bumps raised her skin. She looked at the fading heart she had drawn, the J she had written. Knowing Jared was still watching her she reached out and retraced the heart, the letter J. And after the plus sign, she placed another letter. Another J.

Jared drew in a swift breath of air. "Jenny . . ."

Just her name and her body remembered every intimate caress, every wanton exploration. She moved away from the window, keeping her eyes on his and her body near him. They were so close, she could feel his heat. She wanted him. *Him*. A part of her would always love Steven, but her heart was open to love again. To love Jared.

With steady hands, she faced him and slipped the T-shirt over her head. She stood naked in front of him. Never before had she been so wantonly bold with a man, but before she could let her insecurities take hold, she leaned forward until their bodies fused. "I love you, Jared."

"Jenny," he said again and this time her name was a rough growl of a caress. His arms came around her, and his mouth settled in the soft hollow of her neck, kissing her. Her nipples hardened in response. He wrapped her in his arms. His mouth claimed her, full of passion and possession.

His firm hands gripped her bottom and pulled her tight against him. His erection thrust into her, and she wrapped her arms around his neck wanting him with an intensity that should frighten her but didn't. He pulled her thighs up around his waist and carried her back to the bed they'd recently vacated.

He positioned them so she was straddling his hips. "You don't know what you do to me," he said in a low voice.

Her hot, wet body opened for him, ready and wanting. "Yes, I do. Because I feel it."

At the same moment he drove his hips up and plunged inside of her, a hoarse cry tore out from somewhere deep inside of him. As if he'd been holding that in forever.

Her third climax of the night came hard and fast and simultaneously with his.

* * *

Jenny woke early the next morning to find Jared staring at her. "Morning."

"About time you woke up."

She glanced at the clock and smiled. It wasn't even six. He reached for her, but she scooted away, laughing at his frustrated expression. "Wait. I have a surprise for you."

He pressed the length of himself against her. "My surprise is bigger."

She melted right there, right in his arms. "Considerably."

Later—much later—she was in the kitchen making him a surprise breakfast, though it wasn't much of a surprise any longer. The only way she'd been able to leave the bed was by telling him what she was up to. Even then, he hadn't wanted to let her go. Not that she'd wanted to all that much either. But she'd made him promise to stay put. He'd made her promise to hurry.

She'd already read the directions in her cookbook twice—determined not to screw up the waffles. She read them a third time and then began to make the batter. As she waited for the first one to cook, she put on a pot of coffee and tried to ignore the hollers coming from upstairs telling her to hurry up. She was going as fast as she could, and the adorable rat knew it.

The first waffle was a complete disaster, the second a little crispy. But the third and fourth ones didn't look too bad. Smiling, she put everything on a tray and headed back upstairs.

"About time," Jared said when she stepped through the door.

She held up the tray, immensely proud of her cooking accomplishments. "I made all your favorites."

Naked, he got out of bed and took the tray from her. "You're my favorite." He set it on the dresser and pushed her down on the bed. He followed.

"Breakfast," Jenny began.

"Can wait."

She grinned and ran her hand over his bare chest. "But aren't you the one who keeps telling me breakfast is the most important meal of the day?"

He untied her robe and kissed the soft hollow of her neck, then trailed kisses down until he reached the rounded top of her breast. "I'm an idiot."

She laughed, and neither of them cared that the food got cold.

Sometime around eight, the phone rang.

"Let it ring," Jared said.

Jenny kissed his jaw and decided that morning stubble only added to his good looks. "It's probably my mother, and if I don't answer, she'll drive over."

With a growl of sexual frustration that matched her own,

he gave her a playful push. "We don't want that. But make it fast." His smile was full of wicked promises.

Jenny grabbed her robe and went into her bedroom, the room with the nearest phone. "Hi, Mom," she said automatically, not bothering to glance at the caller ID. Her mother was the only person who ever called this early in the morning.

There was a long pause. "This is Captain Tom Beckett. I'm trying to reach Commander Jared Worth."

For no reason she could define, Jenny suddenly felt cold. Ignoring the impulse to deny that there was anyone here by that name, she said, "One moment, please."

She carefully set the phone down and went back to the other room.

"The call is for you," she said to Jared. "A Captain Beckett, I think he said."

An expression she couldn't read came over Jared's face. Without a word, he got out of the bed, pulled on his Levi's without underwear, and went to take the call.

Jenny sank down on the bed and waited.

She didn't know how much time had passed when Jared walked back in. One look at his face, and she knew. "Tell me."

He didn't join her on the bed. "That was my CO. He not only refused to accept the resignation I gave him months ago, he fought to clear my record." Jared shook his head. "Him and that damn Hart."

"I thought . . ."

His gaze didn't quite meet hers. "What?"

Tears burned the back of her eyes. After last night she'd thought a lot of things. Most of all, she'd thought about a forever with Jared. She'd given him everything—her heart . . . her soul. Her love.

But last night when she'd told Jared she'd loved him, he'd never said the words back to her. He'd taken her in his arms, worshipped her with his hands and mouth. And with his every touch and caress, she'd let herself believe he loved her, too. But now, looking into his eyes, she knew it wasn't true. There was only one love in Jared's life, and it wasn't Jenny.

She swallowed hard. "I thought you were done with the military." It was a pointless question, and they both knew it. Flyboys fly. How could she have forgotten that undeniable truth?

"So did I." He didn't say anything for a moment. "When I tendered my resignation, I accepted that my days of flying jets were over. But now . . ." He stopped, and Jenny didn't need him to say any more.

He had his career back. The life he wanted. A life that couldn't include her. She didn't need him to tell her what this call meant for them. She knew.

Flyboys fly.

She left the room before he could see her tears.

* * *

Jared watched Jenny go. He started to follow her, then stopped. What could he say to her?

What they'd had last night—he knew that wasn't enough to build a life on. He tried to shut out the memories of how much pleasure she'd given him. More than he'd ever received. For the first time in his life, he wanted to wake up next to a woman. To have her right beside him all night so he could reach out and touch her anytime he wanted. Just to make sure she was still there. Last night had been about a hell of a lot more than sex.

I love you, Jared.

Once more he heard Jenny's soft declaration. He knew she believed she was in love with him. Just like he knew she wanted to hear the words from him. Words Jared had never said to anyone. Didn't believe he ever would . . . could. It was yet another thing that proved he wasn't the type of man she wanted. She wanted someone who could say, "I love you." Who could be a part of a family. Part of *her* family. Someone she could cook waffles for on the weekend—

I made all of your favorites. No one else had ever known what his favorites were.

Someone who would be home every night for dinner, be around for family barbeques, birthdays, Little League games, and ballet lessons.

Someone he was not.

Yesterday at her parents' party, he'd let himself believe he could be that guy. But in the light of day, he saw how wrong he'd been. He wasn't Steven. He wasn't a guy who would stick. Who could fit. Who could give her everything she deserved. One call from his CO had proven that.

Flying was the only thing Jared had ever been good at. The only thing he'd ever wanted. He wished he could believe that this time it would be different with Jenny. But the past had taught him otherwise. Eventually she'd see what everyone else had: he screwed up every relationship he'd ever tried having. Disappointment and regret would cloud her eyes, and seeing that would destroy him like nothing else could.

It was better to leave now before he caused her any more pain.

He grabbed his duffel. He stared at the empty bag and silently cursed. He knew better than to unpack. He knew he never stuck around one place long enough to get settled. But just like everything else with Jenny, he let himself forget what he knew to be true. He let himself believe in the impossible. He shoved his clothes into the bag and headed to the bathroom. In less than ten minutes, he was packed and ready to go.

At Jenny's door, he paused. Steeling himself, he knocked.

"Come in."

Her eyes were red and swollen. She looked at his duffel bag, then back to him.

"Just go," she said, her tears flowing steadily. "I know that's what you've decided."

At the sight of the pain on her face, the ache in his chest was like a fist tightening around his heart. He wanted to tell her that his leaving was for the best. The longer he stayed, the more he'd hurt her. But they both knew the real truth: his CO's call had given Jared back the one thing he wanted more than anything. "I'm sorry."

"Just go," she said again. "I know there's nothing I can say to keep you here."

"I'm sorry," he said again, knowing it wasn't enough but knowing it was all he had to give. As he walked out of her house, it felt like someone was ripping his heart right out of his chest.

He jumped on his bike. The engine roared to life beneath him. He looked down the road, wanting to get the hell out of this town as fast as he could. But there was one stop he had to make before he left.

Ten minutes later, he cut the engine and parked in front of Paul's law office. Jared walked past the secretary without a word.

"This is a surprise," Paul said, rising from behind his desk.

Jared's helmet hung from his hand like a leaden weight. "I need your help."

"Does this have to do with Jenny?"

It had everything to do with her. "Draft whatever papers are needed to relinquish any interest I have in Blue Sky Air. That company belongs to her. Only her." He thought of all the successes she'd accomplished in such short time. She'd succeeded where everyone had predicted failure. He was so damn proud of her.

Paul sat back down in his chair. "Care to tell me what's going on?"

"No."

Paul picked up a pen from his desk. "You're leaving. Empty-handed?"

Yes, but not in the way Paul thought. Jared didn't give a damn about the money. "I was never staying."

"Going back to your squadron. Back to flying."

Jared's silence was his answer.

"I thought you were happy here."

Happiness was a fucking illusion. No one knew that better than Jared. "Just write up whatever you have to so I can sign the damn thing and get out of here."

"It's not that easy. Give me a couple of days and—"

"I don't have a couple of days. I need it done now."

Paul stared at him for several long moments. "What you're asking will take some time."

Time was the last thing Jared had. There was no way he could stay around for another couple of days. He'd somehow managed to walk away from Jenny. He didn't know if he'd be able to do it again. He moved toward the door. He needed to get out of here. Now. "Fine. I'll contact you in a few days and give you an address where you can mail them."

Paul's gaze drilled into Jared. "Life's short."

"You think I don't know that?" Each time he climbed into the cockpit he was confronted with just how fragile life could be. Too damn fragile for a woman who had already lost someone.

"No, I don't. There's more to life than flying."

For men like Paul and Steven. But not for Jared.

"You're about to lose the best thing you ever had."

Jared had already lost her. No, that wasn't true. She'd never truly been his.

He turned and walked out.

TWENTY-THREE

∽

For over an hour, Jenny didn't move. She sat on her bed letting the tears flow. Used Kleenexes littered the bed. She reached for a fresh tissue, then realized she'd used up the whole box. She wiped her face with the sleeve of her pajamas. How could she have been so stupid? How could she have given her heart to a man who didn't want her? Who didn't love her enough? Who didn't love her at all.

She didn't want to move. She wanted to stay right where she was, wallow in her heartache until the pain just disintegrated her into a pile of ashes. She couldn't go through this again. She wouldn't survive another broken heart.

But she would. Time had taught her that.

She stood and slipped into jeans and her favorite sweatshirt. As much as she wanted to let her grief overtake her, she had a business to run. She wasn't the same person she'd been when she'd lost Steven. She was stronger now. More sure of herself. More sure of herself as a businesswoman. And Jared had played a big part in helping her see and realize her full potential. While her heart was breaking, she wasn't going to close herself off from everything again. This time, work would be her salvation.

In the bathroom, she brushed her teeth and pulled her hair into a ponytail. She refused to look at her reflection in the mirror. Why bother? She knew what she'd see. A face ravaged by tears. Eyes hollow with grief. She headed downstairs.

The kitchen was as cold and dark and empty as she was. She looked at the remnants of the breakfast she'd made, and fresh tears slid down her cheeks and darkened the front of her sweatshirt like little droplets of rain. Grabbing a paper towel, she dried her face and got to work.

She flipped on the overhead light, put the kettle on to boil, and began to clean up the mess she'd made earlier. It felt better to move, to keep busy. To keep her mind off Jared.

Once the kitchen was spotless, she went to her office and turned on the computer. She was just about to log on to the Internet and check her e-mail for bookings when the doorbell rang. Her hand smacked against the wrong key.

Jared.

She hurried to the door.

A fresh wave of heartache rolled over her when she saw who it was. "Paul."

"Hey, Jelly Belly." Her brother's voice held a note of sympathy that confused her. "May I come in?"

She opened the door wider and stepped to the side. "Of course."

He walked into the foyer, bringing the late morning sun with him. Jenny blinked against the brightness.

"I've called Anna," he said.

"Anna. Why?"

"I thought . . ." He brushed the edges of his suit jacket aside and shoved his hands down the front pockets of his slacks. "Hell, I don't know. I thought maybe having her here would help."

"Help what?"

"Jared stopped by my office before he left."

Left.

As in gone. As in forever.

"So you know." She felt raw and exposed under her brother's gaze.

"Yes." He paused. "He asked me to sign over full ownership of Blue Sky Air to you."

Her head shot up. "What?"

"After I draft the papers and Jared signs, you'll be full owner. Blue Sky Air will be all yours. He doesn't want any part of the company. Not repayment of his loan. Nothing."

You'll be the full owner.

Blue Sky Air will be all yours.

It was exactly what she'd wanted from the beginning. She should feel elated. But she only felt worse. He didn't want her. Any part of her. Signing over the company was his way of permanently severing all ties between the two of them.

A car came barreling down the driveway. Even from inside the house, they could hear gravel flying. Brakes screeched, and within moments Anna ran through the door. She looked at Jenny, then at Paul. "I'm sorry it took me so long. I would have been here sooner, but a cop pulled me over and gave me a speeding ticket. What's going on?"

Even as devastated as Jenny was, her sister's words registered. "*You* got a speeding ticket?"

"Paul said you needed me. He said it was an emergency."

"But weren't you at work?" Jenny asked.

Anna took off her left shoe and held it out the door. Turning the pump upside down, she dumped out several small pieces of gravel. "What does work have to do with this? Paul said you needed me."

"And you came."

"As fast as I could. That's what sisters do."

Jenny felt a surge of love for her sister. "Thank you."

Anna's gaze softened. "You're welcome," she said, putting her shoe back on. "We really should talk about paving that driveway. You've turned your business into a thriving success. You can afford it."

Paul nodded.

"Now," Anna said, straightening, "tell me what's going on."

Jenny drew in a shaky breath. "Jared left." She said it quickly, like pulling off a Band-Aid, hoping that the swifter she told Anna the news, the less it would hurt.

"So when is he coming back?" Anna asked.

Paul put his arm around Jenny, gave her a comforting squeeze. "He's not."

"Why the hell not?"

Jenny leaned against her brother. "Because he doesn't love me."

"Of course he loves you," Anna said, her voice full of conviction.

Jenny shook her head. "No. He doesn't."

"Oh, Jenny." Anna barged forward and engulfed her in a hug. The embrace was awkward—with Paul's arm still around her shoulder and Anna's arms enveloping as much of Jenny as she could hold—but even as elbows dug and heads bumped, it was a wonderful embrace.

"He loves you," Anna said, drawing back. "That's not the question. The real question is: do you love him enough?"

Of course she loved him. She loved everything about him. The way he looked, the way he smelled. The way he dominated a room just by walking into it. Those blue, blue eyes of his that noticed everything. The way he didn't find it necessary to talk incessantly, but when he spoke, people listened. And his smile. God, how she loved his smile. Rare and bone melting—when she coaxed one out of him she felt as if she'd just won a prize of immeasurable worth. He made her feel like she could accomplish anything. Be anyone. He pushed her to be the best she could be, and because of him, she was. She was on her way to being more successful than she'd ever thought possible. And making love to him left her breathless and wanting more. Wanting him in the deepest way possible.

"Yes," she said to her sister, "I love him."

"The question was, do you love him enough?"

Jenny straightened, and her brother's arm fell away from her. She grabbed his arm and put it back around her shoulders, giving him the best smile she could muster. She'd been so wrong to keep her brother and sister at arm's length after Steven's death. She saw that now. She wasn't about to make the same mistake. She looked back to her sister. "Enough for what?"

"Enough for the both of you. Enough to fight for him. He loves you, Jenny. You just have to show him."

"But how?" she said more to herself than to anyone.

Anna gave her a bright smile. "You're a smart girl. You'll figure it out."

*   *   *

All around Jared controlled chaos reigned on the USS *Abraham Lincoln*. Military personnel rushed across the massive aircraft carrier performing their jobs with infinite precision and untiring speed. He paused on the way to the flight line as an F-18 taxied to position. The powerful engines ignited, obliterated any other sound, and intensified the air with the smell of jet fuel. The carrier shuddered beneath his feet as the engines gained power. Moments later, the jet roared and hit the sky.

Jared took it all in: the noise, the smells, the endless blue that surrounded him. *This* was what he lived for. *This* was all he wanted.

Three weeks had passed since he'd left Jenny. Three weeks since he'd gotten his life back. Leaving had been the right decision—the only decision.

Hadn't it?

He shook off the thought and told himself that the only thing he needed to do was get back inside the cockpit. It was the same thing he'd been telling himself ever since he'd rejoined his squadron. And today he finally would. In less than an hour he'd be back up in the skies, the only place he belonged.

Earlier this morning they'd been briefed on their mission. In direct violation of a treaty, a nuclear facility in Tawaitha had been rebuilt. Jared's squadron had been given the directive to destroy it for a second time. Everyone knew the target would be heavily defended, just like everyone knew a confrontation was imminent. American fighters would be mixing it up with Iraqi MiGs. Soon the skies were going to be one hell of a fireball.

Jared wasn't afraid. He had stared down danger more times than he could count. Confrontations like this were exactly what he had been trained for.

He was just about to make his way to his jet when someone tapped him on the shoulder. He turned and saw Kenny Hart.

Ever since he'd gotten back, Jared had been avoiding the kid. Hart was one chatty son of a bitch, and Jared knew that sooner or later he'd mention Jenny. So he avoided Hart just like he avoided thinking about what Paul had said to him. Both guys were bastards who didn't know how to mind their own fucking business.

Hart motioned for Jared to follow him.

They reached a place on the carrier where they could talk, though they still had to shout to be heard above the noise.

"What?" Jared asked, not bothering to hide his annoyance.

"That. You've been in a foul mood ever since you returned."

"Mind your own goddamn business."

"I would, but the guys in the squadron won't let me. They want me to find out what the hell is bugging you and tell you to get over it. Of course, I didn't tell them I already knew."

"You don't know shit." Jared turned to leave, but Hart reached out and grabbed him.

"She's trying to find you."

He didn't need to ask who *she* was. "How the hell do you know?"

Hart readjusted his helmet underneath his arm. "Because she wrote to me asking for help in locating your sorry ass."

Jared heard a roaring in his ears that had nothing to do with the noise from the carrier. He stared at Hart, wanted to put a fist through his pretty boy face. "How the hell did she know how to contact you? And why?" *Fuck all that, and just tell me what she said.*

"Unlike you, I gave her a way to contact me. Since I knew you'd screw it up, I figured Jenny was fair game. I plan on seeing her when we return."

"Like hell you will." Two weeks ago Jared had sent Paul an address; he still hadn't received the papers. He knew it would take some time for them to reach him, and Jared was both dreading and waiting for that day. Until he signed the documents that relinquished any hold he had on Blue Sky, he was still a part of her life. A small part, but it was better than nothing. He'd take whatever he could get.

"Sorry, Charlie. But since you gave her up, you don't get a say."

Jared wanted to punch Hart all over again. Then again, he wanted to smack himself. The second night he'd returned, he'd gotten good and drunk. And Hart had been right there, listening to every whiny word Jared had been unable to stop himself from saying.

"So," Hart prodded. "What do you want me to tell her?"

There were a million things he wanted to say to her. But none of them would change anything, and even if they would, he sure as hell wouldn't use pretty boy as his messenger. This time when Jared turned and walked away, Hart couldn't stop him.

Jared reached his jet and threw himself into the task at hand. He had a job to do, and he'd better get his head on straight and do it. He went through the preflight check then climbed into the cockpit. But as he put on his helmet and connected his oxygen hose, he couldn't stop the memory of when Jenny had picked up his helmet, held it in her hands, and looked at him with those sky blue eyes that tore straight through to his soul.

The Ghost, I know.

She didn't. No one did. He made damn sure of that. If she knew how mixed up he really was, she'd run as fast and as far from him as she could. Instead, he'd protected her by getting the hell away from her.

He motored down the canopy and brought the engine up to speed then completed his primary/secondary and emergency power unit checks, punched in the coordinates, tested the flight-control, brake, and air-refueling system. He cleared his crew chief off the headset and began to taxi. The jet accelerated rapidly, and Jared was airborne in a matter of seconds. As he climbed into the blue sky, he waited for the rush of adrenaline to hit him like it always did. This was it. This was where his magic began.

But this time, there was no adrenaline. No magic.

My nana always told me this lake was magical. This water could heal almost anything.

The roaring in his head grew louder, and his hand slipped on the stick.

Jenny.

Her grandmother had been wrong. It wasn't the lake that held the magic, it was Jenny.

Somehow, with that wondrous heart of hers that was as big and open as the sky before him, she'd shown him that he could put down roots. That he could fit. That he could love. And she did know him. He thought back to all the talks they'd shared—all the things he'd shared about himself.

He loved her.

The truth had been before him all the time.

God, what an utter fool he'd been. He could face an enemy head-on, but one look at Jenny's smile, and he had run away. He'd let the stain of his past muddy his future. And even when Jenny had given him her love, he'd thrown it back in her face, the coward that he was. For so long he'd been running, but she'd seen through every barrier he erected. She tried to show him . . . to tell him . . . but he'd been too stupid to see. He was a guy who could stick—he just hadn't found the right reason . . . the right person, until Jenny. It had taken him getting back into the cockpit and climbing thirty thousand feet for him to see clearly what he'd missed on the ground.

Jared rolled into a thirty-degree bank. For the first time he didn't want to look up; he wanted to look down.

* * *

Jenny frowned at the vegetable platter in her hands. "I don't know. I think you should have put me in charge of chips and salsa. We both know dip is beyond my culinary skills."

"Believe me," Anna said, "I wouldn't have let you make it if I didn't know it would taste good."

Jenny laughed. "So true."

Anna opened the fridge and grabbed the large bowl of potato salad she'd made earlier. "Now come on." She bumped the fridge closed with her hip. "Your guests are hungry."

They made their way out of Jenny's house and across the yard. Under the hot August sun, the lake glistened a stunning silver and blue. Someone had plugged an iPod into a pair of speakers. The Beach Boys were belting out, "And she'll have fun, fun, fun till her daddy takes the T-Bird away." Jenny paused at the edge of the beach and smiled.

Over two dozen of her friends and family were here, with more arriving every minute. Her dad was manning the barbeque they'd moved down from the house. Each time an unsuspecting guest walked by, he'd snag them and proceed to give a five-minute lecture on the proper way to grill salmon. Jenny shook her head. Right now poor Mrs. Murphy was the unlucky recipient of her dad's unsolicited advice.

Mom stood a little ways off to the side, talking to a group of friends. She'd recently discovered a new sculptor from Vancouver and was convinced he was going to take the art community by storm. Jenny had no doubt he would. If Catherine Beckinsale said it was so, it was so.

Cody stood on the left side of the dock, a group of kids around him. The sketch he'd drawn last night of a sand castle was taped to a stick he'd pushed into the sand. The paper fluttered in the soft breeze as Cody directed the kids on what needed to be done to build the most intricate sand castle Jenny had ever seen. As she watched, the kids dispersed, ran to various spots on the beach, and began scooping sand into their brightly colored buckets.

Maddy, Sharron, and several other girlfriends of Jenny's had taken up residence in lawn chairs. While babies slept in portable playpens, the women watched their husbands and boyfriends battle it out at the volleyball net. Even Paul was in the mix. And so was the new lawyer he'd hired, Kara, a tall brunette who was as beautiful as she was smart. Both Jenny and Anna knew it was only a matter of time before their brother fell for her. The only question was how long would Paul take. Jenny had laid odds on a month. Anna had shocked her by giving Paul less than a week. An all-expense-paid spa day was the wager. Watching Paul and Kara, Jenny had a feeling she'd be the one who ended up paying. But she didn't mind. A day at the spa with her sister sounded like heaven—no matter who ended up paying.

The only people who hadn't been able to make it were Steven's parents. They were still in Arizona, but Jenny had called them and they'd talked for over an hour. The phone call had been cathartic—exactly what they'd all needed.

The moment Anna reached the picnic table, she set down her potato salad and frowned. It was the same thing she'd done all day. Jenny wasn't the least surprised when Anna began to once more rearrange all the platters of food. The perfectionist in her just couldn't help it. Jenny grinned when she saw Phillip walk up behind Anna and scoop her into a hug. Anna squealed and then laughed, her face aglow. And when her husband pulled her away from the table and down to the beach, Anna didn't make one word of protest.

Jenny marveled at how much her sister had changed in such a short amount of time. Right after their talk on the Fourth of July, Anna had swallowed her pride and fought for what she wanted. She'd called Phillip that same night and asked him to come home. She told him that she needed him and missed him. And that she loved him. Phillip had been on the first available flight. He'd even made it home in time to see Cody pitch in the championship game.

And just like Anna, Jenny was going to fight for what she wanted. For *who* she wanted. Jared had broken her heart as much as he'd healed it. Now it was her turn to show him just how perfect they were for each other. For three weeks she'd been doing everything she could to try to find him. She grew excited when she learned Jared had sent Paul an address, certain that would lead her to him. After telling her brother in no uncertain terms to forget about drafting up those papers, she set out to find Jared. But the address had proven to be a dead end. So she'd gone back to the drawing board, intensifying her efforts. She exhausted every resource she could think of, and when she was just about to throw herself at whatever high-ranking military person she could find and beg them to help her, yesterday a letter from Kenny had arrived. Jared's squadron had returned to California. Without a moment's hesitation, Jenny had booked a ticket for a six a.m. flight tomorrow morning.

She felt a flutter of worry. Not about Jared but about what she was going to say to him. All she knew was that she wasn't going to let him walk away from what they had. She knew he thought he couldn't be the type of man she wanted because of his past—but he was wrong. And Jenny was going to do everything in her power to prove just that to him, even if it meant leaving Hidden Lake and following him to wherever his job took him. He was more important to her than anything else.

A deep, throaty rumble sounded from the driveway. Jenny smiled—more guests! She set down her vegetable tray and hurried up toward the house to see who it was.

But what she saw brought her to an abrupt halt.

Jared.

His big black Harley rumbled down the driveway, sunlight glinting off his aviators. As he parked, Jenny soaked up the sight of him. Instead of three weeks, it felt more like three years since she'd last seen him.

He put down the kickstand and swung his long, white-clad leg over the back of the bike. He took off his glasses and ran a hand through black hair. He looked around the yard, and then he spotted her. For a long moment, he just stared at her. And then with those long, purposeful strides that triggered a *thump-thump-thump* of remembrance in her heart, he walked straight toward her. It wasn't until he was nearly in front of her that she realized he was in full dress whites. God, what a sight.

"Jenny," he said in that deep, gravelly voice that was so achingly familiar she wanted to throw herself into his arms and kiss him until neither of them could breathe. "Before you say anything, I want to—" Jared broke off, looking at something over her shoulder.

She turned and couldn't believe what she saw. Her family must have heard his arrival, because they were all there right behind her. Along with most of her friends. And they were all listening intently to every word. Someone had even turned off the music so no one would miss a thing.

Jenny glared at them but then realized she didn't care.

All that mattered was Jared. She turned back to him. There was that full, true, wonderfully bright smile that lit up his blue eyes and made her feel like the world had been set right every time she saw it. He reached out and grasped her hands, looking at all the people behind her, then looking back at her, his smile even wider, if that was possible. "Looks like I interrupted a party."

She tried to breathe. "A going-away party."

"Who's leaving?"

"Me."

His smile dimmed as his blue, blue eyes searched her. "Is there room for one more?"

"Are you saying—"

"I want to be wherever you are. I'm sorry it took me so long to figure that out. So, what do you say? Can I go with you?"

Tears pooled in her eyes. She shook her head. "No."

His grip tightened. "I know I screwed up. Leaving you was the biggest mistake of my life. But even if it takes me a lifetime, I'll make it up to you. God, how I'll make it up to you. I love you."

He—had he just said that he loved her?

From somewhere in the crowed, Anna hollered to Jared, "What did you say?"

Jared smiled down at Jenny. "I said I love her."

"About time," her brother added.

"I couldn't agree more," Jared said, still looking only at Jenny. "I've loved you from the first moment I saw you. I was just too blind to see it. Now tell me you'll let me come with you. You're my whole life. Wherever you are is where I belong."

Tears fell down her cheeks, and she smiled through a watery blur. "You can't."

His eyes darkened with determination. "While you're telling me why you *think* I can't, I'll show you why I *know* I can."

Jenny laughed. "No. You don't understand. I don't need to leave now."

The wind picked up and blew her hair across her face. "Why?"

"Because I already found what I was looking for."

He reached out and tucked her hair behind her ear. "And what was that?"

"You," she said, all the love she had for him filling that one word.

"Jenny," he growled from the depths of his soul. "I love you," he said again. "I've never said those words to anyone else before, and it's only because of you that I can say them now."

She wrapped her arms around his shoulders, felt his gold wings press against her chest. "And I love you."

"God, what did I ever do to deserve you?" He pulled her tight against him, kissed her with a passion and a promise that left her breathless. He wiped the tears off her cheeks and lifted up her bare left hand. "I know you wore someone else's ring for a lot of years, but I hope you'll wear mine now."

"Are you asking me to get engaged?"

"No. I'm asking you to marry me. Today. Right now if you want. Please say yes. I'm an impatient man."

She didn't even have to think twice. "Yes."

"Thank you." His solemn words brought fresh tears to her eyes.

Anna was the first to reach Jenny. Her mom, dad, and brother weren't far behind. They engulfed her in a hug, this wonderful family of hers.

"A wedding," Anna and Mom said at the same time.

"I know just the place," her sister said.

"And I know just the menu," her mom added.

Jenny laughed. "And I know just the man." Jared's arms tightened around her.

"Three months?" Anna looked to their mother.

"Six," her mother said. "We'll need at least six months to plan. I know it isn't much time to pull a wedding together, but between the three of us"—her mother looked to Jenny—"we'll be able to do it."

A wedding. The thought sent a flutter of panic through Jenny. Old fears came bubbling up to the surface.

Jared took one look at her and, excusing them from the crowd, he pulled her far enough away so no one could overhear them. Her nana's flowers surrounded them.

"What is it?" he asked gently.

She drew in a breath. "Are you sure?"

"I've never been more sure of anything in my life."

"What about . . ." She looked down, not wanting him to see the fear in her eyes.

His tipped her chin up. "What about what?"

"Flyboys fly."

"I'll quit today if that's what you want." The truth of his statement was in his eyes. "I want to marry you, Jenny. Grow old with you. Watch our children and grandchildren play here on Hidden Lake."

With each word he spoke, her fear receded until it was completely gone. "Children?"

"A dozen. At least." He grinned.

"How about we start with two."

His smile widened. "How about we start trying tonight?"

She laughed. "Impatient man."

"Only where you're concerned." He brushed his hand down the side of her cheek. "And I meant what I said. I'll quit."

She shook her head. "Flyboys fly."

"Even if they're married?"

"Especially if they're married. Just come home to me."

"Always."

"Now, about that wedding my family is planning . . ."

"Whatever you want. I'll marry you today or I'll marry you next month or next year. Wherever, *whenever*, you want. I just want you."

God, how she loved this man. "Seven," she said.

"Seven months it is."

She shook her head. "No. Seven days." Between her, her mom, and Anna, they could pull it off. "I'm an impatient woman."

He laughed and leaned down to kiss her. "Thank God, Cotton Tail. I never considered patience a virtue."

She melted into his embrace and thought about the bunny suit she was going to buy to surprise him on their honeymoon.